FREYA ROBERTSON

SUNSTONE

The Elemental Wars
Book II

ANGRY
ROBOT

ANGRY ROBOT
A member of the Osprey Group

Lace Market House,
54-56 High Pavement,
Nottingham,
NG1 1HW
UK

www.angryrobotbooks.com
Generations

An Angry Robot paperback original 2014
1

A catalogue record for this book is available
from the British Library.

ISBN 978 0 85766 388 7
Ebook ISBN 978 0 85766 390 0

Set in Meridien by Argh! Oxford.

Printed and bound by CPI Group (UK) Ltd, Croydon, CR0 4YY

To Tony & Chris. My Kiwi boys.

PART ONE

CHAPTER ONE

I

Procella leaned on the parapets of the gatehouse known as the Porta and looked down on the Heartwood estate.

The Baillium bustled with people and animals. Knights practiced swordplay in the Exerceo arenas, pages ran errands, horses stood patiently while stable boys tightened their stirrups, and chickens pecked amongst the flagstones fronting the central Temple. The early morning sun had warmed the building's amber stone to a rich gold, and Procella's heart warmed too at the familiar sight of her beloved home.

The Quintus Campana tolled, the bell echoing throughout the complex to mark the end of weapons practice. Usually she barely heard it, the hourly knell as much a part of the background noise of everyday life as the birdsong in the oak trees scattered in the grounds. But this time the resonant peal vibrated through the stone, up through her feet and into her bones, making her teeth ache and her head throb.

Unease rippled through her. The light was too bright. The figures moved too slowly, as if underwater. On the top of the Temple, the glass of the domed roof glimmered, reflecting not the green leaves of the Arbor beneath it but instead a reddish-orange, like the flicker of firelight. The skin prickled on the back of her neck and her stomach churned.

Then she felt a presence at her back, and she turned her head to see Chonrad standing there, looking down at the Baillium. His brown hair fluttered in the light wind. The sight of his handsome, bearded face brought a smile to her lips, and his hand on her hip, a protective gesture that would have irritated her were it any other man, only made her glow.

She blinked. Twenty-two years had passed since the day he had asked her to marry him. So where was the grey in his hair, the scar at his temple he had received in a brief raid on his home town several years later?

An icy coldness slithered down her spine. How come Heartwood – which had been razed to the ground after the attack by the Darkwater Lords – was still standing?

Chonrad raised a hand and gripped her jaw, forcing her to look into his eyes. They burned fierce and intense, as if he wanted to convey something important to her. She shivered and tried to pull her chin away, but he was too strong.

"You should not be here," she whispered.

His blue gaze burrowed into her. Was he about to make some declaration of love? They had never been a romantic couple, but he had always been careful to tell her he loved her every night, to tell her what she meant to him.

Instead, however, he commanded in a low, deep voice, "Bring her."

Growing angry, she pushed at his chest. "Let me go."

His fingers bit into her flesh. "Bring her, Procella." He spoke insistently, both his tone and his stare demanding she listen. Then, finally, he let go of her chin.

She opened her mouth to say something, but a glint of light to her left caught her attention, and she glanced around, the words unspoken.

The windows of the Temple flickered once again with red and orange. Fire was engulfing the building. Heat seared her face and she smelled ash and burnt flesh on the wind. Screams filled the air, and horses panicked and stampeded through the grounds. The crackle of burning wood filled her ears.

The Arbor!

Procella's eyes flew open. Her heart pounded and her chest heaved as she struggled to work out where she was. Gradually, she recognised the master chamber in Vichton – Chonrad's bed, as she thought of it. Chonrad's castle. Even though she had lived there for over twenty years and borne three children there, she still struggled to think of it as home.

She sat up. Stars twinkled through the arrowslit windows, the sun not yet arisen from its bed. A candle guttered, burned low. Early morning, then; dawn a few hours away.

She swung her legs over the bed and pulled on a pair of fur-lined boots, then wrapped herself in a thick cloak. The oak door squeaked as she pulled it open, and she hoped it hadn't awoken anyone. She wanted to be alone, to think about her dream.

She climbed the curving staircase to the top of the keep and stepped out into the cold air. It bit into her lungs and cleared the final dregs of sleep from her mind. She nodded to the guard on duty, who smiled and then politely looked the other way, used to the mistress of the house appearing at all hours of the day and night. Before she entered the army, she had spent years as a Custos, patrolling the walls around Heartwood, and she felt comfortable up high like this, looking down across the land.

The town was quiet; the only sound the occasional bark of a dog from a sleeping household. Rooftops of all shapes, sizes and colours spilled out from the foot of the castle, the streets a tangle of paved roads close to the wall, mudded lanes on the outskirts. A couple of guards walked the streets, distinguishable by their flickering torches, but it was too late for drunks, too early for even the most hardworking shopkeepers. The air smelled of salt from the sea a few miles to the east, as well as the usual aromas of horse from the stables and smoke from the dying fire in the Great Hall.

That made her think about the fire in her dream, and the way it had consumed the Temple. She had been there twenty-two years ago when the Arbor broke through the stone, causing it to crumble. She had been stunned at its sudden destruction, but it had not filled her with the foreboding and fear that the sight of the flames had.

She wrapped her arms around herself, remembering the press of Chonrad against her back in the dream. Never had she missed him so much. His death a year before almost to the day had been sudden and shocking, and yet somehow she had known he wouldn't return from his journey to Heartwood the same man. The Arbor had needed him, as it had needed him all those years ago before they were wed, and just as she had dreaded, he had returned a shadow, practically on his death bed. He had tried to tell her what had happened down in the labyrinth beneath the Arbor, and she knew it was something to do with the tree taking his energy once again, but he had died before he had been able to explain it fully.

Now, she missed and resented him in equal measure. He had put the tree first, before her, before their children. Their children may be full grown, but they still needed their father, and she still needed her husband. But as soon as it had called him, he had gone running, and she hated him for that.

A tear rolled down her cheek. Hated and loved him. "I miss you," she whispered to the wind. But nobody heard.

"Mama?"

The voice behind her made her turn and hastily wipe her cheek dry. Her daughter – the youngest of her three children – stood there, wrapped in a thick cloak over her nightdress, her feet clad in a small pair of leather slippers, her blonde hair snapping around her face in the breeze that had sprung up out of nowhere. Just seventeen, she looked little more than eleven or twelve; small and slight, slender as an arrow.

"You will freeze without your fur boots," Procella scolded, glad nevertheless of the company.

Horada shrugged and frowned. "What are you doing up here?"

"I had a dream." A wisp of the uneasiness that had stolen over her in her sleep returned to flutter in her stomach.

Her daughter clutched the cloak at her throat. "What about?"

Procella shook her head and smiled. "It matters not. It was just a dream."

Horada looked out across the town. Again Procella marvelled at how slight she was, how fragile. So unlike her parents or her siblings. True, Julen was slight too, but he was over six feet tall and dark like his mother, and Orsin was built like Chonrad: broad-shouldered and brown-haired. Horada was almost ethereal, a dreamer who seemed continually in another world. Where had this delicate flower sprung from?

"I had a dream too." Horada pushed her hair behind her ears. "About the Arbor. It was on fire…"

Procella stared. Her daughter had never seen the Arbor – Chonrad had always refused to take her there, even though both their sons had visited it at varying times. "Fire?"

Horada nodded absently. "I could smell it in the air, and feel the heat on my face." She turned concerned eyes back to her mother. "I think…" She hesitated. "I think it meant something."

Words failed Procella. In her head, she heard Chonrad say, "Bring her." Had he been referring to his daughter? But it had just been a dream, she reminded herself. It wasn't an omen or a portent or a glimpse of the future. It couldn't be.

Procella had never experienced a spiritual moment in her life. Like all good Militis, while in the army she had carried out her evening rituals and worn her oak-leaf pendant around her neck, and she still bore the oak-leaf tattoo on her outer wrist, a constant reminder of her past life as Dux. But although she loved the Arbor and would have defended it with her life, it had always been others who'd had the spiritual connection with the tree.

So why was she dreaming about it now? And Horada too? Had her daughter somehow inherited Chonrad's strange connection with it?

"What do you think it means?" she asked.

Horada moistened her lips. "I think it wants me to go there."

Cold filtered down through Procella as if she had drunk a cup of water from a mountain stream. "That would not be wise."

"But–"

"Your father refused to take you there," Procella said sharply. "I have always wondered why, but now I am starting to think he was right. You saw what the Arbor did to him, and maybe he worried it would do the same to you."

"If the Arbor calls, we should answer regardless." Horada's midnight-blue eyes shone with idealistic fervour.

Procella refrained from yelling the sort of swear word she would once have uttered to her fellow Militis in the training ground. She had gained more control over her language since having children and finding out they copied every word she said. But still her back stiffened with resentment. "Should we? Why so?"

Horada frowned. "What do you mean?"

"Why should we go running? The Arbor killed your father, remember?" She clenched her fists, fighting the surge of emotion.

Horada looked up at the stars. "I wish I could have spoken to him about it before he died."

"Yes, well, so do I, but we were not given that luxury."

"I know. And I know that you resent him and the Arbor for that. But he would not have wanted it any other way."

Procella saw scarlet. "Do not presume to tell me what my husband would have wanted. I know he would have been glad to help, but he did not enjoy being at the Arbor's beck and call. The tree revolted him – did you know that?" Horada's startled gaze told her that no, she did not. "He hated the way the tree took sacrifices each year. He could not bear to watch it consume them – it sickened him. Yes, he had a special connection to it. But that did not mean he had to like it." Her voice was sharp enough to chop an oak tree in half.

Horada's bottom lip trembled. "Do not be angry with me. I cannot help it – I can hear it. I can feel it. It is calling me. I must go – I do not have a choice."

"You are not going," Procella said flatly. "Go back to bed."

Horada studied her for a moment. Then, without another word, she turned and walked down the stairs.

Procella smacked her hand on the stone parapet, earning herself an alarmed stare from the guard in the corner who had tried unsuccessfully to ignore her raised voice. It was time for Horada to marry, to have children of her own, to throw off these fanciful dreams and come back down to earth.

But the taste of ash lingered in her mouth, along with the feel of heat on her face. And Chonrad's words, *"Bring her"*, were to echo in her mind for the rest of the day.

II

Demitto roasted slowly in his ceremonial plate armour like a chicken in a pot.

Sweat ran down his back, soaking the tunic he wore under it, and beneath his helmet his hair stuck to his head and his eyes stung. He would have given anything to strip off and dive into the moat surrounding the castle in front of him, even though a layer of scum that covered the surface looked as if it would have dissolved the top layer of his skin if it came within contact.

But he was a trained knight, used to spending hours in the saddle, and his role as ambassador had meant a lot of waiting around over the years. So he sighed and contented himself with shifting into a more comfortable position, and passed the time by keeping an eye on the palm trees and ferns in the bush around him as they rippled in the warm breeze.

He would never have admitted it, but the lush greenery made him nervous. Born in Lassington, a coastal town surrounded by wheat and barley fields, the jungle areas on the southern and western edges of Laxony were alien to him; so different to the oak and beech forests to the east. Every year, it seemed the vines and creepers covered more of Anguis, a slow encroachment, which was nevertheless transforming the countryside he travelled through regularly. This was his first journey so far south, though, and here the thick, dense bush to the west had grown right up to the old castle moat, where surely once the building had stood proud and free, able to look down on the surrounding countryside like a superior nursemaid.

A huge dragonfly flew in front of him, and his horse danced nervously. He patted its neck, looking at the giant pink flowers lining the path to the castle, their leaves as big as his hand. He missed the daisies and buttercups in the meadows, the bluebells and daffodils. It was time to return home, he thought. He had been gone too long.

How long was he going to have to wait out here in the sweltering, moist heat? Mosquitoes were eating him alive wherever they could find a bare patch of skin beneath all the armour. Surely it couldn't be much longer before the castle guard came out to get him? He was from Heartwood, after all. As a royal emissary of the holy Arbor, he was rarely kept waiting for long.

But the sun continued to beat down, and he was just starting to think that he didn't care if the future of the kingdom depended on it – he wasn't going to fry for another minute, when the drawbridge lowered, colour flashed beneath the portcullis, and a small party emerged carrying the blue and silver flag of Harlton.

He straightened in the saddle, watching as the horses approached the waiting party. He had wondered whether the Prince himself would be among them, but the leader was a woman, and she didn't look happy. Tall in the saddle, slender in an embroidered blue and silver tunic over plate armour, she had long dark hair braided back off a severe face, with piercing eyes that turned him to ice in spite of the hot weather.

Even before she introduced herself, he was pretty certain he knew who she was. He had dreamed about this ever since the Nox Aves had given him his quest; had built it up into a historic meeting of great significance; had expected trumpets to ring and stars to fall out of the sky at the momentousness of it. He held his breath, waiting for the speech he was certain would go down in history.

She reined in her horse, rested her hands on the pommel and glared at him. "Come with me." She turned the horse and started back for the castle.

Demitto's eyebrows shot into his hairline. Disappointed, he glanced across at the four knights who had travelled with him from Heartwood, seeing his own resentment reflected in their hot faces.

He kicked the horse forward to walk beside her. "Good morrow to you too," he said as he raised his visor, also irritated that he had been baked like a bun and yet no apology seemed forthcoming.

She cast her dark glance at him again, studied his face and then visibly softened, as if the sun had finally thawed her. "I am sorry. It has been a long day."

Indeed it had, and she had not been sweltering in a steel suit. He didn't say that, however, slightly mellowed by her apology. "You do not seem particularly pleased to see us," he observed.

"It is not you as such," she clarified. "More the situation." She shook her head. "Perhaps we should start again. I am Catena, Chief of the Guard at Harlton Castle."

I know. He didn't say it, though. "Demitto," he returned. "Ambassador to Heartwood."

It was a title that usually made people gasp with admiration. Catena, however, merely rolled her eyes.

He chuckled. "I can see you are a difficult woman to impress."

"Ambassador to a tree." She waved a hand in the air. "I am in awe."

That made him laugh out loud, a reaction she obviously hadn't expected, judging by the way she looked at him with startled eyes. "By the oak leaf," he exclaimed. "Someone must have really stoked your fire today. The Prince, maybe?" Her wry glance told him he had guessed right. "What did he do to earn your ire?"

She slowed the horse and surveyed him with interest. "You are very direct."

"I am interested."

"Do you really think this is an appropriate conversation? Considering that the Prince has been Selected, and I am to accompany him to Heartwood?"

Demitto shrugged. "As ambassador, my role is to improve communication between Heartwood and the neighbouring realms. Besides..." he said, smiling, "I am a good listener."

She let out a long, slow sigh and looked at the rustling ferns. "It is a long story."

"I have been here for hours. Clearly, there is no rush."

The horses' hooves echoed across the wooden drawbridge. Catena nodded at him. "Maybe later. Although I believe you will probably understand the problem very shortly."

Leaving him with that mysterious comment, she dismounted, and he followed suit, handing the reins to one of the pages who had run out to greet the party.

He looked curiously around the outer ward. The castle lay just outside the mysterious Komis lands. Built a hundred years before, its design mirrored the concentric castles found throughout Laxony, but the carvings above the doorways were not the natural patterns he was used to, like leaves and flowers, but instead consisted of geometric shapes – triangles and spirals and dots in the Komis fashion.

Although trade relations in Anguis had improved a hundredfold over the five hundred years since the historic Darkwater attack, and Komis men and women had integrated with Laxonians to a certain extent, there was still something exotic about them that fascinated Demitto. He knew King Gairovald had married a Komis, and supposedly their son – Prince Tahir, soon to be that year's sacrifice to the Arbor – had a very Komis look about him, but Demitto had yet to meet him.

Come to think of it, Catena herself probably had Komis blood in her, Demitto thought, watching her direct the household to secure the rest of the horses of the Heartwood party. Although she didn't have the distinctive golden Komis eyes, her black hair and swarthy complexion suggested an ancestor of that description somewhere in her heritage.

"Come with me." She jerked her head at him, and, removing his helmet, he followed her through the gatehouse into the castle proper.

Like the outside, the castle interior consisted of an intriguing blend of cultures. Demitto recognised the layout: the large central hall, the jumble of rooms, cool out of the heat of the sun. But the large tapestries on the walls depicted geometric shapes rather than the usual landscapes and battle scenes he was used to. Some he recognised as faces and animals and objects like trees, but they were composed of circles and squares, filled in with tiny colourful dots in the Komis fashion. He found them slightly disturbing, like something out of a dream.

Harlton kings had grown rich on the ores mined from the quarries to the west. Thick jungle now hampered the mining operations, but it would be a long while before the wealth they had accumulated vanished. Even in the castle, Demitto could smell the blacksmiths' fires on the air, overriding the usual castle smells of cooking food and ash from the fire, and a strange tang of metal in his mouth set his teeth on edge.

Catena walked forward, gesturing for him to follow, and led him toward the dais. The King and Queen of Amerle sat in elaborate chairs side by side and watched him. Next to them, in a smaller chair, sat a young man who looked down his nose at the Heartwood party. Like his mother, the thirteen year-old Selected had raven hair braided back off his face with gold and jewelled clasps, dark brown skin, and eyes that – even from a distance – were a startling, bright gold. A large hunting dog sat by his side, and the Prince's hand was clenched in its fur, the only sign that maybe he wasn't as relaxed as he appeared.

Demitto approached the dais, stopped a few feet away and bowed. He closed his eyes for a moment and concentrated, remembering his purpose for being there, thinking of the Arbor, the way its leaves rustled when there was no wind, the soft beat of its heart beneath the bark. Then he opened his eyes and stood to face his curious audience. "Greetings from Heartwood."

The King stood and gave him a soldier's salute. Demitto returned it, then stepped forward and the two men grasped wrists and rested a hand on each other's shoulder.

"You are most welcome," Gairovald said. He looked relieved. That puzzled Demitto. "And we are sorry to have kept you waiting. My son was keen to look his best for the Heartwood party."

Demitto's gaze slid to the Prince. He didn't look as if impressing his guests was of particular importance to him. He looked bored and impatient, as if this was all a huge waste of his time. An interesting attitude for a person who was about to dedicate his life to a holy cause.

Demitto glanced at Catena. Undisguised impatience flitted across her face before she caught him looking at her and wiped her expression clear. He filed that look away to think about later.

The formalities continued. Gairovald introduced him to the Queen, then to other members of the court. There were lots of them, people having travelled from far and wide to see the Heartwood party and to say their last goodbyes to the Prince – officially, at least. Demitto noted that nobody paid any interest to the Prince at all. He sat to one side, flipping through the pages of a book, seemingly removed from the festivities.

After the introductions, they all sat down to eat, Demitto and the rest of the Heartwood followers at the high table, everyone else on benches that ran the length of the hall. Servants placed elaborate dishes of stuffed swans resplendent in their feathers, whole roasted pigs and hundreds of cooked chickens on the tables, along with pitchers of ale and large bowls of fruit.

Demitto had a headache after sitting too long in the sun and was desperate to remove his armour and have a long soak in a bath, but he ate politely, made conversation and watched the entertainers, conscious all the while of Tahir's bored and detached demeanour, his superior manner to those around him. Demitto looked longingly at the ale, but purposely steered clear, wanting to keep his wits about him, at least until he had performed his official duties.

Finally the meal ended. Tahir tossed a half-eaten chicken leg onto his plate, got up and walked off behind the dais to the upstairs rooms without a word to anyone, his dog close behind him, earning him a glare from his father, who nevertheless did not rise to go after him. Catena – who'd eaten sparingly at the end of the table near Demitto and answered any questions asked of her in monosyllables – watched the Prince go, then stood and said, "It has been a long day for the party from Heartwood, my liege. They have travelled far and we have to start a long journey soon too. Perhaps we should excuse them for now?"

Gairovald waved a hand, clearly as relieved as his captain of the guard that the day was over. "Yes, yes, of course. Please, show our guests to their chambers."

Demitto rose, bowed and followed Catena out of the hall.

"Thank you," he murmured. "I am exhausted. It was only my armour keeping me upright."

She laughed – the first time she had done so – and it lit up her face like the sun. "I am presuming before you go to your chamber you would like a bath?"

His answer was immediate and heartfelt. "Oh, roots of the Arbor, would I."

"Follow me, then. I think I will join you. This cursed heat has melted my patience."

She led him outside to the bath house – a separate stone building with a hypocaust system under the tiled floor to keep the baths hot. She, Demitto and the other Heartwood knights stripped and sank into the water with a collective sigh.

"Bliss," Demitto said, leaning his head on the back of the bath and closing his eyes. They had added the usual rose petals to the water but it also had a strange smell he couldn't place, something like cinnamon or cloves, sharp on the nostrils. Komir spices no doubt. He didn't like it particularly, but he was too tired to complain and ask for a separate bath.

For a while they soaked in peace, and he let the heat of the water dissolve away the aches in his bones. Heartwood to Harlton was a good ten or eleven days' ride, and he was glad of the brief respite before the return journey.

After a while, Catena spoke. "Following your bath, I expect you will want to retire?"

He opened his eyes and rolled his head on the tiles to look at her. She looked younger without the heavy armour, and strands of her black hair curled around her neck where they had escaped the knot on the top of her head.

"After this I expect to visit every inn in town," he corrected. "I have not had a decent ale all journey."

Her lips curved. "You drink ale? I am shocked!"

"Why?"

"You did not have any at the table. I presumed it was because you had taken holy orders?"

He shrugged and closed his eyes again. "We swear to protect the Arbor, but we are not monks. Those days are long gone."

She fell quiet for a few minutes and they soaked in companionable silence. Then she said, "How long have you been escorting the sacrifices to Heartwood?"

"I have been ambassador for eight years," he said. "I do not escort every year. This is my fifth time."

"And are all sacrifices spoilt brats?"

He opened his eyes again, amused this time. He studied her for a while, long enough to make her shift uncomfortably in the water and say, "What?"

"Did it cross your mind that maybe the Prince is nervous?"

She thought about it. "Honestly? I do not believe that is the case. He is arrogant and thinks he is better than everyone around him because he has been Selected. But he has not won this honour through good deeds, for winning a battle or for being a champion among men."

"It has been a long time since a Selected was picked in such a manner."

"I know." Her brow furrowed. She leaned forward and spoke in a low voice. "Once, those who wished to give their life to the Arbor went to Heartwood to study, and only those who truly understood the nature of their sacrifice were allowed to offer themselves to the tree. Now rich families proffer sons and daughters like produce at a market. Pay the highest price and you can win a place in Animus's kingdom! It disgusts me." Her eyes blazed. "How glorious it must have been for a while, at the beginning of the Second Era, when the land was renewed and everyone's faith was restored. Do you really think Teague and Beata gave their lives so that boys like Tahir would think themselves superior to the rest of us?"

Demitto frowned, still hot and irritated by the strange herb that made his nose itch. "I am no philosopher. I leave the studying to others. As far as I am concerned, these names you mention could just be characters in a story. How do we know the tales are all true? I judge the world based on what is before me – by what I can touch and see. The Arbor needs to consume a living person each year – what does it matter whether the Selected reads scripture or not, whether he or she is holier than you or I? What does that even mean, anyway?"

She stared at him. "You are the ambassador to our holy city. I am aghast that you should speak in such manner." She looked at him as if he had stated that he ate live babies to break his fast each day.

He studied her, watching the way a droplet of water ran from her hair behind her ear and down her long neck. "Have you ever been to Heartwood?"

She glared. "No."

"Then you know nothing about that of which you speak. You have never seen the Arbor, or the city that surrounds it. I expect you envisage it as some shining settlement with streets paved with gold, and holy men and women in white robes singing its praises day and night?"

Her cheeks reddened. "Of course not."

"Perhaps it was that way, in the early days – who is to know? Now it certainly is not. It reeks. Stinks of animal dung and rotting food and sulphur from the smoking mountain behind it. And at night the torches fill the streets with smoke. It is difficult to get near the Arbor itself because of all the pilgrims who stand in line for hours to file past and get one brief touch of its trunk. The King of Heartwood is a fat oaf who is the son of another fat oaf who was no doubt the son of another fat oaf before that, and I doubt they could even spell Oculus or Animus or if any of them would have even heard of the Darkwater Lords. They take money from those who wish to offer their offspring to the tree, and they spend that money on scarlet gowns and golden crowns and venison for their tables. So please do not criticise my faith or my loyalty to that place. It does not deserve it."

He finished, breathless, fists clenched as he sat upright in the bath, back rigid.

Catena studied him wordlessly. For a moment he thought she might knock him out with a fist to his chin and wondered whether he should find something to hang on to. But then, to his surprise, her lips curved.

"Some ambassador you are," she said.

His eyes met hers, and they both started laughing.

"Tell me," she said as they both settled back into the water and stretched out their legs. "Is it true what they say – that Anguis is stirring across the land, not just here?"

Demitto nodded and rubbed his face tiredly, glad she had seen the funny side of it. He really needed to get some sleep before he insulted someone who would really take offence and cause a national incident. "Yes. The weather grows warmer by the day. Throughout my journey I have felt the rumbles beneath the ground. But none as bad as in Heartwood. The mountains behind the city emit smoke and ash on a daily basis."

They fell silent. Demitto surprised himself by wishing he could tell her what he knew and lighten the load a little. But the secret he carried with him could save the world, and he did not have the luxury of sharing it with others.

Instead, he stretched his arms above his head, glad to feel his muscles finally softening, his bones loosening. "By the Arbor, it has been a long day."

Catena pushed herself up out of the water, accepted a towel from one of the waiting pages and began to dry herself off. "Come on. Get dressed and I will take you into the town. The *Fat Pig* has twelve different imported ales for sale at a reasonable price. I wager I can drink more than you before you slide under the table."

"Done," he said wryly, rising to join her. He needed sleep, but the opportunity to drink himself senseless was too much of a draw, and besides, after what he had had to put up with that day, he felt as if he had earned it.

III

It was difficult to walk, stumbling in the darkness with a cloth sack over her head.

Sarra kept her complaints to herself, however, determined not to make a fuss. In spite of her irritation at being treated as if she were untrustworthy, she understood how imperative it was that their destination remain a secret, and that the members of the group remain anonymous. Their lives depended on it, and if she discovered who they were and where they were going before she had established their trust, she had no doubt what that would mean. She would be found floating in the Great Lake with the turtles, and nobody would come forward to claim her. Her body would be taken to the depths of the Secundus District and burned, and nobody would mourn one less mouth to feed. So she remained silent, even though she occasionally stumbled and twisted her ankle or stubbed her toe on a rock, thinking instead of the future, clinging to the hope of better things to come.

Presumably, they thought she had no idea where she was. From their starting point in Pisspot Lane in the Primus District, their course had twisted and turned through the streets until eventually she had lost all sense of direction. But she was able to follow their route by the smells that penetrated the cloth.

The acrid stench of urine and leather from the tanners was gradually replaced by the smell of peat as they skirted the river banks and the weavers' houses, distinguishable by the aroma of dried mosses and pungent dyes. When the tang of fish assailed her nostrils, she knew they were crossing the quay around the Great Lake. Here they moved slowly, keeping to the shadows of the houses – after all, if the Select caught two people escorting another in such a manner, with her head covered, there would be questions to answer and her chance would be over. So she trod carefully over the fishermen's nets and tried not to rattle the turtle shells as the men escorted her along the western edge of the quay.

Their path twisted and turned some more and she lost her sense of direction again. They paused frequently, her guards pushing her into alleyways as voices came towards them. The bustle of people and the stink of perfume oil announced the presence of the whorehouses, which meant they were travelling into the Secundus District. Her heart rate increased even more. She rarely entered the area, preferring to keep to the trade regions and the relative security of the family caverns in Primus. Everyone knew the Select had less control over the inhabitants in Secundus. Overcrowding, poverty, starvation and murder were all commonplace. She clutched hold of Geve's hand, and his tightened on hers in response, comforting her.

The aroma of berry pie told her when they had reached the playhouse. At this late hour, the shows had concluded, but the aroma of baked pastry and cooked fruit still pervaded the air and made her mouth water. The smell made her smile, in spite of her nerves. Rauf had loved pie. He had introduced her to all kinds, brought into the palace from across the sectors, flavoured with fruits and herbs she had never even heard of, let alone tasted before. He had even given her some of the legendary whiskey brewed in the Tertius Sector, although she had not liked it much. He had laughed heartily at the faces she pulled before he took her in his arms and stifled her complaints with kisses.

She pushed the thoughts of him away from her mind. Rauf was gone. The tears she had cried over him could have filled the Great Lake three times over, but she was done mourning. She had to fend for herself now.

They were entering deeper into the Secundus District now. It was late, the alehouses would be full, and she could hear men fighting, the bellow of voices and the crunch of fist meeting bone. In the distance, a woman screamed, abruptly cut off. The air smelled sour and fetid, of unwashed bodies, vomit and other bodily fluids. The men with her moved more quickly, apparently as keen as she was to pass through the troublesome area.

They must be nearing the southern edge now, she calculated, shivering at the thought that one day her body might be disposed of here, the ash washed away over the Magna Cataracta to who-knew-where. But even as she wondered if that was their destination, her feet hit cool water, the shock making her inhale and clutch Geve's hand. They were crossing the river, which meant their destination was away from the waterfall, to the south-western limits of the city. Geve steadied her, guiding her across to the other side, the splash of their feet ringing in her ears. They were heading for the forgotten caves. She had never been this far south. Here the air smelled stale, and sound echoed without people and belongings to soak it up. Most of these caves had been deserted since the White Sickness. The palace insisted the disease had long since died out, but even the poorest in the city refused to cross the banks, in spite of the overcrowding in many areas.

The avenues changed to streets, the streets to lanes, and then they were in alleyways so narrow she could stretch out her hands and brush her fingers against the stone walls on either side. Were there still bodies here? Rumours abounded that the Select had left the sick here to die and just chained off the area. She sniffed cautiously. The air smelled clean with no sign of the sickly sweet smell of rotting flesh. Perhaps it had been too long, and the flesh had turned to dust, and only bones remained. No wonder the group met here – who would ever think to look for them in the forgotten caves?

She shivered, although whether from having wet feet, from the thought of the dead lying abandoned, or from the knowledge that nobody knew she was there, she wasn't sure.

Finally, the men in front of her slowed, and her fingers brushed against a woven door that had been pulled back to let her through. Her shoes scrunched on matting. Whispers and the occasional scuff of feet told her there were other people in the room. Judging by the acoustics, the room was small, but she couldn't make out anything more than that.

Someone led her to a chair and pushed her gently into it, and she sat. She was thankful the journey was over, but her heart continued to pound at the thought of the interrogation she was now going to have to endure.

"Sarra?" It was a voice she recognised. Geve, her friend from the Primus Caverns, the man she had approached in the first place.

She cleared her throat. "Yes?"

"Are you all right? Are you comfortable?"

"Yes, thank you."

"I am sorry that I cannot yet remove the hood, but you understand that secrecy is imperative here."

"I do. I am hot and my nose itches, but I am not distressed by it – please do not worry."

There was a light ripple of laughter. Her chest rose and fell with her rapid breaths, but she forced herself to keep calm. The next few minutes would possibly be the most important of her life. Comfort was the last thing on her mind.

"Tell us why you are here," Geve said. His low voice was gentle and encouraging. He liked her, she reminded herself – he was on her side.

"I wish to know about the Veris," she said.

"Who are the Veris?" he asked.

"A secret society."

"What sort of secret society?"

"You worship the Arbor. You believe in the Surface – a world above the Embers."

There, she had said it. The words were out – there was no going back now. She was either leaving this cave a member of the society or wrapped up in a death blanket.

The room had grown silent, and she had visions of the men and women exchanging worried glances.

"How do you know about the Veris?" a woman asked.

She nibbled her bottom lip. She had thought long and hard about how to answer this question and had decided truth was the best option, although it would not make it easier for them to trust her. "Rauf told me."

Hushed whispers travelled around the room. She waited, letting them process that information.

Eventually, Geve spoke again. "What did Rauf tell you?"

"He heard talk at the palace. The Select know about you."

More hushed whispers. "What do they know?" the woman asked.

"Rauf told me they had heard of a secret group of people who studied the forbidden histories and who believed another world exists on the Surface. He seemed to think it was just a rumour."

"He told you of the Arbor?" Geve asked.

"No." Sarra hesitated. "I… I saw that."

"Saw?" said a man.

"I… see things sometimes. Flashes, like dreams." She took a deep breath. Time to play her trump card. "Of a land, the ground covered in grass. A blue sky and a bright sun. And a tree – a huge tree, arching above me, its leaves fluttering in a warm breeze."

Silence fell. Sarra swallowed. Voices whispered and fell quiet again.

"Search her," a woman commanded.

She waited to feel hands on her clothing, although what they were searching for, she had no idea. But instead someone moved to her side and crouched next to her. "I am going to take your hand," murmured a male voice she didn't recognise. He clasped his hands around hers.

Puzzled, she waited. His hands grew warm, then fiery hot. The heat flooded her veins and sped around her body, and within seconds she broke out in a sweat, burning as if she had a violent temperature. She gasped, but just as she was about to exclaim that she couldn't bear the heat any longer, he stood and released her.

"She is clean," he said. His hands touched her head, and then he lifted off her hood.

Sarra blinked, dazzled for a moment by the bright flame of a single candle that Geve held nearby. Gradually, her vision cleared. The room was small, maybe ten feet square, and there were seven people in it, including herself and Geve with his dark, curly hair, all watching her intently.

The man who had held her hand spoke. "Greetings, Sarra. My name is Turstan." He was slim and dark-skinned with intense eyes but a friendly smile.

She returned it as she said, "You can control fire. You are a member of the Select."

He nodded and lifted the sunstone hanging around his neck on a leather thong from his tunic. It absorbed the light from the candle, glowing a deep orange. Rauf had been a Select too, so she had been aware of the way the palace guardians used the sunstones to channel fire to light the darkness of the caves they lived in.

"And you are a bard," Turstan said.

And this was the bit she had dreaded most. She lifted her chin and shook her head. "No."

He blinked. "I thought you had the dreams?"

"I have not always had them," she said. "Only recently."

They look confused, suddenly wary, even Geve. She had not told him everything, and in his eyes she saw his distrust, his fear that he had brought a traitor into the group. "What do you mean?" he demanded.

She rested a hand on her abdomen. "I am pregnant."

Their faces registered shock and pity. Now they understood why she wanted to escape. And by making such an admission, they would also know she was placing her complete trust in them.

Turstan frowned. "You think the child is why you have the ability to see the Surface?"

"Yes. I think the baby is a bard." She splayed her hands on her stomach. It had just started to swell, although her clothes hid it for now. But it would not be long before the pregnancy became obvious. "He... speaks to me. He shows me scenes of another life on the Surface, of a land rich with growth, where everyone is free."

They nodded, unsurprised. All of the people here, she knew, would have had similar dreams. That was what had brought them all together, except perhaps for Turstan, whose position as a Select would have earned him his place in the society. Could he be trusted? She was surprised he had been allowed in the group. How could they be sure he wasn't reporting everything back to Comminor, the hated Chief Select?

Turstan dropped to his haunches in front of her again. She studied his fine clothing, the silver clasps studded with tiny gems in his braided hair. His sleeveless tunic fit snugly across his broad shoulders and, like Rauf, his arms and thighs were impressively muscled. His bright eyes and strong teeth reflected his better diet, and he smelled of herbs, which meant he had bathed that morning in the clean, fresh waters near the palace.

She shifted in the chair, conscious – as she had used to be with Rauf in the early days – of her shapeless tunic, her unwashed body, her tangled hair. She never wore the silver clasp he had given her; too afraid someone would steal it. And here was this man, reminding her of everything she had once had, and then lost.

Why did Turstan want to escape so badly? He could have whatever woman he wanted, and if one of them got pregnant, he would likely be granted the right for the child to be born. Resentment surged through her, and she let it show in her eyes.

Turstan nodded. "I know," he murmured. "And I understand. I am sure you are wondering why I am here – why I want to leave so badly."

She nodded curtly.

"Two years ago, I fell in love with a girl from Secundus. She was a bard, although I did not know it at the time. She used to tell me stories, late at night when the palace was dark and we were curled in our bed, stories about a green land, about the sun and the way it made the plants grow. About rain that fell from the sky, and wind that blew across the fields. About a tree – a tree so wonderful it made everything else pale in comparison."

Turstan's eyes were far away, seeing not the dim light of the cave and the people around him, but the pictures this girl had painted in his mind of a better life.

"For a long time I thought these were just stories, but as time went by and she began to trust me more, I realised she was not making these tales up in her mind – she was describing another world, where people live on the Surface, in the sun and wind and rain. Where they are not confined to caves and told whether they can and cannot have children, but where they are free to love and marry and have babies with whomever they chose."

He turned his dark eyes back to Sarra, and she swallowed as she saw tears in them. She had suspected the truth from the visions the baby had shown her, but it moved her to have another confirm what she had wondered in her mind.

"And I want that freedom," Turstan said fiercely. "I may have privileges here in the Embers but it is not the same as being free."

"I understand," she whispered. It was what they all wanted. To be free. To live their lives the way they chose.

It was time to reveal her final secret. "There is something else," she said. She glanced at Geve. This bit he did know about, and he nodded now, encouraging her to speak.

"The baby," she said. "He has also shown me the way out."

CHAPTER TWO

I

Julen pushed open one of the hall doors and walked inside. A blast of hot air from the fire in the hearth washed over him, and he stood there for a moment, drinking in the warmth, feeling comforted and welcomed after a morning out on Isenbard's Wall. In spite of it being the height of The Shining, the wind was always brisk across the high hills this end of the Wall so near the sea.

He cast his eye around and saw his mother and siblings eating by the fire, much of the rest of the household dotted around them, the steward directing some of the servants to carry fresh fruit to the tables, maids carrying pitchers of ale from person to person.

Everything seemed normal and in place, from the huge tapestries depicting various battle scenes from his family's past, to the light laughter that rippled around the room as people chatted and relayed the events of their day, to the smell of the fresh rushes on the floor, scattered with lavender and mint, and the aroma of roasted meat that drifted up from the kitchens.

And yet, once again, a frisson of warning ran up his spine.

He put his hand out automatically and Rua's head appeared underneath it, as he had known it would. She stood close to him, cautious and quiet as they both surveyed the room. Could she feel it too? Or was she just picking up on his apprehension?

As before, he couldn't place the problem, so he mentally pushed it away, walked forward and crossed the hall to his family. "Good afternoon," he said, bending forward to kiss his mother on the cheek.

"You are late," she said, running her gaze down him. "And please tell me you are not joining us looking like that."

He glanced down and surveyed his mud-splattered breeches and boots, scratched at the stubble on his face and tugged at his untidy beard. Then he shrugged, climbed onto the bench and sat. "I would not want to deny you a second of my company while I bothered to change," he said as he reached for a loaf of bread and winked at his mother.

Procella's glare faded to a wry smile, and she rolled her eyes and carried on eating. He laughed and cut a thick slice of the bread, winking at his brother, who grinned back. Like the dog sitting beside him, his mother was mostly bark and no bite, although he had seen both of them in battle and knew both to have a savage side that revealed itself when the occasion demanded it. Procella's hair might now be grey, and occasionally in the mornings she moved stiffly until she had worn off the old battles' aches and pains she had gained through the years, but only last week he had accompanied her on a foray into the forest south of Vichton where a group of bandits had been preying on travellers on the road south to Lotberg. She had joined him in hunting them down with her characteristic skill on horseback, and when they caught them, she had dispatched them swiftly, casting aside their vain attempts to defend themselves with undisguised contempt before ending their lives.

Julen had remained astride his horse and had watched her take on three of them in one go, thankful of a situation where she could exorcise her frustration and fury instead of taking it out on him. He loved his mother, but without his father there to lock horns with her and keep her grounded, she rattled around the old castle like a bee in a pot, driven to restless vexation through a lack of activity and physical release.

She was not made for peace, he thought as he took a thick slice of pork and another of beef, layering them with a third slice of cheese on the bread before taking a bite. Procella was a woman built for war, and sometimes he wondered whether she was jealous that he worked for the Peacekeeper.

"So what is the news on the road?" she asked. "Tell us something exciting. It is so very dull around here sometimes."

He glanced at Horada, wondering whether his sister would feel insulted that her mother had described her company as dull, but her gaze was fixed on the candle in the centre of the table, which flickered in the breeze of the open doors, and she did not appear to have heard Procella's words. His eyes followed hers. The candle flame danced, jumping and writhing like a tortured soul in a bright yellow cage. He blinked, seeing bright light before his eyes for a moment as he turned his gaze away.

"I *have* heard something interesting, as it happens." He started to cut himself another slice of bread. "There is talk across the whole of Anguis from Crossnaire to Quillington of an unusual frequency of fires springing up."

"That must be due to the weather." Orsin was busy cutting himself a piece of apple pie. His genial face was relaxed, his beard neatly trimmed, his light brown hair slightly damp, showing he had bathed only an hour before. Orsin liked to bathe, saying women preferred him that way, which was probably true. "It has been incredibly hot lately. The undergrowth must be dry as a five-day bone, and the bracken and dead leaves would make perfect kindling."

"True." Julen concentrated on building another few layers of meat and cheese, and threw a fatty bit of pork to Rua where she lay patiently on the rushes by his feet. "But it is not just in the forest that this has been happening. People have reported it all over the place. In homes, in stables, in market places, in the fields." He wondered whether to mention the rest of his news, then thought about his initial unease on entering the room and decided not to.

He glanced up and paused in the act of placing the last slice of cheese on the top. "What?"

Orsin followed his gaze. Horada's attention had finally been drawn away from the candle, and she and her mother stared at each other for a long moment before both dropped their eyes.

Procella cleared her throat and sliced an apple in half. "How is the Veriditas?"

He met Orsin's gaze and raised an eyebrow. His brother shrugged. Julen wasn't surprised. Orsin had been away for many years, serving first as a page then as a squire at a neighbouring lord's castle, and he had only returned to Vichton after their father's death. Although built like Chonrad with his height and broad shoulders, Orsin had their mother's lack of sensitivity, and this, combined with his long absence, meant he wouldn't have known an atmosphere if it had stood in front of him waving.

Julen took a bite out of his meat and cheese. "Good. The Nodes are attended to regularly."

"And the Arbor?"

"Is good. Tall and strong. The flow of energies is working, Mother, do not fear. What is bothering you?"

"Horada and I... We both had the same dream last night."

He looked up sharply. "The same?"

"Well, similar. We both dreamed the Arbor was on fire."

Cold sliced through him. Suddenly he couldn't swallow the meat and cheese in his mouth. Conscious of his mother's eyes on him, he forced himself to chew several times and took a large mouthful of ale to help the food go down.

He cleared his throat. "How strange."

"I think it means something." It was the first time Horada had spoken. She had gone back to staring at the flame, her brow furrowed.

Julen poured her another glass of ale. "What do you think it means?"

"I think the Arbor wants me to go there." She glanced up at her mother, then away again.

Julen looked at Procella, whose mouth had set into a thin, hard line. "We have had this discussion," Procella said.

"Discussion?" Horada lifted her chin. "We did not 'discuss' anything. You told me I cannot go. That is not a discussion."

Procella's eyes blazed. Julen frowned. His mother had little respect for his sister. Procella thought her daughter weak, not just because she was physically small, but because she had never shown an interest in picking up a sword. Their mother thought all her children should be like her – strong and fierce, able to defend themselves should the need arise, but Horada had proved useless in battle practice and had eventually walked away, refusing to take part. Because of this, Julen was sure Procella secretly despised her.

But what his mother did not seem to understand was that Horada's strengths lay elsewhere. His sister was calm and patient, thoughtful and determined, and although these were not qualities prided by his mother, Julen was sure his father had seen within Horada something of himself. Chonrad's heart had been the size of a mountain, his strength what the Arbor had needed all those years ago when the Darkwater Lords invaded, and almost certainly just the year before, when it had called to him again.

And maybe the Arbor was calling to her now, as the daughter of Chonrad, to come to it and help it. He could understand why that thought scared his mother. He had been shocked when Chonrad had returned from Heartwood, carried on a pallet, too weak to stand. The Arbor had drained him, and Procella – who had spent her life defending the great tree – would never forgive it for taking away the man she loved.

Julen missed his father. But sometimes things happened in

the world that were about more than one person, that were bigger than a love of a man for a woman, or a child for his father. Chonrad had understood that, and in spite of his loyalty to his family, he had left them to answer the Arbor's call, and Julen did not blame him for it. The Arbor had to be maintained – that, if nothing else, the Darkwater Lords had taught them. And who were they to deny it, if it called to them for help?

But Procella knew only that the Arbor had killed her husband, and now it wanted her daughter, and she was clearly going to do everything in her power to ensure it didn't get her.

"Eat your chicken," she instructed her daughter. "You are too skinny."

In answer, Horada pushed away her plate, got up and walked away.

Procella inhaled as if she were about to yell, but Julen stood and held up a hand. "I will talk to her, Mother." Procella glared but nodded and turned her attention to the accounts the steward had brought for her to examine. Julen winked at his brother and left the table, Rua by his side.

He followed Horada out through the doors into the yard. She had already vanished, but he knew where she would be heading. He followed the building around to the east, skirted the stables and barns, and walked through the bougainvillea-covered archway into the herb garden.

She walked slowly along the lines of plants, bending occasionally to break off a dead leaf and rub it between her fingers before taking a gentle sniff. The scents of rosemary, marjoram, chives and garlic rose to mingle in the air as he brushed through them.

"I spoke to Silva last week," he said as he approached her. Silva was a Komis woman who had played a huge role in the healing of the Arbor during the Darkwater invasion.

Horada glanced over her shoulder as he approached, and straightened, shading her eyes from the sun. "Oh?"

"She is putting together a chronicle of medicines." He snapped off a small piece of mint and pressed it to his nose. "I told her that you are renowned throughout Vichton for your tinctures. She is hoping you will write some of them down for her so she can add them to her list."

"I would like to meet her." There was more than a hint of bitterness in her voice. "But that is clearly never going to happen."

He sat on a wooden bench amongst the roses and patted the seat to his right. "Maybe one day we will be able to persuade Mother to let you go."

"Not now." She sank listlessly onto the bench. "I should not have said anything about the dream. Now she will never let me out of her sight."

"It is not good to keep secrets," he said.

That earned him a wry look. "So says Heartwood's greatest spy."

He laughed. "I am not a spy."

"Are you not? You cannot fool me, brother. Gravis the Peacemaker may call you his right-hand man, but I know he makes use of your talent for stealth and your liking of shadows to infiltrate Anguis's darker spots."

He cocked his head at her. "And what makes you say that?" She was right, of course, but he would never admit it. The less she knew about what he really got up to out on the road, the safer she was.

She didn't answer him, just sank back onto the seat and tipped her face up to the sun with a heavy sigh. "Do you know how much I envy you?"

"Envy?"

"No one controls what you do or where you go. You do not know how lucky you are."

He studied her thoughtfully. How would he feel cooped up in this castle day after day with his mother? Frankly, he thought he might have gone mad. "I do understand.

And perhaps our parents have been overprotective. If so, it was only done out of love for you. But you are seventeen now. Many girls are married younger than that. Surely it will not be long before you have a husband and a castle of your own."

Horada dropped her head and stared across the gardens. "Exchange one prison for another?" She turned her dark blue eyes on him. "Would you do it?"

He said nothing, knowing it was a rhetorical question. "What do you want, sweetheart?"

She looked up at a seagull soaring on the zephyrs above the castle. "To be free."

Julen said nothing. The two of them sat in silence. What was there to be said, after all?

II

Tahir was sitting at the high table, breaking his fast, when Demitto finally roused from his pallet at the bottom of the hall. The Prince watched the man push himself upright, stretch, scratch his head wildly until his hair stuck up all over the place, then proceed to get dressed.

The ambassador looked a lot different without his armour, Tahir thought. Because of the heat, the guards at Harlton tended to wear little more than a leather jerkin and breeches on normal days, and even their ceremonial armour consisted of standard flat plates buckled onto the leather. The ambassador's armour had stunned Tahir with its elaborateness. Polished to a high shine and clean even after his long journey, the steel had been finely engraved with entwining leaves and vines, the numerous plates fitting over each other in intricate layers to enable him to move easily. The breastplate sported a picture of the Arbor, inlaid with tiny emerald chips to illustrate the tree's leaves. The helmet was also engraved with complex leaf designs, and a fan of peacock feathers sprouted from the top to fall down the knight's back. Tahir had never seen a peacock, and the shimmering blue and green eyes had sent a shiver down his back.

Although the suit would be impractical for the humid Amerle weather, the ambassador had struck an impressive sight when he first walked through the castle doors and strode toward the dais. The sunlight had slanted through the high windows and bounced off the jewels in the breastplate, dazzling Tahir and enveloping the emissary in a bright aura that Tahir had interpreted as a sign of holy fervour emitting from the knight's very soul.

Now, he realised how mistaken he had been. The ambassador was just a man, and not a very impressive one at that. Barely taller than Catena and about as thin, his hair was long, dark and scruffy, nowhere near as stylish as Tahir's own shiny and braided locks. He was well muscled though, presumably from years of weapons training, which surprised the Prince. He had not expected the ambassador to be a fighting man. He had expected a priest, a righteous, saintly figure who would give Tahir some reassurance that the role he was about to carry out had some purpose other than to provide compost for a plant.

Demitto did not appear to be righteous, or saintly. Having tugged on a tunic and breeches, he walked to the high dais a few seats down from Tahir, burped, farted, then sat and pulled a plate toward him and started eating.

"It is polite to say 'pardon me' if one belches at the table," the Prince said, indignant after years of social grooming.

Demitto looked across at him, still chewing, and surveyed him with an amused gaze. He gave a mock bow. "Begging your pardon, my prince." Then he lifted himself up and farted again, louder this time. Behind them, the servants broke into a ripple of giggles.

Catena approached the table and took a seat opposite them. She had clearly overheard their conversation, but to Tahir's annoyance she didn't reprimand the man. She just rolled her eyes and ladled porridge into a bowl.

Tahir stiffened. The man was mocking him. He noted Demitto's bleary gaze and reddened eyes, the heavy bristle on his chin. How dare the man appear in his presence in such an uncouth manner? "You were out drinking last night," he observed.

Demitto nodded and took a large bite of bread. "Indeed I was. Twelve ales, the inn had, all from various parts of Laxony. I highly recommend it."

"Your behaviour shocks me," Tahir announced.

"So I see." Demitto's eyes gleamed. "May I ask why?"

"Because you are an emissary of Heartwood," Tahir said hotly. "A holy man should not act thus."

Demitto burst into laughter, shook his head and swallowed a large mouthful of ale. "My dear prince, one thing I am *not* is holy." He gave them both a curious frown. "I am beginning to wonder what kind of vision you have of Heartwood down here."

"You represent the Arbor, do you not? You wear its likeness on your breastplate." Tahir clenched his fists on the table as the frustration and fear that had been building over the past year rose to the surface like a piece of wood cast into the moat. "The Arbor is a representation of Animus's love in Anguis. It deserves some respect, especially from those who claim to stand for it."

Demitto swallowed, put down his knife, turned to face the Prince and narrowed his blue eyes. "Now let us get a few things straight, little man. How old are you?"

Tahir lifted his chin. "Thirteen."

"Thirteen. And how many towns and cities have you visited on your travels?"

Tahir's cheeks grew hot. "I have never been out of Amerle."

"You have never been out of Amerle." Demitto's voice mocked him. "Well I am thirty-one, and I have visited practically every town in the whole of Anguis. Mortaire, where they make silver jewellery so intricate it looks like lace. Ornestan, where the great professors teach everything from Philosophy to Law to Science, and where I took part in a debate with the great scholars of the north. Franwar, where the quays are piled high with fish and crabs and lobsters, and where I went diving for coral on the reefs. Henton on the east, where they craft ships so large they can carry a whole army. And even to Darle in Komis – and yes, I can see that surprises you – where they carve wooden animals so lifelike you have to look twice to see if they are real. I have eaten with kings, slept with princesses, fought for princes and got blind drunk with guards. I can speak every language and feel at home at any table. I have seen the world, my friend – I am synonymous with Anguis. That is why I am Heartwood's ambassador – nothing more."

He turned back to his food and bit into an apple.

Tahir stared at him, heart pounding. The man was rude and arrogant, but still, there was something about him... Even though he made himself out to be little more than a mercenary, he emitted a charisma that Tahir had never seen before from anyone at court. Maybe it was just that he had travelled a lot and met many people – that he was exotic, like the peacock plume in his helm. But once again, in spite of his bristles and scruffy hair, he seemed to emit a golden glow, and the sun wasn't even shining.

Tahir's gaze slid across to Catena. Even though he suspected she had accompanied Demitto on his tour of the inns, she looked bright, her uniform clean and her dark hair carefully braided. She had been up for several hours – he had seen her out on the ramparts, organising the daily watch like she usually did every morning. He liked Catena, although he knew she didn't return the affection. But whereas many other courtiers said what they thought he wanted to hear, she always said exactly what was on her mind, even if she knew he wasn't going to like it, and he secretly respected her for that. She had been captain of the guard as long as he could remember, although she couldn't be older than thirty. But even though he knew he irritated her, he trusted her probably more than anyone else at the castle, including his parents.

Now she glanced at him, and he raised his eyebrows, wondering what she thought of the Heartwood ambassador. She looked at Demitto, then back at the Prince. Her mouth quirked. She liked him, in spite of herself, and Tahir thought he could understand why.

He pushed the remains of his breakfast around his plate. Humbleness did not come easily to him, but this man was to accompany him on the long journey to Heartwood, and he had not meant to alienate him. "I am sorry if I offended you. As you say, I have not travelled much, and I am not used to the ways of others."

Demitto met his gaze for a moment, then gave a short nod. He pulled a bunch of grapes toward him, plucked a few from the stalk and popped one in his mouth. "So tell me, young prince. How do you feel about being Selected?"

Tahir shrugged and played with the oak-leaf pendant around his neck. "I am honoured, of course."

"Of course." Demitto's mouth curved.

"You have accompanied the Selected to Heartwood in previous years?"

"Yes. Several times."

"Were they like me?" Tahir despised the way his voice sounded young and weak, but he could not hide his apprehension.

Demitto tipped his head from side to side as he considered. "Some were young, some were old. You are the youngest sacrifice ever to be offered, as far as I know."

"Do you… attend the ceremony?"

Demitto chewed another grape, his eyes on the Prince, then swallowed and nodded. "Yes."

Tahir's heart thumped against his ribs and nausea rose inside him. He picked up his knife and carved a few lines in the table. "Can you describe it to me? Nobody here has been able to tell me what will happen in detail."

Demitto took a swallow of ale from his goblet, leaned back in his chair and crossed his long legs. He exchanged a long glance with Catena, and it seemed as if they had a silent, private conversation before his gaze came back to Tahir. "Surely you would not want to spoil that precious moment by knowing all the particulars beforehand?"

"Like knowing how sausages are made? Because the truth is so disgusting? I am not a fool." Tahir stabbed the knife into the table where it sat upright, handle quivering. His throat tightened, and for a moment he couldn't breathe. His hands clenched into fists, his body went rigid. And then the fear passed, leaving in its wake a wash of emotion that made him sink his head into his hands as tears pricked his eyelids.

He sat there for a moment, breathing heavily, ashamed and embarrassed at showing the feelings he had tried so hard to hide. Along the table, Demitto and Catena were silent, although he was sure they were having another of their silent conversations, mocking him no doubt.

Then Demitto cleared his throat and leaned forward. He pulled Tahir's knife out of the table and turned it in his fingers as he spoke.

"Maybe you have heard tales of the Arbor in the past? No doubt it has been described as glorious, as bigger than any tree anyone has ever seen, as this magical creation, equivalent to dragons and griffons and sea monsters that you can never imagine existing in real life."

He sat back. "The truth is so different, it is difficult to describe. I have tried to explain Heartwood to your captain here. It is not a glorious, shining place filled with holy monks who sing praises to the Arbor day and night. It is a city like any other,

made by men and filled with men, with dark alleyways that
stink of piss, with pickpockets and murderers, with markets
selling cheap necklaces in the shape of an oak tree that break
five minutes after you take them home. Governed – if you can
call it that – by a foolish king who has no more understanding
of what the Arbor stands for or its history than the pauper
eating the bones left by the palace dogs. And the Arbor itself?
It stands surrounded by huge wooden shutters that close it off
to passers-by, overshadowed by the palace to the east and the
houses to the south and west. Pilgrims pay a coin a time to file
through the gateway and along the path to brush their fingers
against its trunk before being ushered hurriedly away."

Tears ran down Tahir's nose and dripped onto the table. He
closed his eyes, trying to make them stop, clenching his hands
in his hair.

"But what most people do not know," Demitto continued,
his voice low and mesmerising, "is that late in the day, when
all the crowds have gone and the world is dark, the gates are
opened to those who can afford to pay for a special nightly
ceremony. I attended this one night when I was younger and
curious about the tree and its power over the land."

Demitto's voice sank even lower, stroking over Tahir's
frayed nerves, seemingly weaving a magical spell around
him, and he opened his eyes to watch the emissary, entranced
by his steady stare. "I was allowed to walk right up to the
Arbor. To say it is huge is an understatement, young prince.
It is difficult to gauge its size from behind the shutters, but it
towers above the surrounding land, the height of ten men,
maybe even twenty. Its leaves never fall – did you know that?
Not even in The Sleeping. It is always green, and the leaves
move as if in a breeze, even if the air is as still as death."

Resting the tip of the blade on the wood, the ambassador
turned the handle slowly, and it seemed to catch the light
of the lone candle in the centre of the table, momentarily

blinding the Prince. Tahir stared at it. Was it his imagination, or could he see the reflection of oak leaves on the shining steel?

"I have also been to four of the five Nodes," Demitto said, his voice warm and smooth as honey. "The Green Giant, the Portal, the Tumulus and the Henge. When you stand on these sites, you can feel the energy running through the earth. The ground literally trembles beneath your feet. You see, the Arbor is alive. And I do not just mean alive like every other tree in the kingdom. The bark is warm, and if you place your ear against its trunk, you can hear the slow, steady beat of the Pectoris inside it. It is *alive*. It lives. It breathes. It knows. It sees inside the heart of every man. Its roots stretch to the ends of Anguis. And it needs you, young prince. So do not be mistaken in thinking that your life is of little value. The Arbor knows your worth. And to it, you are more precious than gold."

Demitto stopped turning the blade. Tahir blinked. His eyes met the emissary's and a shiver passed through him from the roots of his hair to the tips of his toes.

III

Geve watched as Turstan passed his hand across another candle. He had seen him do it a dozen times, but his heart still beat fast every time he witnessed it. Turstan closed his eyes and held the sunstone pendant in his left hand, and then the room grew tense with energy. The very air seemed to crackle with it, and the tips of Turstan's hair glowed bright red. Geve's scalp tingled and his teeth ached. His skin itched as if a thousand tiny marsh bugs crawled over him. And then the torch leaped into life. Turstan opened his eyes and dropped his hand, and Geve's uncomfortable feelings subsided.

Next to him, Sarra blew out a breath, eyes wide. No doubt she had seen Rauf do that before, but it seemed that no matter how many times a person watched the process, it never failed to impress. The first time Geve had seen Turstan do it, he had sworn out loud, causing everyone to burst into laughter.

Nele, who Geve tended to think of as the leader of the Veris even though they had all agreed nobody was in charge, shook out a large mat, and they all sat on it close together in a circle. Nele was older, with untidy brown hair greying at his temples and wrinkles around the corners of his eyes. His was an apothecary, and spent his days developing balms and tinctures to sell at the market.

Turstan stood the second candle in a holder and Geve fitted his in another, and they both placed the holders in the centre, casting the faces of the surrounding seven people in a warm glow.

Sarra was waiting calmly as everyone made themselves comfortable, the men cross-legged, the women sitting on their heels. Geve admired her poise. She had borne the difficult walk to the forgotten caves with only the occasional private grumble to him, and she had answered their initial questions without resorting to melodrama, knowing her words would hold enough drama without the need for added inflection.

He had known her since childhood. They had grown up together in the same sector, and he had seen her often around the Primus District, firstly following in the footsteps of her father as she learned how to catch salamanders, skin them, and turn the skin into usable leather, and then later, on her own, carrying on the trade after her father died.

Once, Geve had watched from the shadows as she came up against one of her competitors, who were also hunting salamanders along the same stretch of riverbank. Her rival had challenged her and Geve had tensed, ready to leap to her aid. But Sarra had defended her territory admirably, emerging the victor in the combat; the other girl had returned home to tend the knife wound on her forearm, leaving Sarra to collect the small pile of lizards she had left behind.

She was tougher than she looked, he thought. With hair the colour of bright firelight and white skin, she was slender enough to appear frail, but her frame belied a resilient and determined personality. Although not rich enough to eat the diet which gave the fruitful curves that their society deemed attractive in a woman, and unable to buy the gold and silver paints the palace women adorned themselves with, her natural beauty had caught the eye of one of the Select. Soon she had become known as Rauf's woman and would probably have ended up marrying him, if he hadn't been killed during the Secundus Rebellion around four months ago.

And now she was alone, and as soon as the Select found out she was with child and single, the pregnancy would be terminated and she would be left to fend for herself.

When she first told him about the baby, Geve had thought long and hard about whether to ask her to marry him. She didn't love him, of course, but he could have lived with that. He felt that he had enough love for the both of them. It had nearly killed him when he first saw her with Rauf, as he had been plucking up the courage to ask her to walk out with him, and at that moment he knew he had left it too late and she would never look at him the same way she did as the man from the Select: with fire in her eyes. And then his heart had broken again when Rauf died and Sarra had fallen apart, from missing the man she loved as well as from the knowledge that she had lost a chance to have a family.

Once again Geve had been plucking up the courage to take her into his arms, wipe her beautiful face free of tears and declare his love for her, when she announced she had been having the dreams.

That had changed things completely. A bard since he was born, haunted by dreams of a different world, Geve had worked with Nele on the docks for many years before one day forgetting himself and making a passing reference to the Arbor, which Nele had picked up on immediately, being a bard himself. The two of them had formed the Veris, and over the last five years, through careful observation and extremely cautious conversations, they had recruited four more to their group, including, miraculously, a member of the Select who was sympathetic to the cause.

Finding out that Sarra was a bard too – which was what Geve had assumed before she admitted to the group that she had only had the dreams since becoming pregnant – had been a dream come true, as well as the end to his reveries of them having a romantic relationship. He had known immediately that he had to bring her to the group and that it had solidified their chances of attempting an escape from the Embers, especially now she had just announced that the baby had shown her a way out. But it also meant the end of life as they had known it for so long. His fantasies of marriage, of being granted their own house and living contentedly for the rest of their days, were finally over.

One of the women, Amabil, older than the rest of them, slender, dark-skinned and dark-haired, had brought a box of small cakes, and they passed these around until everyone had taken one. Sarra glanced at him, seeing how he didn't eat it but let it rest in his palm, and she followed his lead as Nele closed his eyes and started to speak.

"Holy Arbor," he said, "you call to us, you speak to us, you live within us, you are us. We thank you for this gift of food, and we eat it in memory of your love. Bless the Veris."

"Bless the Veris," murmured everyone, and Sarra added her words before solemnly taking a bite out of her cake, along with everyone else.

Geve passed around a leather bag of water, making sure Sarra had a sip. She was painfully thin. The way she sat, her tunic stretched tight across her body, he could see her ribs, the hollow of her stomach beneath them, and then the small swelling of her stomach at the bottom. Hopefully the baby wasn't suffering too much.

Nele finished his cake, swallowed it down with a mouthful of water and wiped his mouth on the back of his hand. Waiting until everyone else had finished, he turned to Sarra and smiled. "We welcome you to the Veris, sister."

"Thank you," she said, dipping her head. "I am glad to be here."

Cross-legged, he clasped his hands in front of him and thought for a few moments before he continued speaking. In the candlelight his hair shone a reddish-brown, curling long around his neck and ears. "We are all bards," he began. "We have all had the dreams since childhood. Images flash through our minds of green grass, warm sunlight, birds flying in a blue sky, and a tree – so big we cannot imagine it to be real – arching over our heads and protecting the land. The tree's roots travel through the earth, stretching to all four corners, transmitting its love, its energy. We all have the same dream. And we believe this is how it is, on the Surface."

Sarra's wide green eyes glittered in the light. "So you believe it is all real? That we are not just dreaming or making it up in our heads?"

Nele nodded. "We believe that the Arbor is speaking to us and showing us another world. Another life. With people like us, living in freedom amongst the green grass, knowing the love of the Arbor. We don't know how or why we ended up here, below the earth, and before now the idea of a way out seemed fantastic, just a dream. But maybe, Sarra, you will be able to lead us there."

They all fell quiet. Sarra looked bemused, and Geve thought he could understand why. Even though he had had the dreams since childhood, he had never really been able to make sense of them. It was only when he had spoken to Nele, and Nele had told him to spend a whole day watching the Caelum, that Geve had really begun to comprehend where they were. Early in the morning, he had found a quiet spot in the docks, lay back, fixed his eyes on the circular disk in the high ceiling above the Great Lake, and stayed there for most of the day and a good portion of the night as well.

He had watched the Caelum change colour from grey to light blue to bright blue, an occasional wisp of white crossing it like a fish through water. In the afternoon, it had turned grey again, and he fancied at one point that he could see a fine mist descend the shaft of light that filtered down onto the lake. Later it had darkened to a grey-blue, then later still to blue-black, and the first stars had begun to glitter like tiny gem chips sewn onto a black tunic.

That was the Surface, Nele had said, on which people stood. And the caverns they themselves lived in were beneath the Surface. Their whole world was under the ground.

Geve's head had spun, and when he stood he had almost fallen over with dizziness. His brain had struggled to make sense of the information. There was a whole world above his head? The Caelum wasn't a magical circular disk stuck on the ceiling, but a hole out into the other world? He couldn't believe he was actually seeing the sky he had dreamed about. And yet somehow it made sense. And that meant the Arbor was up there, existing somewhere, planting its roots in the rich earth above their heads, reaching up to the warm sun.

Nele gave Sarra a few moments to try and process the news. Then he said, "Have you thought about passing on what you know to Comminor?" He was testing her, Geve knew, but still the thought of the Chief Select finding out about their group turned his blood to ice.

Sarra's eyes widened at the idea of talking to the leader of the Select. "No!"

"Do you not think everyone in the Embers should benefit from this knowledge, from knowing there is a way out of here?"

She shook her head vehemently. "He would not believe me. He would think I was trying to stir up discontent, and I would be imprisoned. The Select would not even consider the notion of finding a way out of here. They have power over others and they want for nothing. Why would they want to escape?" She glanced apologetically at Turstan as if she'd suddenly remembered he was also a Select, but he just nodded along with the others. Nele had needed to ask her, but of course they all agreed.

"Can you tell us what the baby showed you?" Nele asked. "Where is the way out?"

Geve's mouth went dry. His heart pounded so loud he could hear it like drums in his head.

Sarra moistened her lips, her gaze passing across each member of the group. Then she said, "I cannot say, because if the Select catch you, they will be able to torture you. If you do not know, you will have nothing to tell."

Nobody said anything, but they all visibly deflated. Geve's shoulders sagged. She was right, of course. It was dangerous for them to have that information. But still, he would have liked to know.

"But how can we be sure you are not lying, just to join our group?" The young woman who spoke, Kytte, did so without accusation. Her black hair was piled into a knot on the top of her head, and tendrils escaped to curl by the side of her pale face.

"You will have to trust me," Sarra said. She gave a little smile. "I am sorry."

Kytte returned the smile. "I understand."

Geve turned to the last woman in the group who had not yet spoken. "This is Betune. She carries with her the hope of the Veris."

Betune had long brown hair braided and tied with a well-worn piece of red cloth. She took the leather thong around her neck and lifted it over her head, drawing from inside her clothing a small leather bag. She loosened the tie at the top, then tipped the item inside onto her palm.

Sarra stared at the tiny object. "What is it?"

"It is an acorn," Geve said. "From the Arbor itself."

Sarra's eyes widened. "From the Arbor?" She held out her palm as Betune offered it to her, and brought the tiny item up close to her face.

"Yes," Nele said. "Betune's ancestors – who were also bards – passed it down to her. You see, they believed we were once on the Surface and, through some misfortune, were driven underground." He picked the acorn up and rolled it between his fingers. "This is our one remaining link to the Surface, and to the Arbor. And we want to return it there. That is our goal, and that it what we have been planning all these years."

"I want to help," Sarra said, and a tear ran down her cheek. "I want to see the sky and feel the grass beneath my feet. I will lead you there, if you will let me."

"We will let you," Nele said solemnly. Geve stifled an almost hysterical laugh. As if they had any other option. They had been trying to find a route out of the caverns for years.

He leaned over and brushed Sarra's cheek dry. He knew the others were watching, but at that moment he didn't care. "Do not cry," he whispered. "Your baby will be born on the Surface, and will grow up in the light and the warmth. We will get you there."

Or die trying, he thought as she leaned her cheek into his palm. What would Comminor and the Select do if they found out that not only was Sarra pregnant, but that she was also now part of the Veris and helping them plan their escape?

CHAPTER THREE

I

The fire seemed hungry, Orsin thought. It chomped greedily on the kindling in the hearth, filling the hall with snaps and crackles as it leapt to life. The flames flowed over the large log in the centre like an orange cloak billowing in the wind. He watched as the log gradually caught light, the bark splintering and turning black, the odd leaf still attached to the twig on the top curling and then turning to ash.

How odd that it seemed alive. Fire had enchanted him for as long as he could remember, and he could vividly recall the beating he had received from the steward who found him playing with a tinderbox in the barn. The straw had caught alight and the barn had nearly burned down, but luckily he had escaped untouched, only to have his backside whipped. Now he understood why he had been beaten, but at the time he had seethed with resentment, angry that the steward had not appreciated his fascination for the flame – that he had felt compelled to light it, enticed by the way he could bring a living thing to life and cultivate it, make it grow.

His fascination had continued through his early teens and twice he had been punished for a fire that had got out of hand. Over the past few years, other things had occupied his mind, his brain and body tiring in physical training at which he excelled, and in women, of whom he had also become something of an expert.

Lately, however, some of his fascination had returned. He had never spoken of it to anyone, aware that his absorption was unusual and that others did not feel the same way. He could not understand how they were not captivated by it. He watched the flame lick over the log, sensual in its caress, like a passionate lover, consuming and obsessive. A hunger grew within him, and he shifted in his chair. He would visit the tavern later after finishing the evening meal. Find a woman there to cool his blood.

"Orsin!"

His head snapped up. His mother was glaring at him, and Julen's lips were twisted in a wry smile. "What?" he said defensively.

"I do swear you are selectively deaf," said his mother. "And just as stupid, sometimes. Have you not heard a word I have said?"

He propped his feet on the chair next to him. "I heard you. I just did not care."

Horada, sitting at the end of the table a little away from them, bit her lip to stifle a smile. Procella continued to glare at him. Orsin finished off his ale, used to his mother's wrath. She had always been stern, but since his father had died she had become even more short-tempered. He put down his tankard and softened a little as Julen raised his eyebrows at him. His brother had told him of her worry about Horada. And he did love and admire his mother, in spite of her sometimes shrewish nature.

"You said you both had another dream last night," he relayed. "About Heartwood."

"Yes." Procella's face etched with worry as she glanced at her daughter. "She asked me again this morning to take her there. I refused of course. Now she is ignoring me."

Horada, who could quite obviously hear every word being said, continued to pick at the strawberries on her plate, not looking up.

Orsin shrugged and turned his gaze back to his mother. "Perhaps you should let her go. Find out what the Arbor wants with her."

Procella banged her goblet on the table and leaned forward. "And let the same thing happen to her that happened to my husband? My family has given enough to the tree. It will not have my daughter as well."

Horada's hand stilled for a moment, tightening into a fist. But she kept her eyes downcast, and went on to pour herself another goblet of wine.

Orsin helped himself to one of the pastries on the plate. "She is seventeen," he reminded his mother. "Some would say she is old enough to make up her own mind."

To his surprise, instead of arguing the point further, Procella leaned back and looked suddenly upset. "You too? I thought you of all people, would have backed me up in this."

Orsin glanced at his brother. "You have said Horada should go?"

Julen hesitated, his hand automatically stroking Rua's silky ears where she had rested her head on his knee. Orsin studied the way the firelight played across his brother's fine features, painting his high cheekbones and the flat planes of his face with golden light. How different they all were, he thought – as if they did not have the same parents. His brother was slim and dark, and although he was the most skilled man with a dagger that Orsin had ever met and a master at blending with the natural scenery, he bore none of the brute strength that Orsin himself had inherited. Julen was also sharp as a meat knife: intuitive and perceptive in ways that Orsin could not comprehend.

He'd been surprised at first when the Peacekeeper had chosen Julen to join him in his work, for although Julen was pleasant, thoughtful and tactful, Orsin had thought it a shame that his brother's talents for stealth and subterfuge would go unused. When they had played hide-and-seek as children, Orsin had never been able to find his brother, who had developed an amazing knack for making himself invisible. Julen would often leave his older brother hunting for ages, before revealing himself to have been hiding in plain sight. What a waste, Orsin had thought! But that was before he realised how much of the Peacekeeper's role involved beneath-the-surface investigation into who wasn't keeping the peace, and setting them straight.

Julen leaned forward, elbows on his knees, and looked into his tankard for a moment. "There is something I must tell you all," he said. "Something mysterious is happening across the land."

Horada raised her head to stare at him, while Procella looked up sharply. "Is this the outbreak of fires you were talking about last night?"

"Connected with that, yes. But it is more than a reaction to a particularly hot and dry Shining." Julen ran his hand through his dark hair. He seemed unsettled – a word Orsin would never normally have associated with his brother. "Over the past year, there has been an unusual scattering of deaths throughout the country. At first, we could see nothing to connect them and thought them random misfortunes. Lowborn and highborn people, rich and poor, men and women. From all four realms, rarely from the same towns."

"What made you think they were connected at all?" Orsin asked.

"Just one thing. They all died in fire – burned to death."

Julen fell quiet for a moment. Then ran his hand through his hair again. "After the Darkwater Lords were defeated twenty-two years ago, the University of Ornestan began some serious research and investigation into the revelations that had come out of that event. Nitesco – the Libraris who discovered the location of the Nodes and the true meaning behind the Veriditas – joined the university and has led the philosophical debates. He has created a group called the Nox Aves. They are based in a group of buildings they call the Nest at Heartwood, consisting of men and women who are involved in carrying out studies into the Nodes and the energy channels in the land. Much has been uncovered, although the whys and wherefores are still under discussion, and therefore the news has been kept in the scholarly circles."

A prickle ran down Orsin's spine. "What news?"

Julen frowned. "The channels in the land that run from the roots of the Arbor do not just conduct energy. They also conduct time."

They all fell silent. Orsin tried to process that information.

Eventually, he spoke. "Huh?"

Procella, too, looked confused. "What do you mean, 'conduct time'? I do not understand."

Julen leaned forward and linked his hands, smiling as Rua tried to push her nose into them. "As you well know, I am no scientist and no philosopher. But from what I understand, the roots of the Arbor connect its form in the past, the present and the future. The Arbor appears to experience all time simultaneously."

More silence.

"Let us say, for argument's sake, that it is so," Orsin said finally. "What effect does it have on Anguis? On us?"

"The scholars believe that the Arbor saw the rise of the Darkwater Lords. It cannot appear to change time, as such, but it can seem to influence it by influencing us."

"Huh?" Orsin said again.

Julen's lips quirked. "Nitesco explained it to me like this. You are watching a man walking on an icy river. You see a crack appear in the ice, but you are too far away for the man to hear if you shout a warning. You cannot stop the man falling into the river, but you can grab a rope and a hook to anchor yourself, and order the servants to get blankets and hot water as you run to his aid. The event itself is fixed in time. But everything else can be moulded like soft clay around it."

Orsin's head hurt. "So how did the Arbor influence the land when it knew the Darkwater Lords were going to rise?"

"Who knows? Its influence could have started hundreds of years ago, and ended with making sure our father was at the Congressus, and that those who attended on that fateful day were people who could help it in its time of need."

"I understand now," Procella said. "A little. What else can you tell us?"

"The scholars believe the Arbor has seen an event in its future – something terrible, maybe even more terrible than the rise of the Darkwater Lords."

A shiver ran down Orsin's back. "What sort of event?"

"It is connected with the fires," Procella said softly.

Julen nodded. "The scholars believe that due to the failure of the Veriditas for so long, the elements became wildly unbalanced. It is like preparing a stew for supper and adding too much salt. This can be alleviated by adding more water, but then the stew becomes watery and needs more meat. It is difficult to regain the right balance. This imbalance with the elements led to the rise of the Darkwater Lords. They were crushed, but the scholars think maybe the imbalance still exists."

"Meaning that one of the other elements is on the rise," Orsin said slowly.

Julen nodded again. "Fire."

Procella leaned back in her chair, her face registering shock. "So this is why there have been fires breaking out across the land?"

"Yes." Julen scratched his cheek, his finger rasping on stubble. "This bit I do not quite understand, but the scholars believe that, in the future, fire elementals have discovered a way to travel along the energy channels from the Arbor. These fire elementals have travelled back into the past – into our time, and maybe even further back. The Nox Aves think that the further the elementals travel back in time, the less power they have. But they do believe they are gradually eliminating the people that they believe the Arbor could call on to help it."

"By burning them to death," Orsin whispered. "What a terrible way to die." *And what a glorious way, too.*

"Yes. The scholars call these elementals the Incendi. They do not know how they work – whether they, like the Darkwater Lords, can somehow take on our form, or whether they are operating in elemental form alone. But it seems as if they are real, and although at the moment they are few in number, they are gradually increasing as we near the catastrophe they suspect is coming."

"So what do they hope to achieve?" Procella asked. "If, as you say, events are fixed?"

"For the Arbor, the events are fixed. For the Incendi? Who knows?"

"You mean they could actually change time? Alter the way the future occurs?"

Julen shrugged. "We do not know. But it is entirely possible. After all, the Arbor can see through time, but it cannot travel through it or alter it, as far as we know. If we return to the analogy of the man on the ice, maybe the Incendi have found a way to transport themselves from the moment they spot the man over to the moment they would reach his side instantaneously. It is then up to them whether they intervene and save him, or watch him die."

Procella touched her hand to her forehead. "This is too much for the likes of us. We do not have the brains of scholars. Chonrad may have enjoyed debating philosophy but I do not. How are we to make sense of all this? Why tell us at all?"

"Because you have had the dreams," Julen said. "The

Arbor has tried to contact you, and Horada. Maybe it needs you. And in that case, the Incendi will know, and maybe they will come after you."

"Let them try," Procella snarled.

Julen banged on the table. "And how, pray, do you propose to defeat these nefarious elementals when we have no idea what form they take or how they appear?"

Procella looked startled. Orsin had never heard his brother speak in that way to their mother. He must really be worried, Orsin thought; that very fact concerning him more than the news of the Incendi did.

"What do you propose?" Procella said, her voice quiet.

Julen took a deep breath and then blew it out slowly. "The Peacekeeper instructed me to fetch you both to Heartwood. I understand your reservations about this, but he feels we must answer the Arbor's call."

"I think if Horada..." Procella's words petered off as she looked along the table to where her daughter had been sitting. The seat was vacant. "Where did she go?"

Orsin shook his head. He hadn't seen his sister leave. "I do not know."

His mother pushed herself impatiently to her feet. "I will go and get her, and we shall talk about it." She marched off toward the stairs to the bedchambers.

Orsin met Julen's dark gaze, and the two brothers smiled wryly.

"I thought she would resist me more," Julen said, leaning back and stroking his short beard.

"I think she is scared," Orsin said. "I would not have thought it of her, but then I suppose one is always scared for one's children."

He looked into the flames that writhed atop the log like figures tortured and made to dance with hot pokers. Would he ever have children, know hearth and home like his father had done? Twice. Orsin's half-brother and sister had lived with them for ten years or so until Rosamunda had married and moved away and Varin had answered the Peacekeeper's call for a small personal army to accompany him on his travels across Anguis. Julen still caught up with him regularly, but Orsin had not seen him for a long time.

Time moves on, he thought, like the stars wheeling in the heavens. How could time be changed? Surely it was as irreversible as the way the fire was currently consuming the log, turning the wood to ash. The ash couldn't be turned back into wood – it just wasn't possible. And he had thought the passage of time was the same.

The log subsided in the grate, and a piece of kindling rolled towards the edge of the brick hearth. Orsin leaned forward and picked it up, watching the flame lick its way up the length of the twig towards his hand. So sensual; fluid, like a viscous liquid. He could just imagine what it would feel like to have it slide over him, stroking, caressing, and teasing him with its white-hot heat…

"Orsin!"

Startled, he dropped the branch into the grate. "What?"

Julen grabbed his hand and turned it over, examining his skin. "The fire covered your hand!"

"No, it did not."

Julen frowned. His eyes met his brother's, and a cold sliver of fear embedded itself in Orsin's stomach.

The moment was broken, however, by the rapid scuff of boots on stone, and then their mother appeared, running along the hall, clearly agitated.

"She has gone!"

The brothers stood, Rua circling them nervously. "Gone where?" Julen demanded.

"I do not know." Procella yelled the words. "One of the servants saw her leave only a short time ago with her travel bag. She assumed Horada was going to stay with Rosamunda, but…" Her voice trailed off.

Horada travelled the short distance to stay with her half-sister on a frequent basis. But Orsin knew that was not the case this time.

"She has gone to Heartwood," Julen murmured.

Procella's cheeks went red as if her head was going to explode.

"I should have foreseen this," Julen said through gritted teeth. He was already buckling on his scabbard. "Yesterday she spoke of her frustration. I know how stubborn she is – I should have guessed she would leave on her own."

"It is not your fault." Procella gripped the back of the chair, her knuckles white. "I drove her to it."

"It is too late for recriminations. We must go after her." Orsin beckoned to a nearby page and told him to go and saddle three horses.

But Julen shook his head. "It is nearly dark and she will not take the main road. She is a good horsewoman and will not fear to travel in the woods. Like me, she has the ability to make herself invisible in the trees. I will follow her – I will be able to travel more quickly on my own and I know the secrets of the shadows whereas you do not."

"What can I do?" Procella reached automatically for the sword at her side, only to find it missing where she wore her casual clothes, and she cursed.

"Go to Heartwood," Julen said. "Take the main road, and gather men on the way from the Wall. We do not know what form the Incendi invasion will take or when it will occur. Spread the word and garner support. Let it be known that we are not going to be taken down lightly." He rested his hand on her arm. "And Mother? Take care. You, too, have received the dreams. The Incendi may be after you also."

He ruffled the fur on Rua's head. "You must stay here, old girl." He bent and kissed her nose. "I do not want you getting into trouble at your age."

He turned to his brother and they clasped hands in the age-old gesture of soldier to soldier. "Travel safe," Julen said. His voice held sincerity, but his eyes were cool. When he turned and walked off without another word, he left Orsin with a vague sense of foreboding and a bitter taste in his mouth, as if he had drunk the oak-leaf tea, acerbitas, reminding him of the bitterness of life without the Arbor's love.

II

Catena hovered in the doorway of the house and leaned against the doorjamb. As always, whenever she visited her childhood home, a sensation of weariness and defeat crept over her, and she had to force a smile onto her face as her mother looked up and saw her.

"Cat!" Imma pushed herself tiredly to her feet and came over to welcome her daughter, kissing her on the cheek. "It is so good to see you."

"And you, Mother." Catena directed her back to the chair. "Please, sit. Do not tire yourself out."

Imma lowered herself back down, already looking worn out by the movement. "It is true, I do feel tired today."

You are always tired, Catena thought, although she didn't voice the words. And no wonder. The noise outside was making her head ache, and she had only been there five minutes. She walked through the small house to the back yard, caught the two boys playing at swords by the scruff of their necks and marched them out of the garden and down to the river. "You can yell all you like down here," she told her brothers sharply. "Give Mother's ears a rest."

The boys continued their play as if nothing had happened, and she walked back through the yard slowly. The vegetables in their rows needed weeding, and the midden at the bottom should have been cleared days ago, the smell making her nose wrinkle. She entered the dark building, noting the way the rough tapestry on the wall that her mother had been so proud of when they had completed it together had faded and was covered in a fine sheen of metallic dust. Half a dozen of the pots on the shelves had been broken and then mended – badly in most cases. Imma still wore the dress Catena could remember her wearing when her daughter had been appointed Captain of the Guard seven years ago, although it had been patched with so many other pieces of cloth that it was barely recognisable.

Catena sat opposite her mother and took her hands. There was little flesh on them, the skin lying over the bones like finest linen draped over thin wooden sticks. Like most mothers, Catena supposed, Imma had given everything she had to her husband and the six children who had been born alive. As the eldest, Catena had watched Imma's body expand and retract over the years until her firm muscles had turned soft like kneaded dough, and the once-bright light of passion and enthusiasm had faded from her eyes to leave them dull and flat like muddy puddles.

So many times Catena had tried to help – with time, with encouragement, even with money once she began to earn her own wage at the castle. But it was never enough. Other babies came from the womb without a breath, and three of her siblings had died in the mines. Sickness and hunger ravaged a house that did not have the food and energy to fight it, and sometimes she felt as if a veil of grief and regret hung over a home that should have been vibrant with the energies of the children inside.

"I suppose you are going," Imma said, looking down at their linked hands. Her once-brown hair hung in a grey curtain, glittering with shining threads like the veins of silver that ran through the castle rock. "I wish you would stay here."

"I know." Catena longed to wrench her hands free from the cold, grey sparrow's feet she held and run out into the bright sunshine, but she forced herself to sit still. "I will be back," she murmured, leaning forward to plant a kiss on Imma's crown.

"Will you?" Imma whispered. "I do not think so, somehow."

After they had said their goodbyes, Catena mused on those words as she mounted her horse and rode away. The house lay on the outskirts of Harlton, and she skirted the town via the coastal road, then re-entered through the southern gatehouse and dismounted on the cobbled street. It was market day and a good majority of the town's inhabitants were in the central square plying their trades. The roads were busy with traffic from Prampton, Quillington and Widdington as carts brought sheep fleeces and hides, sacks of oats, barley and flour, barrels of apples and flagons of wine to exchange for the silver, gold, iron ore and precious gems that the Harlton folk mined from the hills in the west, as well as the superior armour their blacksmiths made.

As she followed the road east, however, the traffic thinned and the day grew quieter. She slowed the horse to a walk and breathed in the salty southerly breeze. Here the city seemed less polluted by the noxious fumes from the blacksmiths, and the jungle thinned, giving way to flowered borders and the occasional village green with its pond, complete with ducks.

She supposed she should have trawled through the taverns to find her father to say goodbye, but she didn't think he would miss her. Her fingers rose to trace the faint scar on her right cheek, caused by a blow from his belt buckle when she was younger. He'd always been a cruel man, and he resented her position at the castle. She would not waste her time tracking him down only to have him shower her with sarcastic comments.

The lane turned south and she dismounted and tied the horse to a beech tree outside the Temple wall. Then she turned the handle on the wooden door and went through.

Catena paused as the path forked, wondering which to take. To the right stood the old stone Temple that had once encased the town's primary oak tree, which had been moved stone by stone thirty feet to the right at the beginning of the

Second Era. The Temple still housed plaques to the dead and places to light candles and pray, but the tree to her left now grew exposed to the elements.

It stood in a ring of grass, surrounded by half a dozen wooden benches for people to sit in quiet contemplation, although now the place was empty; she made her way to one and sat. The sun filtered through the oak leaves, casting a pattern on the grass below that moved and shimmered in the slight breeze like a flock of butterflies.

She released a long, slow breath, not conscious of the tension she had been holding in her body until that moment. She was leaving. Finally leaving. Her heart rate increased at the thought. It would be a long journey to Heartwood, probably at least eleven days, taking into account that the Prince did not ride often and would be saddle-sore within a day or two. Eleven days! She had never travelled further than Prampton, a journey that had taken a day and a half and had required a stop at an inn on the way.

Eleven days with the Prince. Hopefully she wouldn't strangle him before the journey's end.

And eleven days with the mysterious emissary. Demitto fascinated Catena. He was both irreverent and strangely enigmatic. At first glance, as she had ridden out of the castle to escort him, he had seemed like an ordinary man in a very fancy suit of armour, hot and uncomfortable in the sub-tropical climate of the south. Later on, after they had bathed, he had left off his armour and joined her in the taverns in the normal garb of a traveller, and had not drawn a second glance from anyone, save the wenches looking to earn a coin for the night, of whom he had selected two – *two!* – and proceeded up to a room for an hour before emerging with a satisfied smile on his face. Catena had rolled her eyes and ordered another ale, hoping that nobody would recognise him at the ceremonial parade when they left a few days hence.

She knew that was extremely unlikely. Because Demitto the man seemed an entirely different person to Demitto the ambassador. When he had first walked into the hall to meet the King and Queen, it was as if someone had lit a candle inside him. The man had radiated wealth and power, his blue eyes blazing, the tree on his breastplate glittering in the sun and blinding them all as he walked up to the dais. She would have said it must have been down to the armour, but that morning when she had joined him and the Prince at the breakfast table, he had done it again and talked to Tahir in a low, mesmerising voice that sent them both into a trance.

He had played down his role as emissary, claiming he had gained the position only by dint of being well travelled, but she suspected there was more to his gaining the position than met the eye. He had poured scorn on her description of him as holy and on the city of Heartwood and its king, and yet when he had spoken of the Arbor, he had said *It lives. It breathes. It knows.* And his face had been filled with awe and reverence. He had touched the tree, connected with it. Catena suspected there was more magic within him than he realised.

Above her, the oak tree rustled in the sea breeze. A shiver ran through her. Demitto had said the Arbor was as tall as ten men, *maybe even twenty*. Was he using artistic licence? Surely no tree could grow to that height? Its roots spread through the land, connecting every oak tree in Anguis, including the one before her. She had not been to any of the Nodes, but she had heard tales of the energy that could be felt there.

She closed her eyes. Nowadays the earth rumbled frequently. She was used to the tremors, the heat, and the occasional shower of ash in the air. But as she planted her feet firmly on the ground just yards from the oak tree, she was sure she could feel something different, a thrumming, as if someone were playing drums far off in the distance, the sound reverberating through the ground, up through her spine, into her ribcage, into her heart.

She opened her eyes. The sun continued to filter through the leaves, casting tiny gold shapes on the ground. They shimmered and flickered, looking for all the world like flames leaping between the blades of grass.

Unbidden, thoughts came to mind of the way Demitto had turned the blade on the table at breakfast, how the steel had caught the candlelight. She had been hypnotised at the time, the same way she felt hypnotised now. She could not tear her gaze away from the flickering lights. They grew taller, licking up the trunk of the old oak tree, and a scream formed in her throat. The tree was burning! Panic made her chest heave. The fire burned her face and hands. Everything was turning to ash...

And then she blinked and she was sitting in the garden under the tree, the leaves dancing in the sunlight.

Foreboding filled her. The future loomed darkly, like black thunderclouds on the horizon. Something terrible was going to happen. And she didn't have a clue what it was or how to stop it.

III

Sarra hovered on the edge of the crowd, her neck aching from continually craning her neck to look up at the Caelum. Her heart pounded – from the excitement of seeing the White Eye, which had appeared over the rim of the Caelum just an hour before; from the risk of being out in public when she'd been trying to keep a low profile; and from the fact that – tonight – they were due to make their escape.

She kept her gaze fixed on the Caelum, trying not to look around and catch the gaze of one of the many Select patrolling the streets who were trying to keep a presence during the bubbling atmosphere. Everyone was excited – after all, the White Eye only made an appearance every hundred years or so, and nobody living in the caverns had been alive to see it the last time.

Even though the Select forbade the physical recording of historic events, the story of the White Eye's previous appearances had been handed down verbally through generations of families. Most people agreed that last time it had appeared along the lower edge of the Caelum, passing from left to right if you stood by the palace gates looking up, but apparently it was different every time and nobody could predict how much of it would be visible. Various families had tried to calculate when the Eye would next appear, and although people differed on the day, everyone had agreed it would be that year, and several people had forecast that month.

As soon as Nele heard that Sarra knew of a possible way out, he had immediately suggested their best chance of success lay in putting the chaos of the ceremony to good use. It would be a perfect time to start their journey, he had said, when the streets were filled with movement and the curfew was delayed due to merrymaking. It would take several hours for their absence to be noticed. As a member of the Select, Turstan had his own room in the palace grounds, but he was the only one of the Veris. The rest of them slept communally, and on a usual night they would immediately be missed once the curfew bell had rung.

They had quickly begun to plan their escape, not sure exactly when the festivities would begin, and in the end it had only been three weeks before a child had spotted the glimmer of white at the edge of the Caelum. Immediately, everyone had flooded to the Great Lake to watch the appearance of the White Eye with awe. People were saying the whole of the Eye was going to be visible. The Embers had erupted into celebration mode, and excitement filled the air like smoke.

Sarra's heart thudded. She hadn't seen any member of the Veris since the arrival of the White Eye was announced, but they had gone over and over their plans until they all knew them off by heart, so she had no worry that she wouldn't remember what to do.

She breathed deeply, forcing herself to keep calm, conscious that when she was agitated, the baby stirred in her belly. It had been a long few weeks, and she had been jointly comforted and alarmed by the movement of the child within her – comforted at the thought of Rauf's child nestled in her womb, and alarmed that her abdomen was rapidly swelling, and would surely be visible very soon, even through her loose tunic.

Sarra wrapped her arms around herself, staring up at the shining white orb now clearly visible over the rim of the Caelum. Over the past few weeks, the Veris had met half a dozen times, and during each meeting Nele and the others had related to her the dreams that each had experienced over the years. Sarra had listened with wonder to the accounts of the Arbor and life on the Surface, but it had been the stories about the sky that had fascinated her the most. Kytte had been the one with the clearest description, learned through her dreams and tales handed down from generation to generation.

Kytte spoke of the sky above their heads like the roof of the cavern, arching from horizon to horizon so high it would take a hundred thousand years to climb up to touch it. And in the sky was the sun, a huge ball of glowing yellow light that rose above the horizon in the east in the morning and sank down into the west as the day grew old. During the day the sky was blue, or occasionally grey with rain – droplets of water that fell from bunching and furling clouds to fall on your face and hands. At night the sky was black, and sometimes if there were no clouds, the stars came out, tiny twinkling pinpricks of light like the glint of minerals in the black rock down by the river.

This was what they had been calling the Caelum, which appeared to be a hole in the roof through which they occasionally glimpsed the world above. And the White Eye was actually something called the Light Moon, an object in the sky that circled the Surface like the sun did, going around and around them like a ball swung by a child from a piece of string.

Sarra stared at the Caelum until her neck ached and her eyes burned. At first only a thin band of pinkish-white showed, but as a hush fell over the waiting thousands who surrounded the Great Lake, the thin band widened and became a segment. *The Light Moon*. She was seeing above the Surface, up into the sky. It made her head spin.

Around her, people starting singing, a well-known song about the cycle of life they had all learned as children, the haunting melody rising and spiralling towards the ceiling. Sarra hummed along, her eyes pricking with tears. Her mother had sung this to her, and she associated it with the safety and security of childhood, before she had found out what a harsh and difficult place the world was. Or, rather, what a harsh place the Embers was.

How big was the world? Nele had told her it was vast, and it would take a hundred times longer to travel from one side of the land to the other as it did to travel across the Embers. How was that possible? She couldn't even conceive of a place so large.

She dropped her head, ostensibly to massage her aching neck, but taking the time to glance around as she did so. The shores of the Great Lake were choked with people, and the water was also full of boats and rafts on which private celebrations were going on. Stalls had been hastily erected on the quay to sell cheap ale and hot food, as well as crafts made by those with a talent for the creative, to keep as a reminder of the night's festivities, such as small woven bags embroidered with white eyes or colourful decorations for the hair.

The Select stood out with their golden sashes, patrolling the quay and occasionally reprimanding a reveller whose behaviour had got out of hand. More than one of them had an ale in his or her hand, taking advantage of the relaxed atmosphere and joining in with the revelries, but still she shivered as they passed her, and she shrank into the shadows, fearful of drawing attention to herself.

Suddenly she spotted Turstan across the lake, talking to a couple of men who had started a fight and calming them down.

The bell tolled in the palace gatehouse, the watchtowers following its lead and echoing the bell throughout the city, marking the late hour. Turstan stopped beneath one of the lamps hanging from a hook in the wall, and she watched as he grasped his sunstone, placed his hand on the metal cage and closed his eyes. After a brief moment, the ball of flame inside the cage died. Similarly, other members of the Select extinguished every other lamp around the lake, and a cheer went up as the cavern darkened to twilight, the White Eye now dazzling against the black Caelum.

Sarra's heart rate increased. The moment of their flight was drawing near. Nele had instructed them to meet at the western edge of the quay at the next bell. By then the celebrations would be in full swing, most of the Select would have a few tankards of ale inside them, and they would have a few hours before their absence would be noticed.

She turned and made her way across the quay, heading for the Primus District. Lots of people were still to-ing and fro-ing, and she passed unnoticed along the high street, crossed the bridge over the river and headed north into the heart of the district.

She walked calmly, but inside her heart pounded. This would probably be the last time she would ever walk this path. The thought excited her and scared her at the same time. She had spent her whole life walking these streets and knew every lane, every room, every dip and crack in the rock. In spite of her desire to leave to save her baby, the thought of fleeing filled her with a panic she wasn't sure how to deal with. What if the visions she had been receiving were just dreams, images her mind had conjured up to torture her? What if she risked the lives of the others in the Veris by encouraging them to escape, only to find there was no such escape route after all? By the time they realised the truth, their absence would probably be discovered. And the Select – who were always looking for excuses to reduce the population – would waste no time in putting them to death.

As she walked through the unusually quiet trade areas, she

tried to calm herself with thoughts of what it would be like to live on the Surface. Kytte had described how people purchased land and built individual houses of wood and stone as big as they liked, instead of having to put names down on the very long list for one of the new rooms the crews were currently carving out of the rock. It took years to carve new passages and rooms and demand was high, and the newest rooms always went to the richest people, like the Select and guild leaders and the most important merchants. People like Sarra would never be granted new living quarters. When she'd been with Rauf, she might have stood a chance, but alone she was worthless, a nuisance to society, just an extra mouth to feed and a body to house.

But although daydreaming about the grass and the sky had brought her comfort over the last few weeks, this time it only served to heighten her panic. She had never touched grass, other than the abundant mosses that grew down on the riverbanks, and the only trees she had seen were the stunted brackens that grew profusely along with various other plants in the fields on the outskirts of the Embers, where the ground turned moist under foot and made further cave expansion impossible. Her world was cold and dark, hard and cruel. What did she know of warmth and the light?

She turned into the narrower alleyways leading to the living quarters, her stomach churning with nerves. The area was mostly deserted now and she passed only two people making their way towards the Great Lake. By the time she reached her section the only sound came from the rush of the water channel in the middle of the alley, and when she climbed the wooden ladder, she found her communal night room empty.

She crawled over to her corner, curled up on her pallet and fumbled for the cord she wore around her neck. After pulling it out, she grasped the key on the end, slotted it into the lock of the small wooden box that lay to one side of the pallet and lifted the lid.

Heart continuing to hammer, she took out the contents. Regular inspection by the Select made the keeping of any family belongings difficult, but occasionally they would let the little things go by, especially if they were practical. A headscarf her mother had made, painstakingly embroidered with beautiful coloured circles. Her father's skinning knife, recently sharpened, the handle bound firmly with a new strip of cloth. Her bone needles and skeins of coloured threads she had worked so hard to save up for. The silver clasp Rauf had given her, which she took out and kissed. And at the bottom, on a small, thin piece of cloth, the embroidery she had been working on herself, a yellow circle surrounded by green and blue lines – her way of representing the Surface, innocuous to most eyes, and yet full of meaning every time she looked at it.

She put the items in the bag she wore permanently on her hip along with some bread and cheese she had been saving from her daily rations for the very purpose of their escape, and pulled the drawstring tight. Then she pulled up her knees and rested her cheek on them. Now she just had to wait.

She closed her eyes. Her heart pounded so loud it seemed to echo in her ears like the drums she could hear far off in the distance. The dancing must have started, marking the high point of the White Eye across the Caelum. She should get back there and watch it, she thought, but suddenly she didn't want to leave the room.

She pressed her face against her knees. She was doing this for the baby, not for herself. It didn't matter if she was scared. She had to take this risk, because otherwise the baby would die, and how would she feel then?

She bit her lip, ashamed at the temptation that swept over her to abort the baby so she could stay where she was and continue with her life. *Rauf*, she thought miserably, missing him so much it made her ache. *I wish you were here.*

Inside her, the baby stirred. And with the movement came the flash of an image in her mind. Like an eye opening, darkness gave way to light, the sun so bright it momentarily blinded her. Clean air brushed her cheeks, so fresh as it filled her lungs, bringing with it the aroma of the sweet plants, which grew nearby, the smell more beautiful than any of the cloying scents the perfumers could create.

Sarra opened her eyes with a gasp. That moment of emergence from darkness to light stayed with her, though, bringing with it a feeling of hope and excitement stronger than any she had felt before. The baby was trying to tell her everything would be all right.

Pushing herself to her feet, she headed for the doorway and swept aside the leather curtain.

And then she stopped. A figure stood at the bottom of the ladder, arms folded, waiting for her to emerge. The lamp further along the alleyway cast him in silhouette, and all she could make out was his height, the impressive width of his shoulders and the glint of the firelight on his silver hair. But instantly she knew who it was, and the realisation made every muscle in her body tense in fear.

It was Comminor, the Chief Select, the most feared man in the whole of the Embers.

PART TWO

CHAPTER FOUR

I

Horada walked her horse through the town of Vichton so as not to arouse suspicion. She had wrapped herself tightly in a dark cloak and raised the hood, but still she received the occasional nod from shopkeepers and villagers who apparently recognised the horse.

Perhaps she should have taken one of the spare horses rather than Mara, she thought, as a member of the guard spotted her and raised a hand to tip his cap at her. Ultimately though, it didn't really matter. Her family would soon discover she had gone, and they would know she was heading for Heartwood, so she would obviously have left by the western gate. Only once she was out in the countryside could she truly become invisible.

As the gatehouse loomed, she slowed Mara and joined the half a dozen horses and carts making their way out of the town after a day at the market. The stone building passed over her head, casting her briefly into shadow, and as it did so it was as if it also cast a shadow over her heart. A shiver passed through her, and a strong feeling of foreboding arose within her that she would never again ride under this gateway and see her home town of Vichton.

She mounted the horse and set off down the road. Usually the thought of escaping from what she had begun to view as a prison would have filled her with delight, but this time the fear that clawed at her made her turn in the saddle to look back over her shoulder at the city wall. Her father had been instrumental in converting the once-small settlement into a thriving fortified port. She knew her mother had found it difficult to adjust to living permanently in one place and still referred to Vichton as "your father's home", and Horada could understand why. The warm brown stones with which it was built personified him – solid, steady and strong, the wall encircling the town in a similar way to how his arms had once encircled her: protective and proud.

Sadness overwhelmed her. She missed him so much. Although he had often been away from home, he had been a constant in her life, and his sudden death had been shocking and sobering. And now she felt empty, like a shelf that was once full of books but now sat dusty and bare.

The road headed west across Anguis to the mountains, shadowing Isenbard's Wall, which separated Wulfengar in the north from Laxony in the south. Taking the road would be the fastest route to Heartwood, but it would also be the easiest one for her family to follow her. She had no doubt that her mother would come after her and attempt to bring her back to Vichton. And therefore she had to avoid the road and take a more meandering but safer path.

She took the left fork at the main crossing, parting from the Great West Road, travelled along the southern route for about an hour to the tiny hamlet of Farington, then took another fork onto a smaller lane, which headed west toward the forested hills. She knew the countryside as far west as Ransberg, where her half-sister lived, and she had hunted in the forest on many occasions, so she did not fear to enter it, even in the dark.

Still, as the sun sank behind the hills to the west, she glanced frequently over her shoulder at the encroaching darkness and tried to ignore the apprehension that continued to rise like floodwater. Ever since she'd left the castle, she'd had the strange sensation of being followed, although she was certain it wasn't a member of her family. Procella and Orsin would not have skulked in the shadows like thieves, and even Julen – despite his talent for making himself invisible – would not have frightened her thus. No, something else was tracking her, something that did not yet want to announce its presence to her.

The trees ahead parted to accept the pathway, then gathered close around her, turning her away from the entrance and swallowing her up. She breathed a little easier at the presence of the oak and ash trees, and she lifted her chin in an attempt to raise her spirits.

The Laxonian countryside consisted mainly of an eiderdown of fields of oats, wheat and barley, but thick woodland covered the higher hills. As a consequence, many Laxonians spent a lot of time in the forests and enjoyed the company of trees. Most peasants' houses were built of wood, and longbows and crossbows were their main weapons.

But Horada's love of the forest went deeper than that. Although everyone in Anguis followed one of the branches of Animism which saw the Arbor as the manifestation of Animus's love on earth, like Julen she shared a mysterious affinity with the woodland. They had never discussed it, and she had never talked about it with her parents, which she now regretted as she was sure her father may have been able to shed some light on it. She had once caught him watching her when she thought she was alone; she had been in the herb garden, her hands cupped around a dying rosemary stalk. The leaves had unfurled in her hands, the purple flowers blossoming, and she had straightened, content, only to find Chonrad's startled blue eyes fixed on her. She had wondered if he would ask what she was doing, express delight, concern or even fear, but instead he hadn't said anything about it at all. He'd gone on to talk about the location of a salve for one of his horses, and she hadn't mentioned it again, not sure if he was angry with her or if he just didn't want to be reminded of everything he had gone through. She knew he had suffered, and she didn't want to be a constant reminder of his past, so she had kept her talents to herself and never spoken of it.

Similarly, she had never confessed to Julen what she could do. She knew he had a similar talent because she had watched him miraculously disappear before her eyes when they played in the woods as children, blending with the trees as if he himself had grown roots and leaves, but again for some reason they had never discussed it. It was a precious thing, Horada had always thought, a private thing that she did not want to share with anyone else. Now, however, she wished she had spoken to her father about it.

But he was gone and dwelling on it would do her no good. She ducked under overhanging branches and guided Mara along the narrow track west through the trees, the light fading until she could barely see her hand in front of her face, and Mara was just a twitch of ears in the darkness below her.

It had been a long while since she had ridden so far too, and already she felt stiff and sore from the saddle. She would have to stop to rest, even though she would rather ride through the night and get as far as she could from home.

She slipped from the saddle – glad she had worn breeches – took Mara's reins and headed her off the track and into the undergrowth. Once she was out of sight of the track, she sloped down towards the river and found a sheltered spot behind a large oak where the ground wasn't too marshy.

She rubbed Mara down and let her drink, fed her some oats, then tied her up loosely and settled down on the ground a few feet away. The forest had cooled and she was glad of the thick blanket she had brought with her, rolled up on the back of her saddlebag while she travelled.

Tired and weary, she fell asleep quickly. And in her sleep, she dreamed.

She stood beneath an oak tree so tall and with such a broad, leafy shelter that she knew it must be the Arbor. The trunk was so large it would take three people to put their arms around it and be able to link hands. The numerous leaves grew thick and lush, a beautiful deep green with not a hint of blight, and they shivered in the warm breeze that blew over her and caressed her skin.

The side of the trunk facing her did not have the irregular rough bark of the rest of the tree. It looked like it had been carved then smoothed and polished to a high shine. She stepped closer and stared with awe at the carving. Two figures stood wrapped around each other. The woman wore armour, her hair tied in a knot at the nape of her neck, and her beautiful face looked up at the man holding her. His long hair was braided and clipped back with clasps, and he did not wear armour but only a simple tunic and breeches. The most startling thing about his carving, however, were his eyes – the wood of the pupils had been inlaid with gold leaf and they shone in the early morning sunlight.

Her father had once described the figures of Beata and Teague to Horada, but she had never seen them for herself. The part of her mind that knew she was dreaming wondered if she were just imagining them, but she was certain she could never conjure up an image so real, so clear. She reached out a hand and brushed the wooden shoulder of the man and was shocked to find it warm. In fact the whole trunk of the tree was warm, and when she placed her palm over the clasped hands of the couple, she was certain she could feel the slow, steady beat of the Pectoris inside.

Someone moved next to her, and she looked up to see a man standing there. At least she assumed it was a man, as he wore a long grey cloak, the hood drawn over his face. But his height and build suggested he was male. Leather bracers covered his lower arms, and leather straps crossed his body.

Part of her wondered why she didn't feel scared to see the stranger, but there was something about him that she found vaguely familiar, comforting even.

He wore a beautiful pendant around his neck, similar to the one she herself wore, the same that most people in Anguis wore, made of wood in the shape of an oak leaf, although in the centre of his shone a bright orange stone.

Horada turned back to the tree. "She is beautiful," she said, tracing the face of the woman preserved forever in the Arbor like a fly in amber.

The man didn't reply; he just nodded. Perhaps he couldn't speak in this vision – for she was now sure it was such. The air smelled too fresh, the wood felt too smooth, for it to be a dream. The sun grew warm on her body, and she turned her face up to it.

It was only then that she realised it wasn't the sun. It was fire, crackling and leaping in a ring all around them. Her eyes widened and panic roared through her.

She turned wild eyes back to the man. He hadn't moved, and now he turned the pendant on his chest, the stone in the centre catching her gaze like a butterfly in a net and holding it, refusing to let her look away. It blazed with the heat of the centre of a furnace, melting away her terror, tempering her fear.

He reached out and cupped her face.

"Wake up," he said.

Horada opened her eyes. Her pulse raced and her chest rose and fell rapidly with her fast breaths.

She lay in the forest, Mara calm nearby, and all was quiet, but still she knew something approached. And the man in grey had visited her dream to tell her.

Soundlessly, she pushed herself to her feet, picked up her blanket and untied Mara. Some instinct made Horada lead the horse toward the nearby river. Mara – used to being ridden along the beach through the water – followed her into the shallows without hesitation, standing patiently as Horada brought her to a halt. The tumbling water covered the small noises the horse made as she tossed her head and moved her hooves against the pebbles on the riverbed.

Horada reached out and took hold of a branch from a willow tree that grew near the water's edge. Using the ability she had possessed all her life, she sent out a thought to the tree and asked for its help.

The tree responded, arching over her head to cover the horse and her in a curtain of twigs and leaves. She had never been able to describe what happened when she did this – she could only think of it as if the tree reached out with its mind and wrapped itself around her.

She put a hand on Mara's long nose, and waited.

For a short while, nothing happened. She began to wonder if she had imagined it. Maybe nobody was following her. Maybe she had fabricated this illusion of being chased out of some desperate need for validation.

And then she heard it. Scrunching through the dead oak leaves and the dry bracken. She held her breath and willed Mara not to move or whinny. The horse nuzzled her hand, but remained still.

To her surprise, a branch full of oak leaves whispered across her face, forcing her to close her eyes. She did so, aware that for whatever reason, the tree did not want her to see whatever was tracking her.

The footsteps came closer. The person stood by her. Waited. Her skin felt warm, as if she stood too near a fire. A strange sound whispered through the undergrowth, crackling, like someone unfurling a scroll of ancient parchment. Her eyelids flickered, fear making her instinctively want to see who was tracking her. But she could see no figure, only the bright red-orange light of a blazing flame. Her heart pounded in her ears. Then the leaves pressed against her lids, forcing them shut.

Mara twitched but remained still. The undergrowth crunched and rustled. And then the figure was gone. The tree lifted its branches. She opened her eyes to see the forest and the stream.

Horada remained where she stood for a while, too scared to move, but eventually Mara pushed against her arm, and her frozen muscles relaxed.

She led the horse out of the water and put her arms around Mara's neck. Mara whinnied softly. Tears forced their way out of Horada's eyes.

What was that thing?

And why was it hunting her?

II

The room was cool, the hour late, the bed soft and the blankets warm, but Tahir could not sleep.

He lay with his eyes open, looking out of the windows in his room, up at the stars.

Ten days. Possibly eleven, depending on the weather and circumstances of the journey. Ten days until he would give his life to the Arbor, a personal sacrifice for which his name would be recorded in history for evermore, written in the second book of the *Quercetum* that Nitesco the Libraris had begun after the Darkwater Lords invasion all those hundreds of years ago.

Tahir had asked Demitto if the two *Quercetum* books sat in Heartwood's palace, thinking he would feel comforted at the thought that the King would show all the visiting dignitaries the open pages, would read out his name and inform them what he had gone through for the whole of Anguis.

Demitto had laughed at that and said, "I am not even sure the King can read."

Tahir had felt the blood drain from his face. His name would be forgotten. Soon nobody would even remember he had existed.

Demitto's harsh visage had softened. "Like an actor on a stage, the Arbor bears two faces, young prince. One is the public face – the one that the royal family wishes to show visitors. Look at our wondrous tree! Look at how powerful we are! The King has no interest in the sacrifices or in ritual. He attends the ceremonies because his presence is expected, but he leaves study of religion to the scholars."

Demitto had tipped his head, his eyes glowing with that mysterious magnetism that Tahir found so fascinating. "The other face," the emissary continued, "is its private one. Once the actor has finished his performance, he leaves the stage and removes his costume and his rouge, revealing the real man beneath. And so it is with the Arbor. Once the doors have closed, the tourists vacated, the sun has set and the city is quiet, the scholars come out. They call themselves the Nox Aves – it means the Night Birds. They adjust their body clocks so they rest through the day and study when the world is asleep. There is a small college not far from the Arbor. The King is unaware of it – or at least, it is small and insignificant enough to avoid his attention. That is where the serious men and women go, those who wish to know more about the Veriditas."

Something struck Tahir. "Did you study there?" he asked, remembering that the ambassador had said he had visited the university at Ornestan and debated with the great scholars. Had he been a student then?

Demitto considered the question, his blue eyes thoughtful, as if wondering whether to divulge the truth. "Yes," he answered eventually.

"You are one of the Nox Aves?"

"I am many things." Demitto's lips curved. "But it is in the college that the Quercetum are kept. They rest in a cabinet with a glass door, kept out of the sun so its rays do not fade the pages."

"So nobody sees it?" Disappointment left a bitter taste in Tahir's mouth.

Demitto shook his head. "It is not for tourists to paw over, for sticky, dirty fingers to touch." He leaned forward, eyes intense. "The royal family have made the ceremonies a public show. But do not be fooled, young prince. Your sacrifice should not be something for the foolish and unwitting to watch like a puppet show. Your gift is a deep, noble thing. When you are there, you must shut out the crowd and concentrate on the Arbor. When you are embracing the trunk and laying your cheek against the bark, it is just you and the tree. You will become a part of this land – you will exist forever."

A shooting star blazed briefly across the night sky, and Tahir turned onto his side and shivered. The emissary fascinated and repelled him in equal measure. It was as if someone had taken a common rough-as-rats mercenary, an intelligent scholar and a magician, and forged them into one soul. Knight or holy man? Warrior or scholar? Tahir wasn't sure, but he felt certain that Demitto kept enough information to himself to fill an ocean. It was as if he refused to divulge details willingly and would only answer the right questions – and then only if he felt like it.

If he were honest with himself, Tahir supposed he could understand why the ambassador wouldn't give a lengthy, detailed description of what was going to happen in the ceremony. What person wanted to know exactly how they were going to die? And yet Tahir burned to know. Would it be painful? Would it be slow? How dignified would it be – was he likely to scream, to cry like a baby in front of all those people? The thought filled him with horror.

He had known since he was nine that this would be his destiny, and he had tried to prepare himself for it all these years. He had gone over it many times in his head, trying to imagine how he would walk up to the tree, how he would lift his head, act noble and unafraid, so that for years afterwards, people would talk about his courage.

But deep inside he harboured a fear that when the time came, panic would overwhelm him, and he would bring shame to his family. It had happened before, when he had accompanied the

King and some visiting nobles on a hunt. It was his first, and he had been excited to show his new sword skill. He had dreamed of it the night before, imagining how he would be the one to thrust the killing blow. The King would smear the stag's blood across his cheeks and he would bear it like a battle wound, returning triumphant to the cheers of the people.

The reality had been quite different. It had taken hours to hunt down the stag, and by then he had been tired and sore from the saddle, his hands covered in blisters from sawing at the reins and his thighs aching. One of the other nobles had landed the stag, and Tahir had been invited to finish it off. He had approached with his sword, heart thudding, shocked to see the noble creature thrashing on the ground, its eyes wide with fear. He had not been able to bring himself to kill it.

Embarrassed by his weak son, his father had dragged him close to the beast, placed his hand over his son's on the pommel and forced the blade into the stag's heart. Tahir had cried, and then when the blood was smeared across his face, warm and smelling strongly of iron, he had vomited and had to be taken to the stream to have it washed off.

He had not returned a hero.

His father despised him. Catena despised him too – he was sure of it. She thought his manner arrogant and spoiled when in fact he hid his desperation behind a façade of superiority, afraid that otherwise everyone would see what a coward he was inside.

His eyes burned with unshed tears, and so he closed them, shutting out the night sky.

Tiredness swept over him. He was starting a long journey tomorrow. He had to get some sleep or he would fall off his horse. He could only imagine what the impatient Catena and the amused Demitto would say to that.

Sleep gradually drifted over him like a warm blanket.

Tahir dreamed. That, in itself, was fairly unusual. His friends – or, rather, the kitchen and serving boys he sometimes listened to – often talked about their dreams, coming up with all sorts of bizarre stories, but Tahir rarely remembered any of his. Occasionally he would wake with a vague memory of water or fire or screams in the night, but the images soon faded, and he quickly forgot what had made his heart race.

This time, it was different. Once, when Tahir was much younger, a merchant had come to Harlton selling strange devices like leather tubes fitted with mirrors and crystals that enabled a man to see clearly into the distance. The merchant had allowed him to look through one of the devices and Tahir had been unsettled by the view of the forest to the north that suddenly appeared in front of him.

It was kind of like that now. His vision was unclear, blurred, and then all of a sudden the view came into focus.

He stood in a forest. The green canopy of leaves whispered over his head, and his feet sank into bracken and the soft mulch of undergrowth. The tall, straight trunks of trees surrounded him like bodyguards. Nearby, a stream tumbled over rocks.

A man stood next to him, and Tahir looked up, puzzled. He was tall and broad-shouldered, dressed in a dark grey cloak with the hood pulled over his head, his body crossed with leather straps and his wrists covered in leather bracers. His appearance was intimidating, but nevertheless Tahir felt no fear, only curiosity.

The man reached out a hand towards him. Like a child, Tahir took it.

Before them, the trees shimmered, and to his shock he realised a woman had been standing there, holding onto a horse. Leaves had been covering her, shielding her from view, but as he watched, the branches lifted and revealed her small, slender form. She wore breeches and a rustic tunic, and looked for all the world like a peasant woman, but Tahir spotted her breeding instantly in the way her hair was braided and the defiant lift of her chin.

Still, in spite of her obvious spirit, as she led the horse out of the water she pressed a hand to her mouth and leaned against the mare, fear written all over her features. Tahir studied her, intrigued. Who was she? And why was she so scared?

Even as the thoughts entered his head the picture faded and then came into focus again. This time he stood in darkness. It took a moment for his vision to adjust.

He stood in a dark alleyway – a tunnel in fact – as the rock curved up over his head. A lantern hung from a wall further along, and there he could see two figures standing. A man, tall, his hair reflecting the light like a beaten silver mirror. He wore fine clothes, polished boots and a bright golden sash across his body. In front of him stood a woman, very thin and pale, her hair a light gold, dressed in a rough tunic, old scuffed shoes on her feet.

As Tahir watched, the man reached out a hand and cupped the woman's cheek, his fingers sliding down beneath her chin to lift her gaze to his. Like the woman in the forest, this one also had fear written all over her face. But the man with the silver hair only brushed his thumb across her lips, gentle as a feather. The woman's lips parted and she inhaled. Tahir's cheeks grew warm as he watched this private, intimate moment. And then the scene faded again.

He stood on grass, in front of a huge tree. He did not have to be told it was the Arbor. He could not see the city Demitto had told him about, nor the wooden shutters around the tree – it was as if it was so large and so bright it blocked out everything else.

The man standing beside him, still holding his hand, turned him so they faced each other. His face was hidden in shadow, but Tahir sensed something he had not seen from anyone in a long time save, perhaps, Catena on a good day – affection.

"Be strong," the man murmured.

Tahir swallowed and nodded. "I will try."

The man's voice held a hint of humour. "'Tis a good place to start." And to Tahir's shock, the man leaned forward and kissed his forehead.

Tahir's eyes opened. He lay in his own bed, his heart pounding. He sat up, pushed aside the covers and walked over to the narrow window to look out at the stars.

His eyes filled with tears. Who was the man, and why had he kissed him? For a moment – a very brief moment – Tahir had felt a love he had never known as a child. Why had that come into his dreams? If they were dreams. Tahir wasn't so sure.

And who were the other figures the man had shown him? Were they connected somehow?

Perhaps he could ask Demitto on the way to Heartwood, he thought as he returned to bed, his feet cold from the flagstones. It would not surprise him at all if the mysterious emissary had all the answers.

III

Sarra caught her breath. For a moment, she thought she saw a figure standing behind Comminor, a young man with the same golden eyes the Chief Select himself bore. She glanced at the young man, distracted, and Comminor dropped his hand and looked over his shoulder.

"What are you staring at?" he asked.

She blinked, but the corridor was empty. "I thought I saw…" She frowned for a moment, puzzled, and then her gaze came back to his. The sweep of fear returned.

"Would you come with me back to the palace?" His deep voice sent a shudder through her. "I would like to talk to you."

She swallowed, not missing the way his eyes dropped to the muscles in her throat. "Are you asking me or telling me?" she asked softly.

Comminor tipped his head at her, obviously amused. "Well, I am not used to being refused. Equally I am not in the habit of demanding that beautiful young women come home with me. So let us say that I am asking."

She stared, startled at his description of her as beautiful and now thoroughly confused as to his motives.

He smiled and held out a hand. "Please. I just want to talk."

She stared at his hand for a moment. He left it there, seemingly confident of his power, certain she would not refuse him.

What could she do? To refuse the Chief Select would be to draw suspicion upon herself. So she gave a little nod and slipped her hand into his.

They walked back through the Primus District, which was now practically empty, the majority of the population joining in with the White Eye celebrations. As they skirted the Great Lake, Sarra glanced up at the Caelum and saw the White Eye in its completeness, a round silvery pink circle halfway through its mysterious passage across the black disc.

She glanced at Comminor. He had looked up briefly, but otherwise his gaze remained fixed ahead of him as he walked purposefully back to the palace. She felt confused by the way he had touched her, so gentle, when he was said to be such a cruel man. Perhaps the rumours were wrong and he wasn't the monster everyone made him out to be.

Still, she knew she was wise to be scared. But his hand on hers was gentle, and when he spoke, he kept his voice low and comforting, as if talking to one of the many dogs that roamed the palace grounds.

They followed the eastern edge of the lake, avoiding the dancing that had begun on the quay, and headed for the Tertius District. Occasionally people stopped to look at Comminor and dip their head deferentially, but generally in the semi-darkness and the gaiety of the celebrations, they passed unnoticed.

He stopped at the gates to the Tertius District and the guard identified him, bowed and let them pass. She knew he would be aware that she had been there before with Rauf, but still he slowed as they walked through the large entrance cave to the palace. His face showed pride at the gardens he had cultivated since his ascension. The river ran along the west side and the ground here was moist and suitable for planting. Bushes trimmed into geometric shapes lined the pathway, and flowers grew in circular beds, one of the few places in the Embers they flourished. Numerous lanterns filled the whole place with light during the day, and now the few that remained lit cast the gardens in a warm glow.

Comminor bent and picked a single red flower, and he handed it to Sarra. She took it, seeing its waxy petals peeling back to reveal an orange centre, then lifted it to her nose and gave a cautious sniff.

"It is the most beautiful thing I have ever seen," she said softly.

"As are you."

She caught her breath. His golden eyes shone, unnerving her. She had heard of people born very occasionally with these unusual irises, but had never seen anyone with eyes like this before. The lack of visible pupils made his expression difficult to read, but his words and the way he had touched her lips with his fingers told her he liked her, and that was why he had brought her here.

Heart pounding, she followed him into the palace, along the brightly painted corridors, up the long staircase and then back through the state rooms to what she realised must be his private suite. He pulled back a shimmering cloth curtain and gestured for her to precede him, and she walked in, only to stop with a gasp of amazement.

Carved into a second level of rooms above the large state rooms below, the ante-chamber had walls polished to a smooth surface, which were inlaid with silver and glittering gems. Rauf had told her that the palace furniture had been designed by the best carpenter in the city, the ornate table and chairs carved from the rare woody plant that grew near the Magna Cataracta, and she ran a finger over the nearest one in wonder, stunned by the way the wood glowed a deep brown and shone from regular polishing.

But the feature that drew her eye was the wall facing the doorway. It had a long window that ran the length of the room, and as she walked closer, she could see it overlooked the Great Lake. She shivered. He must stand there and watch his people travelling through his city, she thought, like a shadow in the darkness, like the ever-present figure of Death.

Now they had a great view of the celebrations, however, and they stood together quietly for a moment, watching the dancers and listening to the singing as the White Eye continued its journey across the Caelum. She glanced up at him. His expression did not seem malicious or greedy as he overlooked his realm – if anything, she would have said he looked affectionate.

Eventually, he turned. "Would you like some whiskey?" He indicated one of the small jugs on the nearby table.

She glanced at the jug, wrinkled her nose and shook her head.

He smiled. "You did not develop a taste for it when Rauf gave it to you?"

She shook her head again. "It is very strong."

"It is. Maybe, then, you would like to try some wine?"

Her brow furrowed. "What is that? Rauf never mentioned it."

"Most of the Select do not know about it." He lifted the other jug and poured a small amount into a cup. "It takes a vast quantity of berries to make a single jug, so it has to be drunk sparingly. It is sweetened with honeyweed."

Her eyes widened at the mention of the rare herb, and Comminor smiled.

"Yes," he said, "I know. You have to try it." He held the cup out to her.

She took it from him and sniffed it cautiously. The smell appealed to her more than the whiskey, but still she hesitated. Had he drugged it?

As if he had read her mind, he took it from her and, holding her gaze, swallowed a mouthful before passing it back. "It is not drugged," he acknowledged.

Her cheeks warmed. She accepted the cup again, lowered her eyes and sipped the wine, holding it in her mouth and tasting it fully before swallowing.

"It is nice," she murmured.

He poured himself a cup. "I am glad you like it."

They stood at the window and sipped their drinks, watching the dancing. People were weaving white ribbons around a central pole on the quay as they sang. The atmosphere was jovial and infectious, and the melodies spiralled up to the Caelum like smoke.

"They seem happy," she said, unable to stop herself commenting on the exuberance of the dancers.

He sighed. "The mood will eventually turn ugly. The ale will begin to have an effect, the White Eye will vanish and the joy will morph into depression and grief that the daily drudgery will continue as it has always done." He stared morosely at the celebrations. "The arrival of the White Eye means nothing and changes nothing, and when that realisation gradually sinks in, the Select will have to take charge."

She shivered at his words, and at the thought of the cruelty that would ensue.

Casting one last eye over the crowd, Comminor turned his attention back to her. "I suppose you must be wondering why I have brought you here."

She turned and looked up at him, trying to keep her expression blank. She was pretty certain he knew how much she feared him, but she did not want to make it obvious.

"Yes," was all she said.

He reached out and cupped her face the same way he had outside her room and brushed his thumb across her skin.

"Do you really have no idea?" he murmured.

She could only stare up at him, lips parted, confusion and panic filling her.

"I watched Rauf bring you into the palace the very first time." He lifted his hand to stroke her hair. "I could not believe I had not seen you before. I stood here, mesmerised, as you walked through the gardens. I could not take my eyes off you." He smiled at her obvious bewilderment. "You seem surprised."

Her confusion turned to wariness. He was playing with her – he must be. "I do not understand," she whispered.

He slipped his hand to cup the back of her head, holding her in place. "I want you, Sarra. I would not have taken you from one of my Select, even though I had the power to do so. Rauf was a good man and I know he loved you. But now you are free, I would like to claim you for my own." And he lowered his lips to hers.

His mouth was soft and cool. She forced herself to remain there and not to pull away as he kissed her with a gentleness she had not expected.

Was he really asking her to be his mate?

He could have just taken her, of course – he had the right, and the power. Oddly, though, she had not heard of him abusing women in such a way. As far as she knew, he had taken no mate since his wife, Ellota, had died from sickness a few years before. No doubt the Select brought him women from the whorehouses from time to time, but still, that was very different from having a mate.

He lifted his head, his golden eyes gleaming. "You did not slap me," he said with some amusement. "I shall take that as a good sign."

She was too confused to smile. "Are you really asking me to be your mate?"

He continued to stroke her cheek. "I miss the company and the friendship, Sarra. Truth to tell, I am lonely. My life is filled with the harsh reality of life here in the Embers, and I hunger for the closeness of a woman in my bed and in my heart to relieve the cruelty and savagery that has become a part of my days."

She breathed quickly, her chest rising and falling beneath the tunic that she was now conscious was old and dirty next to his bright, clean clothes. She could not believe his words. This was a ruse – maybe he had heard of the baby, or of the Veris, and he was trying to trick her into telling him about it.

"I want to cleanse you in the palace pools, dress you in finely woven garments, highlight your cheeks with silver and gold stars and take you to my bed," he murmured. "Will you let me?"

"Why now?" she whispered. "Why wait until tonight?"

"I wanted to give you time to get over Rauf," he said.

Her back stiffened at that. "It has been but four months," she said. "It will take a lot longer than that for me to 'get over' him."

Anger flared briefly on his face. Not many people had the courage to stand up to him, she thought. Was she brave, or foolish?

He considered her, his golden eyes hard as the metal. "I will not wait forever," he snapped.

She shook her head, her own anger rising to match his. "I find it difficult to believe you are being truthful with me. You could have any woman you want. There would be rich women falling over their feet to be with you. Why me – a poor rag of a woman who has nothing to offer you? If it is just my body you seek, why do you not just take it?"

He tipped his head. "I want your heart, Sarra, not just your body. But I admire your devotion. I envy Rauf, to be loved in such a fashion. Do you think you could ever love me so?" He raised a hand and stroked his thumb across her bottom lip.

She shivered, angry with herself for her body's response to his touch. Though he frightened her, something about him – his power, maybe, or his strange magnetism – attracted her. "I do not know."

He dropped his hand. "I will give you one more month. Maybe in that time you can come to terms with the thought of being with me. Most women would jump at the chance, Sarra. You would live here with me, have fine food and drink, rich clothes – you would never want for anything again."

She lifted her chin. "You would buy my affection?"

He looked amused. "I would treat you like something very precious to me. Is that such a terrible thing?"

"And if I say no? Will you take me anyway?"

He straightened, looking offended. "Is the thought of bedding me so abhorrent? Am I so disgusting that you cannot entertain the thought of taking me as a mate?"

He looked so affronted, she could not stop the ripple of laughter bubbling up inside her. "You look quite indignant," she said, amused at the thought of the Chief Select feeling spurned.

"I am not used to being rejected," he said, a little huffily.

Something inside her warmed. "I have hurt your feelings," she said. "Poor Comminor."

His lips twitched. He could see she was playing with him. Again, she doubted that happened to him on a daily basis. "I am mortally wounded," he said, placing a hand over his heart.

She couldn't help but smile. "I did not think you would be like this."

"A man?"

"Maybe."

He picked up her hand and placed it on his chest. "I do have a heart, Sarra. Can you not feel its beat? Please, do not be the one to break it."

She left her hand there for a moment, then gently withdrew it. "One month?"

He nodded. "One month."

Raised voices sounded from outside the palace and she watched him glance out of the window. Men were pushing and shoving each other around, the ale finally taking its toll as the White Eye began to disappear off the edge of the Caelum. Trouble was brewing, she thought.

A guard appeared in the doorway, stopping as he saw Comminor wasn't alone. The Chief Select took Sarra's hand and kissed her fingers. "Until next month."

She nodded and walked to the door. Outside, she paused just out of sight and listened as the guard spoke. "We are about to suppress the rebellion. We will bring the main perpetrators back here. What should we do with them?"

There was a slight pause, and then Comminor's deep voice answered. "Kill them."

Sarra shivered, and slipped away.

CHAPTER FIVE

I

They had only been travelling for four hours, and Orsin was already bored.

"Where will we stop tonight?" he asked his mother, who rode alongside him on her favourite gelding. He already knew the answer as there was only one hamlet a day's ride from Vichton, but he hoped to prod her into a conversation. She had been very quiet since leaving their hometown.

"At Lipton," she said, confirming his thoughts. "And then tomorrow we shall head for Kettlestan."

That surprised him. The town lay in the Plains of Wulfengar, on the north side of the wall. He frowned. "Julen told us to head straight for Heartwood."

"Julen is not here."

"Yes, but–"

"The decision is made." Her knuckles were white where they held the reins, her back straight and stiff.

He glanced over his shoulder at the four knights they rode with, wondering if they had heard her dismissive attitude towards him. They all looked politely away as if admiring the countryside, but he was certain they must have overheard their conversation. Irritation flared within him. She always spoke to him as if he were a child. Had she not noticed he had been growing his beard these six years hence?

He said nothing more for a while, not quite sure why she seemed so tense. Was she frightened of the coming invasion? Angry that the peace she had fought to gain had been threatened?

Truth to tell, he very rarely knew what was going through his mother's mind. Obviously, he knew she had been Dux of the Exercitus – the leader of Heartwood's army. She had often joined him and Julen in the training ring when they were children before he had been sent away, and she clearly enjoyed the physical exertion. Orsin himself had never seen her in battle, although Julen had related the couple of times she had joined him in a skirmish and said she had fought effortlessly, never seeming in danger.

Still, he had grown up in a very different world to that of his parents. Nowadays Heartwood had no standing army and Anguis was at peace. There had not been war for twenty-two years. Although the law required that all men train with the sword and be able to hit a target with a longbow from fifty paces, and a militaristic life was not forbidden for women in Laxony like it still was in Wulfengar, he did not personally know any other females who were interested in donning armour instead of a pretty gown. The women he mixed with – from daughters of other knights to tavern wenches – would not know how to defend themselves with a sword, nor would they have even a passing interest in battle tactics or the latest designs in armour.

Men were stronger than women – that was a fact, not an opinion. How could a woman best a man in battle, truly? He understood that a fit, swift woman could possibly have the advantage over an unfit, overweight man – but against a young, strong man in his prime, like practically any knight who fought for a living? Orsin could not comprehend it, and had always assumed his mother's role in the Exercitus was a token one, granted to her by an outdated establishment in an attempt to placate their closest Laxonian allies.

He glanced across at her, as surreptitiously as he could. True, she continued to train regularly and remained slim and muscular, although he had heard her complain on wet, cold days that she felt like an old chair that – though once supple and flexible – creaked and groaned when sat upon. He knew she thought herself a superior fighter, and that his father had always spoken of her battle skills with the utmost respect. But how much of that was down to the way a husband would speak to a wife – especially a wife with a shrewish temper? Surely all the stories his father had told him of how she had held off the Darkwater army practically on her own could not possibly be true? If he, Orsin, were to fight her in battle, would she really be able to best him – a man, four inches taller, bigger and obviously stronger than she?

She was looking across at the river, and he took the opportunity to study her face. The fine lines around her eyes and her weathered skin spoke of someone who had spent too many nights sleeping rough. She was striking, but not beautiful, he thought, which puzzled him, because his father had been a rich, handsome man who would have been able to court any woman he wanted. Why had he chosen such a cold, harsh Wulfian woman who wrapped herself in resentment like a thick cloak?

Still, she was his mother, and as he saw her brow furrow in thought his heart went out to her. She had survived the Darkwater invasion and had probably thought to live out her life in peace. She was concerned about Horada and he knew she worried about Julen and his mysterious adventures continuously. His father had told him that when he took a wife, he would need to care for her and protect her from the harshness of the real world. "Is that what you do for Mother?" Orsin had asked. Chonrad had just grinned at that, but Orsin was sure that even though Chonrad pretended he and his wife were equals, deep down he saw himself as the provider and protector.

Orsin reached over and covered his mother's hand with his own. "Do not fear," he said softly. "Everything will be all right. I will be there to protect you should the need arise."

The gelding slowed to a halt.

Procella stared at her son. "I am sorry?"

Orsin reined in his horse. "I was just saying, I will always be there to look after you if…" His voice trailed off at the look on her face. Behind her, one of the knights who had served with her in the Exercitus winced, and the other three's eyebrows nearly shot off their foreheads.

Procella's face turned stony. "Let us get one thing straight." She spoke through gritted teeth, clenching her jaw so hard that her cheek muscles knotted like walnuts. "I am not one of the ladies whose company you like to keep, who talk about nothing but the bows in their hair and the latest length of their overtunics. I trained under the mighty Valens, and I was Dux of Heartwood's Exercitus. Nobody looks after *me*!"

"But you are just a woman," Orsin began.

He wasn't to finish his sentence. Before he could form another word, she leaned over from the saddle and her fist met his face with enough force to take him by surprise, snapping back his head. He lost his balance, grappled for a hold, failed to find one and fell backwards off his horse.

Procella dismounted, sprightly as a cat, and before he could move she straddled him and pressed the blade of her dagger to his throat.

"I do not care if you are my son," she said, and although her voice was little more than a whisper, it rang with such menace that his blood ran cold as a mountain stream. "You *will* show me some respect."

Bewildered, he tried to explain himself. "I am sorry. I truly thought you were scared at the thought of the invasion…"

Behind them, one knight groaned and another cursed and called him a name he couldn't quite catch. But it involved being the son of some animal, and it didn't sound complimentary.

Angry and embarrassed, Orsin pushed up, intending to throw her off, but Procella leaned forward and the dagger bit into his skin. It stung and he knew she had drawn blood. She was going to push the blade up through his throat and into his brain, he was sure of it.

He stopped moving and stared at her. She didn't look scared or fearful. Instead, her eyes blazed with fervour, like a priest afire with his religion.

"I. Am. Not. Scared." She spoke each word slowly, as if he were simple. "While in the Exercitus, I trained for battle every hour of every day. I have commanded armies consisting of thousands of men and have earned their respect. I have killed more men than you have drunk ales – and that is saying something. I have bested men twice the size of you who were twice as strong, with twice the sword skill. I could best you in my sleep, after drinking five flagons of wine and with my hands tied behind my back. I am Procella, the best knight you will ever meet, and if you forget it again, I swear I will make you pay."

He lay still, burning with indignation, and ashamed of being a tiny bit afraid of her. She blinked, and the passion in her eyes died a little. The dagger left his skin, and she pushed herself up and off him. "Come," she said shortly. "We must make haste or we will not reach Lipton by sunset."

They did not speak again for the rest of the day.

Nor did they speak much the following day, and the knights travelling with them also kept their distance, seemingly taking his criticism of the ex-Dux as a personal slight. Orsin grew used to his own company and sank into a melancholic sulk. Instead of improving his respect for her, Procella's actions had only served to increase his bitterness. Why did she have to humiliate him in front of their companions? Already he had to endure constantly being told how wonderful his parents were, what wonderful knights and warriors they had been.

Did she not realise how she had taken away the respect he had built up over the past year in one fell swoop?

On the afternoon of the second day, they crossed the Wall through one of the old gatehouses – standing open since the break-up of the Exercitus – into Wulfengar. Orsin's temper didn't improve at travelling into the other country. He disliked Wulfians with their squat builds, hairy faces, gruff voices and their age-old resentment that refused to die. And even though he might not truly believe women could be as great in battle as men, still he thought of them socially as equals and detested the way the Wulfians refused to let them sit on councils and enter universities. It was archaic, and his mood darkened as they travelled deeper into the land characterised by wide, flat plains, stark and unwelcoming.

They arrived at Kettlestan shortly before sunset. Orsin hadn't met the present lord, Hunfrith, before, but he knew his parents had stayed with him in the past. Following the Darkwater invasion, Chonrad and Procella had taken it upon themselves to ensure the lords on both sides of the wall continued to keep the peace, and Orsin had heard them speak several times about Hunfrith. Procella had called the Wulfian a name that had made Orsin stare at the time, shocked as to why he was always scolded if he used that word but his mother was allowed to get away with it. Chonrad had been more forgiving and assured her that Hunfrith was all talk. Was that why his mother wanted to call in there now – to ensure he wasn't stirring up trouble with the imminent threat of an elemental invasion?

He didn't dare ask her, though, and remained quiet as they approached the town walls and paused at the gatehouse – now closed for the evening – to request entrance. They were kept waiting an inordinately long time while the guard sent a runner to the castle for guidance, and by the time the gates finally opened, Procella's mouth was set in a firm line and Orsin was ready to flatten the first Wulfian he saw.

He restrained himself, however, determined not to give his mother the opportunity to criticise him again, and they led their horses into the town and through the streets to the castle.

They had to wait again to pass through the castle gatehouse, and by this time Orsin knew Hunfrith was doing it on purpose. *This is my land*, the Wulfian was saying. *You pass through here only with my permission.*

"It would have been easier to just piss all around us," Orsin murmured to his mother. Her mouth quirked, but she did not answer him.

Finally granted entry, they dismounted in the yard. As they handed the reins of their horses over to the stable lads, the lord exited the hall doors and crossed the courtyard.

Tall for a Wulfian, Hunfrith had huge shoulders and arms like tree trunks. Orsin could imagine that if Hunfrith stood his ground and refused to move, it would take fifty men to drag him from the spot. The Wulfian walked slowly toward them, an arrogant swagger to his walk.

Orsin had once watched a stallion mount a mare in the field. The mare had resisted him at first, but the stallion had pursued her for what seemed like hours, finally overpowering her with persistence and brute force, the sheer animal power it exerted taking Orsin's breath away.

And as he approached, that was exactly how Hunfrith looked at Procella.

Uh-oh.

II

Catena sat atop her horse, her stomach churning with a mixture of nerves and excitement at the thought of the coming journey.

To one side of her Demitto also sat on his horse, which shifted restlessly, picking up on the emissary's obvious impatience to be on the move. He flew the Heartwood banner – an oak tree

sewn in gold thread on a bright green pennant, and he wore his
ceremonial armour once again, the steel polished to a dazzling
shine and the emeralds glittering in the early morning sun, but
she suspected he would remove it once he was out of sight
of Harlton Castle. She couldn't imagine the irreverent knight
would suffer in the hot armour for the next eleven days.

The rest of the Heartwood party waited behind them, their
faces conveying their pity for the young prince as Tahir said
his last goodbyes to his friends and family.

Catena, too, felt pity wash over her. Tahir stood stiffly before
his parents as a member of the household read aloud to the
waiting crowd an official statement prepared by the King and
Queen of Amerle about how much they were going to miss
their son and how proud of him they were.

They did not look proud, and they did not look as if they
were going to miss him. They looked bored and relieved that
he was finally going, and as the speaker finished and rolled
up the parchment, Tahir's mother did little more than bend
forward and kiss her son on the cheek, while his father gave
him a soldier's salute and didn't touch him at all.

Tahir had made few close friends, more because of lack of
opportunity than anything else, Catena thought as he turned
and waved awkwardly to the groups of young men and
women of his own age who stood on the steps – mainly the
sons and daughters of those who worked in the castle. The
King had a son and heir in Tahir's brother, who was currently
travelling somewhere on the other side of the country to seal
a possible marriage deal, and who hadn't even bothered to
write or send a message to say goodbye. The King had decided
at Tahir's birth that he would apply for his youngest son to be
the new Selected, and as such had never invested time and
energy in getting to know or understand the boy.

Catena puzzled that the Queen seemed so unaffected
though. True, the young prince could be rude and arrogant,

but wasn't the rule that if a child misbehaved one had to look to the parent for a reason why? Tahir's attitude had been born out of neglect and of being given whatever he wanted – horses and exotic pets, rare books, fine clothes and expensive jewellery – in return for keeping himself to himself and not bothering his mother and father.

And now it seemed there was nobody at the castle willing to shed a tear for the boy. Catena watched him give a stiff little bow to his parents, turn and wave to the crowd of castle staff and then walk to his horse. He held his chin high and appeared to look down at the crowd with a sneer as he mounted. Catena knew him well enough though to see the way his hands shook as he took up the reins, and to notice how pale his skin was, and the way sweat beaded his forehead.

At least he had Atavus, she thought, watching the hunting hound waiting by the horse's side. The two of them were inseparable. Part of her had wanted to suggest that Atavus remain at Harlton – after all, what was going to happen to the dog once Tahir had been sacrificed? But she hadn't had the heart to suggest it. Better that he gain some comfort from his one and only friend in the short time he had left.

Not wanting to draw attention to his discomfort in front of everyone, she turned her horse with her knees and led the way out of the castle yard, under the portcullis and across the drawbridge, the horses' hooves echoing above the stagnant water of the moat. Demitto glanced across at her as if aware there was a problem, but he didn't say anything. She waited until they had travelled to where the road curved around the forest and the castle disappeared out of sight.

Then she reined in her horse, gesturing for the Heartwood party to do the same. She kicked her feet out of the stirrups and swung down from the saddle, walked across to Tahir and held out a hand. He stared at her for a moment, then dismounted and took her hand.

She walked him off the road and behind a large bush. And then she rested a hand on his back while he vomited onto the leaves.

She felt a pressure at her shoulder and turned to see Demitto. He stared at Tahir, then flicked his gaze over to her. She wondered whether he would mock the Prince for his display of fear, but the emissary simply took out his water bag, removed the lid, then passed it to Tahir as he straightened and wiped his mouth. Tahir took the leather bag, eyes lowered, drank a mouthful, swirled and spat, then drank again before passing it back.

"'Tis a nice day," Demitto remarked, looking up at the blazing sun. "Perhaps we should take a while to admire the scenery before we continue on our journey."

Tahir rubbed his nose and then lifted his chin. His hand strayed automatically to the dog at his side, as if he found comfort in touching Atavus's soft ears. "No. I am all right. We should carry on."

Demitto nodded, met Catena's eyes again and walked back to his horse.

An uncharacteristic wave of sympathy swept over Catena for the brave boy. Over the years he had done nothing except irritate her, but now she wished she had taken the time to get to know him better. Everyone needs affection in their lives, she thought. The Arbor knew she had been starved of it for long enough herself, and that her loneliness had affected her deeply.

She rested a hand on the Prince's arm as he went to walk past her. "Are you sure you feel well enough to continue?"

Tahir looked up at her, his unusual golden eyes reflecting the bright sunshine; so dazzling she had to blink for a moment to clear her vision. "There is no point in drawing this out," he said. "I just want to get it over with now."

He walked past her, and she followed him slowly. He was right of course. His name was already written in the *Quercetum*, his future imprinted upon time as surely as if it had been carved into stone. Delaying his arrival would serve no purpose now. The time for worrying, for debating, for anything but action had long gone.

She mounted her horse and they set off again, and for the rest of the day they spoke little. Tahir remained pale but composed, Demitto seemed lost in thought and the Heartwood guards talked in low voices amongst themselves, so Catena spent her time looking around, enjoying the chance to see something of Anguis for once.

It surprised her how much the countryside had changed since her last visit to Prampton several years before. The bush had encroached a lot further across the landscape and in places it had covered the road so much that they had to push aside ferns and vines to continue their journey. Sub-tropical insects buzzed between lush vibrantly coloured flowers, while to the east what had once been fertile fields of wheat lay parched and barren.

Catena looked to the west, where the range of mountains that ran down the centre of Anguis reared above the jungle, disappearing every now and then into the clouds. At their bases where the earth's crust thinned and lakes pooled, geysers erupted regularly, while the occasional plume of smoke curled into the air. The whole world seemed to be bubbling, she thought, a pocket of unease settling in her stomach. She had grown used to the tremors that ran through the ground, but she was sure they had increased in frequency and severity since she was a child. Why was that? What was causing the land to boil like a hot stew?

She cast a glance across at Demitto, sure he knew more than he was letting on about the current situation. There was no doubt the mysterious emissary was a lot more than he made himself out to be. She had watched him captivate Tahir with his tales as if casting a spell over him, and there was something… otherworldly about him that marked him out as much more than a simple ambassador.

As she had suspected, halfway through the day when they stopped to refresh the horses and partake of some lunch, he had unbuckled his fancy armour, wrapped it carefully in cloth and stowed it in the panniers on the back of one of the spare horses. Now there was nothing to mark him out as anything other than a standard traveller, dressed in breeches and boots and a thin sleeveless tunic; his dark hair once he had removed the helmet in its usual disarray. And yet still he exuded a strange aura that she could not quite put her finger on...

The day passed slowly and by the time they reached the small hamlet halfway between Harlton and Prampton she was ready for rest. They handed their horses over to the inn's stables for rubbing down and looking after. It was too warm to sit inside the inn so they stretched out in front of one of the streams and the landlord's daughter brought their food and ale to them outside.

She tried to engage the others in conversation but Tahir was sullen and Demitto seemed distracted, so in the end she played dice with a couple of the guards and then went to bed.

The rooms were warm and stuffy, and although she managed to doze for a short while, she tossed and turned restlessly and eventually sat up, uncomfortable and irritable, wanting a drink of water. Tahir lay quietly on the pallet beside hers, Atavus at his feet, and the other guard in the room with them also appeared to be asleep, so she rose soundlessly and left. The tap room was empty, everyone abed, so she made her way outside.

The night was clear, the Light Moon on the wane high in the sky. It cast an eerie silvery-pink glow over the dozen buildings in the hamlet, filling the place with shadows and shining patches wherever it hit metal.

Beneath her leather boots she could feel a faint vibration in the ground. At first she thought it was one of the rumbles they had been experiencing, but instead of stopping after a few seconds like it normally did, this time it continued, as if a hundred wild horses were galloping along the road towards them.

Frowning, she walked through the buildings, seeing no sign of what could be causing the vibration. She rounded the last house and stared up the road to the north, still not spotting anything suspicious, but as she walked a little way away from the hamlet, the vibrations seemed to increase, travelling up through her bones and making her teeth ache.

She walked about a hundred yards up the road. Here the bush hadn't quite sunk its claws into the countryside and so the road was flanked by natural forest, oaks and ash trees, the undergrowth choked with bracken and nettles.

The vibrations increased. Heart pounding, her brain told her that she should go back to the hamlet and get Demitto to come with her, but her feet refused to wait and crunched through the bracken towards the source of the rumbling. Chinks of moonlight slid through the network of branches above her head, coating every other leaf in silver.

Something moved in the trees and she stopped and slid behind the trunk of a large oak, then gradually made her way forward to what appeared to be a tiny clearing. A figure – a man – sat in the centre, legs crossed, his hands thrust into the grass in front of him.

It was Demitto.

Catena stared. As her eyes grew used to the darkness, she saw that his hands rested on a wooden object pressed into the earth. He was mumbling something under his breath, and it was only when a reply came that she realised with shock that another figure stood in front of the emissary. And yet it wasn't a real person. The shape of a man shimmered against the leaves – an illusion, composed of shadows and light, a tall figure cloaked and hooded – and it was from him that the rumbles were emitting.

Before she could think better of it, she gasped aloud. The figure immediately vanished. Demitto's head snapped around. He stared at her, and Catena's breath caught in her throat, terror filling her at the sight of his eyes flickering with orange-red flames.

III

Sarra walked back along the quayside, her arms wrapped tightly around her body, looking across the Great Lake. The White Eye had nearly disappeared across the rim of the Caelum, and the crowd were beginning to realise that there wasn't going to be a great revelation – that basically the appearance of what she knew to be the Light Moon in the sky meant no significant change in their lives, and everything would carry on as it had always done. The rich would stay rich and the poor would stay poor, and nobody would be saved.

The mood had turned from joyful to rebellious, and the Select had poured from the palace, distinct in their gold sashes, and were breaking up the crowd and sending everyone back to the districts. It was taking a while, though, excitement and despair and anger making the people unruly, and above the raucous singing the occasional yell or scream rang out, along with a splash as someone got pushed into the water. Occasionally an individual got frogmarched back through the palace gates.

Sarra couldn't stop herself glancing up at what she now knew were Comminor's private rooms. There were no lanterns on the wall at that height and therefore the long window remained in darkness, which was probably why she had never noticed it before. She could not see a figure there, and it was possible he was somewhere on the quay helping to regain order, but still a shiver ran down her spine at the thought that he could be standing there, watching her.

Her head was still spinning. The Chief Select was interested in *her*. She would not be a woman if she wasn't immensely flattered by that. Of all the females in the Embers, all the rich women who would have done anything to be chosen, he had picked her.

She was baffled by his decision. Mirrors were rare in the Embers, but she knew from the occasional glance in the blade of her eating knife that she did not possess the sort of beauty so prized by their society, nor the plumpness that marked one out as wealthy. She had been puzzled enough when Rauf had shown interest, let alone his superior. She was nothing special.

Because of this, she could not help but feel convinced that Comminor had an ulterior motive. Perhaps he thought to gain her loyalty and then she would spill the details of the Veris like the sliced stomach of a salamander would spill slimy intestines.

His affection had seemed genuine though. His kiss had been soft, his eyes filled with amusement and interest, not determination or curiosity. She had been frightened of him because she had heard such awful tales of his cruelty, and yet standing there before him, she had found it difficult to believe in them. Was it possible for a man to be so gentle and tender one minute, so cruel and hard the next?

She shook off her doubts. Comminor had not known she was pregnant. His affections – even if they weren't real – would not have been so fervent had he known.

Reaching the edge of the quay, she looked across the Great Lake to the far side. Nele was just visible, standing in the shadows by a shop that sold plates and bowls made from turtle shells, their agreed meeting point. Along from him she could see Turstan walking down the edge of the lake, ostensibly in his role as Select, but privately waiting for her to join them ready for the journey they were supposed to start that night. She could not see Geve, but she knew he would be there, as would the others, waiting for her.

They would be wondering where she had got to. They had agreed to meet just after the evening lanterns had been extinguished, but now she was an hour late, and she knew they must be starting to panic.

There was still time, she thought as a fight began just fifty feet away from her and numerous Select rushed to break it up. She could circumnavigate the lake and make her way to the others, and then they could slip away into the shadows and begin their journey.

She looked up into the darkness. Was he there? Was he watching her at that moment? Did he know they were supposed to be leaving that night – was that why he had chosen to find her during the ceremony? Or was it just a coincidence?

She could not risk it. Turning, she slipped through the crowd and made her way back through the Primus District to her rooms.

Sarra was standing in line in the communal food hall the next day when she felt a presence against her back and glanced over her shoulder to see Geve there. Her mouth curved automatically into a smile, but when he met her gaze, his eyes were stony and his lips stayed in a firm, hard line.

Her smile faded, and a peculiar ache twisted her inside. She had spent most of the night lying awake dreading this confrontation. She had tried to convince herself that he wouldn't be angry, but it looked to be as bad as she'd feared.

"What happened?" he murmured, glancing around the hall to make sure they weren't being watched.

She looked down at her hands miserably. They used to talk openly, but since she had entered the Veris, their communication was always conducted in whispers and in secret. She missed the gaiety of ordinary life, and she missed her friend. Why had she got herself caught up in all this?

"Comminor came to me," she whispered.

Geve went still. "He knows?" His words sounded tight, forced out through gritted teeth.

"No." She swallowed. "It was nothing to do with... anything. He wanted... to see me."

"You?"

She moistened her lips. "He expressed an interest in me."

For a while, Geve said nothing. They shuffled forward in the queue, and when they reached the table, she held out her bowl for that morning's helping of porridge. The dark oats that grew in the northern Primus caverns cooked in goat's milk did not look particularly appetising, but she knew she had to eat for the baby's sake.

Geve received his breakfast and joined her at one of the tables. Luckily, following the celebrations, with most of the population having a hangover, the room was nearly empty and they were able to speak in privacy.

"Was he serious?" Geve asked.

Sarra met his gaze. For a moment she was speechless. She knew how he felt about her, had always known, right from when they were young. And she liked him. Who wouldn't like the curly-haired joker with his teasing comments and his quick wit? But although she knew he would have liked to take their relationship further, she had never felt about him in that way. He had always been more like a brother.

Until she met Rauf, she hadn't really understood why she had never urged Geve to court her. Geve was not harsh to look upon, he was gentle and considerate, and he liked her. He would never rank highly in the Embers' strict social hierarchy, but she had no expectations in that regard and knew he could provide a stable enough existence for her.

It was only when she met Rauf and fell in love that she realised what had been missing in her relationship with Geve. She did not love him, and once she had tasted the strength of that emotion, she knew she could not have a relationship without it. Rauf had made her heart thunder, and no man yet had done the same.

Briefly she thought about Comminor, and how she had felt when he kissed her. Then she pushed the memory away.

Was he serious? Geve had asked.

"I... do not know. Maybe. Although I cannot think why."

Geve gave a wry smile as he ate his porridge. "I know you cannot. That is part of your charm, Sarra dear."

"Geve, do not tease me. I am hardly the epitome of beauty. I am so thin my ribs show through my skin, and my hair does not shine like that of the ladies from the palace. I am not educated in literature or music, and I have no outstanding talents to speak of."

He continued to look at her, the hardness in his eyes softening. "There is something within you that shines forth like a lantern," he said. "I cannot explain it, but it has always drawn me to you. Rauf saw it, and now it seems that Comminor has seen it. I am not surprised."

He wiped his lips and studied her thoughtfully. "Are you considering his offer?"

"Geve! How can you even say such a thing?"

"I would not condemn you for it," he murmured. "Marriage to the Chief Select? You would never want for anything again."

"It was not marriage he was proposing, and do you really think I would even think about it for a moment?" She leaned forward, guilt at the memory of how she hadn't pulled away from Comminor's kiss, forcing her to fake indignation. "I am part of the Veris, and I have sworn to guide you to the light. I do not go back on my word. Besides, he does not know I am pregnant. Can you imagine what will happen when he finds out?"

Geve shrugged. "Maybe nothing, if he wants you that much."

"He would not want to raise another man's child!"

"You know him so well, Sarra? He wants you – you do not

know what lengths he will go to get you." Her friend's blazing eyes betrayed his jealousy. He knew he could not compete with the most powerful man in the Embers, and it burned him to the core.

She laid a hand on his arm. "He has given me a month. So we must escape within that time. I am still not sure he is not using me to get to the group. I am not as convinced about my ability to charm men as you are." She winked at him.

He dropped his gaze and pushed the porridge around his bowl. "I am sorry. I should not be jealous. I have no claim on you."

"You are my friend – the best friend I have. Of course my welfare is of importance to you."

His eyes rose to meet hers. "You know you are more than a friend to me, Sarra. You know I would wish to be more to you than that."

Words stuck in her throat as if she had swallowed brambles. "It would not be wise for us to pursue a relationship while Comminor insists he is interested," she said cautiously. "He will be watching me. We should not even be talking really."

Geve's shoulders sagged. "Yes. Of course." He went to rise.

She caught his arm. She could not bear for him to lose hope. He was a good man and he had set his heart on having her, but she knew he would never force himself upon her, and there were many men who would. He would make a good husband, and even though he did not make her feel as Rauf had done, she should not turn her back on such hope for her future, for her baby's sake if not her own.

"Geve… If we do make it out of here, make it to the Surface and start a new life…" She hesitated and met his eyes. "I would be yours. If you will have me."

He held her gaze. Passion and hope flared in his eyes, and for a brief moment Sarra saw him how he truly was – a man, not the young boy she had known all her life, thin and scrawny and with a high, infectious laugh. Although still slender, his shoulders had broadened and his muscles were firm, and for the first time she could imagine them under her fingers, her hands sliding beneath his tunic over his skin. He would make a good mate.

"Until the Surface," he said, his voice husky.

"Until the Surface." She watched him walk away.

Two men, she thought. Two lives that could not be more different. Both tempted her for different reasons. One was safe, promised security and protection for her and her child. One risked everything for the chance of a better life. Or maybe both terms could apply to each option? The thought made her smile wryly. Each choice had its risks. And its rewards.

Which should she choose?

CHAPTER SIX

I

Julen tracked Horada as far as the forest, only to find that her trail vanished about halfway into the woods. He had long suspected that she possessed similar talents to himself and that she knew perfectly well how to make herself invisible should she truly desire, and so the distinctive – to his eyes – blurring of the leaves down by the stream and the sudden absence of her aura did not completely surprise him. But he was concerned as to why she had suddenly had to employ her abilities, especially once he saw the charred footprints amongst the dry leaves on the ground.

With no other option, and not wanting to wander aimlessly through the countryside on the off chance of picking her up, he exited the woods and headed for Esberg, two days' ride from Vichton.

The town was busy, filled with traffic passing through the countryside from west to east and also from the lands in southern Laxony up to the Wall, taking cartloads of wheat, oats and barley, plain and dyed cloth, and armour from the expert Laxonian blacksmiths to exchange for Wulfian beef, pork and fish, the superior crockery from the kilns on the clay lands to the east, and the jewellery and fine silverwork from Hanaire.

Julen passed unnoticed through the streets, blending in with his surroundings with his natural ability to camouflage himself wherever he went. He had never been able to describe how he did what he did to anyone, including his father, who had been the only one on whom it had not worked.

Julen's nurse had come looking for him to tell him it was time for dinner. He was only seven, and, playing by the river and enjoying his game, he had watched with amusement as she hunted up and down the riverbank, yelling his name, unable to see him even though he sat in plain sight, his back against a tree trunk. She had gone back to the castle and returned with his father, and Chonrad had walked along the riverbank with her as she called Julen's name, stopping a few yards down as it became clear she could not find him.

"Perhaps you would return to the castle and see whether he has come home," Chonrad had said. "I will have one more look."

The nurse had returned, grumbling, and when she had vanished, Chonrad had turned and looked straight at his son.

"Hmm," Chonrad said, hands on hips.

Julen had stared back, shocked to find that his special trick hadn't worked on his father.

"That is a very useful skill you have there," Chonrad said. "How do you do it?"

Julen had just shrugged, because he had no idea. "I just think of myself as part of whatever I am touching and suddenly nobody can see me."

A frown had flitted across Chonrad's brow. "Does it work against stone?"

"No. Only trees and grass, and sometimes water," Julen had replied, and it was true that his camouflaging ability was most successful when used with natural objects. To his surprise, his father had hugged him rather than scolded him for being late for dinner, but no more was said about his special ability, not even – Julen realised – to his mother.

As time had passed, he had been able to adapt his ability for most other substances, and now he found that wherever he was, be it city or countryside, he was able to blend himself into his surroundings and remain invisible to most eyes.

He still didn't know why his father had been able to see him that day. He guessed it was something to do with Chonrad's unique connection to the Arbor, and that his own skill was also somehow connected to the great tree.

Now, as he rode through the streets of Esberg, he drew the city's anonymity around him like a blanket and used the shadows to blend in with the townsfolk. The bustling shopkeepers and tradespeople paid him hardly any heed. He reached the Silver Boar Inn without any hassle, left his horse with the stablehand to be rubbed down and fed, and entered the inn.

As he had been riding for several hours and was hungry, he ordered himself a meal of bread, cheese and sausages and a tankard of ale to wash it down with from the innkeeper.

"How are things in Esberg these days?" he asked the innkeeper as he poured the ale.

"So-so," the innkeeper said. "Usual. Busy on market days like today. A bit hair-raising earlier in the week with the fires and all."

Julen's heart thumped in response, but he kept his pose casual. "Fires?"

The innkeeper passed him his tankard and then dried a couple of cleaned ones with a cloth. "Aye, strange it was. Flared up out of nowhere, as if a mighty dragon had flown overhead and breathed life into roofs and trees from the west gate to the east. Half a dozen there were, and nobody could say whence they started and who was to blame. Took us half a day to put them all out. Did some damage, I can tell you."

"I can imagine." Julen took a mouthful of his ale, but had to force himself to swallow. Was it the same elemental that had passed through Esberg that was hunting Horada? Icicles descended his spine at the thought. *Arbor keep her safe*, he prayed. He had hoped to protect her himself, but how was he to do that when she was purposely avoiding him?

He took his meal and ale to the fire and sat there to finish it. The person he was supposed to meet had not yet arrived, so he had a while to himself. Used to making the most of the precious spare hours he had, he pulled his hood over his eyes and promptly dozed off.

A kick to his feet, forcing them off the table, jerked him awake. He sat up, startled, hand already on the hilt of his sword, only to sag back with relief when he saw the man sitting opposite him. He had greying curly hair and a boyish look to his face, in spite of the fact that he was in his forties. He wore plain leather breeches and a nondescript brown tunic and cloak. Nobody would have guessed that he was the ambassador known as the Peacemaker.

"Gravis," Julen said, glancing over at the bar. Only a few patrons were left, showing that the lunchtime rush had passed. Early afternoon, he thought. He must have slept for a few hours. Probably because he hadn't had much sleep the night before – he had spent most of the night tracking his sister.

The Peacemaker linked his fingers and studied the younger knight with amusement. "Catching you sleeping, Master Barle? Thank the Arbor the invasion had not begun while you examined the inside of your eyelids!"

Julen smiled wryly and finished off the inch of ale he had left in his tankard. "I would have woken should the need have arisen."

"If you say so." Gravis looked over his shoulder at the innkeeper and signalled for two tankards. The innkeeper brought them over.

Julen studied the older man while he drank his second ale. When feeling nostalgic – which wasn't often – and willing to relate some tales of the old days, his father had spoken much of the twins, Gravis and Gavius, and of the importance they had played in exorcising Anguis of the presence of the Darkwater Lords. Julen knew that Gavius had died at the hand of the

Komis king after opening the portal of the Green Man carving in Komis, and that Gravis had opened the portal at the Henge in Dorle and then returned to Heartwood for the Last Stand.

Once thought the quieter twin, Gravis had shown his true worth after the Arbor destroyed its Temple and the country had to pick itself up and mend the broken alliances that had led to its downfall in the first place. He had displayed a surprising ability for diplomacy, and the man who headed the new Heartwood Council – Dolosus, the one-armed knight whose body had been made whole again by the Arbor – had lost no time in enlisting Gravis's help as an emissary to the four lands to encourage them to maintain a truce and turn their attention from war to peace.

And Gravis, in turn, had enlisted Julen shortly after meeting him three years before, when he had accompanied Chonrad on a visit to Heartwood.

Julen realised shortly after he began working for the Peacemaker that Gravis's role involved a lot more than merely talking nicely to the leaders of the four countries of Anguis. Gravis had spies in every town, and he worked closely with Nitesco and the University of Ornestan to utilise skills other than those involving the five senses to track down troublemakers and problems, which was one reason why he had asked Julen to join them.

"What is the news?" Julen said. "The innkeeper told me about the fires here this week."

Gravis leaned forward, elbows on his knees, and cupped his tankard. "Yes, we have had more and more reports of similar outbreaks across Anguis. Nowhere seems immune – from northern Hanaire to western Komis, the world burns."

"It will be soon then?"

Gravis nodded. "We think so."

Julen hesitated. "I think the Arbor is beginning its call."

To his surprise, the Peacemaker just nodded again. "I know."

"You know about Horada?" Julen asked with a frown.

"Yes."

"How do you know already? I only left two days ago!"

Gravis grinned. "You are not my only spy in Laxony."

Julen's lips twisted wryly. "So I do not need to relay the details then?"

"I know that your sister took off in the night and you lost her in the woods. And I know your mother and brother have set off for Kettlestan and are probably there by now. I am not sure of the sense of that plan. Hunfrith recently called five other lords to his castle – your family will not be in friendly company."

"We are at peace," Julen reminded him with amusement.

Gravis rolled his eyes. "You know as well as I that Wulfians do not really understand the meaning of the word. They have always resented the fact that a woman headed the Exercitus, and that she is such a strong woman only jars the more. A couple of the lords, like you, were not even born when the Darkwater invasion happened. They hunger for war – it runs in the blood. There are old scores to settle and debts to pay. They will not be immune to the current problems, and they will plan to make the most of any weaknesses they perceive."

He put down the empty tankard and linked his fingers. "We must crush the Incendi invasion before it happens. Nitesco believes Chonrad's children will play a prominent role in this, and it is imperative that we get you all to Heartwood as soon as possible."

"As you so rightly pointed out, I lost Horada," Julen said. "Not even I can track her when she is camouflaged."

Gravis pushed himself to his feet. "I think I have something that can help you there." He beckoned with his head for Julen to follow him.

His interest piqued, Julen rose and followed his mentor out of the inn. Gravis led him through the town streets towards the quieter southern district, and Julen realised they were going to the town's temple.

Esberg's oak tree was old, maybe nearly as old as the Arbor, so the records said. Although only a fraction of the size of the great tree, it was still impressive and arched over the walled-off area, scattering fragments of light like scoops of butter across the grass.

A couple of travellers were paying their respects and Gravis and Julen waited politely until they finished their quiet prayer and left. In spite of the fact that the Arbor had told Chonrad it did not want to be worshipped, it was difficult to erase a lifetime of habit from the common people's lives. Although many rituals had been eradicated, it would take a lot longer for everyone's beliefs to follow the same path.

When they were alone, Gravis led Julen underneath the tree's branches. Casting a glance around to ensure they were not being watched, Gravis took the cord holding the oak-tree pendant that hung around his neck and lifted it over his head. He held it out to Julen.

Julen stared at it, not wanting to be rude. "I already have one." He indicated his own pendant that he had worn since birth, which felt almost as much a part of him as his arms and legs.

Gravis smiled. "It is no ordinary pendant." He turned it, and Julen saw it held an orange stone in the middle that sparkled in the sunlight.

"What is that?"

"A sunstone."

"I have not heard of such a thing."

"I am aware of that. Several of them were discovered recently in the bowels of the labyrinth beneath the Arbor – almost as if the tree wanted us to find them. I am interested to see what happens when you hold it."

A tingle ran across Julen's shoulder blades as he held out his hand, and Gravis placed the wooden token with its shining stone on his palm.

At first nothing happened, and Julen looked up guiltily, wondering if he had spoiled whatever surprise his mentor had planned for him. And then it began.

A warmth spread across his palm, then up his arm, moving rapidly through his body until he glowed with a pleasant, joyful feeling that made his face break out in a smile. He stared at Gravis in shock, having never had such an emotional reaction to an object before.

"What is it?" he asked.

Gravis reached out and touched it almost reverently. "It is from the Arbor."

Julen blinked. Unlike other trees, the Arbor shed neither leaves nor branches, remaining whole and complete from The Sleep to The Shining. Taking a piece of the live tree was strictly forbidden.

"How…?" he whispered. "Why?"

"It is from Cinereo."

Julen had heard of Cinereo, the mysterious leader of the Nox Aves, but he had not yet met him. He had once asked Gravis about him, but the Peacemaker had been unusually reluctant to share details.

Gravis rubbed a finger across the wood. "Cinereo believes that the tree is trying to communicate with us – with Horada, with you, with many others – to stop the Incendi invasion. Because of this, he asked the Arbor for help, and right there in front of him, a branch broke off and fell to the ground. This happened at almost the same time that the sunstones were found." He touched a second one around his neck. "Nitesco had the wood made into pendants, each set with a sunstone. We are to give them to those who will play a part in the denouement. This is yours, and I have another you are to deliver to Horada. It will guide and protect you."

"I would if I could find her," Julen murmured, his fingers still tingling at the thought that he held a part of the great tree.

"More of that in a moment. But first… I want you to think of fire. Concentrate on the thought of it burning, and imagine a flame dancing here, on your palm."

Julen frowned, but did as he was bid. He thought of a roaring log fire, imagining the heat searing through his veins.

Then, to his shock, a flame leapt to life on his palm. He yelled and dropped the pendant. The flame disappeared, and Gravis laughed.

"Do not worry. It will not burn you. The holder of a pendant is immune to fire. But remember that you can use it whenever you need light."

Julen's heart pounded – he had never experienced anything like that before. He picked the pendant up again, surprised that it was untouched, and not hot. "Arbor's roots."

"Indeed. And now for the second part of its magic." Gravis beckoned him closer, and crouched down to the ground. Julen followed.

"Hold the pendant and push one end into the earth," Gravis said.

Julen did so.

"Concentrate," Gravis instructed.

Julen closed his eyes. He focussed his attention on the spot between his eyebrows, reached out like he did when he camouflaged himself and connected with the grass and the tree before him.

Immediately he felt the difference. It was as if he had plugged himself into the energy channels that he knew ran beneath the earth: the roots of the Arbor that stretched from one side of Anguis to the other, connecting all four corners of the world.

Energy zapped through him, hot and fierce, and he gasped as for a brief moment he felt himself torn into tiny pieces, present in every person, every leaf and every stone in Anguis at the same time. A creature loomed before him: a giant bird with outspread wings that spread for miles, formed of flame, huge and menacing. Its eyes danced with hatred and retribution, rendering him rigid with terror.

"Concentrate on Horada." Gravis's voice cut through the sensations, and Julen held onto it and pulled himself free of the fire.

He thought of his sister, concentrated on her long blonde hair, her beautiful face, her gentle voice. To his amazement, his consciousness travelled along one of the channels, and before he knew it, he could see her. She had her arms wrapped around her body, and he sensed she was camouflaging herself, but for once she was clearly visible to him. She sat outside an inn, and he recognised the carving of a large oak tree on the inn door – she was heading for the hamlet of Franberg, on one of the smaller roads to Heartwood.

Gravis touched his hand, and he opened his eyes. He was back in Esberg, in front of the old oak tree, the Peacemaker's face creased with concern.

"Did you see her?" Gravis asked.

Julen nodded. His mouth had gone dry and he desperately needed a drink. "I saw more than my sister," he said, his voice hoarse. "I think I saw the King of the Incendi."

II

Demitto pushed his way through the trees angrily, unmindful of the branches whipping his face. He could not believe Catena had found him in the middle of the ritual. He had tried so hard to sneak away from the hamlet quietly, waiting until all their party were asleep. He had poked his head into her room and seen her lying quietly, and had assumed he would be safe. He hadn't accounted for the fact that the vibrations might awaken her.

And now she had stormed off yelling something about betrayal, and if he wasn't careful she'd blunder back to the inn and inform the whole party – including Tahir – what was going on.

He saw her ahead of him, exiting the trees, and increased his pace. As she crossed the road, he sprinted forward and caught her arm. "Catena!"

She snatched it away and whirled around, eyes blazing. "Let me go, *traitor!*"

He caught her again and began to drag her back to the trees, but he had forgotten she was not one of the women of the court, simpering around in a fine dress with nothing on her mind except for which rich man she should target for a husband. Catena was a knight, trained for battle, and as he tugged her arm she whipped out her sword and it came whistling through the air, missing his throat by an inch.

He bellowed and drew his own sword, and for a brief moment found himself on the back foot, fighting for his life. Part of his mind recognised her skill and rejoiced in it, certain it would be needed within due course, but the other part could only boil with anger and frustration as he widened his stance and met her blow for blow. She was good, but she was no match for a warrior who had seen action in all four countries, who had headed the vanguard in numerous battles, who had mounted sieges, protected kings and killed more men than there were leaves on the nearest tree.

Using brute strength to overwhelm her, he knocked her sword from her grasp and pinned her against an oak.

"Wait," he hissed. "Let me explain."

"And let you fill my mind with poison?" She spat in his face. "Think again."

He wiped his cheek on his shoulder and leaned on her until she ceased to struggle. "There are things of which you are unaware," he snapped. "And I will share them with you, but you have to stop fighting me."

She met his gaze. Her chest rose and fell rapidly, but he was holding her so firmly that she had little option but to nod her agreement.

He released her, wary in case she immediately lunged at him, but she just bent and retrieved her sword and sheathed it, her mouth set in a firm line. "So tell me this amazing story," she said.

"Prove to me that you have the Prince's best interests at heart."

With surprise he realised that her primary concern was for Tahir's safety, not her own. She was worried that he was leading them into some kind of trap. She obviously treated her responsibilities seriously.

He led her to a fallen tree trunk, sat astride it and motioned for her to join him. She sat opposite him, the moonlight painting her in streaks of silver. He examined his hands, wondering where to start. He had not planned to tell her the truth, and he would still not be able to tell her everything, but clearly he had to divulge some of the facts or she would not trust him, and her being able to trust him was imperative to saving the world.

"Do you remember that I said I was part of the Nox Aves?" he began.

"The scholars at Heartwood?"

"Yes, although I am not based there, like all the others – I am more of a mercenary than a regular member. They are viewed by most as eccentrics disconnected with the real world, who bury their noses in books and hearken to days gone by. And to an extent that is the truth. But they are so much more than that."

He picked a leaf from the nearby tree and curled it around his finger as he thought about how best to tell her. The truth, he decided, was probably the best way. "As I explained to you and the Prince, I have travelled much over the years. I have an ear for languages and a talent for diplomacy, and my name soon came to the ears of the Nox Aves, who were looking for someone to carry out a role for them. You see, as I said, they are much more than eccentric scholars. They are historians, who carry within them the knowledge of the past, and of the future."

He glanced up at Catena, wondering what she was thinking. She remained quiet but as his gaze fell on her she said, "Go on."

"Beneath Heartwood lies a room known as the Cavus."

She nodded. "Which leads to the location of the fifth Node."

"Yes. The Nox Aves maintain it, which is common knowledge, of course, but what is not well known is that it also houses a secret library. Chronicles of everything that has happened over the last five hundred years, as well as both volumes of the ancient *Quercetum* – the first one that the legendary Nitesco translated before the invasion of the Darkwater Lords and the second which he began after that event – are kept down there. And they tell a very interesting tale."

He shifted on the hard log, wishing he could take her back to the comfort of the inn, but he knew he had to ensure complete privacy. "After the Darkwater Lords were vanquished, the scholars at Ornestan University – including Nitesco – carried out years of study into the nature of our existence and what this meant for our future. And they discovered something incredible, which is very hard for our small minds to grasp – that the Arbor's roots travel through time, as well as through the land. To the great tree, the past, present and future are one, and although it cannot change time or alter major events, it can warn its people of disasters yet to come."

Catena's eyes had widened with a mixture of incredulousness and curiosity. "Truly?"

"Truly. And it has been recorded that twenty-two years after the Darkwater invasion, something happened in Anguis – an event that is somehow linked to one which will occur very shortly, as well as one which will come to pass many, many years in our future. The Nox Aves call this the Apex, emphasising that the three events, though separate, will all converge at the same point, like the three sides of a pyramid. Do you understand? The Arbor can see each side of the pyramid. It cannot change these events, but it can ensure that we are best prepared for them when they occur."

She said nothing for a while, obviously trying to process that information. "So what event is supposed to happen to us shortly?"

He stood and stretched, and looked up at the stars, at the constellations turning slowly above his head like a cartwheel. Then he leaned against a nearby tree trunk and looked back at her. He couldn't tell her the whole truth, of course, but he could hopefully tell her enough to make her trust him. "Even though the Darkwater Lords were defeated, the elemental powers remained unbalanced. From the beginning of the Second Era, the element of fire has been on the rise. That is why the climate has changed so much, and why fires so often break out in unusual places out of the blue."

"There is going to be another invasion?" she asked, wide-eyed.

"Yes."

"When?"

He hesitated. "I cannot tell you that." At the roll of her eyes, he added, "I am sworn to secrecy. The future of the country is at stake. The Nox Aves believe that time is malleable – that although certain events are fixed, other paths shift and move, guided by our actions. So although the invasion in the future is inevitable, its success will be decided by the choices we make. This is why what happened in the past has not become common knowledge and has been kept secret amongst the great scholars. They know what will happen at the Apex, but they do not know the details of the events leading up to that intersection."

"It is a lot to take in," Catena said.

"Do you believe me?"

She considered him thoughtfully. "I am not sure. I think maybe I do because it seems too fantastic an idea to make up. Why bother? And besides, oddly, a lot of it makes sense. I was wondering just yesterday why the climate has changed so much since I was young. But what I do not understand is, what part do you play in it all?"

"I am just one of many people the Nox Aves have accepted into their circle over the years to help bring the threads together. We all have a part to play. It is just that some of us know more about our journey than others."

"Hmm," she said. Her eyes gleamed.

"What?"

"I think you are playing down your role. You are far more than an ambassador sent to deliver the Selected."

"Am I?"

She lifted her chin. "What were you doing in the forest? I saw you pressing an object into the ground."

She had seen more than he had realised. He gave her a wry look. "And if I were to tell you that was a secret?"

"I will just ask you every minute of every day until we reach Heartwood, and make a complete nuisance of myself."

"More than you are already?"

They smiled at each other.

He sat on the tree trunk again, leant forward and linked his fingers. He liked her. She was brave and honest, and she genuinely seemed to care for the young prince. And of course, he knew the role she would play in the Apex, and it was not inconsiderable. He could not divulge her future. But he surprised himself with his desire to want to share more with her. Maybe it was just because he had been alone for so long, and he was tired of carrying such a burden. Or maybe he just wanted her to like him.

"What do you know of Nitesco the Great and his part in the Darkwater invasion?" he asked.

"I know that he discovered the *Quercetum*, and he was the one to first understand the link between the elementals and how one could transform into another."

He nodded. "Nitesco was also responsible for crafting these." He reached into his tunic and pulled out the oak-leaf pendant around his neck. It mirrored the one that everyone wore since birth, except it held within it a round, shining sunstone. "It is made from the Arbor and it is very old. It retains a special link to the great tree."

Her mouth had dropped open. "This is made from the Arbor?"

"Yes."

She touched it reverently, then brushed her fingers across the gem in the middle. "What is this?"

"It is a sunstone. They are found deep underground, and whereas the wood has a connection with the Arbor, the stones have an ancient connection with the fire elementals. Watch." He held the pendant in his left hand, opened his right and held it palm up. A dancing flame appeared in the middle.

Catena gasped. "How did you do that?"

"The Nox Aves believe the sunstones hold a memory of fire within them. I do not understand it completely, but I know that when I concentrate on it, I can conjure up a flame. And the holders of the pendants do not feel the fire – they remain immune."

She nodded, clearly in awe of it. "And this is what you pushed into the ground?"

"Yes. When placed in the earth, it enables the bearer to access the channels that run beneath the ground – the roots of the Arbor which run not only from east to west and north to south, but also through time itself. The fire elementals – which are known as the Incendi – have been using these channels to move through time and to influence events leading up to the Apex. Those Nox Aves who own these pendants can sometimes use this strange connection between earth and fire to observe these events and find out what they are up to."

"Who was the person you were speaking to, the one in the grey cloak?"

"His name is Cinereo. He is the leader of the Nox Aves."

"It is fantastic," she whispered. She glanced over her shoulder, towards the inn. "And Tahir also is to play a special part in the Apex?"

"He is a Selected. He is essential to the whole plan."

Her face softened. "I am glad."

"You thought his sacrifice was meaningless?"

"I thought people saw it as such, even if the Arbor did not. I am comforted to know his role is important."

That was the understatement of the Second Era, but Demitto did not say more. "It is advisable that Tahir knows none of this," he said. "Whilst it is encouraging to know one's role is important, knowing you are the saviour of the world is sometimes a little too much to handle."

She met his gaze. He could say no more, but he saw in her eyes the final understanding. Through the centuries their people had climbed a mountain, and they were currently nearing the peak. The lines of time were converging, and the result would be a conjunction like the meeting of great stars in the sky. They were writing history with every step they took, and they carried with them the weight of the future and the very existence of their kind.

"Are you all right?" he said, wondering if her head were about to explode.

Catena nodded.

He stood and held out his hand, and she rose and placed hers into it.

Together, they walked back to the inn.

III

Geve stood in the shadows and waited.

Around him, the hustle and bustle of daily life in the Primus District continued. He stood in front of the smithies, and the place was filled with the hiss and steam of the forges and the clash of hammers on iron. Furnaces blazed, reflecting off the beaten metal and sending dancing flames around the walls; the forges flashing occasionally with the glint of gold. The air tasted gritty, rich and sharp, the tang of metal setting his teeth on edge. Young boys walked past carrying buckets of water from the stream that ran through the western part of the district, and occasionally a cartload of ore from the mines at the northernmost edge of the Embers trundled past.

In spite of the busyness of the area, Geve soon picked out what he had suspected – the shine of the golden sash denoting a Select, who was walking casually along the central road, his sharp eyes darting from room to room.

Geve was being followed.

He remained still, but his mind worked furiously. Why was he being trailed? Was it because the Select suspected he had a role in the Veris? Sarra had made it clear that Rauf had known about the – as they had thought – secret society, and maybe they were trying to track the members down.

Or was this about Sarra herself? Over the last few days, since the White Eye celebrations, he had been conscious that every time he spoke to her, he would turn around to find a Select in the room watching him. Their presence in the district wasn't unusual, as that was how they maintained order – by making themselves a part of the daily lives of people, an ever-present reminder of the law and order of their society, as well as an encouragement that for those who worked hard, promotion into the ranks was always a possibility. What was unusual was the way Geve had caught them watching him on more than one occasion, making him certain they were targeting him in particular, and that they weren't just there to keep an eye on the room.

Sarra had told him all about what happened on the night of the celebrations, and that Comminor was apparently interested in her, and had given her a month to think about a relationship with him. If that were the case, maybe the Chief Select was keeping an eye on her, seeing who her friends were, making sure nobody else had staked a claim on her.

Geve wasn't a hundred percent sure whether Comminor's interest in her was personal or connected with the Veris, but either way he sensed they had picked up on the fact that he was friends with her, and Comminor had instructed them to keep an eye on him and report back his comings and goings.

Day-to-day, this wasn't necessarily a problem as he didn't do anything that would arouse suspicion anyway. But today he was supposed to meet with the Veris to discuss their future plans in light of their failure to escape on the night of the celebration, and he could hardly lead the person tailing him to their secret hiding place.

The Select walked past him and continued down the road, so Geve slipped out of the shadows and walked in the opposite direction. As he turned into the main road, he paused and pretended to look at the wares of one of the shops selling engraved metal boxes. As he stared at the polished tin, the reflection of the Select appeared around the corner of the road, pausing as the man stopped and pretended to examine a display of cutlery.

Geve cursed under his breath and began walking again. He was going to have to be clever to lose this one.

He didn't bother winding his way through the maze of roads and alleyways that formed the upper Primus District but instead took the main road, walking casually as if he were a man with a purpose, but no rush, to get where he was going. He walked through the leather makers, past the claymakers coiling tubes of rolled clay into pots, past the weavers and the dyers with their blue and red stained hands, past the bakers where the warm and comforting smell of cooking bread made his stomach rumble. He walked and walked without turning around, and then when he reached the shell-cutters busy joining squares of turtle shell with tiny iron loops into shimmering curtains, he stepped suddenly into the shadow of one of the shops and pressed himself against the wall.

He waited until the Select had passed the entrance, still walking casually as if certain the man he followed had just turned a corner, and then Geve walked quickly along the narrow alleyway that led through to the merchants' district, picking up speed once he was certain he wasn't being followed.

Exiting the alleyway the other side, he walked more quickly now through the brightly-coloured clothes shops, the jewellers setting gems into silver and gold rings and pendants, the barbers sweeping tufts of hair into bags, the apothecaries measuring tinctures and pastes into tiny leather pouches. When he reached the quay, he circumnavigated the lake and made his way into the Secundus District, pausing every now and again to check behind him, certain by now he wasn't being followed.

Nobody stopped or spoke to him, and thus it took him completely by surprise when – halfway across the district as he left the playhouse behind him and entered the more threatening areas of the underworld – someone grabbed a handful of his tunic and drew him into a side alley.

He exclaimed and went to wrestle with his assailant, but a flame flared briefly from the man's hands and in the answering light he saw it was Turstan.

"Roots," Geve swore. "You scared me."

"Stay still," Turstan murmured in his ear.

The two of them waited, silent, listening. Geve's heart sounded loud in his ears. He could hear the whisper of the Magnus Cataracta in the far distance, the yells of men having a fight somewhere to his right in one of the alleys, the crash of a glass breaking. The stench of the filth running down the channel in the middle of the alleyway rose up, cloying and overpowering, even to his nostrils that were accustomed to the smells of the tanners. Turstan's breath was hot on his neck.

Gradually, the other man's fingers relaxed on his arm and Turstan moved back. "Sorry. I thought you were being followed."

"I was," Geve said. "I gave him the slip back in Primus."

"I think maybe we are all being watched," Turstan said. His dark brows met in a straight, heavy line.

Geve's mouth went dry. "You think they know who we are?"

"Sarra said Rauf was aware of us. That must mean Comminor is too."

"I am not so sure. She also said although he enjoyed his position and privileges, Rauf was sympathetic to our cause."

"And now he is dead."

Geve stared at him. "You think Comminor had him killed?"

Turstan shrugged. "We cannot prove it either way. But it would not surprise me. The Chief Select is very skilful at removing opposition to his rule." He backed down the alleyway. "Come on. They will be waiting for us."

Geve followed him down to the river and crossed with him to the opposite bank. "Does that not worry you – that Comminor may know you are part of the Veris?"

"Yes, it worries me. Which is yet another reason for us to reorganise the date of our departure for as soon as possible."

The two men continued in silence. Geve had passed on to Nele what had happened to Sarra on the night of the celebrations, and he knew Nele would have passed it on to the others. They would all be worried that Comminor's interest in Sarra was to cover his interest in the Veris. Geve, however, was still certain the Chief Select's declaration that he wished to get to know her stemmed from a more personal desire.

The alleyways grew narrower and darker, and Turstan let a flame dance on his palm to guide them in between the lanterns, which were few and far between in the outer regions of the district. It took them a while to reach their meeting place, which was in a different section to the previous one. Turstan swept aside the curtain covering the door, and Geve entered the room.

Everyone was there, and he and Turstan joined them where they sat in a circle on the floor. Geve took a place next to Sarra, warmed by the way she smiled at him, clearly relieved to see him there.

"Were you followed?" Nele asked Geve.

"To western Primus. Then I lost him."

Neve's brow furrowed, and his gaze slid across to a pale but composed Sarra. "Perhaps you can now explain to us what happened the night of the White Eye, Sarra."

She would have known that he would have passed on what she had told him, Geve thought, but she related it again anyway, obviously realising that they would want to try to assess the truth of her words. She told them how Comminor had appeared at her night rooms, how he had asked her to come back to the palace, and there how he had told her he wanted her for his own. They asked many questions, and she answered them all.

When she announced he had given her a month to decide, they fell silent.

"Why a month?" Kytte asked.

Sarra shrugged. "He wanted to give me more time to recover from Rauf's death. I suppose a week was too little, a year too much."

"So we have a month before he will come for you," Kytte said.

Sarra nodded.

Amabil, the older, dark-haired and dark-skinned baker who always brought the cakes, leaned forward and took Sarra's hand. "Do you think he is sincere about his affections for you?"

Sarra hesitated. "I do not think so. I saw him briefly once or twice when I went to the palace with Rauf, and he never even looked in my direction. He could have any female he wants in the whole of the Embers, whether they are willing or not! I am not being coy, but I cannot imagine why he would decide I am his ideal woman. It seems too much of a coincidence that he would choose now to show his 'love' – just after I joined the Veris."

"Do you think he knew we had planned an escape that night?" Turstan asked.

She thought about it. "No. And Rauf never spoke of any knowledge of plans to leave the Embers. He just thought the group was a place to talk about the dreams. I do not think Comminor has considered we would try to leave. I think he is more concerned about us stirring up hope and rebellion in the city's inhabitants."

"The Arbor forbid," Geve said, and they all smiled wryly.

"So you do not think we have a spy in here," Betune said. She still wore the ragged red ribbon tied around her long, brown braid, and Geve wondered absently if it had been given to her by a loved one who had died, as he knew she did not have a husband. Her dark gaze rested evenly on Sarra as her hand fingered the leather pouch around her neck, the one that supposedly contained an original acorn from the Arbor.

Sarra went still. "I have not betrayed you," she whispered.

Nele blew out a long breath. He had drawn his straggly brown-and-grey hair back into a ponytail, and it seemed to accentuate his high cheekbones and the brightness of his green eyes. "I do not think we should start talking about spies. Madness dwells down that route. We will be too busy watching each other to look out for the Select. We all have a huge amount invested in this group. We are all bards and we all want to see the Surface. I do not believe any of us would sacrifice that."

"So what do we do now?" Geve asked Nele. "We have lost the confusion of the White Eye celebrations as cover. When do you think we should attempt it again?"

"I have been thinking about that," Nele said. "In nearly three weeks' time, there will be a market day."

Geve's eyebrows rose. "How do you know this?"

"There was a meeting for guild members in the merchant district," Nele said, naming the location of his apothecary shop. "One of the women who is married to a Select said she had heard them discussing it at the palace. I think there will be an announcement over the next few days."

They all sat up a little straighter. Geve's heart lifted at the thought that an opportunity for escape still existed. Market days were only held once or twice a year because – like at the celebrations – they raised the people's spirits a little too high and often chaos followed. But the Select would no doubt have picked up on the drop of the people's mood after the celebrations.

"That makes sense," he said. "So we aim for that day?"

Nele nodded, and looked at Sarra. "What do you think?" He glanced at her abdomen, which showed a clear bump the way she was sitting. "Are you comfortable waiting until then?"

She rested her hand on the bump. "I am not sure I have a lot of choice really. I would like to leave sooner. The thought of waiting – both because of the child and because of Comminor – fills my heart with panic. But I know it makes sense. I am happy to abide by your decision."

Nele nodded. "We will plan for market day, then. Same plan as before, same positions, but let us say at the midday bell this time. I think it best we do not meet again, unless someone has an urgent issue that must be addressed. They are obviously watching us, and if we can allay their suspicion for a few weeks, it will be good for us."

Amabil took out her cakes. "Let us have the ritual."

Geve bent his head and closed his eyes, trying to calm himself. Images flickered behind his lids of the dreams he had had the night before of a cool breeze – something they did not often feel in the Embers – blowing across a blue sea. He could not even imagine such an expanse of water while awake, but in his dreams he saw the ocean, topped with white waves, rolling up a golden beach. He wanted to stand on that beach with a longing that made him ache, and nothing would make him happier than to have Sarra standing by his side.

He opened his eyes, studying her face as the others prayed. She appeared calm, but he knew her well and saw the fear flicker across her features. She was scared, and as she gave a light stroke to her bump, he knew the child was moving again.

Was she tempted by Comminor's offer? He was still not as certain as the others that the Chief Select wanted her only to get to the Veris.

Would she sell them out for a life of peace and comfort?

CHAPTER SEVEN

I

Procella sipped her ale and cut a small corner from the piece of beef on her plate. She chewed slowly as the men around her talked of the latest developments in armour and weaponry and pretended to be listening, but all the while her gaze flicked around the room, taking in the numbers of Wulfians sitting around the table, the men standing in the shadows – noting the arms they bore, the mail that glinted beneath their overtunics.

It was no coincidence that half a dozen Wulfian lords were present, she thought, fully armed and with mean eyes in their smiling faces. This wasn't dinner. This was an ambush.

She looked across the table to where her son sat next to Hunfrith's son, Alfrid. Orsin was busy tearing into a hunk of bread, dipping it into the meat gravy left over from his beef pie, but when he looked up and met her eyes, she saw the wariness in them.

She glanced at the table where the knights who had travelled with them from Vichton were sitting. The Wulfians had put a man in between each one, ostensibly as a social tactic to make them feel comfortable, but she was aware it was a clever tactic to separate them. She knew each of the knights well; two of them had fought with her in the Exercitus, another two were from Vichton's castle guard, good, solid, sturdy knights she trusted. Each would fight to the death for her and Orsin, and she had complete faith in their abilities against any foe one-on-one. But in a room full of hostile Wulfians who had too long been denied the taste of Laxonian blood?

Her gaze fell back on her son. Her and Chonrad's eldest son and heir had seen little battle action, and she was not even sure he had ever killed a man. True it was no fault of his own – unlike Julen, who had seemed to be around whenever a raid struck, Orsin had always happened to be absent. When Chonrad had sent him to learn how to be a page and a squire with an old friend in the Castle of Lacton in Perle, some seventy-five miles away, Procella had been surprised. Lacton lay a long way from Isenbard's Wall and Wulfian territory, and miles from the sea, so it did not even suffer from coastal smugglers' raids. At the time she had puzzled as to why Chonrad would not want his boy in the thick of it, learning how to live on his toes, how to defend himself, but now she wondered if he had somehow tried to protect his heir, to wrap him in velvet so his life would never be in danger, the same way he had refused to let Horada travel to Heartwood. That was fine all the time they were at peace, but clearly the Wulfians were stirring up trouble for the first time in two decades, and now Orsin stood untried and untested.

She herself had overseen her sons' training and ensured they knew how to fight to the standard of any knight of the Exercitus, so she wasn't worried about his ability to hold a sword. But Valens – the great leader who had taught her practically everything she knew about the art of warfare before he died at the hands of the Darkwater Lords – had once put her in charge of those knights new to battle as part of her training. At the time she had complained bitterly about the role, annoyed that she had to waste precious battle time looking after those still wet behind the ears.

But the task had proved invaluable. She had learned that the biggest, strongest, most arrogant warriors could be those who shook at the first sign of blood, and that many men and women who had thought themselves brave cried for their mothers when they suffered a wound. And she had developed a priceless instinct for guessing a knight's true worth, for knowing whether their brave talk and threats of chalking up the kills would ever come to fruition, an instinct that had saved the day in battle on more than one occasion when she had pulled a knight off the front line, knowing they would break as the enemy closed in.

Now she studied her son and wondered whether he would hold his own if the Wulfians sprung. But for once, she could not be sure. He was a roguish man and never tried to hide his love of ale and women – unlike his brother, who she was sure had experienced his share of female companions but never flaunted them in front of her. And Orsin was one of those men who could talk a good talk, who thought he knew all the best tactics and battle patterns, even though his sword had seen little more action than a brief skirmish once on the beach during a bandit raid some years before.

It was too late to worry about it now. When the moment came, she would not be able to protect him. She had already embarrassed him in front of the other knights, and he would not forgive her easily for that, even though he had insulted her prowess and talked to her like she were any other woman. He would have to do his best, as everyone always did in battle, and even though they were vastly outnumbered, she thought they would give the Wulfians a run for their money.

She finished off her ale, knowing it had been foolish to walk into Hunfrith's hands. She had thought to scout out the territory and test both his temperature and that of her countrymen before travelling on to Heartwood. Well, she had done that well enough, she thought wryly. Whether she would leave the castle with her teeth intact would be another matter.

She put down her cup and rose to her feet.

To her surprise, Hunfrith rose with her. "Madam," he said in Wulfian. "Perhaps you would take a stroll with me? The gardens are pleasant at this late hour."

Taken aback, Procella just stared at him. Chonrad had been her first and her last love, and she had adored him because he had treated her as both a woman and a knight, sacrificing neither for the other. Social niceties had never been her strong point, and she would rather knock a man on his backside than take a compliment or a gift, sure that accepting either could be interpreted as weakness.

Hunfrith did not move, just stood watching her, clearly interested to see her reaction. She swallowed and glanced at Orsin, but his gaze was fixed on the candle in front of him, as if he were entranced by the flickering flame. She frowned. Maybe it would be best to separate Hunfrith from his followers. Perhaps he knew something about the Incendi he wanted to share with her.

She nodded and followed him across the hall to the doors. Cheers echoed around them, and warmth stole into her cheeks, which made her angry. Embarrassment was an emotion she was neither familiar with nor liked. She slipped through the doors as he held them open and let the cool evening air stroke her skin.

"Come this way," Hunfrith demanded.

Procella bit her tongue and followed him. He led her through the castle yard, past the squabbling chickens and the mangy dogs, around the castle to the gardens at the back. He hadn't lied – unusually for a Wulfian lord, he sported large, carefully tended lawns and sculpted bushes, with rows of pink and red flowers nodding in the evening breeze.

"Very tasteful," Procella said, unable to hide her sarcasm. "Is this what peace does to a Wulfian lord?"

He stopped by a tall, leaf-covered arbour, turned to look at her and studied her carefully. For a moment she thought he was angry, and then she saw what it was that glittered in his eyes – not anger. *Desire*.

He stepped closer to her, and to her shame she took a step backwards, only realising he had her pinned when she felt the arbour wall at her back.

"Dux of the Exercitus," Hunfrith murmured. He reached out a hand and cupped her cheek, his big, calloused thumb stroking her skin. "I always wondered what you would be like in bed."

"I snore," said Procella. She pushed his hand away. "What do you want?"

"I think you know what I want." He stepped even closer. He was taller than Chonrad had been, broader in the shoulder: a fine figure of a man. But whereas her husband had made her heart pound whenever he got that look in his eye, Hunfrith made her skin crawl.

"Are you proposing to me?" She raised her chin. "I am no man's whore."

His lips curved, thick and fleshy beneath his bushy brown beard and moustache. "I already have a wife. But Chonrad has been dead these past two hundred and fifty days or so. That is a long time for a woman to have an empty bed. And I wager you are a woman with hungry appetites."

Procella went stiff with resentment and indignation as he leaned close to her. "Step away," she said icily, "if you wish to keep your head atop your shoulders."

Hunfrith chuckled. "I thought some of your passion would have dulled after all those years of peace, but it appears I was mistaken. Let me taste a little of that heat."

Procella placed both her hands on his chest, alarmed as he moved forward. "Get off…" But he smothered her words with his lips.

Incensed, she acted automatically and raised her knee, but Hunfrith surprised her by being quicker than she and pushing her back hard against the wall. The movement made her exhale in a sharp *whoof*, and before she could gather her breath he closed his mouth over hers again and shoved his tongue between her teeth.

Procella gagged and struggled. Part of the reason for her outrage was that the last person to touch his lips to hers was her husband, and somehow this spoiled his memory, turned it to ashes in her mouth, as if she had somehow betrayed him.

But the major part of her ire was due to sheer fury at this man thinking he could best the Dux of Heartwood's Exercitus and take from her something she did not wish to give.

She shoved hard against his chest, but he caught her hands and twisted them against her back, pinning her against the wall with his body, his hip against her stomach and his thigh parting hers. His fingers felt like iron manacles around her wrists, and when he dropped his hand between her legs, there was nothing she could do to stop him. He chuckled with victory as he probed the material of her breeches, and a wave of rage like nothing she had ever experienced before swept over her.

She bit down hard on his lip, then drew her head back the remaining inch or two left to her and smacked her forehead onto his nose as hard she could. The bone gave with a loud crack, and he bellowed and drew back.

Procella moved away from the wall, conscious of being restricted, and tried to draw her sword, but Hunfrith threw his weight forward and before she could brace herself she fell back into the earth, him on top of her. He kissed her again, hard.

She heaved up with her body, but he was too heavy, and once again he caught her hands and pinned them above her body.

Procella yelled, aware of the shock value of a loud protest, kicked out with her legs and twisted beneath him, but all it did was make Hunfrith laugh and squirm on top of her, and she realised she was inflaming his desire by struggling. He lowered his head to her neck and sunk his teeth into her flesh, and she squealed, turning it into a bellow as anger overtook the pain.

She was *not* going to be taken on the earth like an animal, especially by this ignorant, bumbling mule who thought he could have her now that her husband had died and she was alone. She was not weak and she was not an object for men to have their pleasure with whenever the mood took them.

Blood dripped from his nose onto her face, and she spat as some of it found its way into her mouth. She ripped at his ear with her teeth, then managed to get enough leverage to swing one elbow into his face, where it struck him in the tender spot beneath the eye. She hit hard enough to make him gasp, and she seized the chance and reared up. He fell off to one side, and she leapt nimbly to her feet, drew her sword and backed up a few yards, intending to give herself time to steady her stance and prepare herself. Her neck throbbed where he had bit it and she realised he was going to be a hard foe to bring down, that he knew how to use his height and weight to his advantage. As he rolled to his feet, she shook her head to clear it and took a deep breath.

It happened before she could react, before she could even draw a breath. She stood two feet from an oak tree, a small, rather weedy specimen, but in the blink of an eye it sent out half a dozen roots that wrapped themselves around her, encasing her in a cocoon of wood and leaves. One snaked across her mouth, stopping any oath that may have slipped from her lips, and the roots tightened so that within seconds she was immobile.

Hunfrith steadied himself, drew his sword and turned. And stopped. His gaze scanned the space in front of him, combing from one end of the garden to the other. Procella blinked, certain he must be able to see her, but as he yelled a curse and strode down the garden, she realised that not only had the roots wrapped around her, they had somehow camouflaged her from his view.

Hunfrith disappeared, still yelling. Procella's chest rose and fell with her rapid breaths, but still the roots remained tight. Fury and confusion wrestled for prominence inside her. She wanted to march into the hall and tear the Wulfians apart with her bare hands. She would show them the Dux was not a woman to be trifled with.

And then a voice murmured in her ear. "Sometimes a battle leader should know when to withdraw."

The root across her mouth withdrew. She gasped and glanced over her shoulder. The place was in shadow, but she could see a figure cloaked in grey, the hood pulled over his head. Leather bracers covered his lower arms, and she wondered if he were an archer.

"Orsin must travel his own path," the man said. "Here your fates divide, and you must follow your own course."

"I must go in," she whispered furiously. "They need me."

"The battle has already been fought," the man said, "and the Incendi have made their move. Returning there will be certain death. Follow your son, Procella. He knows well the benefit of subterfuge."

It took her a moment to realise he was speaking of Julen.

"What of Orsin?" she said, her voice rough as she thought that the fire elementals might have somehow taken over the castle and were threatening her offspring. "Must I leave him to die?"

"Take to the shadows," the man urged. "Gather your followers. Trust your children to carry out their own destinies. And meet them at Heartwood. That is where you will be needed."

That was not Procella's way, and she hesitated, hating the thought of abandoning Orsin to his fate.

"Trust your children," the man repeated. "They carry your and Chonrad's blood in their veins. They are all strong in their own way. Trust that we will protect them."

We? She knew not of whom he spoke, and yet something within her trusted this stranger. She had taught her children well, she thought, even Horada. Maybe it was time to let them find their own futures.

She nodded. The roots withdrew and, even before she turned, she knew she would find no one there.

Procella sheathed her sword, glanced over at the castle then backed away and let the shadows swallow her up.

II

There were times when Tahir thought the journey would go on forever. For hours and hours, the only thing that existed was the lurch of the horse beneath him, the feel of wind or rain or sun on his face, and the scenery that rolled past him in a blur of greens, vibrant blues and oranges as the countryside displayed its best fancy clothes for the passing Selected.

Before he had left, he had dreaded the thought of the journey with its lack of entertainment and its physical discomforts, but in truth he found himself fascinated by the panorama of hills to the east marked out by square fields of crops, the occasional river winding its way through them like a blue silk ribbon threaded into a patchwork quilt.

He could see the battle occurring with the dense, verdant jungle to the west that crept ever closer, its pace almost visible to the naked eye as it crawled across and consumed the arable and pastoral Laxonian land. He could see that Demitto hated it, could tell by the disgust on the emissary's face that he saw it as an invasion of his homeland.

Demitto rode on his right most of the time, Catena on his left, Atavus ran at his feet, and the four Heartwood guards rode behind them, talking quietly amongst themselves. Something had happened the night they had spent in the hamlet, Tahir was certain of it. He had risen the next day and the atmosphere had been slightly frosty, and since then his chief of guard had kept her distance from the ambassador, although Tahir often caught her studying Demitto thoughtfully when he wasn't looking.

He puzzled over it for a while, but she refused to tell him what had happened and he didn't dare ask Demitto, and after a while he forgot about it, his attention caught by the tales that Demitto wove as their horses plodded along.

The emissary told him all about Laxony – indeed about all the four lands, both in the present and past. Tahir learned more in a day than he had ever learned from his tutors at home. Demitto explained how the warmer southern country had always been renowned for its crops, for its oats, barley and wheat, and for the magnificent ales and whiskeys the expert brewers had learned to create. He went into great detail about how the rivers in Santerle soaked through the peat-heavy land, and this lent the whiskey a strong medicinal flavour that was an acquired taste but exquisite to those with a trained palate. Tahir thought the ambassador seemed to know a little too much about the various beverages available, but still he found him fascinating to listen to.

Demitto spoke of everything with great enthusiasm, carrying the Prince along on his passionate tales. He related the old troubles in the north and the way Isenbard's Wall – long since decayed, the stone carried off for building by the locals – had once threaded all the way across the land from Heartwood to the sea, and Heartwood's army had manned it, trying to keep the peace. He spoke with glowing eyes of the glorious University of Ornestan, of its pointed arches and sweeping buttresses and amazing stained-glass windows, of the knowledge that hung in the air like smoke. He described the way the fact that the Wulfians were mainly a fishing people, and this had found its way into their art: it was common to find paintings and sculptures of fish and the sea, and their clothing often had silver fish shapes woven into the fabric.

He told of the quiet lands of Hanaire, of its gentle and serious people who placed family above all else, of the large groups of happy children who wove ribbons around the oak trees on the day of the Veriditas ceremony. He seemed to bring to life the high plains that looked over the vast expanse of the northern seas, and their cool winds, and again he seemed angry and saddened by the fact that the jungle had crept up from the Spina Mountains and clawed its way almost up to the Portal – the Node that still had to be maintained for the Veriditas to work.

And Demitto told Tahir about Komis, his own mother's land, about which Tahir knew very little. His mother had never spoken of it, and as its people kept themselves to themselves for the most part, there had never been anyone else to tell him about it either. But Demitto spoke of the land as still mostly covered in forest, of the way the trees surrounding the Green Giant Node transformed in The Falling, coating the ground in a layer of gold and red that made it feel as if you were walking through fire. He told the Prince how the Komis people had never really recovered from the devastation of the Darkwater Invasion, when the vast army that had descended on Heartwood had been drowned. The remaining population had lived quietly ever since, driven mainly by women in the absence of the men who had died, and their society had evolved into a much more peaceful one that focussed on strengthening their own culture rather than taking over others. Their carpenters were the best in all four lands, Demitto explained, and their cities still existed in the treetops, formed by trees carved into the shapes of animals and linked together by rope bridges, with houses built over vast platforms, which stretched from one side of the forest to the other.

Demitto's voice had a kind of soporific quality, Tahir thought as he fought to stay awake while the ambassador debated which country served the best food. The Prince was not bored, but his eyelids kept drooping almost as if he were in a trance. Maybe it was the rhythmic plodding of the horse, or maybe he had eaten too much at dinner, but gradually his eyes closed, and while he slept, he dreamed.

The Arbor called to him. Its voice – or maybe it was the thousands of voices of all the Selected who had joined it over the years – reached out to him, wrapped around him with velvety arms. *I need you*, said the tree, and deep within himself, Tahir felt a longing he had never experienced before, a *be*longing, in fact, as if that was where he was meant to be, as if that had been his destiny since even before he was born.

All his life he had thought of his role as one decided by financial means. He knew he had been Selected because the King of Amerle had been able to offer the biggest "contribution" to the King of Heartwood. He had never viewed his role as holy, or indeed anything but unfortunate.

And yet now, it seemed as if he could see his part in the history of Anguis as if from a distance, as if he were a tiny cog in the mechanism of life, just one star in the billions in the sky, and yet without him the world would stop turning and everything would grind to a halt.

I need you, said the Arbor, and around it, fire flared.

Tahir's breath caught in his throat. The air was filled with ash and smoke, and everything around him was burning. The tree screamed, and Tahir's heart nearly shuddered to a halt. The Arbor was frightened, could see its imminent death. Leaves flared, crisped, turned to dust, and flames licked up its branches causing it to contort in agony. The heat was unbearable, and Tahir could feel his skin burning as the flames licked towards him. The fire was going to consume him along with the tree. He twisted and turned, but he could not escape. He was going to die...

A fist caught hold of the back of his tunic and wrenched him out of his trance, and he blinked, confused by the sudden

raised voices and yells echoing around him, the twist of bodies
and flailing of hooves. It was nearly dark, and ahead he could
see the lights of what he assumed was Realberg Castle, but
before they had reached the safety of the town walls, they had
been ambushed.

It had been Catena who had grabbed his tunic, and now she
dragged him unceremoniously from his horse onto her own.

"What is going on?" he said, breathless, seeing figures
appear out of the night cloaked in black, swords drawn.

"I do not know." She drew her own sword, brought it
down on a hand that reached up for the Prince. "They have
come for you."

"For me?" He looked down as another figure reached up for
him. He was used to seeing his mother's eyes, golden like his
own, and did not find them as startling as most people, who
often found it difficult to tear their gaze from him. But this
man's eyes were filled with dancing flames, and once again his
dream flared, the memory of burning.

He kicked out, and the man grabbed his foot, but again
Catena was there to save him, hacking down with her sword
until their assailant fell back with a squeal. Next to them,
Atavus leapt up at the arm of another man, who howled
with pain. All around them sounded the clash of blades as the
Heartwood knights fought to defend the Prince, and his heart
pounded at the sudden realisation that they may not get to
Realberg Castle at all.

One of the men reached up to Demitto and grabbed him
by his belt, but Demitto kicked his heels into his horse and it
reared. His belt broke and the man fell, and the horse's hooves
came crashing down onto him with an almighty crack.

I need you! the Arbor whispered in Tahir's ear.

Demitto turned, grabbed Catena's reins and yanked the
horse around. Without another word, he set off towards the
castle at breakneck pace, and Catena kicked her heels into the

horse's side and leaned into the saddle, holding Tahir tightly.

The horses thundered along the path and Tahir didn't dare look behind them to see if they were being followed. He glanced down at the ground rushing past, relieved to see Atavus racing alongside them.

"Should we not head for the woods?" Catena yelled across to Demitto.

"They will not follow us into the city," he yelled back.

They closed the distance quicker than Tahir had expected, and Catena had to saw at the reins to get the horse to skid to a halt before the gatehouse. Demitto leapt out of the saddle, the horse still moving, and ran to the gate to talk to the guard. He relayed something urgently and showed him the seal of the ambassador of Heartwood he carried in his pocket. The guard nodded and opened the doors, and as the three of them entered, so Tahir saw half a dozen knights mounting horses, ready to go and see if they could help the Heartwood knights.

"Should you help them?" he said to Demitto, who was now leading both horses into the city.

"You are my first priority," Demitto said, glancing over his shoulder and up at the boy. He leaned across and gripped Tahir's hand hard. "I will *not* let them take you."

Already half in love with the mysterious, irreverent knight, Tahir felt a sweep of relief at the thought that he had both Demitto and Catena there to protect him. The chief of guard's arm was still tight around his waist, her sword still drawn. She had leapt to his defence immediately, he thought, the notion making him glow inside.

"Who were they?" he whispered as the ambassador turned off the main road and headed east, soon losing them in a maze of streets. Tall buildings towered over them and cast the roads into shadow, but people spilled out of the alehouses and some shops were still open, and gradually Tahir's panic faded. Atavus stopped for a quick drink in a puddle, then ran up to join them again.

Demitto glanced up at him. "They were Incendi," he murmured.

Catena stiffened behind the Prince.

"Who?" Tahir asked, puzzled.

Catena ignored the question. "How did they know he would be there?"

"He connected with the Arbor," Demitto said. "I could not stop him. He fell into a trance and accessed the energy channels that run through its roots. The Incendi monitor them and use them to gain information. They knew immediately where he was."

Tahir did not understand, but he did get one thing from the ambassador's words. "It was not a dream?"

Demitto smiled wryly. "No, young prince. The Arbor spoke to you."

Tahir wavered in the saddle. "How… why…?"

"First we get you something to eat," Demitto said firmly. "Then we will talk."

III

The days ticked by slowly. Sarra seemed to spend every waking moment breathless, desperate for the time to come when they could finally be free and there would no longer be all this waiting.

The Select were a constant presence, even in the evenings, and other people even began to remark on it, so Sarra knew it wasn't her imagination. The reason might still be unclear, but Comminor was keeping an eye on her. She felt his gaze on her whenever she circled the Great Lake, and no matter where she went now, she would only have to look over her shoulder and a Select would be standing there.

But she went about her daily life as usual, trying to keep calm. Hunted salamanders by the river. Ate her dinner in the food hall. Went to the Primus evening entertainments where the tradespeople sang or played musical instruments, or where people danced, trying to ease the drudgery of the day with movement and song. She liked dancing, and the baby was not so big yet that it altered her natural flowing steps. Dancing cheered her, and she joined in most evenings. Sometimes she paired with another, sometimes she just danced on her own, but always she left the hall with spirits lifted and a smile on her lips, her fate temporarily put to the back of her mind.

It was one such night that she walked down from the dance hall, singing to a particularly entrancing melody one of the lute players had come up with, that she bumped straight into a Select. The tall woman, distinct in her gold sash, did not apologise for getting in her way, just looked – rather curiously – at her, and arched an eyebrow.

"You are to come with me," she stated, and turned and walked away.

Sarra froze, feeling as if her heart had risen into her mouth. Out of the corner of her eye, she could see Geve staring at her. It took every ounce of willpower she possessed not to turn and look at him. He had danced with her that evening, and although they had not discussed it, she had seen the desire in his eyes, the hope that her prediction would come to pass. He wanted her for his own, and she had promised him that if they escaped, she would be his. What would he think if now she walked away from him and went with the Select?

Not that she had a choice. *I have two weeks yet!* she wanted to protest, but Comminor had clearly changed his mind. Her spine stiff, she nodded as the Select turned and made an impatient gesture with her hand, and walked towards her.

The Select led her through the Primus District and south to the Great Lake. Sarra did not bother asking her where they were going – that much was obvious. She wondered what the woman thought of her. Was she puzzling as to why the Chief Select wanted such a poor, insignificant woman? Or had Comminor made it clear to his followers the reasons why she was important to him?

And what were those reasons, exactly? She still wasn't sure.

They circuited the lake and headed for the palace gates. Sarra resisted the urge to look up, certain he was watching her as she approached. She also fought the desire to stroke her bump, a habit that had been forming over the last few weeks – the mother's instinct to calm and protect. That was the last thing Comminor needed to know.

The guard on the gates let them through without a word, and she crossed the gardens, which were now brightly lit, filled with an amazing number of plants and flowers she had not seen before. But she was too nervous to stop and admire them now.

As she approached the palace, two guards stood by the main entrance. To her alarm, one of them was Turstan. As she mounted the steps, she risked a quick glance at him. His eyes met hers briefly, sparking with alarm, and she was sure he twitched as if wondering whether he should do something. She gave a quick shake of her head, though, and continued past him, and he did not move to follow her.

She followed the Select into the palace and up the same stairs where Comminor had taken her last time. At the top, she passed two more guards and entered the large foyer with its window looking down across the lake. But it was empty, and the Select did not stop there. She walked across to a door on the opposite side, pulled the curtain back and then waited, her gaze finally coming to rest on Sarra.

Sarra walked slowly towards the door. The curtain was made of tiny squares of turtle shell interlinked with golden hoops, and it shimmered in the light of the lanterns. When she reached the door, she paused and glanced up at the Select. The woman looked down at her, and although her face was impassive, her eyes were gentle.

"Go on," the woman whispered. "He is waiting for you."

Sarra swallowed and walked into the room, and the Select let the curtain swing behind her.

It was Comminor's personal bedchamber. In the centre against the wall stood the largest bed she had ever seen, waist high, covered with a magnificent dark blue blanket embroidered with silver and gold stars. Beautifully carved wooden furniture – a table and chairs, a large coffer – stood against the wall containing the doorway.

On the opposite wall hung a huge tapestry. It was formed from geometric shapes using threads of all colours, and to the untrained eye it looked like a beautiful abstract pattern. However, it reflected Sarra's embroidery clearly enough for her to realise that whoever had made this was a bard. The blue "sky", round yellow "sun" and green "grass" stood out amongst the other bright colours. Darker triangles depicted birds in the sky, while two arcs with their tails crossed represented fish in the sea. And on the far side, the long brown rectangle topped with hundreds of green circles – surely that represented the Arbor?

Comminor stood in front of it, studying it, and he did not turn immediately as she walked in. She took a few steps forward and waited, heart pounding, trying to calm herself.

"It is beautiful, is it not?" Comminor said after a moment, and he reached out a hand and traced the curve of the white ball she was sure represented the Light Moon.

"It is amazing," she said truthfully.

"What do you think of the design?" he asked, finally turning to look at her.

Only one lantern was lit in the room, and Comminor's face was in shadow. She swallowed and looked back at the tapestry. "It is… unusual. Lots of different shapes. But they fit together well." Was he trying to see whether she recognised the pattern? She thought of her embroidery back in her sleep room, in her private box. Had the Select been through her belongings? Had Comminor seen her work?

He moved forward, his face coming into the light, and to her surprise it held neither harshness nor recrimination.

He glanced back at the tapestry, and his expression showed only pleasure. "A team of five artists worked on it. I am very pleased with the final result."

Who had designed it she wondered? Because clearly the person dreamed of the Surface. She longed to ask him, but did not want to draw attention to the design, and anyway, he was now turning his attention away from the tapestry, and focussing instead on her.

"Sarra," he said, and moved a little closer to her.

She looked up at him, speechless. He wore a long silver tunic that matched his hair, and he seemed to glow in the semi-darkness. The room smelled of expensive incense, something musky and exotic that stirred her senses.

She had heard others speak about the Chief Select, about whether he held some kind of magical power that enabled him to have a hold over his followers. Turstan had dismissed this, saying Comminor was a man who knew how to reward those who did as he said, and who had no qualms in punishing those who did not. But standing before him, Sarra wondered, because the man's golden eyes were mesmerising, and he emitted an aura of power such as she had never seen before in anyone in the Embers.

He raised a hand and cupped her cheek, and she shivered.

"You said you would give me a month," she whispered.

"I could not wait," he replied, his deep voice stroking all her nerve endings just as his thumb was stroking her cheek. "I have observed you walking the lake every day, seen you at work, watched you dance in the evenings."

She gasped, not having been aware of his presence at any of the music performances. "You watched me?"

"Always," he murmured, slipping a hand into her hair. "You have captivated me, Sarra. I do not know why, and I am not even sure that I like it, but I cannot stop thinking of you. When I see you, I light up inside. It is like I have a fever

– I cannot think of anything else." He moved closer, so their bodies touched. "I have to have you, or I will burn."

He lowered his lips, and Sarra stood frozen, her heart pounding. His words flattered her, but she could not be sure he meant them. What if this was all just a way to find out about the Veris? To get her to relax her guard?

And yet his desire seemed genuine, and when he raised his head, she could see only tenderness and need in his eyes.

"Say yes," he murmured. "Say you will have me."

She moistened her lips. "And if I say no? Will you have me anyway?"

He brushed his lips against hers again. "I promise you, you will not be disappointed. I have never had any complaints before."

Between them, her hand rested on her abdomen. She could not hide it any longer. If she did not agree to be his mate, he would take her anyway, she was sure of it, and either way she could not keep the baby secret any longer.

She stepped back, grasped the hem of her tunic and drew it over her head, then let it drop to the floor. His eyes blazed. She did the same with her more finely woven under tunic, and stood before him naked.

His gaze raked her, and then stopped as he discovered what she had been hiding all along.

His eyes rose to meet hers.

"I am sorry," she whispered, and steeled herself for the full onslaught of his fury.

CHAPTER EIGHT

I

Horada stood at the edge of a small cluster of trees and shivered as she looked across the expanse of countryside separating her and the large Forest of Bream, two days' ride to the west. Between them lay the hamlet of Franberg, her current destination.

Even though whatever had been following her had come awfully close to finding her in the trees, she still felt more comfortable within them, as if the Arbor itself had sent its children to protect her. But out there, in the fields where there was little cover and an unusual bout of light rain, she would be exposed and vulnerable, an easy target for whatever strange entity it had been that had decided that stopping her reaching Heartwood was its ultimate goal.

Still, she couldn't stand there all day. Her only hope, she felt, was to keep going and put some distance between her and her stalker.

She nudged Mara forward with her knees, aware that the horse also appeared strangely reluctant to leave the forest's skirts, and guided her along the pathway leading between the two hills ahead of her. The rain, which was more like a heavy mist really, soon soaked into her cloak and made it hang heavily, but Horada didn't mind the weather. Oddly, in contrast to what she had felt before exiting the forest, she found her spirits lifting the further they went, her mood echoed in the way Mara's ears pricked up and her tail swished as she trotted along in a lively fashion.

She puzzled on this as they passed the fields of wheat, the ripening sheaves a blurred golden yellow through the rain. She remembered that moment she had tried to open her eyes in the forest, the heat she had felt on her skin, and the way the leaves had been turned to ash when the tree finally released her. And there was also the information that Julen had imparted, about there being strange fires springing up all over the place.

Unbeknown to her mother, Horada and her father had often discussed the Darkwater Lords' invasion in great depth. Chonrad had confessed to his daughter that Procella didn't really understand the love-hate connection he had with the Arbor, and he didn't want to burden her with things she couldn't – or wouldn't – understand. But Horada's willingness to listen, and the fact that she seemed to comprehend what had happened, meant that he had told her everything of the events of twenty-two years ago.

The history had rung a bell deep inside Horada, her understanding somehow more than just mere comprehension. It spoke to something within her, in her blood maybe, an emotion or a knowledge concerning the elements and the balance that the Arbor tried to control that Chonrad hadn't needed to put into words. She had known intuitively that the wars and the people's disconnection with the land had led to the imbalance which had subsequently made the rise of water possible.

And now, just as instinctively, she knew the same thing was happening with fire.

She lifted her face and let the misty rain fall on it. Perhaps this was why she felt more at ease in the open air? Even though she had thought the Arbor could not protect her out here, somehow the wet weather meant the fire elemental – if there were such a thing – would not be able to travel, or at least its power would be subdued, like throwing a bucket of water at a house on fire.

She thought about what Julen had said about another attack on Heartwood and the Arbor. That was worrying, because the Arbor itself had broken down the Temple that protected it, telling her father it did not need protecting in that way. It had told Chonrad that, providing the love of the people for the land was strong, it could defend itself. And since then, the Heartwood Council, headed by Dolosus, had made great efforts to maintain the Nodes, honour the Veriditas greening ceremony and keep the energies flowing. So what had gone wrong?

She pondered on the question as Mara trotted through the puddles, heading for the hamlet of Franberg. Country lanes diverted every now and then from the main road, and they passed the occasional house or workers in the field who raised their hands as she passed, but otherwise the road remained quiet, with no sign of anyone following her, even though she looked over her shoulder frequently to check.

She arrived in Franberg as the sun was beginning to set and went straight to the small inn. The innkeeper's son took Mara to rub her down and feed her, and the innkeeper's wife sat Horada in front of the fire with a plate of stew and cup of ale. She tried to engage her in conversation, and Horada chatted for a while, finding out that there had been a few fires in the neighbourhood recently, which the woman thought strange because they had seemed to spring up out of nowhere.

The woman finally went back to sweeping the floors and serving the other couple of travellers in the inn, and Horada finished her stew and curled up in the chair, tired and comfortable.

She studied the fire as her aching bones – unaccustomed to hours in the saddle – gradually began to relax and her eyelids drooped. The flames leapt around the log like dancing figures, dressed in yellow, orange and red. She watched as they danced higher and higher, the figures more twisting and writhing than dancing, like tortured souls bound by invisible chains.

Something thrummed in her ears, a rumbling like the tremors that could supposedly be heard in the middle of the Spina Mountains. They passed up through the legs of the chair and vibrated through her, until her heartbeat seemed to match the steady pounding like a deep bass drum. For a brief moment it was as if her body had melted and soaked into the ground and become one with the earth – she felt that if she stretched out her arms she would be able to touch the sea on one side of Laxony and the mountains on the other. It was a glorious sensation, a merging, and her heart swelled.

Almost immediately, a noise filled her ears – a bellowing roar, like the backdraft of a fire as it engulfs a house. Heat swept over her, as if the flame had entered her fingertips and travelled along her arteries and veins. Pain made her open her mouth in a soundless scream as her whole body stiffened. She was going to burn...

And a voice said, "Halt!" and abruptly the roaring noise stopped, the pain dissolved and the heat disappeared. She opened her eyes slowly, panting with exertion, only then realising her eyes had been closed.

In the inn, a man stood before her, dressed in a long light grey cloak topped with leather bracers and straps across his body, and a hood that covered his face.

She pushed herself to her feet and glanced around. The half-dozen people in the room looked like statues, frozen in various poses, and the air had a strange, shimmering quality to it.

She looked back at the man.

"Hello, Horada," he said.

Heart thumping, she glanced around again, noting that the people still hadn't moved. "Who are you? What have you done to everyone?"

"I have done nothing to them," he said, his deep voice mellow and soothing to her frayed nerves. "The Arbor has paused the passage of time to enable us to have a conversation. And in answer to your first question, my name is Cinereo. I am from the Nox Aves."

She recalled the name of the group from Julen's conversation, although not the name of the man. She couldn't think what to say. In front of her, the air glimmered as if the sun had highlighted silver dust motes. A shiver ran through her. Something magical was happening, way beyond her understanding. But if the man standing before her *was* from the Nox Aves, she knew she could trust him.

"What do you need from me?" she asked. "I want to help. What can I do?"

The air shimmered around him. "The wheels are in motion," he said, "the chess pieces are moving into place. It is nearly time, Horada."

"What can I do?" she repeated.

He passed his hand in front of her in an arc, and the air glittered again. An image appeared before them. She had not seen anything like it before, but her father had described one to her once when he had journeyed to the University of Ornestan many years before.

It was an hourglass. It tipped slowly in the air, the sand trickling from one bulb to the other, marking time.

She stared at it, not knowing what it represented in this context. "I do not understand," she murmured.

"You are the Timekeeper," Cinereo said, his voice deepening, resonating through her.

"The Timekeeper?" She watched the hourglass turn, the movement reminding her of the wheel of the stars in the sky above her head at night.

"You must be ready." His form shimmered, and for the first time his voice sounded faint. "They are coming, Horada. The

Incendi – the fire elementals – they use the Arbor's roots to move through space and time. They use them to find you."

Her eyes widened. "That is who was following me in the forest?"

"Yes." He disappeared, then reappeared briefly. "You have a natural link to the Arbor. But be careful how you use it – the Incendi are coming!"

He vanished.

At the same time, Horada opened her eyes to see the fire in the grate leap up a foot high. She stood so suddenly her chair toppled over, only then realising that the people in the room had started to move again, and were exclaiming as the fire spat scarlet embers across the floor to light the rushes. Flames sprung up all around the room, and in her half-daze, Horada was sure she could see figures within them.

The innkeeper's wife squealed, grabbed a bucket and dashed outside, and Horada followed suit, finding a pail outside the front door and following her to the large water butt to one side of the building. They dipped the buckets and ran back into the inn, and proceeded to douse the floor with water.

For a brief moment, Horada thought they weren't going to be able to get the blaze under control and she was going to be responsible for burning down the whole inn, but then the flames gradually sputtered and died, and the emergency was over.

They put down the pails, panting and wide-eyed. Horada wrapped her arms around herself, close to tears.

The innkeeper came forward and rubbed the top of her arms. "It is all right, no damage has been done."

"They found me," Horada said, shaking.

The innkeeper's wife frowned. "Who found you?"

But Horada couldn't reply, knowing none of what she said would make any sense. Had it all been a figment of her imagination, a dream born out of tiredness and exhaustion? Or had Cinereo really been there? There was no way of knowing, and because of that she couldn't afford to stay there any longer and put herself – and all these people – in jeopardy.

"I have to leave," she said, turning to pick up her bag. "Please, let me give you some money in compensation for the mess."

The innkeeper's wife waved a hand, concerned. "It is my fault the fire was not well tended – I should have placed a guard around it. Please, stay a little longer."

Horada took out some coins and shoved them into the woman's hand. "No, I have to go." Too upset to talk further, she walked out of the inn and round to the stable to collect Mara, led her to the road, mounted and set off at a fast trot, aware of the innkeeper's wife's anxious face watching her as she left.

Tears poured down her cheeks, joining with the rain, which had grown heavier since she had arrived at the hamlet. What was happening to her? Had Cinereo spoken the truth? Were these Incendi really hunting her down?

And what had he meant by calling her the Timekeeper?

II

Catena's uneasiness grew the more miles they put between themselves and Harlton.

She had thought she would enjoy the adventure of travelling all the way to Heartwood, seeing the changing countryside, meeting new people, new places. But instead she found the whole process unsettling. The food – even in the cities – tasted different: bland and without the usual spices she was accustomed to. The air, absent of the tang of metal from the forges and the dust from the mines, smelled strangely sweet, reminding her of the cloying odour of rotting meat. Her joints ached from too many hours in the saddle, and the water in the bathhouses was never hot enough to relieve it. The wine was sour. Even the beds were uncomfortable.

She had thought the experience of meeting people from other lands would be exciting, but ultimately she discovered the inhabitants of all cities had the same old prejudices – the same bad attitudes, the same grumpy moods and irritations with life – as anyone else in her home country. The sense of humour was different, and they made jokes about things that left her staring blankly. The men seemed lewd, the women interested only in what other women were wearing and which members of the opposite sex were available for marriage. She could find nothing to connect with them at all, and longed to return home. She had thought her life in Harlton dull at times, but now she ached for her rooms in the castle, for the peace and quiet of daily life, for the nights she would spend patrolling the castle walls, letting her thoughts trail off into the star-scattered sky.

Part of her unease was due to the strange story that Demitto had told her, and the events of a few nights before. When they had reached the safety of the city of Realberg, Demitto had sat down with them both to tell Tahir what he knew. As the story had unravelled, it had become very clear that he had not told her everything. He revealed that the Incendi elementals were able to manifest by entering people – that anyone around them could in fact be an Incendi, and the only way they could tell was the eyes, which always lit with the fire that raged within them.

Catena had exploded with rage, demanding to know why he hadn't told her this essential piece of information. The emissary had just shrugged in his usual inimitable fashion and said he had told her what he thought she could deal with at the time.

Catena had told him icily that she would decide what she could and couldn't deal with and, as she was the one in charge of escorting the Prince until they got to Heartwood, Demitto was not to withhold information from her any longer. He had nodded, straight-faced, but she knew he would not impart anything further unless he decided it was time.

Since then, she had hardly spoken two words to him, spending her time instead focussing on Tahir, who had been badly shaken by the assault outside Realberg's walls and by the revelations that Demitto had given him. The four Heartwood knights accompanying them had died in the skirmish outside Realberg, and she could see that Tahir thought himself responsible because of the way he had connected with the Arbor.

The Prince – who was still pretty much a boy even though his fourteenth birthday loomed – was facing an immense moment of his life; after all, not many people had the knowledge of exactly what day they were due to die on. Being Selected was not his choice, and it wasn't even as if he could approach being sacrificed in privacy or with only herself to accompany him. Instead, he had to do it all in public so everyone could see the fear that would no doubt show itself at the moment of his death.

Everything else was irrelevant, she decided. Tahir's peace of mind in the days leading to the Veriditas was all that mattered, and the only thing for which she was responsible. And she wasn't even responsible for that, really – her only task was to ensure that he arrived at Heartwood in one piece. His emotional state did not rest in her hands. And yet she was the closest thing to a friend he had, and she found she could not abandon the boy or ignore his well-being just because she was impatient to return home.

After their argument, Demitto had left her alone, and he travelled mostly in silence. Most of the time he seemed lost in thought, his mood seemingly darkening the closer they got to Heartwood.

Catena pretended to ignore him, but she made sure to watch him carefully. At the time of his little revelation on the night she'd caught him communicating with Cinereo, she had believed him wholeheartedly, caught up in his spell the same way she knew Tahir had been. But she could see Demitto was a skilled manipulator, and therefore she was aware he must also be affecting the way she thought, too.

Was it purely through the power of words that he had been able to convince her? She wasn't sure. There was no doubt he had a strange... *quality* she couldn't put her finger on. It was more than a charming personality or a knack for turning conversation. The Prince was besotted with the emissary – she could see it in his eyes – and she had watched Demitto play on his emotions and use them to get what he wanted. And she was certain he had done the same to her, to convince her that he was the hero in all this.

There was something about the mysterious ambassador she did not trust. It was only after the attack outside Realberg that she remembered the way his eyes had been filled with flame when she had interrupted his strange ritual. And even though his story made a kind of strange, surreal sense, and he had joined in with the fight against their attackers, she could not be convinced that everything he said was the truth. There was no doubt he hadn't told her everything. What other important information was he withholding?

With every mile and every minute that passed, her concerns grew. They played on a lifetime's worth of suspicion of Heartwood and the holy tree, of stories told by travelling merchants of the way the city had fallen to depravity. She wanted to believe in the Arbor and its power, but how could she when young, innocent children were picked without choice as its sacrifices simply because their father offered more money than anyone else? How was that religious or holy or dignified? How was it something that she – as a follower of Animus – should believe in?

And why should she deliver Tahir to Heartwood only to have him offered for sacrifice like some kind of crude entertainment for a king who did not deserve the title? Demitto had admitted to her the chicanery of the celebrations, and however much he insisted the meaning beneath them was true and noble, she began to find it more and more difficult to think of handing Tahir over to dance for his supper like a bear in chains.

The boy had withdrawn into himself, going a little crazy, she thought, as the event to come played on his mind. His previous arrogance had faded away like mist, and she began to realise how much of it had been a result of his loneliness and isolation in the castle, his haughtiness a by-product of his efforts to show everyone he didn't care that he had few – if any – friends of his own age to play with. She began to wish she had taken more time to get to know him, and now, as she rode beside him and thought about how his mother had not shed even one tear when he left, her heart went out to him.

By the time they reached Lornberg, Catena had made up her mind. Tahir was bleary-eyed and in a half-trance most of the time, and she was sure fear was the main cause. The boy did not deserve to die, and certainly not for a cause that she wasn't sure she believed in any longer. What use would he be to the Arbor, other than to act as manure? There was nothing spiritual about his sacrifice, and therefore surely they could find somebody else to fulfil the role.

Gairovald, Tahir's father, would be furious if the ceremony didn't go ahead and would see it as a public humiliation. If she decided to take this action, she would not be able to return to Harlton. She would have to take Tahir away somewhere, find a job in another city or maybe even working on a farm, and live in relative obscurity. Much as she knew she would miss her old rooms and job, the idea appealed to her, and she was certain the thought of escaping would be a relief to him.

She dwelt briefly on Demitto and wondered how far he would pursue them before deciding it would be easier to find another sacrifice. He could talk until he was blue in the face about destiny and fate and what was meant to be, but ultimately if Tahir vanished, the emissary would have to find a replacement. Let someone else give up their life for others' entertainment.

That night, they found lodgings in a hamlet just north of Lornberg, two small rooms in an inn. Demitto kept the Prince with him at all times now, ostensibly to protect him from the Incendi, but Catena thought secretly that he was afraid the boy would try to escape at the last minute once he realised how little his sacrifice actually meant. She would not be able to get him out of the room without Demitto waking.

So she slipped a little packet of herbs into his ale.

The enigmatic emissary snored louder than Atavus, she discovered. When she crept into the room late in the night, Demitto didn't even twitch, although Tahir woke as soon as she laid a hand on his arm. He looked younger, she thought, without his fine clothes, his face untouched by the frown lines he had gained when awake.

"What is the matter?" he asked, rubbing his eyes. His hand automatically strayed to Atavus's fur as the dog came over to see what all the fuss was about, tail wagging.

"Dress and come with me," she whispered. "Quietly now."

He stared at her, puzzled, but did as she bid and slipped on his tunic and breeches while she stuffed the remainder of his belongings in his bag. She wrapped his cloak around his shoulders and held out her hand, and he blinked and took it, following her out of the inn into the cool night air, Atavus at his side.

"Where are we going?" he asked when they were outside.

She stopped and turned him to face her. "Tahir, do you want to go to Heartwood?"

He stared at her. "What do you mean?"

"I mean, for the first time in your life, someone is asking you: do you want to be a Selected?"

He said nothing for a moment. The Light Moon hung low in the sky, three quarters full, and the Dark Moon was just rising in the west. The clear sky glittered with stars, but the night was warm, unusually so. The thought of the Incendi flickered through Catena's mind, but she pushed it away impatiently.

"It is my destiny," Tahir said eventually.

"It has been decided it is your destiny by your father and the King of Heartwood who is accepting your sacrifice in exchange for gold," she said flatly. "That is not destiny. It is a transaction."

She took his hands and looked earnestly into his golden eyes, which shone almost silver in the moonlight. "You are just a boy teetering on the edge of adulthood. You deserve to have a life, to fall in love, to have children if that is your wish, to have adventures, see the world. To live until old age. Not to be public entertainment in a pointless ritual. I know the ambassador tried to convince you that ultimately what you are doing has meaning, and that you have some affection for him. It is your choice. So I ask you once again. Do you want to be a Selected?"

The Prince blinked and looked across at the Light Moon for a moment. Then he looked back at her.

"No," he said simply.

Catena smiled. "Then come. We shall leave Demitto behind, and find ourselves another life to live."

III

Sarra stood naked before Comminor and rested her hands on her swollen belly as if she could protect her unborn child, an instinctive gesture as she knew that ultimately, when he chose to unleash his wrath on her, there would be nothing she could do to stop him. She shivered, although whether it was from the cold or from fear, she wasn't sure.

He saw the shiver, and to her surprise he removed one of the thick blankets from the bed and wrapped it around her. She clutched it, shocked at his reaction, having expected anything but sympathy.

"Come and sit down," he said, gesturing to the bed.

Instinct told her to flee, but he would just send for his guard to find her, and she could not hide forever – the Embers was not that big a place, not when the Chief Select was after you. Instead, she climbed onto the mattress, which was thick and soft, the grasses fresh rather than the ones in her own bed which were a month old and squashed flat. The herbs in them lent the air a flowery perfume.

She continued to clutch the blanket around her, wondering what he was going to say, unable to believe he was reacting so calmly. There were numerous stories of him breaking into rage at discovering women with unplanned pregnancies, and ordering his Select to drag these women to the palace apothecary, who strapped them down and removed their babies dispassionately. She hadn't questioned the validity of these stories, but now she wondered whether they were rumours spread by the Select to ensure the people of the Embers remained afraid of him. Usually there was no light without a lantern, though. Which meant the stories probably had a foundation in truth, and that meant his mood could change on a whim. The thought of him having the ability to be kind one moment and cruel the next sent a ripple of unease through her.

Comminor sat down, his arm brushing her drawn-up knees. His face was expressionless so she could not guess what he was thinking, but the cloak around her shoulders told her that maybe he wasn't angry, or not angry enough at that moment to do her harm anyway.

"Can I get you anything?" he said.

She shook her head. "No, thank you."

He glanced down at her abdomen. "It is Rauf's, I presume?"

"Yes."

He nodded thoughtfully. Then, for a while, he said nothing. He sat with head bowed, his silver hair painted orange from the lantern's glow.

"Are you very angry with me?" she whispered, wishing that if he were going to turn on her, he would do it and get it over with.

He looked up then. A smile touched his lips. "Angry? No." His brow furrowed, and he reached out and stroked her cheek. "No wonder you looked so shocked last time. And now I understand why you were so wary about beginning a new relationship."

Relief overwhelmed her, the rush of emotion catching her by surprise. She pressed her hand to her mouth as a tear tipped over her lashes. Spirited by nature, she would never normally have let her vulnerability show, but she supposed the baby had changed things about her other than her appearance.

Comminor moved her hand away. He leaned forward and touched his lips to the tear on her cheek. Then he moved his mouth to hers.

Stunned at his reaction, she sat unmoving and let him kiss her. Her heart beat a rapid tattoo beneath her ribs and the baby fluttered, no doubt responding to the emotions coursing through her.

When he eventually lifted his head, she said, "I do not understand. Why are you not angry with me?"

"I have tried to ignore my feelings for you, but they will not go away. I wish you were not carrying another man's child. But he was a Select, one of my own, and because of that I am prepared to look after the babe as if it were my own. It changes nothing. I want you, Sarra. Say you will be mine."

She caught her breath. His golden eyes warmed her, and his deep voice rang through her like the hourly bell. Was he speaking the truth? Did he truly want her so much that he was prepared to take on another man's child? Or was this all a ruse – was he hiding his anger because he wanted to find out about the Veris?

Ultimately, she realised, it didn't matter. If she refused him because she was afraid of being found out, he would become suspicious and that would make things difficult for her and ultimately the Veris too. What woman – especially one in her situation: poor and single and with a child on the way – would turn down a chance to be the Chief Select's mate? He would provide for her and her baby, and she would never know hunger or poverty again. She would have new clothes, a comfortable home and the respect of the other citizens. She did not love him, but love and pride were not luxuries people in her situation could afford.

That was what he and others who knew nothing about the Veris would think, anyway.

She looked up at him, a shiver passing down her spine at his intense look of desire. Rauf had loved her and had been affectionate, but he had never looked at her like this, as a thirsty man looks at a cup of clear water. Comminor was a handsome man, his arrogance and power making him strangely magnetic. It scared her and aroused her at the same time.

"Let me love you," he said hoarsely, his hand dropping to her breast.

Sarra nodded and let the blanket slip from her shoulders, her blood heating as his eyes flamed.

Later, she lay there and listened to him breathing in the semi-darkness. His arm was heavy across her ribcage, just above the bump where the baby lay, and his head rested near her shoulder.

His lovemaking had been as she had expected – skilled, passionate, with the strange touch of tenderness she was beginning to realise lay beneath his outer harshness like the flesh of a berry lay beneath its tough skin. He had kissed her belly and spoken to the child within her, which had touched and disturbed her at the same time.

She looked up at the ceiling, only then realising it had been inlaid with tiny silver stars that glittered in the low light from the dimmed lantern. How strange. That and the tapestry on the wall led her to believe the person who had decorated the room was a bard. Did Comminor have any inkling of what the art represented? Was that why he was interested in the Veris?

Too many questions, and not enough answers. She lifted a hand and traced from star to star, imagining she was drawing the constellations that Kytte had described from one of her dreams. Would she ever get to see them in person? Would she ever lie on the grass out in the fresh air and look up at the real sky?

Aware of a growing warmth on her skin, she lifted her head and looked down at where Comminor's hand rested, palm flat on her ribs. She had forgotten he wore a sunstone pendant and was thus able to conjure fire. The tell-tale red aura surrounded his hand, sparking in response to some dream he was having. It had happened to Rauf from time to time, and it touched some inner part of her to think he was connected to Rauf in this way.

She lowered her raised hand onto his hair. Lightly, she stroked the silvery strands.

She had thought she would hate him, but now she could not conjure up that emotion. Could a man really love with such tenderness one moment and then be so harsh the next? Surely his reputation must be a façade, created to keep order?

She closed her eyes, biting her lip. This was so hard. The baby had shown her a way out of the Embers, a way to the Surface, but she could not be sure how much of it was truth and how much a figment of her imagination. The journey would be long and hard, fraught with who knew what dangers. It would be so much easier to stay here, in this bed, with Comminor lying beside her, breathing softly. To be cared for. To be loved.

And what of Nele and the others, she thought. What of Geve? Thinking of her old friend brought a pain to her chest. She did not love Comminor, but she did love Geve. It may not have been the sort of love he wanted, but she had a deep and abiding affection for him. He had been there to look after her when her parents died, and she could not throw away his love for her because she wanted an easy life.

Beside her, Comminor shifted and mumbled something in his sleep. She stroked his hair again and wondered if Turstan had told Geve that she had been called to the palace. If he had indeed relayed the event to the Veris, they would be panicking, afraid of what the outcome would be. They would be afraid that she would turn them in for the lifestyle they had all envied for so long.

She may long for a comfortable life, but she would never sacrifice the Veris for it. And hopefully Geve knew that.

Then she thought about the beautiful words Comminor had murmured in her ear as he made love to her, the promises he had made. *You're tempted*, she thought fiercely. *Only because of the baby*, the little voice in her head said defensively. But her heart knew the truth.

Comminor mumbled. Sarra was thinking about Geve, and at first she didn't register his words. But then he spoke again, and her hand stopped stroking his hair, her body going rigid at his words.

"Birds," he murmured. "Fly like the birds."

Her heart thumping hard, she held her breath. Where had he heard that phrase? It was nothing anyone in the Embers would have said naturally as there were no birds in the caves and even the memory of them had faded from the minds of everyone, save for those bards for whom the ability to remember and carry the history in their minds and hearts remained strong. Had he found out about the birds from the same person who had decorated his chamber?

"Through the clouds," he murmured.

"Ssh," she soothed, her hand shaking slightly.

"They do not know," he whispered.

She stroked his hair. "What do they not know?" she whispered back.

"The moon in the sky," he muttered. "The White Eye. The Light Moon in the sky." He twitched. "The Arbor!" His hand warmed against her skin. And suddenly, she understood.

Comminor was a bard.

The Chief Select himself knew a whole land existed above the Embers. He must have designed the artwork in his chamber himself, Sarra realised. He had commissioned the patterns without relating what they meant, describing them in abstract terms so the embroiderers and the gem makers had no idea of what they represented. He had surrounded himself with his dreams made real. And, like all bards, at night he dreamed about the Surface.

Was that why Rauf said Comminor had known about the Veris? Did the Chief Select want to talk to people like him who knew about the world above? Did he long to see the Surface too?

Or was he afraid that if people knew of the world beyond their world, they would try to escape? Was he merely afraid of losing the power and station he had acquired?

Sarra's head spun. Suddenly his seduction of her took on much more meaning. Had someone told him that she carried a bard? Turstan maybe? Maybe all along he had thought to take her, then destroy the baby?

What would happen when he awoke?

CHAPTER NINE

I

Orsin opened his eyes slowly.

The first thing he became aware of was the dull pounding on the right side of his head, and the fact that he couldn't seem to move his arms. He felt groggy, and it took a few minutes for him to remember what had happened, as if he were standing there watching a scribe writing down the events on a piece of parchment.

The memory formed gradually. The Wulfians had sprung an attack once Hunfrith had taken his mother outside. He had not expected it, had not been prepared for it. Although he had been aware that they had separated each member of the party, the lords present had been amiable enough, plying him with food and wine, and Orsin had actually begun to enjoy himself. The Wulfian wench who had poured his wine had pressed her breasts against his arm – a promise for later – and after the dull ride and the unpleasant confrontation with his mother, he had looked forward to an enjoyable evening.

But one of the lords had suddenly stood and let out a bellow, and before Orsin had even had a chance to draw his sword, the warrior sitting next to him had delivered a blow to the side of his head that knocked him out cold.

His hands were tied behind his back, he realised, and he lay on the ground on his side among the rushes. They appeared to have dumped him in front of the fire, and the log that lay burning in the hearth spat tiny sparks at him every now and then.

Voices were lowered in conversation at the tables behind him. Not wanting to draw attention to himself, he remained still but moved his head slightly to look around him.

No sign of the knights who had travelled with them from Vichton. Were they dead? Somehow he didn't think they were sitting up there with the Wulfians, drinking wine.

And what of his mother? Had Hunfrith taken her outside to kill her? At the thought of Procella dead, Orsin's throat tightened and for a moment he couldn't breathe. She had embarrassed him, she was harsh and strict and sometimes he even hated her, but he did not wish her dead. Maybe she was just lying somewhere like he was, bound and captured. He prayed to the Arbor that was the case.

Someone banged a tankard on the table and the voices rose. He stilled and strained his ears, hoping to gain an insight into his predicament. They spoke in Wulfian, but his mother had taught him that language at an early age, and he could understand them well enough.

"Enough!" said a voice Orsin recognised as Hunfrith. "The time for talk is over. Too long we have waited for our chance to take back the Wall. But Chonrad is dead. The Heartwood Council is distracted by the nonsense talk of elementals once again. For the first time in twenty years, the lands on the north side of the Wall are being held by lords sympathetic to our cause. The time is ripe!"

"And what of Procella?" said another lord. "If she puts out a call, the whole of Laxony will rise up against us."

Hope reared in Orsin's chest. She wasn't dead!

"Procella is gone," Hunfrith snarled. "She can do nothing to stop us."

"You should have killed her," a man snapped.

"She is weak and alone," Hunfrith said, "and long gone by now. Do not piss your pants over her. She is but a woman. Let her do her worst."

So his mother had escaped. Orsin felt stunned. She had fought off the mighty Wulfian lord, and left him there! Her eldest son. How could she have done such a thing? Anger flared within him. Clearly she thought so little of him she did not even think him worth saving. She had spoken as if she had the power of twenty warriors, as if she could have charged into the hall and defeated them all with her own hand. But instead she had slunk away into the night to lick her wounds.

"What of the boy?" another said.

Orsin froze, sensing them glance over at him.

Several men laughed. "He sleeps like a baby," said one. "I only tapped him on the temple."

"Chonrad's heir," said another. "I wager he turns in his grave with disappointment." They laughed again and went on to talk about plans to attack the lands south of the Wall.

Resentment knotted Orsin's stomach and tears of humiliation stung his eyes. Would his father be disappointed in him? How in Arbor's name was he supposed to live up to Chonrad? His father had saved the world. Everything Orsin did would be sure to fall short of that goal. True, Chonrad had never made him feel inferior personally and he had always felt his father loved him, but every time a visitor came to Vichton and the topic of the Darkwater invasion was raised, the visitors' eyes would shine with admiration as they looked on the saviour of the Arbor, and Orsin would sit mutely, jealous of his father's fame.

He knew his parents had been impressed by the way the Peacemaker had enlisted Julen. His brother had always outshone him – he was smarter, wittier, and he often looked at Orsin like he was a simpleton. At the time of Julen's announcement, he had wished he had a special role, something to make them proud of him. But what could he have done? They were a country at peace – if you didn't listen to the Wulfians – and there were little to no chances for a man to prove himself. He knew his mother was impatient with the way he enjoyed his ales and his women, but the truth was – what else was there to do? Should he start a rebellion just to prove he could lead an army?

He pulled angrily at the rope cutting into his wrists. The Wulfians thought to truss him like a chicken, and then what? Ransom him back? Kill him when it amused them? Well, he was done being everyone's plaything. He was not a boy – he was a grown man of twenty-three, and maybe he didn't have extensive battle experience, but he was not a child, and he was not a fool.

Before him, the fire flared. His eyes widened as he looked into its depths. As always, the beauty of the flame mesmerised him. Red and orange. A halo of gold. He could not shake the feeling that fire was a living thing. It had too much life and energy – it ate and it grew and it danced.

He blinked. There was a shape in the flames.

He was imagining it. He must be. Like making pictures in the clouds.

But the more he stared, the clearer the shape became. A creature – a bird. Huge, with wide wings and golden eyes.

He thought about what Julen had told them in Vichton – that the Incendi were fire elementals bent on destroying everyone who could help defend the Arbor. Is that what this was? A fire elemental come to take his life?

He waited for panic and fear to rise in his chest – but it didn't happen. Instead, all he felt was excitement.

"Do it," he whispered. The thought of the fire licking over him, consuming him, made his muscles clench in pleasure.

But the firebird didn't move.

I am not here to kill you.

Orsin frowned. The words had sounded in his head, but they had been as clear as a sharply tapped bell.

The flames around the firebird moved, leapt, but the eyes remained fixed on him.

"What do you want?" Orsin whispered.

You.

He licked his lips. "I do not understand."

You are my link, Orsin of Barle. You have always been my link. You think yourself inconsequential, but to me you are the most important person in the whole of Anguis.

He stared. "What do you mean?"

You love fire. Always have. I have watched you since you were a child. You have never shown fear of it. And you have the ability to control it.

"I…" Now he was speechless. Control it? What did they mean?

Fire does not burn you, the voice said. *It lives in your blood.*

His heart pounded. He thought of the way the flames had poured over his hand in Vichton, how his brother had been alarmed that he had been burned, but he had remained untouched. And of course, the incident in his childhood, when he had nearly burned down the stables but emerged unscathed.

It lives in your blood? What did that mean?

Join me, whispered the firebird. *I am the King of the Incendi. You know the sensual power of fire. Come, welcome me inside you.*

He couldn't look away from the gold-and-blue eyes. The King?

You have always been mine, the voice said. *And you always will be. I know your true worth. I salute you. You will be my first – my link with the world. Come, join with me.*

Heat flooded his veins. Maybe this was why he had always felt like an outsider, as if he didn't belong. This was what he had been waiting for his whole life. Meaning. A purpose.

He thought briefly of his mother, of Julen and Horada, but deep down he knew they would not miss him. He didn't belong with them. He belonged in a different world entirely.

The firebird danced. He watched, fascinated, as a finger of flame crept out of the grate and along the floor towards him. His chest rose and fell quickly with each heave of his breath. The flame reached his foot and, to his shock, slid into his boot and licked his toes. White-hot, it seared, and yet the pain was exquisite, like no pleasure he had ever experienced before.

The flame caressed his toes, then slid between them to enter his feet. His muscles went rigid with agony and he arched his back and opened his mouth in a soundless cry as the heat entered his veins and burned around his body. The firebird swept over him, around him, inside him. Pain and pleasure made him convulse and twist.

Flames brushed up his legs and spread across his torso. Turned the rope around his wrists to ash. Danced on his chest and licked his face. Covered him in fire.

In some part of his consciousness, he heard the yell from the men sitting at the table, felt the thunder of their feet as they rushed over to him. Water sluiced over his body, but the firebird ignored it and laughed as it danced.

Orsin pushed himself to his feet, stood and looked at his hands. Flames flared from his fingers, ran down his body.

You are mine, said the King of the Incendi in triumph.

Orsin tipped back his head. Fire raced through him, bursting forth from his mouth in a roar of flame that swept across the hall, lighting the rushes and burning the curtains. Men yelled and ran, but Orsin reached out his fiery hands, grasped them and watched with fascination as their skin blackened and peeled, and the smell of cooked flesh filled the air.

He had never felt so alive, so sure of himself, so powerful and so free. He swept his arm across the room and watched sparks fly through the air to set light to cloth, wood, hair. Tables groaned and broke, metal melted and ran like ale. Men screamed, shrivelled, died.

Yessssss, breathed the voice in his head, encouraging him, spurring him on.

He reached fiery arms up to the rafters, brought them crashing down. Broke the beams like biscuits, scattered stones and crushed tiles like snail shells beneath his boot. And still the fire did not stop.

It burned higher, hotter, faster. It rushed down his throat and into his lungs, filtered into his blood and raced around his limbs. He *was* fire, born to it, part of it.

For the first time in his life, he belonged.

The Wulfian castle crumbled around him, and Orsin walked free and into the night, lighting up the trees as he passed.

Hiding in the darkness, Procella watched. And for maybe the first time in her life, she was scared.

II

"Fire!" said Tahir, and sat bolt upright.

The woman beside him immediately roused and stroked his arm, murmured, "Ssh, ssh, everything is all right, young prince." Beside him, Atavus rose and nuzzled against him, sensing his distress.

His heart hammering, he looked around, trying to get his bearings. The dream had been vivid, and it took a moment for him to realise he wasn't in a burning room; that his clothes weren't on fire.

"Another one?" Catena asked.

He nodded, comforted by her touch and her presence. When they had lived in Harlton, he had always thought she didn't like him much. She had seemed permanently impatient and annoyed with him, and because of that he supposed he had played up, acted the pompous royal prince to prove that he didn't need her approval or friendship. Now, though, she was concerned and gentle, more like a mother to him than his own mother had ever been.

"Have a drink," Catena said, passing him a water bottle.

He sipped it, looking around him. They lay on blankets, surrounded by green plants and flowers big as his hand. She had taken him deep into the bush, conscious of Demitto's wariness of the lush jungle and using her skills to travel through it, hoping to dissuade the emissary from following them. Around them, the long, narrow leaves of ferns unfurled in the early morning light, while palms arched, tiny birds flitting from broad leaf to leaf as they announced the dawn.

He was soaked with sweat, he realised, and peeled his tunic away from his body with distaste. "Do I have a fever?"

She pressed the back of her fingers against his forehead, but shook her head. "It is the weather. It grows warmer by the day. It is difficult to believe it is only The Stirring. What is it going to be like when it is The Shining?"

"Do you think that is due to the Incendi?"

She hesitated. Tahir had voiced his concern that he was abandoning the Arbor, that he was somehow contributing to helping the Incendi win, but Catena had brushed his fears aside impatiently, saying his father had purchased his status as Selected and he could damn well go and purchase himself another. She had ended the diatribe with a string of colourful curses, including one or two that Tahir had not even heard of.

He knew fear for him lay beneath her anger, and he was touched by that. But still, he could not shake the memory of Demitto's words from his head. *The Arbor spoke to you*, Demitto had explained when he had fallen into a trance outside Realberg. He had also said, *You are my first priority... I will not let them take you.* Just the memory of the words made him shiver.

Catena thought Demitto a charlatan, that he would say anything to get Tahir to Heartwood because that was what he was being paid for. Tahir, knowing himself innocent where relationships were concerned but intelligent enough to know it was possible he could be played, had said nothing to this, agreeing that the emissary certainly had a way about him that somehow made a person believe everything he said when he was standing in front of them.

And it was true, his father *had* purchased the Selected status for him. It was hardly a holy calling, and although he had always known it would be his ultimate purpose when he reached the age of fourteen and had acted as if he were special because of it, deep down he had always harboured a fear that he would not be good enough, that the Arbor might reject him because he wasn't anything special.

But now... *He connected with the Arbor*, Demitto had said. *He fell into a trance and accessed the energy channels that run through its roots.* Catena had not spoken of this, but the words played in Tahir's head. How had he done that? Was the Arbor connecting with him because it knew he was the Selected? Or was it something deeper than that? Had he always been meant to be the sacrifice and the Arbor had somehow engineered it so his father had been the one to pay the most?

He pressed the heels of his hands into his eyes. His head ached from thinking about it. All he knew was that the dreams continued to plague him since leaving Demitto behind, and even though he didn't want to die and certainly not in front of an audience, the thought that he had abandoned the Arbor – and therefore Anguis – to its fate made him ashamed.

"Come on." Catena pulled him to his feet. "We should get going."

He rose obediently, rolled up his blanket and put it in his bag, and hefted it over his shoulder. He carried his own bags now, made his own bed. She had explained to him that they could not return to Harlton – not that he had any desire to – and that her plan was for them to disappear. No longer was he a prince and she a captain of the guard. They were just two travellers with a dog, and he was now her nephew, she had said. Her plan was to head south, deep into the bush, to skirt the base of the Spina Mountains and then head west into Komis. He clearly had Komis blood in him, and she hoped they would find a quiet hamlet or town where they could find work and settle down. If they didn't like it there, she had said, they would go north to Hanaire.

These were all just names to Tahir and he knew they would

have to travel long distances to reach them. He tried not to think about it, or about Demitto and how the emissary had said *I will not let them take you*. He could defend himself, he thought stubbornly, lifting his chin. Catena had given him her dagger, and she had been showing him simple moves with it should the need arise. Not that it would, she had insisted. They were nameless now, of interest to nobody but themselves. The other dangers they had to worry about were bandits and thieves.

Still, as they walked he noticed she looked over her shoulder repeatedly, scanning the forest, and her face remained grim, free of the smiles he knew hid beneath the surface.

"Is something concerning you?" he asked eventually when she looked over her shoulder for the fifth time.

She glanced at him, her green eyes dark as the river they had just crossed. "I think we are being followed."

His eyebrows rose. "Demitto?" A flash of pleasure lit him up, along with relief. He hadn't realised until then how safe he had felt with the emissary.

But Catena shook her head, her brow furrowing. "I do not think it is he. And I think there is more than one. Come, we must pick up our speed."

Atavus padding at their side, they crashed through the undergrowth, almost running now, as much as the dense bush would allow them anyway. Fear lodged in Tahir's stomach, and his heart pounded from it as much as from the exertion of moving so fast. He was not used to hard physical exercise, and the long horse rides and walks had left him stiff. His muscles ached and he had a stitch in his side. But he didn't protest, aware from Catena's pale face that they were in danger.

It seemed like they walked forever. They must have lost the people following them, he thought, his feet moving forward one after the other in a rhythm he felt he could not have broken even if his life depended on it. Left, right, left, right, left, right. The bag across his shoulders dug into his skin, but

Catena continued to walk, and he didn't want to complain.

Left, right, left, right, left, right. The motion lulled him, made his eyelids begin to droop. He could not be tired, he thought, he had only awoken an hour or so before! But his head felt heavy, his muscles loose and relaxed. The ferns and broken palm leaves beneath his feet would make a soft bed, he thought. He imagined lying there, sinking into the ground, becoming one with the earth. The ferns could creep over him, the tree roots drag him down. He would become a part of Anguis forever, melt into the mulch, stretch out his arms and legs from coast to coast. Nobody would ever find him.

His hands grew warm. Catena was right, he thought, the climate was changing. Sweat ran down his back, soaked his tunic again. His body burned.

Catena stopped, so abruptly that Tahir bumped into her, shaking him out of his trance. She put out her arm and pushed him behind her. He peered around and whispered, "What is it?"

Ahead of them the bush was moving. At first he wondered if it were an animal – there were plenty in the jungle, although they tended to keep to themselves and were not people-friendly. But then the ferns parted, and he saw it was a man.

Atavus bared his teeth, crouched and snarled.

A rustle sounded from behind them, and he turned quickly to see two further figures emerging, one man, one woman. All three wore nondescript clothes – plain woollen breeches, brown tunics, much patched; their hair was unkempt and their faces dirty. Brigands then, he thought, who live at the edge of the forest and prey on unwary travellers like themselves.

And then, as the brigands neared, he noticed the eyes of the man in front. They were orange and red, dancing with tiny flames.

"Incendi," Tahir breathed into Catena's ear. Elemental spirits that had somehow taken over these penniless brigands. Panic filled him, and he remembered the way his body had grown hot. He had fallen into a trance again, he thought. Demitto had said before, *They knew immediately where he was.* They had used the energy channels to find him, and he had let them.

Catena drew her sword, and he drew his blade, trying not to notice how his hand shook.

"You will not take him," she announced firmly, and he saw with pride how fierce she looked, how determined.

The man in front of him just smiled, however, and drew his own blade. Keeping Tahir behind her, she turned and backed away until she had all three of them in her sight.

"When I start fighting, you run!" she whispered furiously to the Prince.

He said nothing, frightened, confused. He didn't want to leave her. Where would he go if he was completely alone? He knew nothing about the world – he had no money, no idea of anything he could do to earn it. He could not defend himself, could not even find his way out of the jungle. What was the point in running?

The first man lunged, and Catena parried his blade easily. The second did the same, and she parried that too. The two of them alternated thrusts, testing her, toying with her, occasionally swinging at Atavus, who remained just out of blade range, waiting for an opportunity to leap. They were not skilled with the blade – even Tahir could see that – but they had Incendi inside them, and their eyes blazed with power, making him shiver in his shoes.

The woman had stood to one side, watching them, but as he glanced over, Tahir saw suddenly why she had removed herself – she carried a bow and was about to release the arrow. It whistled through the air and, shocked, he had no time to warn Catena; all he could do was knock her arm, and the arrow whizzed by her ear and embedded itself in a nearby tree.

The woman bellowed and reached behind her for another arrow, and Catena doubled her efforts against the men. She landed a blow on one of them, numbing his elbow and forcing him to drop his sword, and she took advantage of his weakness and thrust the blade down into his neck. Tahir watched, horrified, as blood bubbled in the man's mouth and he dropped to his knees. Catena pulled out the sword and readied herself immediately for the next man's attack, but Tahir could not tear his eyes from those of the dying man. A hideous burbling screech sounded from the man's lips, and then – shocking Tahir – a spurt of flame. It hit Tahir full in the chest, running down his body like water, and immediately his clothes caught light.

He squealed and dropped to the ground, rolling, only half-conscious of Catena still battling it out with the other man while Atavus sank his teeth into the man's arm. Tahir only half heard the whistle of another arrow, and this time, the dull smack like a side of beef hitting a table as the arrow met flesh. He rolled, aware that his sweat-soaked tunic was probably the only thing that had saved his life from being burned to a crisp, smothering the flames beneath him, and then raised his head as someone fell beside him.

"Catena!" Fear fired through him fast as the arrow that had rooted itself in her chest. He crawled toward her, but before he could reach her, the man had covered the distance between them and threw a bag over his head, shutting out the light.

He screamed, kicked, but burly arms clamped his arms to his sides and lifted him over a shoulder. Atavus barked and the man holding Tahir jerked as the dog launched at him, but a high pitched squeal filled the air, and Tahir knew the man must have hurt the dog. He cried out in anguish. And then the world went black.

III

Geve waited in the shadow of a doorway until Sarra was level with him, then reached out and yanked her in with him, placing a hand over her mouth.

Sarra fought him, but Geve whispered in her ear, "It is me," and when she turned her head and saw who it was, she ceased to struggle. "Keep quiet," he said. "You're being followed."

He removed his hand from her mouth, grabbed her arm and led her along the narrow passageway. They were on their way to meet the Veris in the Secundus Quarter, and Geve now knew he was being followed and was therefore sure that the Chief Select would definitely be having her followed too, whatever his reasons for his interest in her.

He led her out of the passageway and across the river. Lanterns here were few and far between and they stumbled often, but he knew it also meant the person trailing them would have more difficulty finding them. They threaded through darkened alleyways and dim rooms, doubling back and changing direction until he was sure they had lost their tail. Only then did he take her to the new meeting place, at the opposite end of the caverns to the previous time.

Sarra hadn't said a word the whole time they were walking, and Geve had kept silent too. Turstan had come to find him the previous evening and had related that Comminor had called Sarra to his chamber. All night, Geve's imagination had tortured him with what might be happening to her. Obviously the Chief Select had been unable – or unwilling – to wait for her any longer. What had he done when he found out she was pregnant? Was she lying dead right at that moment, or strapped down in the apothecary's chair as he cut the baby from her? He had feared the worst and had hovered around the quay all night, waiting to see if they brought out a sack-covered body to send to the Burning Caves. But the next morning, she had walked out, crossed the quay and returned to the Primus District, and although she was still not big enough for the baby to be obvious beneath her loose tunic, Geve's careful eyes had seen that the slight bump was still present.

That could only mean one thing, surely.

Geve's hands had curled into fists and nausea had risen in his throat. He hadn't followed her back to Primus but instead had remained on the quay, trying to deal with his jealousy and confusion about what this meant for the Veris.

Now, he felt a little calmer, but he couldn't be sure he would stay that way once she began to tell her tale. He glanced across at her as they walked. Her head was down, her face pale. She looked tired and dispirited, and he longed to reach out and take her in his arms, stroke her hair, kiss her fears away. But he kept his distance. There was more at stake here than his love for her.

They arrived at the designated room, and Geve pulled back the curtain to let her enter. He followed her in. The other five were there, seated around a lantern, and Sarra walked over, took a place between Kytte and Amabil and sat quietly with her hands in her lap.

Geve sat next to Nele and they exchanged a glance.

"She was followed," Geve confirmed. "We lost them before the river."

Nele nodded. "We are all being watched. Comminor knows about the Veris, and clearly he knows we are all members."

"But why have we not been arrested?" Amabil wanted to know. She glanced at Sarra, her thin face worried and sullen. "Everything was fine until Sarra came into the group."

"And we will not start blaming anyone for the way things have gone," Nele scolded. "Without Sarra we would have no hope of an escape, no way to make our dreams real. We have to trust each other. Comminor clearly knows about the Veris and about us, but obviously he is waiting to make his move."

"Maybe he knows we meet, but he does not know why," Kytte said.

"He knows," said Sarra.

They all looked at her.

She licked her lips. "I think he knows because... I am certain he is a bard."

Nele's eyes widened. The others gasped. Geve's heart seemed to stop.

"What makes you think that?" Nele asked carefully.

"He... talked in his sleep." Sarra lowered her eyes and stared at the lantern.

Geve had meant to keep calm, to keep his emotions in check, but jealousy and anger bubbled out before he could stop them. "How could you?" he said, forcing the words out through clenched teeth.

Nele put a hand on his arm. "What happened when he found out about the baby?" he asked her.

"He said he would look after the babe as if it were his own," Sarra said.

They all stared.

"Truly?" Betune, her hand rising instinctively to the pouch around her neck that contained the acorn, spoke in a whisper of something like awe.

"So he said." Sarra spoke calmly. She looked briefly at Geve, met his angry gaze and lifted her chin. She was refusing to feel guilty about what she'd done, he thought, and something twisted inside him.

"He wants you to be his mate?" Nele asked.

"Yes."

"Do you believe him?"

She hesitated. "I do not know. He seemed sincere. He genuinely seemed to care for me. But can I be sure that he is not using me to get to the Veris? No, I cannot."

"Of course he is using you!" Geve could no longer hold in his anger, and he shook off Nele's hand. "How could you lay with him? You have heard the stories about his cruelty. He is harsh and heartless. It makes me sick to think of you with him."

"I had no choice," she snapped. "What do you think he would have done with me if I had refused him? Why would I refuse him?"

His hurt must have shown in his face, because she corrected herself, "I mean, why would a woman in my position refuse him? Nobody in their right minds would, and he knew that. He promised me a life of security, where I would be warm, well-fed, respected and loved. Whether that is true or not, it is not something any other woman would turn down. To do so would have aroused suspicion."

Geve opened his mouth to tell her she was fooling herself. Comminor could have the pick of all the women in The Embers. Rich ones, beautiful ones, clever ones. He could bring them all running with a snap of his fingers. Why would he choose Sarra – a penniless daughter of a leather merchant, skinny and carrying another man's child?

And yet as he sat there and saw her eyes blaze, her defiant and courageous spirit rising up to meet his, the words faded on his lips and he found himself speechless. Something shone within her, radiating forth like the sun he had once hoped to see, and although he could not put it into words, he knew Comminor had seen it also, and had wanted it for himself. Could he really blame the man for that?

Nele cleared his throat. "You said he talked in his sleep?"

She tore her eyes away from Geve's. "Yes. He spoke of birds in the sky, and clouds and the White Eye being the moon. And he said the word 'Arbor'."

Kytte raised a hand to cover her mouth. The others looked distressed.

"How do we know he had not heard these words from someone else?" Turstan said.

"Have you seen his private chamber?" Sarra asked him. When he shook his head, she continued, "It has stars on the ceiling. And a tapestry on the wall representing grass and the sky and the sea, and animals on the Surface. I cannot be sure – maybe you are right and he knows of these things through someone else, but I think he commissioned that tapestry because of his dreams. I think he has heard of the Veris and he is curious because he did not realise there were others like him."

Nele raised his eyebrows. "So what are you saying? That he wants to meet us to compare notes?"

She blushed. "No, of course not. I think he likes his position here, and the thought of someone leading everyone else to freedom would mean the end of his control. I do not think he is quite the ogre that the rumours say, but equally I think he has no qualms about quashing those who stand in his way."

Nele gave her a firm look. "You must tell us now, Sarra, what your plans are. We do not know what lies outside the Embers or how dangerous our journey would be, especially for someone in your condition. If you stay here, perhaps Comminor tells the truth and he will look after you and keep you healthy and well. I would not blame you if you could not turn your back on that. But we need to know. Because if you plan to do so, we must call an end to the Veris now, before we are found."

Geve watched her. She looked down at her hands, studied them in the light from the lantern. He sensed that maybe she had been asking herself the same question, maybe ever since Comminor had first shown interest in her. His heart ached. Why had he not been born a Select, privileged and able to offer her a better life? Why would she choose him, and an uncertain life for her child, over security and safety?

She lifted her head. He could almost hear everyone holding their breath.

"I cannot say I am not tempted," she said. "He was kind to me, and I find it difficult to believe everything he said was a lie and the affection he showed me was just a ruse to earn my trust before he made me tell him about the Veris. But... I cannot be sure." She hesitated. "There is no doubt that many women have had their pregnancies terminated, and that has been at his command. He explained to me last night how he has to control the population because of our limited resources. But he said so coldly, with no sign of emotion behind it. Part of me fears that he is able to be cruel one minute, tender the next. That scares me more than the animal they have made him out to be."

She rested her hand on her belly. "The dreams are getting stronger, more vivid, as the baby grows. I can feel the wind on my face, the rain, see the clouds in the sky. I can feel myself standing beneath the Arbor, and I look up and see its leaves shaking in the breeze." Her eyes took on a faraway look. "The sun streams through them and scatters golden fragments across my arms and face. And... I know this sounds strange, but I can feel its love."

Relief showed in her face as the others nodded, Geve included. He, too, had dreamed of the Arbor and felt enveloped in the warmth of its love.

"The Arbor wants us, needs us," she said. "We must get to the Surface." Her eyes blazed. "This urge within me to take my child there overwhelms every other feeling I have. It overpowers me, makes me shake with its intensity. I have to go. It is as simple as that. It does not matter if Comminor promises me all the gold and food in the Embers, none of it could replace the feel of the sun on my face as it has been in my dreams."

Geve felt dizzy with a mixture of emotions; relief that she had not changed her mind, exultancy that they were still to escape, and a strange kind of despair that lingered at the thought of her in Comminor's arms, lying with him. She had promised herself to him, Geve, if they made it to the Surface. He thought she might even honour that promise, would do so for her child's sake. But at that moment, he knew she did not – and probably never would – love him.

The thought settled over him like ash.

Nele nodded. "It is done, then." He shifted on the ground, making himself comfortable. "Let us make our plans."

CHAPTER TEN

I

Horada reined Mara in and sat looking ahead of her at the Forest of Bream. It stretched to her left and right for many miles, the road she was on leading straight into the trees, bisecting the finger of woods that separated Esberg to the north and Ransberg to the south.

She could, of course, go around the forest. Although she usually liked being amongst the trees, her experience in the hamlet had suggested she was better in the open air, and she felt nervous at the thought of entering the woods again.

However riding around them would mean a detour of probably two days either north or south, time she could ill afford to waste. The urge to get to Heartwood seemed to increase with every minute, and the memory of Cinereo's words and the way the Incendi had nearly set fire to the inn made her think she should not loiter just because of an uneasy feeling.

Mara pranced beneath her, clearly picking up on her tension. She patted her neck, trying to think calm thoughts. She would ride as quickly as she could through the trees, and before she even realised it, she would be on the other side. She was only three days' ride from Heartwood now, and it wouldn't be long before she was in the presence of the great Arbor, and she would be able to take advice from the council and others who knew far more about the problems of the Incendi than herself.

Lifting her chin, firming her resolve, she kicked her heels gently into Mara's flanks and the horse trotted forward.

The forest closed around her in a swathe of green. The air smelled of mulching leaves, rich loam and the freshness of new growth. The trees – mainly oaks, some beeches and ash – shook in the light breeze, and she could almost taste green on her tongue, making her mouth water, like the tang of metal in the air when riding nearby a forge.

Her mother had once confided she felt uneasy in forests, stating they were like graveyards and smelled of death and decay, the trees like tombstones and the air unnaturally still. She had admitted that had a lot to do with spending much of her time walking the walls of Heartwood, high up, open to the elements and with panoramic views in every direction, or on patrol on the Wall, where the north wind blew across wild plains and nobody could creep up on you without being seen from miles away. Forests lent themselves to stealth and secrets, and Horada could understand her mother's dislike, even if she didn't feel the same. She felt the opposite, and had always thought of them as nurseries, focussing on the new buds and twigs instead of the dead leaves underfoot, and thinking of the ancient trees as caring for the newborn seedlings.

That day, though, for the first time she thought she could understand Procella's wariness. The trees whispered, looming above her, and the undergrowth seemed filled with shadows, with plenty of places for people to hide. Where were the animals, the rabbits and squirrels, the numerous crawling insects, the birds that usually hopped from branch to branch, following her with interest? The smell of rotting leaves rose up to fill her senses, and she couldn't stop thinking of the way the leaves were falling to the floor to decay. Why did everything suddenly smell of death?

Her heart pounded as she rode, her mouth going dry with

nerves, although she didn't dare stop for a drink. She felt
frustrated at the slow pace, but she couldn't speed up because
the path zigzagged through the trees. Clearly, it had not been
tended for a while. What had happened to the forest rangers
who maintained the roads, the poachers and hunters who
knew the natural pathways almost as well as the animals? She
had worried that Mara might fall into a trap, but after a while
the feeling grew on her that nobody had passed through the
forest for a long while. That in itself was worrying.

Branches reached across to whip her face, and Mara
stumbled occasionally on fallen logs and vines that snaked
across the path. Horada let her go at her own pace, the last
thing she wanted was for her horse to break a leg.

For a while she rode quietly, stiff and tense in the saddle,
but as nothing happened and the sun climbed high in the
sky she began to relax and think maybe she had imagined
that the danger would be greater within the trees. Cinereo
hadn't said thus, had just said she should be wary of her
connection to the Arbor, and she had assumed he meant
that being in the presence of trees would make it worse. She
was being foolish, she told herself – she had to be careful
not to let her imagination run away with her. A permanent
optimist, she made herself roll back her shoulders and let
the dappled sun fall on her face, let the fresh smell of nature
fill her nostrils.

She had just thought she must be about halfway through
the forest when she felt it: a presence behind her, a feeling
of being watched, so clear and sharp it sent a frisson up her
spine and made the hairs on the nape of her neck stand
on end.

She turned in the saddle and looked over her shoulder,
searching the trees. For a moment she could see nothing and
thought, again, she had imagined it. And then, far off into the
distance, she saw it.

Fire.

Her heart seemed to rise into her throat and choke her as the reddish-orange glow flared in the trees. The forest was on fire, and even as she watched, she saw it spread from left to right, the dry brush and dead leaves catching light and flaring to reach for the higher twigs and branches.

It was too late to conceal herself – they knew she was there, and camouflage wouldn't save her against fire. She kicked her heels into Mara's sides and urged, "On, Mara!" The horse leapt forward, and Horada leaned close to Mara's neck to avoid the branches whipping above her head.

Glancing over her shoulder as the horse thundered through the trees, Horada felt panic flood through her at the sight of the red-tinged greenery. The sound of crackling as the flames chomped on the undergrowth rose in her ears. For the first time, smoke filled her nostrils, and as she looked forward, she saw the fire spreading in her peripheral vision.

Heart in her mouth, she urged the horse on. Mara needed little encouragement. Clearly she could hear the fire and smell the smoke too. Her ears flat to her head, nostrils flaring and mouth flecked with foam, she wove through the trees, leaping over fallen trunks and skilfully dodging the branches that seemed to reach out to grasp them.

For the first time in her life, Horada felt that the forest was working against her, trying to slow her down. Twigs caught at her clothing and hair, vines threatened to catch around her neck, and only staying low and close to Mara saved her from being snagged and pulled from the horse.

It could not be much further, she thought desperately. Instinct told her the edge of the forest wasn't far, and yet the trees clustered close ahead of her, with no sign of daylight to lift her spirits. Though she knew it was sunny, the canopy of leaves above her head grew dense and thick, and here deep in the forest there were no rays to light their way. Shadows

loomed, reached grey hands for her, while the fire clawed
its way forward like a huge beast dragging itself on flaming
arms, closing around her until she could feel the heat on
her skin.

Mara whinnied, and a moment later Horada thought
she heard someone call to her right. She risked lifting her
head a little and saw through the darkness of the trees an
even darker shape – a figure in a black cloak, riding low like
herself, matching her speed. Her heart rose into her mouth
again, but even as panic swept over her, she heard him call,
"Horada!"

It was Julen, she realised – her brother must have been
tracking her, and had seen the fire and knew she was in
danger. She would have turned the horse towards him, but
she didn't want to interrupt Mara's agile dodging of the trees,
and instead just called back, "Julen!"

He called something else, but she had to duck again to
avoid a branch and missed his words. *Brother!* she thought,
but could not find the breath to shout. The knowledge that
he had come to find her – while annoying in one way that
he hadn't trusted her alone – made her heart swell. He had
always looked out for her. How had he found her? She had
thought she'd covered her tracks well. But she was relieved
he had used his tracking skills to hunt her down. If only she
could exit the forest, she thought maybe she would ask him to
go with her to Heartwood.

On her right, he moved closer through the trees, his horse
matching her pace, but still the forest refused to part ahead
of her, remaining a wall of green like a tidal wave coming
to sweep over her. The fire crackled loudly behind her, hot
on Mara's heels, and the horse's eyes shone white with fear.
Horada urged her on, patting her neck, but the horse had been
running hard for some time now and Horada wasn't sure how
much speed she had left in her.

"Not much further, not much further," she said to herself, although she couldn't be sure. Julen had closed the distance between them, and now she could see him just feet away, his horse weaving the same as hers, avoiding the uneven pattern of trees. She managed a glance across and saw his grim face, his frown of concentration.

"Faster!" he yelled, and she kicked her heels, let the horse feel her own panic.

Heat wafted over her, smothering in its intensity. Tree trunks fell and ash rained down on them both, soft as snow but smudging black on her skin. The forest was burning. The forest was burning and she was going to burn along with it.

Was that a glimmer of light through the trees ahead? Her heart lifted. "We are nearly there," she urged Mara. "Come on!"

Heat engulfed her, and she risked a glance back over her shoulder, only to fill with panic at the sight of the bushes only feet behind them bursting into flames. The fire was spreading at an incredible rate, clearly unnatural, and for a moment she thought she could see the shapes of creatures in the flames, figures running on two legs, racing on four, crashing through the undergrowth after her.

She wasn't going to make it. Even as the thought filled her head, in her mind's eye she saw a vision of Cinereo as he had appeared to her in the hamlet, cloaked in grey.

"Ride, Horada," he whispered on the wind, and the ground trembled and the air thrummed with a low humming like the reverberation of a bell.

The Arbor, she thought. The Arbor was sending her what power it could to aid her flight. She would make it. Light angled through the trees ahead of her, welcoming arms of sunshine to encourage her into the daylight. The trees cracked, crackled and burned, but she was going to make it...

And then Mara stumbled. Her stride broken, her pace slowed, and Horada screamed in frustration as the fire caught up with them.

The flames swept over her, enveloping her in a wall of heat. The world became a blur of scarlet and gold.

The last thing she remembered was seeing Julen's horror-stricken face. And then everything faded away.

II

Demitto opened his eyes. For a moment he just lay there, bleary and groggy, trying to focus on the walls of the inn. His mouth felt like he had been licking the floor with it, and his head pounded. Had he been drinking the night before? For a moment he couldn't think. He had drunk a few ales the night before they left Harlton, but since then he had been careful with his drink, wanting to stay alert, especially since the incident outside Realberg.

Finally able to focus on the ceiling, he lifted his head and looked at the bed next to his, where Tahir had lain the night before.

It was empty.

He glanced across the corner to the curtained-off area where the pisspot lay, but the curtain was drawn back, the small cubicle empty.

Alarm shot through him, but his body refused to respond. It took a few moments for him to push himself upright, wait for the room to stop spinning and then gingerly rise to his feet.

He padded out of the room and into the one next door, only to find that empty too. Catena's bag and clothes were also gone.

She had taken the boy, he realised. Left him behind and gone who knew where.

He should have expected this. She had withdrawn from him over the past few days, but he had been so preoccupied with the news he received from the Nox Aves every day that he had assumed his talk with her had convinced her of the seriousness of the matter, and that she understood why it was imperative that the young prince accompany him to Heartwood.

Clearly, he had not conveyed his anxiety well enough.

Cursing, he returned to his room and quickly packed away his things. Hefting the bag onto his shoulder, he went downstairs, paid the innkeeper and discussed them delivering some of his belongings to Heartwood – mainly his ceremonial armour, and a few other bits and pieces that weren't essential for the detour he was now going to have to make.

With just the one bag left, he headed out of the door. It was well into morning, the sun rising in the sky, the air already humid. Sweat dampened his tunic and did not improve his befuddlement. Catena must have drugged him, he thought as he made his way around to the stables. Annoyance and worry sharpened his wits a little, and while he waited for the stable lad to saddle his horse, he ate a bread roll and drank a cup of water, and that also helped him clear his head.

Where had they gone? He had no idea. He doubted Catena would have taken the boy back to Harlton. There would be no welcoming committee waiting there for him, no flags hung out on his return. His father, the King, would only be embarrassed and angered that the sacrifice hadn't gone ahead. Catena would be disgraced and removed from her position, and the boy probably sent straight back to Heartwood on a horse. Demitto couldn't believe she wouldn't think of that.

Equally she would not be taking him to Heartwood, of that he was certain. She had obviously hoped that if she spirited the boy away, he, Demitto, would lose heart and return to Heartwood to find someone to take Tahir's place. She didn't understand the vital role that they would all play in the coming confrontation – that they were all of them essential figures in the chess game that was coming together piece by piece. She didn't understand because he hadn't told her, worried about confiding too much, fearing she wouldn't be able to handle the truth. And now he had lost her.

Cursing again under his breath, trying to stave off the guilt and panic that threatened to wash over him at the thought that he had failed the Nox Aves, he took the reins from the stable lad, mounted the horse and turned it to head south out of the city. She would either have gone east or west. His instincts told him west, into the bush. She was more comfortable there than he, and would feel more at home than she would in the wide open fields of east Laxony. Kicking his heels into his horse, he set off at a canter, scattering dogs, chickens and people in his path as he raced through the city centre.

Outside the walls, he headed south for a few miles before turning off towards the bush. The jungle undergrowth had already crept east to entangle the road, and the horse threaded through vines and lush palms for a while before it eventually became too dense to ride any further.

Demitto dismounted and withdrew the wooden pendant around his neck. Checking around him briefly, making sure he wasn't being watched, he dropped to his knees and pressed the pendant into the soft earth.

As usual, for a few moments, nothing happened. The earth felt soft around his fingers, sticky from mulch and plant decay. The chirrup of cicadas sounded loud in his ears. The smell of rich loam filled his nostrils, and he closed his eyes, imagining he was reaching down into the ground, plunging his hands deep, deep into the earth, searching for the channels he knew ran from the Arbor to all corners of the world.

The connection, when it came, took his breath away, sharp and almost painful, as if he had plunged his hand into an icy stream or grabbed hold of a hot iron bar. He gasped, the energy washing over him, and he had to struggle to concentrate, the winds whipping at his consciousness. He was still under the influence of whatever drug Catena had given him, he thought, and if he wasn't careful his mind would be torn to shreds. But he didn't have the time to wait.

He focussed on Catena, imagining her long dark hair, braided and looped over her ears, her bright green eyes with the habitual frown between them, her firm mouth, set in its usual stubborn line. Almost immediately he found her, a few miles to the south-west, as he'd thought, in the heart of the jungle. He concentrated, tried to reach out to her. Her energy was still, like a stagnant pond. She wasn't moving. Dead? His heart gave a strange thump. Her form gave a shallow pulse like a small ripple in the pond. No, not dead then. But not good. Not healthy.

He turned his attention to the Prince, imagining his face, his dark hair, and those strange, unsettling gold eyes. This time he could not make a connection. He stretched out his feelings into the energy channels like reaching out with a stick to grab something in a river, and for a brief moment he thought he felt a flicker of a presence far to the west, but then it vanished. Instinct told him the Prince wasn't dead either. But something had come between him and the Arbor's reach, cutting him off from contact.

Cursing again with a vast and colourful array of swear words, this time he switched direction and reached out to Heartwood. As he reached the boundaries of the city, he felt the usual dislocation, the movement beneath the earth of the channel junctions like cogs moving into place, the opening up of one time to another, three sides to the pyramid.

At the centre, he found the man he knew only as Cinereo. He knew Cinereo was a member of the Nox Aves, but he did not know his identity, which was kept secret because of the ever-present Incendi threat.

"Demitto," Cinereo announced, appearing before him as a figure in a hooded grey cloak, criss-crossed with leather straps.

"My lord." Demitto bowed his head.

"You have news?"

"I do, but not of the good kind, I am afraid. I have lost Tahir and Catena. I can feel the latter through the network, but the Prince's presence is absent."

Cinereo said nothing, but Demitto was sure he could feel his frustration flooding through the energy channels.

"You *must* find them," the grey-cloaked figure insisted. "Time is not written in stone, emissary. Although the tablet may remain, its inscription has yet to be carved."

"I understand." Demitto's head throbbed. He cursed himself silently for being foolish enough to let Catena drug him. Why had he not anticipated such an event?

"Do not berate yourself overmuch," Cinereo said, his voice holding amusement and some gentleness.

"I should have anticipated something like this," Demitto said bitterly. "I was wary of telling them too much because I thought it might scare them–"

"And it is always nice to be the one in the know," Cinereo said, still sounding amused.

Demitto said nothing. It was true – he had enjoyed the knowledge he possessed, had coveted it, finding comfort and pride in knowing the Nox Aves had entrusted him to carry out their precious task. And now he had failed them. That was where pride got you.

"You have not failed," Cinereo said as if reading his thoughts. "This is not the end, just a... setback."

"I am sorry, nevertheless."

The grey-cloaked figure gestured with his hand as if in dismissal. "Find the woman," he said. "Then contact me again. I will help you locate the boy." The cloaked figure shimmered. "I must go now. Farewell, emissary."

"And you." Demitto lifted the pendant free of the earth. The connection broke, the figure disappeared, and the deep humming in his ears stopped. He sat back, drenched in sweat, not realising until then how much heat had been flowing through him. The Incendi searched for him, knew he used the channels to contact the Nox Aves, but with the shield of fire that the Night Birds had created around his pendant, the fire elementals had not yet been able to hunt him down.

He retrieved his belongings from the horse, gave its rump a whack and watched it head back towards the city. Then, passing the handle of the bag over his head and resting it across his back, he set off into the bush.

It closed around him quickly like a green fog, cloying and suffocating with its heat and humidity. Demitto hated the bush. He longed for the wide open countryside: the breeze that played across the high hills, the fields of golden wheat that rippled, the wide rivers and narrow streams that chattered over rocks to the sea. This knotted and tangled jungle was a nightmare from which he thought he would never wake. Vines wrapped themselves lovingly around his neck, choking him, while lush flowers and leaves tempted interest, belying their poisonous, deadly nature. He didn't mind forests, with squirrels and foxes and badgers, cuckoos and owls, caterpillars and worms, but here the insects bit and burrowed into the skin, the shrill birds flaunted colour that seemed unnatural amongst the dull green of the bush, and the animals consisted of varying species of climbing furred creatures and insidious snakes that he secretly feared.

Still, this time in the jungle he had a purpose, and he focussed on Catena, stopping every now and again to plunge the pendant into the ground to search for her presence. In the end, he found her easily, only a couple of miles from the spot he had entered the bush.

Atavus lay next to her, but stood and shook himself as Demitto walked up. He had blood on his fur, but his tail wagged furiously, and his leaping about showed he wasn't too badly hurt.

Demitto gave him a quick hug and kissed his head, then fell to his knees beside Catena, alarmed at the sight of the arrow shaft in her chest, the paleness of her face.

"Catena," he murmured, lifting his bag to the ground and retrieving his water bag. He dribbled some of the water into her mouth and tapped her cheek lightly. "Catena?"

She stirred and opened her eyes. To his relief they didn't look feverish.

"Demitto?" she mumbled. She turned her head and looked around. "Where is the Prince?"

"Gone," he said.

She stared at him, and to his surprise, tears filled her green eyes like a river filling a rock pool. "I am sorry," she whispered. "He was frightened – he is just a child. I did not think he deserved to die."

"That is not your decision to make," he said, more irritably than he had meant. He stroked her hair as a tear spilled down the side of her face. "But do not worry about that now. We will find him again. But first we have to get this arrow out of you."

He took a roll of cloth from his bag, a bottle of whiskey and a jar of ointment. Straddling Catena's limp form, he took his knife and ripped away her tunic to expose the wound.

"By the Arbor," she swore as he tore almost to her waist, and she tried to cover herself weakly. "That was my best tunic. And do you really need to expose my entire chest?"

He pushed her hand away, needing to view the wound and with no patience for modesty at that moment. Atavus came forward for a look, sniffing at the wound.

The arrow was embedded several inches above her right breast, deep in her shoulder. Demitto braced his left hand on her arm, knelt all his weight on the rest of her so she could not move. "On the count of three," he instructed. She nodded, a sheen of sweat on her forehead.

"One," he said. "Two." And pulled.

The shaft slid out, and to his relief it was not barbed or it would have brought half her shoulder with it. She screamed and then sobbed, making Atavus nuzzle her ear, but Demitto ignored her pain for a moment, pouring water onto the wound to clean it, then finishing with some of the whiskey, sighing at the thought of wasting the drink. He smoothed a fingerful of ointment from the jar onto the pad of cloth and placed that over the wound, then bound it to her shoulder, winding the bandages around her arm and chest and knotting it securely.

The last thing he did was to place his hand over the wound and push the pendant back into the earth. For a few minutes he channelled the Arbor's energy into her shoulder, aware of her watching him, and knowing she must be able to feel the heat that flooded between them. He finished by placing his hand briefly on Atavus, hoping that the heat would heal the wound the animal had obviously suffered to his ribs, probably from a firm kick.

He pulled her to a sitting position. She turned and spat a mouthful of blood and spittle onto the grass, then grabbed his whiskey bottle and took a large swallow, ignoring his raised eyebrow. Finally she gestured to her bag and said hoarsely, "Please find me another tunic so I do not have to ride on with my breasts out for the world to see."

Smiling wryly, he fetched her tunic and helped her take the old one off and replace it with the new.

"How do you feel?" he asked, pleased to see some colour back in her face.

She rolled her shoulder, winced and gave him a curious look. "It is sore, but not as bad as it should be. What did you do to me?"

"Made you better." He did not elaborate and got to his feet, took her other hand and helped her up. "We should be going." He hefted her bag onto his back along with his own.

"Where?" she asked, puzzled. "I do not know where the Prince is. They carried him off, and I could not even tell you which direction."

"We will head west," he said. "Towards the mountains. Something tells me the timelines are converging there."

"The timelines?"

"Yes," he said, turning and walking off into the undergrowth, Atavus at his side. "We are going to rescue Tahir. And then we are going to save the world."

III

Comminor sat behind his desk, which was covered in sheets of paper ingrained with his small, neat handwriting. He had a steward who kept the tally of resources in the Embers. This included the number of sacks of moss oats in the storage rooms and how many rolls of goats' cheese remained wrapped in leaves, a count of the men and women in the city and how many in each age group, how many goats there were and when kids were born, any incidences of disease, and careful observation of relationships which might lead to the occurrence of a child.

He leaned back and ran a hand through his hair as he read that three more women had become pregnant. The day before, he had been walking through the Secundus District when a woman had thrown herself at his feet, begging him to let her keep her baby. He had commanded the Select with him to remove her and take her to the palace apothecary, but that one had weighed heavy on his mind overnight.

More babies meant more strain on their resources. It would have been easier to regulate the birth rate by separating the men and women completely, and only allowing relationships on a controlled basis. He had considered it on more than one occasion, rejecting it each time for several reasons; the difficulty of implementing segregation on a population that would obviously resent and rebel against such a decision, the difficulty of maintaining it even if they were to achieve it, and the effect on morale should they be able to achieve it *and* maintain it, which he sincerely doubted.

Morale was an issue that weighed heavily on his mind. Standing at the long window in his foyer, looking down at the Great Lake and the busyness of daily life, he sometimes thought he could feel the depression his people exhibited at times like a tangible thing, like a fog that descended on them, enveloping them and causing their spirits to sink, their enthusiasm to wane. It happened after festivals, market days and other important events, and also at other times of the year, when there seemed little for the people to look forward to. Taking away his people's mates, refusing them sexual relationships, closing down the whorehouses, effectively turning the place into a prison – that would not go down well. He understood the need for companionship, for sexual release – that was perfectly natural, and the only way the Embers had survived for so long was by maintaining their humanity, by ensuring they continued the way of life that they had known before they were cut off from the world.

Bored with statistics and records, he pushed the papers aside, stood and went to the entrance to his chambers. Most of the time he kept the embroidered curtain pulled back, but now he let it drop, signifying that he did not want to be disturbed.

He walked across the room to the cabinet that stood in the corner. Innocuous and plain, it did not draw a second glance from anyone who came into the room, which was how he liked it. He took the key from around his neck and unlocked it, opened the doors and withdrew one of the large books that lay within. Carefully, he carried it over to his desk.

He sat and looked at the cover. It was made of the skin of some animal unknown in the Embers, and although the ink on the front had cracked and peeled slightly, he could still make out the words.

The Nox Aves Quercetum II.

Carefully, he lifted the cover and began turning the pages.

He spent a while looking through the book, more out of a need to remind and reassure himself of his purpose than out of a wish to read the text. He knew most of it off by heart anyway, could recite long passages due to the fact that he had read the book numerous times from cover to cover.

It contained the accounts of members of the group who called themselves the Nox Aves from their creation many thousands of years ago up to its latest and only member – himself. Here lay the history of Anguis in two volumes, including the writings of Oculus, the invasion of the Darkwater Lords at the beginning of the Second Era, the rise of the Incendi, and the event that had led to the creation of the Embers itself.

He smoothed his fingers over the crackled parchment. Touching the book always filled him with a sense of awe, of reassurance. He had accepted the role of Chief Select from his predecessor knowing that he had the combination of personal characteristics that the role required: vision, empathy and the necessary ability to be cruel, because no leader can rule purely out of the goodness of his heart. And in such a place as the Embers, governance would always demand hard decisions for the general good of the people.

Still, he had doubted over the years, especially lately. The dreams had been coming thick and strong, vivid and real, and it made it even harder for him to continue to hold onto his control, not to doubt himself. Not being able to share his knowledge had been hard. Reading the words of those who had come before him comforted him, made him feel less lonely. There were reasons, he told himself, for his harsh decisions, and if everyone knew what he knew, they would not question him.

He turned the page and came across the passage written by his predecessor about the presence of bards within their society. Though he knew the words, he read them again, tracing the ink with his fingers as his eyes followed the words.

There are families in the Embers who seem to carry within their blood a memory of the old days, Comminor read. *These men and women keep alive the world on the Surface, and pass on to their successors the dreams of the green and blue, the birds in the sky and the creatures of the earth. They keep their gifts secret, their abilities buried within themselves. They are special and extraordinary, and they are to be hunted down and destroyed at all costs.*

Comminor's finger paused, then retraced the last sentence again.

His predecessor had not known that Comminor himself was a bard, and Comminor had not disclosed it, mainly because he had not even been aware of it himself until he read the Nox Aves book. His high birth and confident personality had let him rise quickly amongst the ranks until the previous Chief Select had noticed him, and he had been careful to keep his dreams to himself.

But it was only once he read the *Quercetum* that he realised what he had been dreaming about. And by then it was too late for him to take the path of anything but Chief Select, bent on destroying those with whom he would otherwise have been seeking to collude with. There was no point in seeking them out now. He had read the book. He knew the truth. And he knew there was no other way to keep the people in the Embers alive than to kill those who dreamed of another world.

The bell outside the door rang, and he called out, "One moment," before closing the book and replacing it in the cabinet. He locked the door, hung the key around his neck, and only then walked across to the curtain and pulled it back.

His eyebrows rose to see four Select standing there, as well as his two guards. They were breathing heavily, although whether from exertion or emotion he was not sure, because although their chests heaved, their eyes flickered with fear.

"What is it?" he demanded.

Viel, one of his most loyal followers and the leader of the small hand-picked group closest to him that he called the Umbra, leaned towards him and murmured in his ear, "It is about the Veris."

Comminor's eyes narrowed. "Come in."

He turned and walked back into the foyer, and the members of the Umbra followed. One of them shut the door, and they all turned to face him.

"So?"

Josse, a young Select with wild dark hair that refused to be tamed, spoke up. "Sir, I managed to get close enough to overhear a conversation that Nele the apothecary had with another member of the Veris. And they were discussing plans to leave the Embers – tonight."

Comminor stared at him. "Who was the other member?"

Viel hesitated. "You are not going to like it."

Comminor just glared at him.

"Turstan," Viel said.

Fury lit Comminor up like a lantern. He had picked the young Select himself, impressed by the lad's record and abilities. "Fire and ash! Where is he?"

"We brought him back to the palace prison. We have been trying to get him to talk, but so far he will not reveal anything."

"What did you do with Nele?"

Josse shifted from foot to foot. "We let him go, although there is a Select tracking him. I was not sure what to do."

Comminor supressed his anger. He had instructed them to follow the Veris only and not to alert them to the fact that they were aware of their presence. They were right to take Turstan, but he could not have expected them to arrest Nele and go against his earlier command.

He strode out into the corridor, the rest of them scurrying to keep up with him. Viel managed to get ahead to sweep aside the curtains covering the doors, leading the way through the huge palace to the caves at the back in the deepest, darkest part of the Tertius District.

Viel stopped outside one of the cells and instructed the two Select on guard to open the door. Comminor marched in, immediately seeing the young Select tied to a chair in the centre of the room, shrouded in darkness.

The Chief Select held his pendant and passed his hand over the lantern on the wall, and it flared into life. He turned and surveyed the sorry figure sitting in the chair.

Turstan had slouched forward to the extent of his restraints, and his head hung down, his hair matted with a mixture of sweat and blood. Drops of red also dripped from his face onto the floor, pooling at his feet.

Comminor dropped to his haunches before him and pushed up his head. The Select had been badly beaten. Both eyes were swollen almost shut, his nose was broken and covered in blood, his lip was split and several teeth were missing.

Comminor stroked his cheek with his thumb. "Turstan?"

The young man opened his eyes as far as he could. He blinked a couple of times and focussed on the man in front of him. Comminor was not surprised to see a spark of fear in his eyes.

"Sir," Turstan said hoarsely. He turned his head and spat onto the floor, a mixture of saliva and thick red blood.

Comminor surveyed him thoughtfully. "Josse overheard you talking to Nele," he said. "You were discussing leaving the Embers, I understand."

Turstan said nothing, just surveyed him dully.

"I know about the Veris," Comminor said calmly. "I know about Nele, Amabil, Kytte and Betune. And I know there are others, whose identity I will discover in the very near future."

Turstan spat on the floor again.

"Tell me what time you are planning to leave," Comminor said, "and where you are meeting."

Turstan tested his teeth with his tongue. "Beat me all you like," he said. "I will not tell you anything more."

"I have no intention of touching you," Comminor said. "How is Orla?"

Turstan stared at him.

"Yes," Comminor said, "I am aware of the whore you frequent on a weekly basis. I know that you loved Iriellor, and that since she died you have been lonely. And that you have been keeping Orla company instead. And I encourage that – man was not made to live alone. I know you do not mean to marry her. But equally, I know you have affection for her." He shifted position to get more comfortable. "Shall I bring her here? Torture her in front of you?"

Tears filled Turstan's eyes. "Please. Do not harm her."

"I will do it, and I will force you to listen to her screams." He stood, lifted Turstan's head by his hair to force him to look up at him. "I am Chief Select, and I am in charge of the Embers. You will tell me everything you know about the Veris. I will not have citizens under my rule thinking they can leave and leading the rest of our society to destruction!"

Turstan gave a kind of gurgling half-laugh, half-cough. "You really think you know everything, don't you?" He licked his lips. "Did you know Sarra is a member of the group?"

Comminor stared at him. Ice slid down his gullet and into his stomach, as cold and chilling as if he had drunk from the Magna Cataracta itself. "Sarra?"

Turstan's eyes gleamed. "You did not know."

"I…" For maybe the first time in his life, Comminor was speechless. He had not known. His love for Sarra had been completely separate from his role as Chief Select, one of the few pure things he had allowed himself in his life. The moment when she had accepted him willingly in his bed had been one of the best moments of his life. She had a quality that fascinated him, an inner surety and purity that he had had to possess, as if in making her his mate, he could somehow gain a little of it himself. The thought that she was a member of the Veris – that she had kept that secret from him, brought the fire scorching through his veins to flame in his palms.

Turstan saw his fingers spit sparks and lifted his chin. "The baby is a bard," he said. "And not just any bard. It knows the way out. It has showed her in a dream."

"Where is she?" Comminor grabbed the Select's throat, squeezing his fingers until the man's eyes bulged, flames licking from his fingers and scalding the other man's skin. "Tell me where she is or I swear I will bring Orla here and pull out her fingernails one by one, remove her teeth and slice her into tiny pieces until the room fills with blood!"

Turstan gurgled. "They have gone," he managed to say. "They will have left when... they knew you... arrested me. You are... too late..."

Anger roared through Comminor, bursting from him in a wave of flame that swept over the man before him. Still he continued to squeeze until Turstan's tongue turned blue and he grew limp, and his skin blackened and bubbled, popped and burst beneath the heat of the fire that burned within the Chief Select.

Comminor dropped the man, stood back and let the fire roar from him. It engulfed the room, sending the others scurrying outside, billowing in folds of red and orange and gold until the whole room glowed.

His anger burned, but the hurt at Sarra's betrayal burned even hotter. He had loved her, and she had deceived him. He would hunt her. He would track them all down, bring them back to the Embers, and then he would make her pay. He was the Chief Select, and the future of the city and its people was his task and his alone. He would not be held accountable for its destruction. He would not be the one responsible for bringing it down.

He clenched his fists, forced the anger down deep inside him. The fire flared briefly, then died. He stared dispassionately at the charred remains of the man before him, then turned to the door and opened it to see his Umbra, their faces showing their willingness to do whatever he commanded.

"Come on," he said. "We are going on a hunt."

PART THREE

CHAPTER ELEVEN

I

Procella sat with her back against the wall of the barn and wrapped her arms around her knees. The place was filled with the usual smell of horse and cow dung, and the rustle of animals in the stalls, the skitter of rats across the rafters. But at least in her corner the straw was clean, and the night was warm, so it didn't matter so much that she didn't have a bed for the night.

Not that she could have slept anyway. Although the tiny hamlet was silent, the candles in the dozen or so houses were extinguished, and the Light Moon shone down on the empty streets, the comfort of sleep eluded her. She kept thinking about the events of the previous night, and wondering what was happening to her children.

Her head fell back on the wooden plank as sadness filled her heart. Although she had done plenty of guard duty at night in Heartwood and on the Wall, she had spent very little time alone in her life. In the Exercitus, army life had always been communal and busy with even basic tasks like eating and bathing carried out together, and she had always found comfort in the presence of others. It didn't necessarily have to involve speaking – the Militis were brought up to follow rather than question, and talk would revolve around armour and weapons and tactics, or occasionally storytelling in the evenings to pass the time. Emotions were not high on the list of topics discussed, and she had grown used to keeping her feelings to herself.

Meeting Chonrad had meant a vast change in her daily life. The destruction of Heartwood as she had known it, getting married, having children – her whole way of life had been turned upside down. And she had borne it as best as she could, because there was little place for a soldier in peacetime, and she had enjoyed for a while the task of raising her children and being a wife to the man she loved.

It had taken time for her to learn to share herself with someone. Chonrad was probably the best knight she had ever met save the mighty Valens who had trained her, but he had not led the life of a soldier the way she had. He had been married before he met her, had raised two children, had rebuilt Vichton and learned about trade and the economy, had had the responsibility of looking after the people of the town ever since he was a lad, raised to follow in his father's footsteps. Although he had admitted to her that his relationship with his first wife had not been close, still he had been used to sharing a bed with another, to listening to her dreams and complaints, to helping her through the days, bad and good.

At first, Procella had baulked at Chonrad's gentle encouragement to share her innermost thoughts. What was the point? Why burden him with her worries when talking about them didn't do anything except mean that both of them ended up worried? Physical intimacy was one thing and she enjoyed sharing her body with him, but emotional intimacy was something entirely different, as was adjusting to being part of a couple. She didn't like compromising and adapting. And she was never sure she liked him knowing what was going on in her head. He had understood her so well it scared her, and she had fought against that closeness for a long time.

Fights she could deal with and almost enjoyed, and there was no doubt that his temper – although hidden deep inside him – flared with as much brightness and heat as her own. She preferred to tease it out of him, to goad him into a vocal and passionate response when they disagreed, because first they would shout, and then things would turn physical, and then he would kiss her to shut her up. They would end up making love, which she enjoyed and which ultimately diffused the friction between them.

But Chonrad was calm and patient, and as the years went by, he had learned how to deal with her frustration, and to understand that ultimately she was scared of sharing herself, and of learning to love. In her world, a soldier lived for the day, because no matter how strong and fierce the warrior, a stray arrow could easily take one's life away in the blink of an eye. She had loved and lost Valens, as well as many of the men and women who had served under her, and she couldn't bear the thought of losing Chonrad too. And he had understood this and slowly teased her out of her tight shell like a periwinkle. He had encouraged her to express her love for him and her children, and the harsh and regimented soldier had gradually relaxed into motherhood and family life. She knew she had been strict with her children, and that Chonrad probably deserved someone who returned his love with the warmth and affection he himself portrayed, but he had never once expressed regret for taking her as his wife, and she had grown to love him deeply.

And then he had left her. She closed her eyes and her hands tightened into fists as the grief that she had thought would be long past welled inside her once again. How could the knife of pain still be as sharp as when it had plunged into her ribs the day they brought Chonrad home, inches from death? The force of her feelings had shocked her. She was a soldier – death had always been a part of everyday life. Why had it come as such a blow? But it had shaken her world like an earthquake, and after he died, she knew he had taken part of her with him.

Her children had gathered around her, but she had turned away from them rather than pulling them close and allowing them to comfort her. Never again would she allow death to affect her so, she had vowed. They were all but dust in the wind, and love was an emotion she had no interest in and no desire to continue to nurture like a seedling.

She pressed a hand against her heart. It felt hollow, like an old tree stump, a resting place for mice and hedgehogs. She had grown used to being cared about, she realised. To leaning on others like a crutch and letting them support her. To caring. But no longer.

She thought of her children and wondered where they were. Her daughter, Horada, lost deep in the countryside, tied to the Arbor by the same silken strings as Chonrad, and responding to the tug of the holy tree whenever it felt like pulling, just like he had. Procella knew she was too impatient with her daughter, that she didn't know how to talk to her, because she was so different to herself. Where was Horada now? Had she got to Heartwood? Or had she been caught by the fire demons Julen had told them about?

Thinking about her youngest son brought a pang of angst, and she rested her face in her hands. Julen had always been independent and fearless, and she had no worries about him coping alone. He spent weeks travelling by himself doing Gravis's bidding – preferred his own company, in fact. And she had seen him defend himself, had privately been surprised and pleased at his inherent skills. But still, he was her son. And now he, too, was Arbor-knew-where in the countryside, chasing his sister. Perhaps both of them had already been caught, been killed? Would she know? Would she be able to feel when they left the earthly world?

And as for Orsin… Procella regretted being so rough with him earlier on their journey. She had embarrassed him – had done it on purpose, impatient with his foolishness and embarrassed by his idle boasting. All he cared about was wine and women, and while she appreciated these things were at the foremost of most normal men's minds, still she had expected her own son to have some appreciation for the more important things in life. In nearly all ways he fell short of Julen, and she had never bothered to hide her disappointment. Now, though, she wished she had not been so harsh.

She wrapped her arms around herself and fought back the tears that she had shed so little of throughout the years. She missed Valens. She missed Chonrad. And she missed her children.

For the first time in her life, Procella was lonely.

The tears ran silently down her face. In the barn, mice rustled, a horse snorted, one of the working dogs got up and shook itself, turning around a few times before settling back down.

Procella's thoughts were turned so inward that for a moment nothing seemed out of the ordinary. As she leaned her cheek on her knees, she could see through a wide crack where a plank had slipped, where a sliver of Light Moon lay on a puddle like the blade of a scythe, stars around it glittering like white stones. Chonrad... she thought, fighting the ache inside her. I miss you...

It was the age-old warrior's instinct she had carried for so long that finally made her stiffen, her senses sharpening. For a moment she remained motionless, holding her breath, straining her ears to catch whatever it was that had alerted her. A jingle of horse's reins. A whisper of conversation on the wind.

She pushed herself quietly to her feet, her tears drying on her cheeks. Silently, she crept to the doorway and peeked through.

At the end of the street, a fire burned. She blinked and focussed, trying to make out the men who stood around it. Several figures, Wulfian obviously as she was still north of the Wall. One she recognised. She would never be able to rid herself of the memory of his huge frame pinning her into the dirt, the smell of his breath on her cheek. Hunfrith would die at her own hand – of that, if nothing else, she was certain.

Two of the men with him she thought she recognised from Kettlestan – other lords of the lands north of the Wall, greedy and desiring money and land over peace. They must have escaped the burning castle, and now Hunfrith was on the hunt for her.

She turned to the horses watching her patiently, went over to the one she had decided earlier would be the most suitable for her purposes – a riding horse, a gelding, fifteen hands high, solid and sturdy. She had already selected a saddle and reins from those hanging on hooks to the side, and she took them now and saddled him quickly. An expert horsewoman, it took only minutes before she was leading him out of the wide doors at the back.

The gelding was dark grey with a black mane and blended nicely in with the long shadows and bleached landscape. Procella led him around the barn to the west and mounted him swiftly. Then, casting a final look over her shoulder, she urged the horse towards the forest.

Within seconds, she heard a cry behind her. Kicking her heels into the gelding's flanks, she sent it racing towards the trees.

Voices yelled behind her. She leaned forward, urging the horse to pick up its speed. Its hooves thundered on the dry ground, and then trees flashed by her, branches tugged at her hair, and the welcoming darkness of the forest closed around her.

Procella turned immediately south, heading for the Wall. She needed to get back into Laxony, although the nearest fort and passage through was several miles west. The Wulfians would know that was where she was going, and would try to head her off before she got there. She had a long hard ride ahead of her, on a horse she didn't know, at night, in a land less familiar to her after years spent south of the Wall. The odds weren't in her favour.

But those were the kind of odds she loved, the kind of risk that made her heart race and her blood pound in her ears.

Feeling more alive than she had felt in the past twelve months, Procella hugged the horse's neck and prepared for a challenging journey.

II

Catena had never been so deep into the jungle. The going was tough – they had to fight their way through creepers and vines that laced between the trees, and they were obviously nearing the base of the mountains because sometimes huge boulders forced them to detour. Tropical flowers grew thick and lush, and multi-coloured birds also hopped between the ferns, a kaleidoscope of primary colours amongst the dark green vegetation.

She was glad she had brought the ointment they used in the mines to counteract insect bites. The oil contained some kind of herb that repelled mosquitoes and other insects, and without it she was sure they would have been eaten alive. Atavus snapped constantly around him, irritated by the buzzing, and eventually she put some drops of the oil on a cloth and tied it around his neck. He seemed better after that.

She tried not to laugh every time she looked at Demitto. Clearly, he was also hating every minute of their journey west. He had stripped off his leather jerkin, rolled it up and strapped it to his backpack. His linen undershirt clung to his upper body with sweat, and he had pulled his long scruffy hair back off his neck and tied it with cord. Deep frown lines cut into his forehead, and she could hear him muttering from several paces away.

Still, in spite of his obvious resentment, he pushed on, and she was pleased that he seemed so determined to rescue the Prince. She had wondered whether he might have told her that, because she had taken the Prince away, he would not help her rescue him and would in fact return to Heartwood to find another sacrifice as she had originally hoped, but he hadn't. However, he had hardly said two words to her since binding her shoulder, and he was clearly angry with her.

She rolled her shoulder as they walked. She wasn't quite sure what he had done to her before binding her shoulder. He said he had 'directed the Arbor's love' when she queried him again, and she had seen him push the pendant into the ground. Was it true that energy travelled beneath the earth from the Arbor? Had he truly channelled that energy into her? Her shoulder was sore, but it should have been throbbing a great deal more, and there was no sign of infection, the skin already healing nicely.

She mused on the enigmatic emissary as he stopped to hack at a trailing vine with a dagger. He portrayed himself as a sword-for-hire with less spirituality than a piece of rock, but that didn't explain the way he had healed her, or the fervour that shone through him at times, lighting him up like a lantern.

He pushed forward through the greenery, Atavus leaping elegantly over a fallen log, and she trailed after them, wondering what Demitto would say if she asked if they could stop for a while. She was thirsty and could do with a bite to eat to keep her strength up, but his rigid spine and stony face discouraged her from asking. She would wait until he had to stop. Surely he would have to stop at some point?

On cue, he came to a halt so suddenly that she bumped into his back. A query hovered on her lips, but before she could voice it, he sank to his haunches and gestured for her to do the same, putting a hand on Atavus to stop him running forward.

Catena moved forward and parted the undergrowth, peering through to the scene in front of them. Two men stood there, in the middle of the jungle, motionless as if carved from the rock that reared behind them. They wore plain brown clothes with various fancy pieces of plate armour engraved with a design Catena had never seen before. It was only when she looked at their eyes that she realised what the design was, because it was reflected in their gaze – dancing flames, the red and orange irises sending a shiver down her spine.

They stood with hands braced on the hilt of their swords, the point resting on the ground. For a moment, she thought they *were* statues, but then a beautifully coloured butterfly alighted on the pommel of one of the swords. The knight twitched, and the butterfly flew away.

Demitto studied them silently, then withdrew back into the undergrowth, pulling Atavus with him. They walked back silently the way they had come until they were sure they would not be overheard, and then crouched beneath a huge fern, hiding in the shadows.

"Who were they?" Catena whispered.

"I do not know." Demitto fumbled in his jacket for the pendant. He pulled it out, then hesitated. "I need to speak to Cinereo. Do you promise to remain quiet?"

She nodded, wanting to see what he did, pleased that he wasn't going to send her away. His eyes met hers briefly. Then he lowered them and plunged the pendant into the ground.

She sat with her back against the trunk, one arm around her knees, one around Atavus's neck, and watch Demitto concentrate, his eyes closed, his head bent. A lock of his hair that had escaped the tie at the back fell forward, curving around his cheekbone. He was too thin, she thought – he looked as if he could do with some good home cooking and a woman to look after him. Too much time spent on the road missing meals, existing on ale and hunks of dry bread from his saddlebag. What a life he must have had. Part of her envied him, part of her felt sorry for him. Was he lonely? He couldn't be any lonelier than her, she thought, and she'd spent a lifetime surrounded by people.

She blinked. The air before him was shimmering. For a moment she thought she was imagining it, but then it grew stronger, the air blurring as if she were looking through heavy rain. Atavus growled low in his throat, and she murmured to him and stroked his fur reassuringly.

The shadows around them lengthened, thickened, darkened, and she felt the same sense of something crawling over her skin that she had felt the previous time she'd watched him do this, the rising of hairs all over her body. A shape began to form before them, sinister in the twilight – a figure cloaked and hooded in grey, his lower arms covered by leather bracers, leather straps across his body. She shivered, trying to ignore the fear that rose within her.

Demitto raised his head and opened his eyes. "Cinereo," he acknowledged.

The man nodded a greeting. "You have reached the mountains?"

"Yes. There are two knights in the jungle, guarding something. I think it might be the entrance to the caves."

The caves? Catena frowned. She hadn't seen the entrance to any caves.

"The Prince lies within," Cinereo confirmed.

Demitto nodded. "You wish me to enter?"

"The Prince must be retrieved at all costs."

"I understand. But the guards suggest the Incendi have more followers bound to their will. I know neither where they have drafted these from, nor how many they have. We are but two. If–"

"At. All. Costs." The words dropped from the grey-cloaked figure like stones.

Demitto dropped his head, subservient for once. "I may not be able to contact you within the caves," he murmured. "The ground will be rock and the pendant will be unusable. Do you have any further instructions?"

"Pyra is attempting to force the Apex to a location and time that gives him the advantage. We must avoid that. Do not fail me."

"I will do my best." Demitto hesitated, and Catena had the feeling he was suddenly conscious of admitting a weakness in her presence, but he went ahead anyway. "I am uncertain how to find the Prince once we are inside the caves."

"Use Catena," Cinereo instructed. "She is a Saxum." The figure shimmered. "I must go, I have much to do."

Abruptly, the figure faded like early morning mist. Atavus rose and went over to sniff where he had been.

Demitto slid the pendant beneath his clothes and glanced across at Catena.

"Well, he was friendly," she said. The manner in which he had spoken to the emissary had shocked her. Suddenly she understood the pressure Demitto was under, the responsibility that rested on his shoulders. Why was he doing this? What was he getting out of it?

His mouth curved wryly. "He has his reasons."

"Who is he? How do we know we can trust him?"

His mouth curved more. "Oh, we can trust him. Do not worry about that."

"Have you met him? In person, I mean?"

He sat back, arms around his knees, fingers linked. "No. But I do know he speaks for the Nox Aves. And I trust them with my life." He spoke simply, and his eyes were clear. He was telling the truth, she decided.

"So what did he mean, 'use Catena'? What is a Saxum?"

Now Demitto's eyes turned thoughtful, his expression interested. "It is a term I have not heard used for a long time. Tell me, your father is a miner, yes?"

"Yes. So?"

"Has he ever spoken to you about his work?"

She gave a laugh that held no humour. "My father rarely speaks to anyone or anything except his tankard. Why would he talk to me about his work?"

"Was his father a miner before him?"

"And his father before him." Now she was confused. "I do not understand."

"Often within families of miners, there runs in the blood a kind of..." he thought about how to describe it, "special ability. The miners themselves are not always aware of it, and it is stronger in some than others. But some people have the talent for listening to stone."

She stared at him. "Now I know you are jesting. 'Listening to stone'? Are you telling me I have to have a conversation with the rockface?"

"Maybe," he said, a sliver of humour in his words. "I do not have the talent so I cannot tell you how it works. It is an innate ability, like how some people can paint the likeness of a person. We cannot explain why one person can sing and another makes us cover our ears. So it is with those of us who connect with the elements."

She shook her head, still disbelieving.

He frowned. "It is like when I channel the fire as I hold the sunstone. How can I explain it...? Although I do not have an elemental inside me, I can feel the fire in my veins, and I only have to think of it and it bursts through my skin."

"So what are you saying – that you think I can connect in a similar way with... what? Rock?"

"Saxum traditionally have the ability to sense the harder elements – they can often find the ores, gold and copper and such, within the mountains. They have a skill with gems and crystals – they know where to find them, and how to cut them to avoid flaws. Hanaire people have a high percentage of Saxum, which is why they are so skilled with silver work. And traditionally those from Harlton and the far south have been known to have this connection. Perhaps they have absorbed it into the blood over the years of working in the mines, like breathing dust into the lungs. Who knows? But it seems that Cinereo thinks you have the talent. And maybe that is why..."

She stared at him. "Why..."

He shook his head and pushed himself to his feet. "We should go. It will be dark soon and, with you injured, I would rather we fight these men while we can see them."

"It will be even darker in the caves," she said, rising with him. What had he been about to say?

"True, but I will be able to use the sunstone to guide us." He drew his sword, being careful not to let the steel sing as it came out of the scabbard. "Are you ready?"

She withdrew her own sword, hefting it in her right hand. She could feel the pull of the weight on her shoulder, and she knew she would feel the wound once they started to fight, but she would not let it stop her. "Ready."

"Then let us do it." They moved forward until they saw the glimmer of the men's swords through the leaves.

Demitto met her gaze. Above their heads, the Light Moon climbed high in the sky and his eyes glittered, making her shiver.

"Now," he said, and they leapt forward with a yell.

III

In the southernmost part of the Embers, the lanterns became further apart, and their journey became a fumbling through black passageways interspersed with patches of weak yellow light.

"I presume everyone is thinking what I am thinking," Amabil said as she stumbled and almost fell for the third time.

Betune put a hand under her arm and steadied her. "You mean, what are we going to do without Turstan to light our way?"

The thought had played on Sarra's mind too. Once they left the Embers, the caves would be unlit. So far she had trusted her instincts that they would find a way to guide themselves, but the worry that her blind faith was a mistake grew more in her mind with each step. Still, she knew she had to reassure them. She had led them this far – she had to hope the baby would continue to guide her. "The way will become clear," Sarra said with more conviction than she felt.

None of the five people with her said anything. Sarra wasn't surprised. Nele's face was carefully blank and she knew he wouldn't question her, although she was sure he was worried. Geve's expression showed his obvious concern, but again, he wouldn't question her. Betune and Kytte both looked nervous, and Amabil continued to look belligerent, although she too remained quiet for now.

The news of Turstan's arrest had shocked them all, and she knew their hearts must be pounding, their mouths dry the same as hers. They wanted to believe her. But doubt loomed like towering shadows in their minds.

"Where are we going?" Geve whispered to her. They travelled in single file through the narrow alleys, and he was behind her, holding her hand.

She shook her head, not sure whether he could see her in the dim light. He wanted her to confide in him, to trust him to support her, but instinct told her to wait until they arrived at the first checkpoint before she revealed their destination. She knew it wouldn't please him. Since Comminor had taken her to his bed, Geve had been quiet and reserved, hurt shimmering in his eyes. *What choice did I have?* She wanted to yell the words, but knew he wasn't interested in the truth. His heart would rather she had refused the Chief Select, even if it had meant her arrest and probably her death. She understood, but it made her sad.

The passageway twisted west, and the faint rush of water that had accompanied them the last five minutes grew to a loud chatter. The tunnel opened to reveal the river channel that led from its source in the far north of the Primus District, through the Great Lake and then all the way through the Secundus District to the Magna Cataracta not far from where they were.

As they walked quickly along the riverbank, Sarra wondered what was happening to Turstan. She had no doubt he was being tortured and that Comminor and his Umbra were forcing him to tell them about the conversation they had overheard him have with Nele. Would he have told them anything? Was Comminor hot on their trail now, already making his way through the District towards them?

The thought sent cold filtering through her, and she picked up her pace, crossing the river over the old bridge and leading the rest of the group to the opposite bank. Already the bag she carried grew heavy on her back, the weight pulling on the muscles around her stomach. She rested her hands on the bump that swelled above her pubic bone and stroked it lightly. Was it her imagination, or had it grown since that morning? She wore breeches beneath the tunic, and the waistband stretched tightly around her waist. It had not been that tight when she dressed. Had it?

She pushed the thought to the back of her mind. She had more important things to worry about than the tightness of her breeches. At that moment, it felt as if her whole life hung by a thread. The literal and metaphorical path they were on stretched ahead of her, rocky and dangerous, and she could not yet see how the future would pan out. Her gut clenched with fear, and part of her wished she had stayed, become Comminor's mistress, lived a life of ease and brought her child up in safety.

But inside her, the baby stirred, a constant reminder of her dreams and the urge she felt to reach the Surface. The baby did not want her to stay. She did not yet know whether their journey would be a success, but she did know that she had to try.

The rush of the river in the channel below them grew to a roar, and she knew they were nearing the Magna Cataracta. Here the riverbanks grew lush with mosses, and the humid air wrapped around them: thick, wet and heavy as a sodden blanket. The water ran deep, shining black like the large crystals they mined in the north of the Primus District, and it thundered past them with frightening speed and strength. If she stepped into the channel, she would be swept off her feet, right down the Cataracta. The thought frightened her, and her heart thundered along with the water.

The edge of the waterfall was marked by large boulders and she climbed them hesitantly, afraid of slipping on the wet rock. The others followed, slowly making their way to the centre, where the river disappeared down into the darkness. One large lantern had been nailed into the rock above their heads many years before, and it cast its yellow light eerily across the scene.

Sarra reached the large boulder on the river's edge and waited for the others to join her. Their faces were pale in the lamplight, solemn but resolute. The dreams gave them all hope that this journey would ultimately be rewarding.

Nele crouched beside her and raised his voice over the thundering river. "Where now?"

She waited for Kytte and Amabil to bring up the rear, until they could all hear her. Then she took a deep breath.

"We have to go over," she said.

They stared at her.

"Over," Geve said dully.

"Over," she repeated. "We have rope, and we have to lower ourselves."

"Down?" Betune said. "How can the way to the Surface be down?"

"Down, then up," Sarra said. "I promise."

"It is impossible." Amabil looked incredulous. "There is no way we could survive that."

"We can and we will," Sarra said firmly. "It is the only way out of here."

"How do you know?" Amabil's eyes blazed. She turned to the others. "It is crazy to put our lives in her hands!"

Nele's eyes met Sarra's. "We have trusted her thus far," he said, but his words sounded weak to her, his uncertainty ringing through.

Sarra turned to Geve and took his hands. "It is the only way," she insisted. "Do you believe me?"

He hesitated. "I do... but Sarra, over the Cataracta? It is certain death."

She began to pull the rope from her bag. "The lantern above is hung from a solid hook that has held for many years. I came here a while ago and tested it – it is firm and will not give. We must tie our ropes to it and lower ourselves down. It will not be easy, but I promise you, it will work."

Betune caught her hand. "In your condition? You have to think of the baby."

"I am," Sarra said simply. "I have dreamed of this every night for weeks. He shows me again and again the river, the Cataracta, the way down."

"And what happens when we reach the bottom?" Kytte asked.

It was Sarra's turn to hesitate. "I am unsure of that. I believe he will show me when the first part of this journey is done."

She turned her attention to the lantern and its hook, embedded in the rock. Her hands shook, but she ignored them and began tying the rope. It was the sturdiest twine she had been able to find, plaited from numerous strands of the thickest moss in the Embers. She had made hundreds of yards of it, stopping only when instinct told her, but still she was not sure she had made enough. While the others talked among themselves, she tied it repeatedly in knots to the hook as her father had taught her, over and over again until it would have needed to be removed with a blade.

She finished and turned to them, brushing her hands down her tunic. "Well?"

"It is a huge risk," Nele said.

"I know." She leaned on the rope, tested its weight. "But we have no time to lose. I am sure Comminor tortured Turstan, and he will be here soon, no doubt." She moved along the rock, peered over the edge. The water tumbled, glistening occasionally in the light of the lantern until it finally vanished into darkness. She swallowed, and then looked back at them. "Well I am going. I cannot stay here. Maybe once I had a choice, but if I stay, Comminor will kill me. I must go."

Geve stood. "I will come with you. There is nothing here for me anyhow."

Nele took a deep breath. "We will all go. We have all dreamed of the Surface. We all know it is our only option. We will not let fear rule us."

The others stood, even Amabil, and Sarra's heart soared.

"Let us do it."

As the leader of the group, Nele went first, bracing himself on the boulder at the edge of the river as he climbed over. He had looped the rope over his shoulders and beneath his armpits, and all the others except Sarra began to lower him down slowly. His face betrayed the fear he had been determined not to voice.

The water churned around him, white on the rocks, black where it coated the walls and fell into the darkness. He tried to keep to the edge of the tunnel, but the water still soaked him within seconds.

Sarra watched him descend, her heart in her mouth. All of them were used to physical work and had strong arms and muscular shoulders, but even so she was unsure how she would fare. They had no idea how far they would have to descend or how strong the force of the water would be.

"How goes it?" Geve yelled down once Nele's head disappeared into the black hole.

"It is difficult with the weight of the water," Nele yelled back. "But at the edge here the rock is uneven and there are plenty of footholds."

Geve – his arms taut and veins popping on his forehead – glanced at Sarra and moved close to murmur in her ear. "Do you really think you can do this? Do you have the strength?"

She nodded, although her mouth had gone dry. "I will do it. I must."

"You will go next," he said. "I am strongest – I will go last. I will have to climb down the rope."

She turned her head and met his gaze. His eyes were firm, brooking no argument. Her mouth curved. "Thank you for caring about me."

His expression softened. "Always." A flush touched his cheekbones, and he turned away and looked over the edge. "Well, of course, it depends on whether Nele makes it to the bottom or not."

His attempt at humour didn't lighten their mood. From time to time he yelled up a report, but eventually the crash of the water drowned him out.

The rope gradually unfurled. More and more of it snaked over the edge. Sarra watched it disappear, heart pounding. What if he ran out?

"How will we know if he reaches the bottom?" Betune wondered.

Geve, his hand still holding the rope, turned worried eyes to them. "I suppose he will try to signal us somehow."

"Is the rope still taut?" Sarra asked.

"Yes."

So clearly Nele was still hanging onto the other end.

Whether he was still alive was anyone's guess.

Minutes passed, and the waiting four women and Geve grew restless. The rope continued to disappear as they lowered it gradually over the edge.

Eventually, Geve released the last piece, and it hung straining from the hook, going directly down into the darkness.

"He has reached the end of it," Amabil said, biting her lip to stop it trembling. "He could be miles from the bottom."

"And he could already be there." Geve spoke firmly, but his eyes continued to look fearful. "We should–"

"What?"

He pulled on the rope. "It has gone slack."

They waited, turning worried eyes to each other. Silently, Geve began to pull in the rope. It took a long time before he reached the loop that Nele had placed around his shoulders. The loop was still intact. But they had no way of knowing what had happened to Nele.

"Maybe he is at the bottom," Betune suggested.

"Or maybe he has fallen," Kytte whispered.

"It matters not," Sarra said. She took the rope from Geve and pulled the loop over her head and under her arms. "We have to go. We have no choice."

Geve took up the slack, and the others grabbed a hold of it too, their faces white in the lamplight.

Sarra met his eyes and wondered what to say to him. Her heart pounded, nausea rose inside her, and she felt frightened for the baby. What if the dreams were just that – dreams? What if she were about to kill the child when she had been given the perfect opportunity to give it a long and happy life?

Too late, she thought. The decisions had been made, the journey begun; like the ingredients of a pie placed in an oven, there could only be one result. The only way was forward.

She could think of nothing to say. In the end, Geve leaned forward and kissed her, his mouth soft and warm on hers.

He lifted his head and nodded, then began to lower her over the edge of the Cataracta. The sensation of going over was terrifying. The water pounded around her, loud in her ears, soaking her within seconds. She gasped at the coolness of it, at the force of it on her shoulders. She gripped hold of the rope, planting her feet on the rockface behind the water. She was not going to fall! She was going to get to the bottom and find Nele, and then she was going to help the others descend and lead them all to the Surface. It was the adventure of a lifetime, and one day the baby in her belly would tell tales of this to her grandchildren.

The water filled her mouth, tumbled into her eyes. She tossed her head and shook the droplets away. She was over the edge, and now it was just a matter of finding the bottom.

Geve lowered her down. And the darkness swallowed her up.

CHAPTER TWELVE

I

Horada opened her eyes, slowly rising to awareness like a piece of wood in the depths of a river.

The room was dark, lit only by the glow of torches in sconces on the stone walls. She lay on a stone floor, iron chains binding her wrists to the wall behind her.

Her memory came back in a rush. She had been fleeing the Incendi elementals, racing through the forest with Julen, the trees and undergrowth bursting into flames all around her. It had overtaken her before she could urge Mara to the forest edge. She had lost consciousness, and could remember nothing of what had happened from that point until she opened her eyes.

Where was Mara? What had happened to Julen?

And where in Anguis was she?

She sat up and looked around. Her first thought was a castle dungeon. Orsin had taken her down into Vichton's dungeons once. Barely used, they had been clean but damp and cold, smelling of moss and earth and guttering candles.

This place was different – the dry air smelled faintly of sulphur. Her teeth ached from the taste of metal. And the walls and floor, although made of stone, were warm to the touch. The room was bare, although on the walls she could see marks in brightly coloured paint, red and orange and blue, but in the semi-darkness she couldn't make out the patterns.

She stood, wincing as the iron manacles chafed the delicate skin of her wrists. Tears pricked her eyes and her bottom lip trembled, but she bit it hard and took a few deep breaths to gather her courage.

She was alive! After the events in the forest, she had to be thankful for that. Chafed wrists were a small price to pay when the alternative was being roasted like a duck. Clearly, it had been no ordinary fire that had swept over her, and therefore she was not certain that Julen and Mara had perished. Maybe once the Incendi had got what they wanted, they had let her brother and the horse go free.

She leaned against the wall. The Incendi. Where had they taken her? Did they have a base somewhere in Anguis? Or had they taken over a castle belonging to one of the Laxonian lords?

A noise like the crackle of burning twigs filled the quiet room, and she turned with alarm to see a small square of the wall flame with light. The light died down after a few moments to a dull glow illuminating a grille in a doorway she hadn't realised was there.

Moving to the extent of her chains, she raised herself on tiptoes and peered through the grille.

Outside, two figures stood in a long corridor stretching out of sight to the left and right. Although they vaguely looked like men, the figures were formed from fire, their shape constantly moving as the scarlet flames jumped and danced the same as any on a burning log.

Horada gasped and pressed fingers to her mouth. As one, the two figures turned and looked at her. Their faces blurred and shimmered, but their eyes burned into her like brands, and she stepped back in shock, heart pounding.

She pressed her back against the wall again and slid down it to the ground. *Incendi.* Fire elementals in their pure form. And they had kidnapped her and spirited her away. What did they intend to do with her?

She closed her eyes as panic threatened to overwhelm her. Where was Julen? Had he followed her to this place, wherever it was? Would he come and rescue her? She wanted to believe so, but found it difficult to summon any hope.

Her mother had been right – she should never have left Vichton. Shame and resentment burned inside her. Along with an irresistible urge to get to the Arbor, she had also wanted to prove to her mother that she knew best – that she was old enough to make her own decisions and could cope on her own. How stupid she had been. Clearly, she was unable to defend herself. For years she had scorned the swordplay her mother had tried to force her to practise, insisting she would never need those skills. But then she had never foreseen that something like this would happen.

She could imagine the look that would appear on Procella's face should she find out what had happened to her daughter. An unappealing mixture of frustration, irritation and regret. Horada cringed to think of it. She was a disappointment to her mother – Procella had never bothered to hide that fact. Orsin, too, fell short of the ex-Dux's incredibly high standards. Only Julen conjured any sense of approval within her, and that always seemed begrudging.

How could her father have loved her mother so? Horada saw Procella as permanently irritable and bad-tempered, superior and forceful, not at all a suitable mate for her mild-mannered father. Her half-sister, Rosamunda, had once told Horada about her own mother, describing her as meek, mild and gentle. She would have been a far more suitable wife, Horada thought, although by all accounts it had not been a love match, whereas her own parents' marriage appeared to have been, even though she couldn't understand it. Who could possibly love Procella, with her sharp tongue and high ideals? And she had only got worse since Chonrad's death.

Father, Horada thought, a sudden burst of grief leaving her empty and hollow. She missed him so much at that moment it felt as if she'd lost a physical part of herself. She understood why he had answered the Arbor's call as she herself had felt the same draw, but still, it was difficult to think of it as anything other than abandonment. He had left his family to answer the tree, and she couldn't help the feelings of hurt and betrayal that caused in her.

Drawing up her legs, pressing her forehead to her knees, she conjured up an image of him in her mind. *Help me,* she whispered. *Don't leave me here alone. Send me a sign you are still with me.*

For a moment, nothing happened. She could still hear the crackling noise that she presumed was the Incendi outside her door. The unpleasant smell of sulphur continued to fill her nostrils. Her heart felt heavy and empty at the same time.

And then the hairs stood up on her arms and the back of her neck. And she got the unmistakeable sensation she was not alone.

She raised her head and inhaled sharply. A figure stood before her, tall and straight, wrapped in a dark grey cloak, head bowed beneath the hood.

"Cinereo!"

His figure looked vague and insubstantial, and as she watched, it faded from sight briefly before reappearing, as faint as before. He didn't say anything, just raised a hand and passed it before him from left to right. A glittering dust emanated from his fingers, sparkling in the light that bloomed in a sphere around the torch. The air shimmered, and Cinereo vanished.

Horada blinked. Sitting next to her on the stone floor was a young man, maybe a few years younger than herself. He had long black hair braided back, but untidy wisps had escaped to hang around his pale face. When he turned his head to look at her, his eyes were the colour of beaten gold.

They stared at each other for a moment, too shocked to speak.

Eventually, Horada found her voice. "I have seen you before. By the stream. I thought I saw a young man for a moment, and then you were gone."

The young man's eyes widened, and then he nodded. "I saw you too. I was asleep and dreaming. A man came to me in the dream, dressed in a grey cloak." He spoke in Laxonian and she could just understand his words, but he had a strange accent, and his words had an odd intonation.

"Cinereo!" Horada's heart thumped. "He was just here. Before you appeared."

"Who is he?"

"I do not know. I have never seen his face. But I think he is a friend."

Tahir agreed. "Last time he took me by the hand and led me to you, and also to another girl, in the darkness, with a man with silver hair…" He shook his head and looked around the room. "Where are we?"

"I am not sure. I was captured by the Incendi. Do you know of them?"

He studied her warily. Then he gave a cautious nod. "I have been told of them. We were attacked by brigands in the forest. They had fire in their eyes. I think Incendi had possessed them."

Horada frowned. "I thought they did not have the ability to possess people."

"We were also attacked on the way to Realberg. Demitto told me those who attacked us were also possessed by the elementals."

"Demitto?"

"The ambassador to Heartwood." The young man looked at his hands. "He was escorting me there. I am the Selected."

Startled, Horada ran her gaze over him. He did not look like the Selected she had heard Julen describe – devoted and wise scholars who dedicated their lives to study of the Arbor. Neither had she heard of this Demitto. Gravis was the only ambassador she knew of.

The air around the young man shimmered. Horada blinked, her attention distracted. The room darkened, and the glittering dust seemed to gravitate together to form a shape in the middle of the room. It was an hourglass, the sand trickling from the top bulb into the bottom, and as she watched, it tipped to start transferring the grains back.

You are the Timekeeper. Cinereo's words rang in her ears.

And suddenly she understood.

"You are from the future," she whispered as the hourglass faded. "What is your name?"

He frowned. "Tahir. But what do you mean, the future?"

"Something is happening," she said, heart pounding as pushed herself up to sit on her heels. "I do not understand it perfectly. My brother Julen told me that the timelines are converging – that the past and the future are becoming one."

"The Apex," Tahir murmured.

"You know of it?"

"Demitto told me about it. He said an event in the past, one in my present and one in the future will unite."

"I have been told the same."

"Who are you?" Tahir asked curiously.

"I am Horada." She licked her lips. "Cinereo called me the Timekeeper. My father was Chonrad of Barle."

Tahir's eyes widened. "I know this name. Surely not the Chonrad who saved the Arbor during the Darkwater Invasion?"

She smiled, her heart lifting. "The one and the same."

"But that was at the beginning of the Second Era."

"Twenty-two years ago for me," she said.

"Nearly five hundred for me," Tahir stated.

They stared at each other, stunned into silence again. Horada found it difficult to process her thoughts. This young man was from five hundred years in the future. How could that be? What made that possible?

The Arbor, she thought. Somehow the great tree had enabled them to connect. But why?

"Have you been kidnapped too?" Tahir asked.

She nodded. "I think in my time the Incendi exist only in

elemental form. Julen told me they are able to travel along the Arbor's roots through time. I think maybe they are aware of those who will play a part in the Apex. I wonder if they are trying to destroy us before we can complete our destiny."

Tahir paled. "If that is the case, how can we hope to stop them?"

"I do not know. Cinereo and the Nox Aves are trying."

He nodded. "Demitto has told me about them."

"Is he a member of theirs?"

"I am not sure. He is mysterious – he says he is just doing a job, but then when he speaks about the Arbor, he lights up inside."

Horada remembered the way her father used to light up whenever he thought about the tree. He used to shiver whenever he spoke about what had happened the day of the invasion and sometimes spoke harshly of its hold on him, but she knew the love he bore for the Arbor was far greater than his dislike.

"But I still do not understand why we have been brought together," she said.

"Perhaps to know the other is there," Tahir said. "To know we are not alone."

"Maybe." A frisson of unease ran down her spine.

He looked over his shoulder and frowned as if he had heard a sound outside. "The other girl I saw in my dream... I think maybe she is from our future."

"The third part of the Apex," Horada murmured. "I wonder if she is here, in this place in her own timeline."

He looked over his shoulder again, distracted. "This does not feel right. Why did they not just kill us?" He turned back to her, his golden eyes unnerving. "I have to get to Heartwood. Demitto was very clear about that."

The unease turned to ice in her stomach as realisation dawned. "They are trying to move the Apex."

Tahir stared at her. "How?"

"By forcing the three timelines to converge earlier than they should." Her heart pounded. "We must stop them."

"But how?" He looked over his shoulder for a third time, and fear lit his face. "They are coming for me."

At the same time, her doorway lit once again with flame. "And for me. She reached out for him, but her hand met only glittering dust, his image as insubstantial as mist. "Stay strong, Tahir. We will meet again," she said with more determination than she felt.

He opened his mouth to reply, and then vanished.

The lock on Horada's door clicked and the door swung open.

She pushed herself to her feet. She could not allow them to move the Apex. They were all supposed to meet at Heartwood, at the Arbor, at a particular time. What would happen if they met too early? Horada didn't want to find out.

But as a flaming form filled the doorway, she realised she didn't really have a choice.

II

Tahir blinked as the young woman before him faded away, her glowing form disappearing like the setting sun, leaving him in semi-darkness. His chest rose and fell with rapid breaths as he struggled with the knowledge that not only was he alone again, but someone was about to come through the door to his cell, and almost certainly that would not end well.

He missed Catena and Demitto, and he missed Atavus more than anything.

He struggled to his feet, leaning against the stone wall as his knees trembled and failed to support him. *Have courage*, he thought, remembering how brave Horada had seemed, her blue eyes flashing with fervour as they spoke about the Incendi. Was she truly the daughter of the hero, Chonrad, stepping through the fabric of time to talk to him? It was difficult to believe, and yet how else could he explain her appearance, and the way she had mysteriously faded from sight?

The door opened, and he clenched his fists behind his back to stop his hands shaking, refusing to show these people how frightened he was.

Two men came through the door and walked up to him. One looked Laxonian, tall and sturdy with brown hair and beard. Tahir thought the other might be from Komis judging by his night-black hair, but instead of the distinctive golden eyes, both men's eyes danced with flame, indicating to Tahir they were servants of the Incendi, possessed by fire elementals. They were dressed in sleeveless tunics to the knees and wore no breeches, presumably because it was so warm, and their brown skin shone with sweat.

"What do you want?" he demanded, hoping his voice didn't portray his fear. But the men acted as if he hadn't even spoken. One unhooked his chains from the wall, leaving the manacles around his wrists, and then they led him out of the cell and into the corridor beyond.

Tahir looked around him, heart pounding. When they had attacked him and Catena, they had placed a cloth bag over his head and had not removed it until he reached his cell, so he had no idea where they had taken him.

He found himself in a stone passageway, and as he stretched out his arms and brushed them with his fingers, the stone felt warm to the touch.

"Where are you taking me?" he demanded, but again, they refused to reply. He thought about dropping to the ground and refusing to walk, but they would probably just lift him up and carry him. Although his heart felt as if it was going to jump out of his chest, and tears trembled on the edge of his lashes, he tried his best to gather his courage. He couldn't give in and let Demitto down. He had to do his best to fight.

The two men led him along several corridors and past other cells. Cries and screams filtered occasionally to his ears, presumably from prisoners being held in the cells. Were those unwitting souls about to be filled with elemental forms? Was that going to happen to him?

The corridors grew warm and hazy, and sweat broke out on his forehead and ran down his back beneath his tunic. The air became thick and cloying, almost as if he were breathing underwater. He realised the haziness was due to ash floating in the air. It stung his throat and lungs.

They rounded the corner, and to Tahir's surprise the corridor opened up into a vast chamber. It had high ceilings, and the upper half of the chamber was filled with ash and steam curling up from a scarlet liquid that moved slowly in a wide channel around the edge of the room. *Magma*, he thought, his skin already pouring with sweat from the heat. He had never seen it, but he had heard the miners speak of its presence in the mountains.

Was that where he was? Deep in the Spina Mountains, miles from Heartwood and his home?

Holy Arbor, protect me.

A bridge crossed the channel, leading to a huge raised rock in the centre of the flowing magma. Atop this rock perched a wide seat with a high back similar to Tahir's father's throne.

And sitting on the throne was a man.

Tahir's knees trembled, but before he could fall, the men holding his chains led him across the bridge and up the roughly hewn steps to the flattened portion at the top.

They brought him before the man and jerked Tahir to his knees before chaining him to a huge iron ring embedded in the rock in front of him.

Then the men withdrew.

Tahir stared at the man's feet, unable to stop himself shaking with fear. The man wore brown, soft leather slippers and a simple scarlet tunic to his knees that looked as if it could have been made of linen. His light brown skin shone like polished oak.

Gradually, as the man remained silent, Tahir raised his gaze to take in the rest of his appearance. His bare arms bore numerous gold bracelets, and a golden circlet rested on his red hair. His face was handsome but unremarkable – straight nose, heavy brows, square jaw, but his eyes blazed with scarlet flame, and the imperious look on the man's face made him cower.

The man raised one eyebrow. "*You* are the Arbor's Selected." He spoke flatly, unimpressed.

Tahir's mouth went dry. "Yes."

The man's eyes burned into him. Tahir couldn't look away. "Who are you?" Tahir whispered.

It seemed as if the eyes were hot brands, boring through his pupils into his brain, as if the man was searching inside his mind to read his thoughts. "I am Pyra. I am King of the Incendi."

Tahir could only stare. He knelt in front of the King of the fire elementals. "But you are a man..." he stuttered.

Pyra laughed. "I have taken the body of many men over the years. This is but the latest in a long line." Power radiated from the King, hot and fierce as the magma bubbling in the channel. Sweat poured down Tahir from the heat and the fear.

"You think you are a challenge to me?" mocked the King.

Tahir shook his head. "No, sir."

Pyra leaned forward, elbows on his knees, to glare at the young prince. "Do you think you are anything to me but an ant crawling on the ground? I could shrivel you to ash with a flick of my fingers." His voice seemed to make the air rumble like thunder, and Tahir was sure he felt the ground tremble.

He said nothing, bending his head so low it almost touched the rock. However, deep inside him, something struck like a hammer on a bell. If the King was so powerful, if he could remove him from the world with a blink of an eyelid, why hadn't he killed him?

"Get up," the King snapped.

Tahir lifted his head and sat back on his heels. Terror made him shake, but still he nurtured the small seed of light within him that repeated the words, *why hasn't he killed me?*

"You were being taken to Heartwood," Pyra said. "To the Arbor."

"Yes." Tahir's teeth chattered, but he made himself lift his chin and look the King in the face. He was a prince, the son of a king, he reminded himself. He was neither this man's minion nor his slave.

Pyra studied him, eyes narrowed. "What will happen when I kill you and the Arbor has no sacrifice?" His voice held a hint of scorn, as if he knew the answer and was mocking the Prince.

Tahir's hands tightened into fists, but still he met the fire king's gaze. "They will find another. My death will mean nothing to them but an inconvenience."

Pyra's eyes gleamed, dancing with fire. "That is not what I have been led to believe. The Selected are not just individuals chosen at random. They are distinct and unique. They are written in the fabric of time, their names are fixed points we cannot change. You lie by pretending they are meaningless. You think you can fool me?" Again the ground trembled beneath Tahir's feet.

Still the Prince remained upright, drawing his courage around him like a cloak. "That is what I believed. My father paid the most money. He bought my place as a Selected."

Pyra's lips curled. "You are the most foolish child I have met since I became flesh. You think because it appears the sacrifice is a game of chance, the tree has not chosen you?"

Tahir stared, speechless. The King's words echoed Demitto's, *The Arbor knows your worth. And to it, you are more precious than gold.* Could it be true that the Arbor had in fact chosen him? His heart swelled.

And then he blinked, his brief euphoria dying. It could not be true. He was not special, or brave, or clever, or anything exceptional.

But maybe once a person was Selected, the Arbor saw them as belonging to it. Maybe being Selected had made him special, and now the Arbor knew of him, it did not want to let him go.

The King of the Incendi had brought him and Horada here, somewhere in the mountains, because he wanted to control the convergence of the timelines. Maybe the third line – the young girl he had seen in the darkness with the man with the silver hair – was on her way there too. The easiest thing would be to destroy them, to change history, to make it impossible for the Apex to take place.

But although his eyes flamed and his temper shook the room, the King had not killed him.

Maybe he couldn't.

Tahir's heart pounded and for a moment he thought he might faint from fear. He couldn't believe he was about to do what he was about to do. He expected his life would end here, in this pit of molten rock. His life back in Harlton was over – he could never return there. If the King raised his hand and turned him to cinders, he probably wouldn't feel a thing. He had nothing to lose, and for the first time in his life, he felt a flutter of faith that maybe he *was* special, perhaps he *did* have something to give to the world.

He pushed himself to his knees, then his feet, and stood before the King.

"If you truly believe I belong to the Arbor, then kill me now," he shouted.

The King's eyes widened, and he stood to face the young prince. He was tall – taller than any man Tahir had ever met – and he towered over him, his power and anger as imposing as his physical build. His eyes spat sparks and around them the magma bubbled and smoke filled the air.

"I can fell whole forests with one breath!" boomed the King. "I can melt glaciers and turn gold and rock to rivers. I can change the very fabric of this world!"

Tahir shook so hard his manacles rattled, but still he stood his ground. "But you cannot kill me," he guessed. "The Arbor will not let you take me."

Pyra struck him across the face. Tahir had never been hit before, and he collapsed with a cry, his cheek throbbing with pain.

"I can kill you," the King snarled. "Do not mistake me. I let you live because crushing you now would not be as powerful as waiting for the right moment. Let me elaborate." He reached down, put a hand under Tahir's arm and hauled him up. Half-leading, half-dragging him, Pyra led him across the bridge, through the doorway and along the maze of corridors. Tahir stumbled beside him, tearful and frightened. The King could not kill him, but he could hurt him, and he feared pain beyond almost anything else, even beyond death.

They walked for what seemed like miles, and then they turned a corner and passed through a large doorway. Tahir blinked, confused by the sudden change in atmosphere. He stood in a large open space, and although still obviously underground, the ceiling was much higher, what seemed like miles above his head. He stood on a small platform overlooking the huge cavern. On one side, blacksmiths forged iron into weapons, the water used to cool their metal adding more steam to the fog-filled air. On the other, soldiers marched or practised swordplay, the immense army stretching as far as the eye could see.

Tahir looked over his shoulder, only then realising what sort of building he had been in. He stood about halfway up a huge pyramid formed from solid blocks of stone. The base seemed miles wide, and the three walls narrowed to a point that almost reached the ceiling, which was filled with carvings, inlaid with gold, jewels and coloured paints. Many had faded, the carvings worn almost smooth, and Tahir gained the impression that the pyramid was ancient. The Incendi had been there for millennia, he thought, gradually growing in power and size. Horada had mentioned that the elementals hadn't been able to take human form in her time. Over the last five hundred years, Pyra had developed a way for his followers to possess men so he could enter the earth elementals' realm, and now he was building an army to take over the world.

"I *will* crush you," the King snarled, thrusting him forward to the balcony and holding him there. "And then the element of fire will be in the ascendancy once again. I swear on the souls of every Incendi under my rule."

And Tahir believed him.

III

Comminor had reached the bottom of the rope.

He hung there for a while, exhausted, the tumbling water weighing heavy on his shoulders like a thick cloak.

He had reached the Magna Cataracta just as Geve – the curly haired friend of Sarra he hated so much – disappeared over the edge. Comminor had rushed up in time to see Geve's look of alarm as he lowered himself down the waterfall, and the Chief Select's first thought was to hack away at the rope and let Geve plunge to his death. Nothing would have given him greater satisfaction than to hear the screams of the man who had dared to dance with Sarra, the girl who haunted his dreams.

But if he wanted to stand any hope of catching the rebel party before they reached the Surface, he had to follow them over the falls, and as they didn't have any rope themselves, it meant using the one they had tied to the lantern.

Comminor had reached over to try and pull the rope up, but even with the five of them it had proved impossible against the weight of the water. And then the rope had gone slack, so he knew Geve must have reached the bottom – or fallen. Either way, it was time to follow them down.

"We are going down there?" Josse, the youngest Select, stared at the mass of tumbling water with wide eyes.

"We are." Comminor climbed onto the edge of the slippery rocks. "I will go first. I will try to send you a signal or tug the rope, to let you know when I am at the bottom. If I cannot and the rope goes slack..." He hoisted himself up onto the middle of the rocks and held tightly to the rope. "It is up to you whether you follow me."

"We will follow," Viel said, and the three others with him nodded.

Comminor nodded. "I will see you at the bottom."

His stomach had flipped as he lowered himself over the edge into the black tunnel, but once he disappeared into the darkness he had settled into a rhythmical movement. It had seemed to go on forever, descending hand over hand, one leg wrapped around the rope to try to keep himself stable. It had proved difficult, the weight of the water thundering onto his shoulders, and he was half blind with it most of the time; not that it mattered as the light faded quickly above him, and soon all he could see was the faint shine of the water around him from the last remnants of the lantern's light.

But he had kept going, and then all of a sudden his foot slipped off and he realised he had reached the end.

He hung there, swinging a little from side to side. How far was left until he reached the bottom? Should he just let go and hope it was only a few feet? Would he fall onto rocks or into a pool? Perhaps the members of the Veris had all fallen and perished, and his body would join theirs and float away into the darkness.

What alternatives did he have? To climb all the way back up to the top? Even if he could do that, and he was not sure he had the strength, it would mean admitting failure. He would never know what had happened to the Veris, and that was unacceptable. He *had* to pursue them and stop them trying to escape. He had made that solemn vow when he joined the Nox Aves, had promised to keep the population of the Embers safe, and after a life of dedication to that cause, he could not now go back on it.

Plus, deep down, he could not bear the thought of letting Sarra go.

Reluctant to release the rope, he threw his head back out of the force of the water and reached out a hand. As he swung, it just brushed the other side of the tunnel. The water had obviously carved out a channel for itself over the thousands of years it had plunged through these caverns. But it gave him no idea how much further the water had to fall.

He strained his ears. Was it his imagination, or did it seem as if the already deafening noise of the water increased somewhere below him? He was sure it did, which suggested the bottom. But was that bottom water meeting rock, or the churning of water meeting water?

There was no way of telling. He had no choice but to take the plunge, literally.

His heart in his mouth, he let go of the rope.

He fell about twenty feet, the weight of his bag pulling him so he landed on his back in the water, and plunged beneath the surface. His arm struck rock on the way down and pain shot through him, and an involuntary gasp forced water into his mouth and gave him a moment of panic. But he had swum often in the Great Lake as a child and in the palace pool since becoming Chief Select, and he was used to the water. He kicked hard and ignored the pain to swim strongly upwards.

His head broke the surface and he gasped air, taking a few minutes to get to grips with his situation. He was in complete darkness, the river crashing into the pool a short distance to his right, but he had no idea how big the pool was or where he should swim. He forced himself to stay calm, to regulate his breathing, and he listened carefully to see if he could tell which way to go.

To his left the river continued to tumble, and he sensed it carried on its journey along a channel in that direction. So he should swim either forward or backwards and see if he could find the riverbank. He chose forward, knowing he had to get out of the way of the water in case the next member of the Umbra followed him down and fell on top of him.

He kicked out and swam with strong thrusts of his arms, wincing as pain shot through his shoulder. He had done some damage striking that rock, but at least he had not landed directly on it – he could have broken both his legs.

He was alive! Exultancy shot through him. At least he had that to be thankful for.

He stopped for a moment and trod water. No sign of the bottom. Something brushed against his legs and he recoiled, kicking out. Probably just a turtle or a salamander, he thought, but still, who knew what creatures lurked in the darkness?

He swam a few more feet, and then suddenly his knees bumped the ground, taking him by surprise. He lowered his feet and stumbled out of the shallows onto the river bank, collapsing onto the silty surface. He'd done it. He'd reached the edge.

He lay there for a while, gathering his strength, waiting. His shoulder throbbed, but he couldn't tell if it was bleeding while everything was soaking. The air was warm, but still he shivered. He would have to change into the clothes he'd wrapped in the treated leather bag – hopefully it wouldn't have let in much water. But first he had to find out what kind of place he was in.

He sat up, grasped his sunstone pendant and held out his hand. He imagined fire flooding him, flowing through his veins. The flame leapt to life on his palm, and he raised it to look around.

His breath caught in his throat. The Embers consisted of a series of natural caverns that had been added to over the years by generations of its inhabitants, the irregular walls gradually polished to smooth rock, but here and there in the outer reaches, the natural surface remained. This was what he had expected – a roughly hewn cavern, untouched and irregular.

Instead, his gaze fell on a large square room. The waterfall descended through a hole that took up a quarter of the ceiling to his left, the tumultuous water tumbling into a pool that stretched from the ground at his feet to the opposite bank some thirty feet away. The water then fed into a river that hurried away to his right through a wide corridor flanked by a walkway on either side.

Slowly, he pushed himself to his feet, wincing at the ache in his shoulder, and turned in a circle to look around the room. The walls glimmered in the light of the flame, and as he neared them he could see why. They were covered with paintings and gold leaf, thousands of shapes, some patterns like triangles and dots and wavy lines, some that looked vaguely like figures painted in reds and oranges, and lots and lots of flame shapes filled with yellows and golds.

"Incendi," he murmured. He had read about them in the Quercetum. And he knew what they had done.

Moving around the room, he reached the corridor where the river flowed away, and peered around the corner. There was no sign of the Veris, and no bodies left lying around the room. Presumably they had all made it down the Cataracta intact, and had swiftly moved onwards.

He itched to follow them, but knew he had to wait for the Umbra to arrive. A strangled yell at that moment made him turn, and he saw a figure falling through the hole in the ceiling to plunge into the pool below. He paced to the bank, held his hand aloft to light the way, and waited for the person to rise.

Viel's dark head broke the surface, and he coughed and spluttered, shaking the water out of his eyes as he turned to find the source of the light.

"Swim this way," Comminor instructed. "The water is shallow here – mind your knees."

Viel swam strongly towards him, face filled with relief. "It took me ages to let go of the rope," he admitted as he dragged himself onto the bank.

"Me also." Comminor helped him up.

Viel turned and sat, waiting for his strength to return. "I thought I might land on rock. I seemed to fall forever." He looked around, wiping his face. "Where are we?"

"Not quite where I expected," Comminor said wryly. He walked forward and tried to look up the hole in the ceiling, but the torrential downpour of water forced him back. "Who is next?"

"Paronel."

They waited a while for her to descend, walking around the room and inspecting the pictures on the wall.

"Who are they?" Viel ran his fingers lightly over the painted figures.

"I do not know." Comminor was not ready to share the history of the *Quercetum*. His Umbra followed him unquestioningly, and although he knew it might be useful in the future to share his knowledge, now was not the time. "I think I hear something."

They both walked to the edge of the river and, sure enough, in a few moments Paronel came hurtling down and landed with a squeal in the water.

"Azorius is next," she panted as she hauled herself to the side. "Smoke and fire, that took some courage to let go of the rope." She looked at Comminor as she wrung out her long blonde hair, obviously noting how he held his arm. "You are hurt?"

"It is nothing." He did not reveal how much his shoulder throbbed.

He let Viel answer Paronel's questions about the room and waited for the next arrival.

He did not have long to wait. A scream filled the room and Comminor's body jerked towards the water automatically as Azorius plummeted down only to land flat on the rock that Comminor had struck his arm on.

Comminor did not have to go over to the body to know the Umbra was dead, his neck and back broken, his eyes lifeless. Anger and futility flooded him, and he tipped back his head and let out a howl.

Josse followed not long after, missing the rock by a hair's breadth. He surfaced and stared silently at the lifeless figure before swimming to the side.

"Should we bring his body over here?" Paronel said, teeth chattering.

Comminor shook his head. His throat felt thick with emotion, but his voice, when he spoke, was firm and clear as ever. "We do not have the time." He turned away from the body. "Let us see if any of us has any dry clothes. We will get changed, and then set off after the Veris."

He tipped the items out of his own bag and they began sorting through. Had all the Veris made it to the bottom unharmed? It didn't look as if anyone had died or they would probably have left the body there, too, he thought.

He pulled on his other tunic and breeches, which were only very slightly damp. Inside, rage boiled. It was Sarra's fault that Azorius was dead. He could not believe he had taken her to his bed, and all along she had been planning to leave.

He would make her pay for that.

CHAPTER THIRTEEN

I

When the fire washed over Horada, Julen roared with rage. If he could, he would have turned and ridden back into the forest to try to rescue her, but his horse bolted, too scared of the flames. It was all he could do to hang onto the reins as the horse exited the treeline and fled across the fields.

It took him several minutes to calm him and bring him under control, and by the time the gelding finally slowed to a halt, they were both trembling. Julen was sure the whites of his eyes were as visible as the horse's.

"There, there," he murmured comfortingly, even though his own heart continued to pound. He slid from the saddle and led the horse over to a fence bordering the field. "The fire will not get you here."

He glanced over his shoulder to make sure that was the case, seeing to his surprise that the flames in the forest had already died down. Waiting a few minutes until the gelding had calmed, Julen walked back across the field to the edge of the forest.

To his shock, the trees were for the most part untouched. Some of the undergrowth had been turned to ash and several trees had fallen, but it was as if the flames had picked and chosen which branches and leaves would burn, and had left the remainder. How was that possible? Clearly, it had not been a natural fire. The Incendi had snaked their way through the forest, and the only places to catch fire had been those the elementals had touched.

He drew his sword – although what good the blade would do against a fire elemental, he wasn't sure – and walked into the trees. Silence enveloped him, the birds and creatures having fled, even the wind dying down to a whisper. He wove through the trees until he reached the spot where he was sure Horada would have fallen.

There was no sign of her.

There were, however, the smoking remains of her horse.

Julen stopped in front of the skeleton, his chest heaving with indignation at what they had done to Mara. She had possessed a sweet and gentle nature and had been Horada's favourite for several years. Now her hair and mane had been burned away, her flesh charred, and the smell of roasting meat arose to assail his nostrils. He scanned the remains to make sure none of the bones belonged to a woman, but he had no doubt, Horada was not there.

His gaze raked the forest, but she had vanished. The elementals must have taken her, he thought.

He wished he had the time to bury Mara, but the forest would gradually welcome her into its arms. He did not want to waste a moment now he knew the Incendi had taken his sister.

As he made his way back to his horse, he took comfort from the fact that they did not appear to have killed her. Although the Nox Aves had come to the conclusion that the mysterious deaths occurring across Anguis had been caused by the Incendi removing those it thought important for the Apex to occur, for some reason it appeared they wanted Horada alive. Although pleasing, that in itself was puzzling.

He reached the horse, untied his reins and walked with him a little way to a stream where he let the gelding drink and graze for a while. Moving a short distance away, he knelt down by a clump of bushes and took the pendant Gravis had given him from around his neck.

He stroked his thumb across the wooden oak leaf, enjoying the frisson of warmth that spread through his hand. Knowing he carried a piece of the Arbor against his chest brought him comfort and strength during this time of uncertainty. The sunstone in the middle gleamed, catching the sunlight and giving him an unwelcome reminder of the flames in the forest.

Giving the wood one final brush, he pushed the pendant into the earth.

For a moment, nothing happened. Then, as before, the ground began to tremble. Heat rushed through him, and briefly he was swept up in the energy from the Arbor's roots, the channels that spread across the whole of Anguis.

He tried to quell the wave of fear he felt at the memory of what had happened last time. A creature had appeared before him: a firebird, with eyes that had branded him with white-hot heat. He had been certain it was the King of the Incendi, and he had never been so frightened at the thought that his enemy had seen him and knew where he was.

Afterwards, Gravis had reassured him that it was possible for him to remain out of the King's vision – that the sunstone protected him. "We picked you for your special connection to the Arbor," the Peacemaker had reminded him. "Now you must begin to turn that to our advantage."

Focus, Julen told himself, remembering Gravis's instructions on how to protect himself while using the pendant. Just like when he used his abilities to camouflage himself, now he drew his energy tight around him, imagining himself like a shadow, unobtrusive and invisible to the untrained eye. And then he was ready to begin.

First, he thought of his sister. Last time, he had found her almost immediately. He had pictured her in his mind's eye, painted her face and hair and thought of her bright spirit and teasing sense of humour, and the connection between them had sprung into place, drawing him straight to her.

This time it was different. He imagined her standing there before him, but although he felt himself travel to the west and reach out towards the mountains, there the trail stopped as if he had run into a stone wall. She was alive – that much he could tell. But the connection refused to form.

How was he to find her when he had no idea where she had gone?

Looking for comfort, he reached out instead to his brother, only to find once again the connection failed to form. Confused, he deepened the search, stretching out his senses as far as he could, but all he could get was an image of fire, of burning houses, trees aflame and bodies lying charred on the ground.

Nausea rose inside him, threatening to choke him for a moment. Did that mean Orsin was dead? He couldn't be sure – he hadn't been doing this for long enough. He didn't get the same feeling he got when he thought of his father – a sensation of peace and rest, of completeness. Instead he felt unease and anger, a sense of being scattered, of being lost. His brother was alive, he thought. But not happy, and not whole.

His throat tightened, and his concentration waned. He became aware of his hands resting atop the warm wooden pendant, and the coolness of the earth. The stream sang merrily off to his right, and he could hear the quiet munching of the gelding as it snacked on the grass.

He went to sit back and release the pendant, but as he did so, found his hands somehow glued to the wood. He couldn't move. He opened his eyes and looked up, alarmed to see the air before him glittering. The morning darkened as if storm clouds had moved overhead, although the sun still shone way off in the east.

The sparkling air darkened even more, the particles

drawing together to form a shape. A figure, cloaked in grey, face covered by the hood, silent and still in the semi-darkness.

Julen froze. "Who are you?" he whispered.

"I am Cinereo," came the deep voice. "Founder of the Nox Aves. Do not be afraid."

Julen's panic died down. Gravis had told him of the man, and he trusted the Peacemaker with his life.

"How are you here?" Julen asked. "Are you in Heartwood?"

"I am in many places," Cinereo said. "The Arbor grants me the gift of travel along its roots. Our pendants connect us, young Viator."

Julen frowned. "Viator?"

"It is the name the Arbor gives to its personal messengers."

A glow spread through Julen. The Arbor thought of himself as its messenger?

"Can you see where my sister and brother are?" he asked. "They are both lost to me, and I fear for their lives."

Cinereo said nothing for a moment, his head bowed. Then he said simply, "They live. But Orsin is weak. He has not the strength to fight the Incendi. He has succumbed to temptation and is lost to us."

Julen clenched his jaw. "I will not believe that."

"Trying to change what cannot be changed is like trying to swim against the current," Cinereo said.

"I will not lose faith in him," Julen said hoarsely. "He may not be perfect, but he is my brother, and all the time he lives, he will never be lost to me."

Cinereo said nothing. Julen swallowed, unease rippling through him at having spoken back to the obviously powerful scholar. But he refused to give up on Orsin, even though he drove him to distraction with his irreverence and flippancy at times.

"What of Horada?" Julen asked. "I traced her to the mountains but lost her there."

"She lies within the rock," Cinereo stated. "Pyra, the King of the Incendi, has taken her."

Julen went cold. "Is that who I saw last time I used the pendant?"

"Yes. His spirit lay beneath Anguis for many millennia, trapped there by the Arbor and kept in place by bonds too strong for the Incendi to break free. But the elements are once again out of balance and the bonds are weakening. Fire is rising, and one day it will sweep the world."

Julen saw images of whole towns bursting into flames, of sheets of fire consuming vast forests, turning every living thing it passed over into ash.

"Then all is lost?" he murmured.

Cinereo held up a hand. "It is never the end while we have love, faith and hope. And you have all three in abundance, my friend."

Julen swallowed. What use were those emotions when the world was doomed?

"Nothing is certain," Cinereo murmured as if he had read the young man's mind. "The battle will be won by those who are strongest of heart, and the Arbor's followers have hearts strong enough to lift mountains." He let his hand drop in a sweeping motion, and the glittering dust felt across Julen like rain. "Believe."

Julen's eyes closed at the brush of dust on his lashes, and immediately he saw in his mind's eye his mother, tall and strong, her greying hair in its customary knot at the nape of her neck. The connection formed immediately, his energy reaching out to her, linking them together.

She was north of the Wall, west of Kettlestan, the darkness of the forest close around her. He could smell the rich loam and the green trees, and he could feel the race of her heart and her grim determination to flee, so he knew she was being pursued. The Incendi? Or was someone else after her?

He had never known his mother to portray fear, but for the first time in his life he could sense her anxiety. She had lost her daughter, lost Orsin, and now she thought herself all alone. He thought of them – his sister, his brother, his mother – all lost, all alone.

Cinereo's words echoed in his ears, ringing through him like a bell. *It is never the end while we have love, faith and hope. And you have all three in abundance, my friend.*

Julen's father had only ever discussed his part in repelling the Darkwater invasion once. Oh, Chonrad had enjoyed relaying the events of the Last Stand at length after a few ales, and Julen had lost count of the number of times he had heard his father retelling the story to friends and family. But although he described the water warriors, the great battle at the end and the wonder with which they had all watched the Arbor grow, he had only recounted the moment he opened the fifth node in the depths of the labyrinth once.

He had related how the Arbor had told him it required something from him. Chonrad had not known what he could possibly possess that the Arbor would need. But it had turned out to be his strength. Not his physical strength, although that was more impressive than most. But the strength of his heart. In spite of his fearsome ability in battle, Chonrad had been courageous, compassionate and kind, and the Arbor had seen this, and asked him for help when it needed him most.

The pendant grew hot in Julen's hand, and he inhaled as he let the love for his family sweep through him. He thought of his father – how much he had loved and admired him, and he thought of his siblings and his mother and how glad he was that he had been born into that family and no other, much as sometimes they clashed and drove each other mad.

And as he thought of the Arbor, the love he bore for the tree and the land in which it grew, so the tree loomed large in his mind, as clear as if he stood beneath it in the shade of its leaves. He had only been to Heartwood on a few occasions, but as he knelt there holding the pendant carved from part of the holy tree, he connected with it as surely as if he stood there with his hands on its trunk, feeling its heart – the Pectoris that Dolosus had been compelled to dive to the bottom of the ocean to recover – beat beneath his fingertips.

Energy shot from him, pure and clear, rushing along the Arbor's roots to his family, enveloping them in his love, and carrying with it the message he carried in his heart.

I love you. I am here for you.

You are not alone.

II

The tunnels were stiflingly hot, the semi-darkness like a woollen blanket laying over them, thick and suffocating. Demitto wanted to push the damp air away from his mouth, almost choking on the humidity.

Anguis's weather had changed over the last few years, growing steadily more tropical. In the past, he had trekked through the jungle, descended into some of Hanaire's deepest silver mines and spent a week in Wulfengar's famous hot pools, so he was well aware of the changing climate. But he had never encountered anything like this.

Catena held up a hand, and he stopped walking and closed his fist over the flame that had danced there. Atavus bumped his nose against his legs, subdued and uneasy underground. They plunged into darkness as if falling into a vat of black treacle, and he clutched hold of the rock wall, heart pounding at the sensation of being lost in an infinite void.

"I have you," Catena whispered, and her small hand crept into his. He said nothing but clutched hold of it gratefully, using the feel of her warm skin to anchor him to reality.

"What can you sense?" he murmured, his mouth close to her ear.

She moved beside him, and then a faint glow appeared around the hand she had pressed against the rock. Demitto watched her concentrate, admiring the way the silvery light painted her cheeks and nose.

"We are getting closer," she whispered.

He didn't bother to hide his sigh of relief. They had been walking for what seemed like hours, although he was sure it couldn't have been that long. The intricate maze of tunnels led deep into the mountainside, and he had been lost within the first few minutes after half a dozen twists and turns. Numerous times they had had to duck into side passages to avoid people walking through the tunnels, and twice they walked around a corner straight into guards.

He had been impressed with the way Catena handled a sword. Although in Laxony it wasn't unusual for women to enter the standing army of a local lord, there had generally been peace in the four countries over the last hundred years. The world had grown lazy, and highly trained soldiers of either sex were few and far between.

But Catena had defended herself and dispatched the Incendi guards with skill. He reminded himself she was Chief of the Guard at Harlton, in charge of training the castle watch, and clearly not to be underestimated.

But at that moment, her skill with the sword was not the most impressive thing about her. He knew of the Saxum and their skill in reading stone, but he had never seen one in action before. Catena appeared as surprised as he by her new talent and had initially been reluctant to use it, sure Cinereo had been mistaken. But Demitto had encouraged her to try it, and just moments after she placed her hands on the wall of the tunnel, her eyes had widened, and he knew she was receiving sensations through the rock.

She opened her eyes and her hand dropped. "This way," she whispered, "the passage is clear."

He formed a flame on his palm and then they were off again, turning seemingly indiscriminately this way and that into the heart of the mountain. He buried his hand in Atavus's fur the same way Tahir had done, finding comfort in the presence of the dog beside him.

Once again, it seemed as if they walked for hours. Demitto was glad he wasn't wearing his armour. The sweat ran down him in rivulets, dripped into his eyes and made his palms slippery. They drank regularly from their leather water bottles, but he worried they would eventually run out, and that would not be good. The only way out of these tunnels would be by walking; he didn't think he would be strong enough to carry Catena if he was dehydrated, and there was certainly no way she could carry him!

Catena slowed and then stopped, and turned to look up at him, puzzled. "Can you hear that?"

He could, and had been aware of it for some time – a low rumble through the rock, almost more of a sensation than a sound, vibrating up through his feet and legs, up his spine, making his head and teeth ache.

"What is it?" she asked.

"I do not know." He had a feeling it couldn't be something good. He didn't think he had to put that into words though – the look on Catena's face expressed his thoughts.

As they moved forward, he stumbled on some loose rock and reached out to get his balance. Then he exclaimed out loud.

She turned, eyes wide. "What is it?"

"The wall." He rested his palm on it. Ever since they had entered the tunnels, he had been surprised that the rock was warm rather than cool. When delving into Anguis's depths, the mines and caves usually became dryer and colder the deeper one went.

But this time, the rock was hot. He could not leave his palm there for longer than a few seconds before having to pull it away.

Catena did the same, concern flickering in her eyes. "What does it mean?"

He shook his head, unease filtering through him.

They walked down a long passage, met another at the end, and she turned right. The air grew thick and moist, as if someone had placed a damp cloth over his mouth and nose. The rumbling increased, and the heat became intense.

They rounded the corner, and both of them stopped dead in shock. His hand tightened in Atavus's fur, stopping the dog from leaping forward. The passageway opened into a large chamber, the pathway running around the edge of the room several feet above the floor. The reason for this was that the entire floor consisted of rock heated to such a temperature that it became liquid, flowing in a scarlet river that burped and boiled and spat.

"Arbor's roots," Catena swore. "I have never seen anything like it."

Demitto just stared. She had never seen anything like it because there had never been anything like it in Anguis before. The country was not – nor had ever been in written history – a volcanic one. He had read of such places in far distant lands, where the rock turned molten and mountains spat ash and lava that ran down into the valleys to cool eventually into folds of grey stone, but he had never seen such a phenomenon himself.

The magma fascinated him, and he could not tear his eyes away from it. Although the heat seared his skin and it was hard to breathe, the moving liquefied rock hypnotised him. It swirled in ridges of yellow and gold, and darkened in the centre to a deep red-black. It was almost like smoke, and he could imagining it wreathing around him, entwining him like tree roots, loving and tender in its touch…

"Demitto!" Catena shrieked and grabbed his arm, and at the same time Atavus leapt forward and sank his teeth into his tunic, holding him back. With alarm, he realised he was teetering on the edge of the platform, about to plunge into the fiery depths. The river spat sparks at him that burned into his clothing. His face flared with pain, and he was sure his eyebrows had been seared off.

He fell backwards, and Catena rushed to flick off the hot rock eating into his clothes like acid, squealing as her hand touched it. Atavus licked his ear.

"What were you doing?" Her heartfelt sobs wrenched at him.

"I do not know." He lay back, panting, heart pounding at the thought of what he had nearly done.

"I nearly lost you." Tears ran down her face, drying instantly on her cheeks. "You cannot leave me – I cannot do this without you."

"It is all right, I am still here." He put his arms around her, trying not to wince at the tenderness of his burned skin, and held her close. "I will not leave you."

She buried her face in his shoulder and cried. "I have to find Tahir. He will be so scared without me. I cannot leave him to the Incendi."

"We will find him," he assured her. Once again, the feel of her soft skin, the smell of her hair, grounded him, and pulled him back to reality.

She lifted her head to look at him. Her tears had dried immediately, leaving her cheeks streaked, her eyes red, but she was so beautiful she took his breath away.

He pushed away Atavus's inquisitive nose, slipped a hand into Catena's hair, and kissed her.

She didn't return it, but neither did she pull away. He pressed his lips against hers once, twice, then lay back.

They stared at each other for a moment. Then they looked at the bubbling magma.

"We should go," she said, and he nodded and let her pull him to his feet.

They made their way up the platform through the chamber of molten rock. Demitto cursed himself under his breath, keeping well to the side away from the edge. What in Arbor's name was wrong with him? Why had he been entranced by the magma, and why in all Anguis had he kissed Catena? That had been the last thing on his mind, with his hair singed and his skin raw from the heat.

Uneasy, slightly embarrassed and thoroughly fed up with being drenched with his own sweat, he followed her, Atavus hot on his heels, as the platform sloped upwards and led through a doorway.

And once again, they came shuddering to a halt, astounded at the view in front of them.

This time, the room wasn't just big – it was vast. The platform they stood on jutted out from the rock halfway up the wall, and ran around three sides of the roughly square cavern. Dark doorways led from it on all sides into more passageways, leading off into what Demitto now realised was a complex far greater than he had imagined lay beneath the Spina Mountains.

The fourth wall was partly obscured by a gigantic pyramid.

Demitto stared, mouth open, stunned into silence. Formed by rectangular blocks of stone, the pyramid's three walls reached up to a point only feet from the roof of the cavern. The entrance on the side facing him looked ten times taller than a man, fronted with huge doors that stood open to reveal a glittering, golden interior. The doors were flanked by two massive statues, painted and decorated in gold leaf to look like leaping flames.

All four walls of the chamber were also covered in paintings. Demitto had seen ancient art in caves in Hanaire, and tree carvings from hundreds of years ago in Komis, but again, nothing like this. Bright colours covered faded pictures, building layer upon layer of Incendi history. Hundreds of scenes showed battles between tribes, worship of gods, kings rising and falling, sacrifices and deaths. The cavern portrayed a whole civilisation, which had obviously existed for thousands of years.

But what chilled him more than the thought of this whole world existing beneath his own were the thousands of men and women working in the cavern below them. On the far side, he could see numerous furnaces making armour and weapons, and people training with those weapons, building up their strength and skill. Even from up high, he could see their red eyes, and he knew they had all been possessed by Incendi.

It was an army in the making, and although sweat still rolled off him and steam swirled in the air, he felt as if he had swallowed ice.

"Arbor help us," Catena whispered, and he knew she had also realised what was happening. He had known the elementals were now taking over people, but he had not realised the extent of their possession. They were building an army to take to the surface, to take over Anguis and defeat the element of earth for good.

Catena's hand crept into his, and his fingers tightened on it. Cinereo and the Nox Aves had no idea. They had sent him to save Tahir so he could help save the world, but how was he to find him and rescue him now?

Demitto knew he was a confident man – maybe even an arrogant one. He had great faith in his own abilities, and when the Nox Aves had approached him during one of his random visits to Heartwood, he had accepted their mission without giving it much thought. His initiation into the group and their stories about how events were unfolding had shocked and fascinated him, but even though he believed everything they told him, it had not affected him on a deep level.

He was a man who lived for the moment, who appreciated the food, drink, people, countryside and events occurring right in front of him. He wasn't prone to analysing life, and concentrated on the physical world rather than the emotional or metaphysical one. He understood what was happening with the Incendi and desired to stop them, but his faith wasn't deep or strong and thus hadn't been threatened by what he'd learned.

For the first time, though, real, true panic flared inside him. This threat wasn't some imaginary force dreamt up by scholars interpreting Arbor-knew-what from ancient tomes and fabricating threats. This was real. Anguis was in huge danger.

And he and Catena were the only ones standing in the way of the Incendi.

He gritted his teeth. Good to know there was no pressure.

III

Although a burning fear filled Sarra that pushed her to keep on moving, she reluctantly agreed they had to stop for a while to rest. Even though she did her daily perambulation of the Embers' main roads the same as many of its citizens, she had never walked so far for so long. Her leg muscles ached, and she felt that if she sat for too long, her eyes would close and she would probably sleep for weeks.

Part of her tiredness was due to a matter that had become apparent the further they walked from the Embers. At first she had thought she was imagining it, conjuring it up out of a combination of tiredness, fear and panic about the fact that she was supposed to be leading the group, and she had no idea where she was going. She tried to concentrate on her surroundings, her fingers trailing over the paintings on the walls as they walked, her ears straining for any sounds of others ahead, but she grew to realise that although the drawings spoke of an ancient civilisation, they were there no longer, and the place felt deserted, the corridors silent and cold.

And because there was little else to distract her, her companions as silent and withdrawn as herself, she couldn't help but notice the changes in her body, and eventually had to admit the truth.

The baby was growing.

And not just that – the baby was growing *fast*.

It had been moving for a while, but since they left the city its kicks had grown stronger, and her bump had grown to the point that she had to loosen the belt around her waist. She had not been with child before, but she had observed many pregnancies in those around her, and she knew enough about the process to understand that what she was experiencing was unnatural.

Still, she kept the news to herself, aware that her condition was the least of their worries at that moment. For Kytte – who had struck the rock during the fall from the Cataracta into the pool and almost certainly broken a couple of ribs, if not more – was in great pain and obviously finding it difficult to walk at any speed.

Sarra watched Geve and Amabil tend to her while Betune stood beside them, holding up the bag she carried around her neck. Sarra's gaze was drawn by the bag, which glowed with a golden light, illuminating the small party where they sat in the corner of an empty room.

To the amazement of everyone – including Betune – she had emerged from the pool to find herself lit up, and on realising the glow came from the bag, she had withdrawn the acorn inside and held it on her palm for them all to see. It was almost too bright to look at, shimmering as if sprinkled with golden dust, a lantern for them to follow in the darkness of the caves.

None of them had had an answer as to why it had reacted in such a way. As they gathered initially, supporting Kytte and trying to bind up her ribs to ease her pain, they speculated that the Arbor knew they were coming and was trying to guide them, leading them on to their new life. The thought gave them hope at a time when despair kept rising inside them, and made them feel the Arbor was there, supporting them, and that this wasn't a futile journey – that the reward was there waiting for them. It had lifted their spirits as they comforted Kytte, and had given Sarra heart.

But even though the acorn still glowed, Sarra's heart was beginning to sink. She had heard a bellow far off in the distance, and although she couldn't be sure, instinct told her it was Comminor. He had followed them down the rope. He would not let them go free, and the thought of his anger and what he would do to her if he found her had kept her heart pumping and her legs moving with the intent of putting as much distance between them as they could.

But they couldn't walk forever, and she had no idea how far it was to the Surface. She had hoped that once they left the Embers, the knowledge would flower in her mind and she would receive the image of some sort of map, or at least a strong instinct of which way was correct. But so far nothing had happened to guide her. She had wandered along the maze of passages blindly, turning randomly, too worried to admit to the others that she didn't know the way, and too afraid to stop and wait for the knowledge to come.

Perhaps she had been mistaken and it had all been a dream, something her mind had made up to fool this poor, pitiful woman – who had barely anything to call her own – that she mattered, that her life was worth living. Maybe it had been a creation of a mind intent on survival, even to the extent of trying to fool the body in which it resided?

She pressed the heels of her hands into her eyes. She could not give up hope or she wouldn't be able to take another step. She had to believe it was all real. The glowing acorn, the baby's rapid growth – these must all be signs that they were nearing the Surface, and that the road they were on – literally and metaphorically – was the right one.

She lifted her head. "We should get going."

Nele met her gaze, his eyes glinting in the golden light. "I do not think Kytte can carry on."

She looked across at the injured girl. Kytte lay on her side, her face bleached of all colour, features racked with pain. Her breath rattled, and blood already seeped through the bandages they had tried to wrap around her.

"I think the broken ribs have damaged organs." Amabil struggled to hold back tears, and anger flared her cheeks red.

"This was such a stupid idea. We should not have left home."

"We had no choice," Geve said calmly, although Sarra could see the worry etched in the lines on his face. "The Arbor sent the dreams of the Surface to us for a reason. We were meant to escape and find our way to it."

Tears ran down Amabil's cheeks and she dashed them away furiously, but as she opened her mouth to reply, Kytte gave a strangled cough, turned and vomited blood onto the floor.

They gathered around and tried to calm her, but it was clear to Sarra within moments that the young woman was beyond help. Her body twitched for a while and more blood issued forth, but her movements slowed, and eventually her chest failed to rise and fall, her eyes glassing over.

"Is she…?" Betune couldn't bring herself to say the words.

Geve nodded, swallowing, and closed her eyes.

"We cannot just leave her here," Amabil whispered.

Sarra pushed herself to her feet. She wanted to weep and wail and take the time to burn the body in their usual tradition, but the thought of Comminor hastening through the corridors urged her on. "We do not have the time."

Amabil went scarlet. "I am not leaving her here like this!"

"Then you carry her." Sarra picked up her bag, hardening her heart.

When she turned, however, and saw the tears in Amabil's eyes, she melted and put her arms around her. "I am so sorry. My heart feels broken too. But we cannot wait, we simply cannot."

"I know." Amabil sobbed into her shoulder. "I know we had no choice in coming, and that we have to go on now. By why did she have to die, why?"

"I do not know." Sarra held her tightly, meeting Geve's gaze over the top of her head. His eyes held pity, but he gave a small smile at the sight of her comforting the other girl.

Sarra itched to get going, but she made herself wait until Amabil's sobs died down. Together, they all laid Kytte's body out and crossed her arms over her chest, cleaned away the blood around her face and covered her with one of the wet blankets. Then they collected their belongings together and left the body behind.

Sarra led the way, with no more idea than before of which way to go, hoping the decisions she made were not random choices but instead some inherent ability she was unaware of to sense the right path. Truth to tell, though, she knew they were lost. The air grew cool and stale, each tunnel and cave so similar to the one before she wondered if they were going around in circles. Certainly it didn't feel as if they were going up. The paths remained level, each passage seemingly the same width, with the same smooth walls and faded paintings that she couldn't quite make out.

And then finally one of the tunnels widened, and without warning opened out into a largish room of a size similar to the first one with the pool. They all filtered onto the raised platform and stared around silently. The platform ran around the walls above a floor that looked as if it should be filled with water, but instead all that remained was rock. But instead of the surfaces they were used to, like the irregular surface in their own rooms, the polished floor of the palace or the earthen texture near the riverbanks, the rock here looked like grey bread dough kneaded and folded and then left so the rolls softened and blended into one another.

"What has happened here?" Nele wondered, but none of them had an answer.

The platform sloped upwards at the far end, so Sarra led the others around the room and up towards the doorway, wondering what they would find when they exited.

Nothing could have prepared her for the vista before them.

The cavern dwarfed even that containing the Great Lake, being maybe four times its size, stretching away from them far into the distance and to either side to such an extent that for a moment Sarra felt dizzy. She had never been in a place so big, and found it difficult to get used to the perspective. Geve clutched her, and as she glanced over, she had the feeling he felt the same, because he held onto the wall with his other hand, and his jaw had fallen open, his eyes wide.

She looked back at the view. How could she see? She looked up and realised there were small holes in the roof like the Caelum in the Embers, through which light filtered down to cast the room in a dull, dusty glow. The far end of the room was filled with an enormous pyramid. She knew the shape from childhood mathematic lessons, but had never seen it put to use for buildings. It was difficult to comprehend just how large the structure was, reaching almost to the roof and filling a good two-thirds of the width of the room. What in Arbor's name was it?

The floor was littered with small structures and debris, bits of metal, tools, broken pots, strips of cloth, all covered in dust. As in the corridors, paintings filled the walls, old and faded so she had difficulty making them out, but she thought they had probably been brightly coloured once, and would have brought the whole place alive.

Now, though, it was deserted, so silent that when Nele's shoe scuffed on loose rock, the noise filled the air and echoed loudly for some time.

"What is it?" Betune's whisper rustled around them like the feet of a hundred small creatures.

"I think it was a city," Nele said, his voice hushed even though nobody could hear them.

Geve moved forward to peer over the edge of the platform. "I wonder how long it has been deserted."

"It must be hundreds of years," Nele said. "Maybe thousands."

Amabil shivered. "How odd to think of people living here, not far from us. Do you think they lived here at the same time as people lived in the Embers?"

"I do not know," Nele said. They had talked long and hard about how and when the Embers had been created. Because the keeping of histories was forbidden, the only record they had was anything that had been handed down orally, and although they had worked out that the Embers had existed for at least twenty generations, they had not been able to decipher exactly when it had begun.

Sarra felt Geve's hand slide into hers. They couldn't afford to waste time staring around. She thought of Comminor marching through the passageways, coming for her, and wasn't sure if it were that or the cool air that made the hairs stand up on the back of her neck.

"Come along," she said. "Perhaps it is not much further now."

Betune guiding the way with the light from the acorn, they walked along the platform and began to descend the steps to the cavern floor.

CHAPTER FOURTEEN

I

Orsin wasn't sure where they were taking him. They had been travelling west for days towards the Forest of Wings – the dark, closely wooded area in west Wulfengar that most people avoided like the pestilence. The road wound around the outside of the forest, apparently as reluctant as people to enter into the shady depths. But the elementals he travelled with came off the road and plunged into the trees, weaving through the tightly-knit trunks towards the mountains.

He didn't care that he didn't know his destination. At that moment, he felt as if he could have ruled the world. He had the strength of a hundred men, the passion of a hundred lovers, and he burned with a determination he had never felt before.

What had happened to him? Some small part of his brain remained puzzled over the transformation. He couldn't quite remember what had occurred in Kettlestan. He had been feasting at the table, wondering where his mother had gone with Hunfrith, and he had been staring into the flame, and then...

He looked down at himself seated astride a horse, then across at his companions. They did not ride horses. And they were not men. They stood tall as men on horses though, slender and willowy, their forms flickering like candles in a draught as they ran beside him. They were not human, and inside, he turned to ice.

296

But even as fear filtered down him, fire ran through his veins and filled him with an intoxicating excitement and power that knocked all other thoughts out of his head. He didn't care what had happened to him. He liked feeling this way, liked the energy and the power, and he had no desire to go back to being the person he had been before.

He rode through the night, heading ever west, and reached the edge of the mountains as the sun began to rise. The six fire elementals with him lit up the forest so the entrance to the cave stood out clearly as they neared. He reined in outside, dismounted and tied the horse to a tree.

Then he followed the elementals into the cave.

In turned out to be the first of a series of caves and tunnels, leading deeper into the mountains. The air became humid and stifling; sweat soaked his hair and clothing, stung his eyes. Still they went deeper, the elementals' fiery skin making the crystalline rocks sparkle as they passed from passageway to passageway and cave to cave.

As the air grew thicker and the walls hot to the touch, they rounded a corner and the passageway opened up to a larger cavern. Orsin stopped, taken aback at the size of it – which was bigger than the Great Hall in Vichton Castle – and the strangeness of its construction. Circular in shape, most of it was filled with a pit of boiling magma that bubbled and spat flecks of scarlet onto the pathway that ran around the edge. The pit led to a river of red that ran through a doorway on the other side of the cavern and disappeared into the distance.

The intense heat seared his skin and made his hair crisp and his eyebrows shrivel. He gasped, the dry air burning down his gullet, and backed up to the wall, stopping as he felt rock behind his shoulders. He wanted to flee, but equally the molten rock called to him, and part of him wanted to throw himself into its fiery depths and let it consume him. He had always had a fascination for fire, but never anything as intense as this. The need frightened him, and his chest heaved as he fought with himself for a moment, gaze fixed on the thick scarlet and gold viscose liquid that swirled and popped and called him to come.

Inside him, something twisted, and he grabbed hold of the rough wall as his body shuddered and stiffened. Fear overwhelmed him again and he opened his mouth to cry out, but as he did so his voice refused to come. Instead, burning heat rose inside him, up into his throat, choking him momentarily, and he panicked as he couldn't breathe, his fingers scrabbling on the rock. He tipped his head back and tried to scream, but instead of sound issuing forth, he vomited a stream of magma that arched over the path towards the pit, disappearing into its fiery depths.

Orsin dropped to his knees, retching at the feel of the thick, slimy liquid passing through his throat, and gasping as it finally left him and his airways cleared. How was he still alive? And yet although the heat from the pit blasted his face, his insides appeared untouched from the heat of the thing that had possessed him.

On hands and knees, he watched the fiery stream join the magma pit. He was sure a long sigh filled the cavern, or was it just the wind soughing through the tunnels? The elementals that had accompanied him circled the cavern, taking up places at regular intervals on the path as if waiting, and he stared into the pit, heart pounding at the realisation of what had happened.

He had been possessed by the Incendi king. He remembered now. That was why he had felt so powerful. Now that the elemental had deserted him, his thoughts remained his own, and his head spun at the knowledge that one of the creatures standing before him had been inside him. It frightened and invigorated him at the same time. What strength, what power! He was almost disappointed it had left him, and yet equally the thought of it entering him made him nauseous.

As he watched, the pit churned, boiled and then, to Orsin's alarm, the whole pit reared up before him in a wall of dripping magma.

He fell back, pressing himself against the wall in fear as the wall hovered in the air, then gradually took the shape of a creature. A long body formed with a flaming tail and wide, wide wings that stretched across the room. It was a firebird, but on a scale Orsin had never seen before – filling the room, the wingspan a hundred feet wide and with eyes of fire that seared his skin as they looked at him.

The creature beat its wings and moved forward, and the elementals bowed as it passed. Clearly it was their leader, and Orsin's stomach turned to water as it stopped before him.

"What are you?" he whispered, the words sounding as insubstantial as a dandelion puff in the wind.

But the salamander heard him. "I am Pyra, King of the Incendi." It surveyed him thoughtfully. "Good morning."

Orsin blinked. Had the King of the elementals really just exchanged pleasantries with him?

"Thank you for allowing me the use of your body," said the King. "It was… an interesting experience."

"For me also," Orsin said, his mouth dry.

A fiery tongue flicked out, flamed heat onto his skin. "You enjoyed the experience?"

Orsin cleared his throat. "Maybe enjoyed is the wrong word. But it made me feel…" He thought about how he had felt when the creature had been inside him. Strong, powerful. "Alive," he finished, puzzling himself with the answer.

The firebird swept across the room, magma dripping from it and falling into the pit. "You have been a follower of mine for a long time."

Orsin frowned. "I am not your follower."

"Words do not make it so, but neither can they unmake the truth. Fire has always fascinated you. You have always been drawn to me."

Orsin could not deny it. That the element enchanted him, he could not refute. But that did not make him a follower of the Incendi king. That was traitorous talk, and horror filled him at the thought. He loved the Arbor, and although he did not consider himself a religious man and was struggling with his role in life, he did not wish the holy tree harm.

"I will not betray my people," he whispered, trying not to think of how he had incinerated a room full of people in Kettlestan, burning forests and cremating animals along the way. *It was not me*, his mind insisted, but deep down he knew he had enjoyed the power.

The firebird flicked out its tongue, but did not reply. Instead, after a few moments, it merely said, "Come with me."

It turned and beat its wings, floating above the magma to the room beyond. Orsin swallowed, wondering whether to try to flee. But the six elementals hovered around him, and he knew that the moment he tried to escape, they would burn him to a crisp.

He pushed himself weakly to his feet and lurched along the pathway to the door. He had burns on his arms and legs where flecks of magma had eaten through his clothing; his face felt sore to touch, and his mouth was dry as a desert. But he had no choice, and so he almost fell through the doorway, collapsing onto his knees at the edge of the cavern beyond.

He stared, his eyes on stalks, unable to believe what he was seeing. The river of magma fed in a wide, deep channel through the room, and the firebird flew above it to the centre. It swooped in a circle to face Orsin, scattering burning fragments across the floor.

"All this can be yours," it hissed. "Can you really deny your heart's desire?"

The room was filled with gold. Coins and objects made from the valuable ore were stacked in huge piles to the ceiling. From doors on either side, fiery figures marched through with more objects that they scattered on the heaps as if they were valueless stones. Obviously the elementals had a fascination for the metal, and as coins ran down the piles and slid into the pit, the firebird dipped its claws in and raised them, letting the discs melt and slip through to mix with the swirling magma.

Orsin had never seen so much wealth in one place, and his jaw dropped at the King's words. "Mine?"

"All this and more." The firebird raised its wings.

Before Orsin, the magma pit boiled and a curtain of steam rose from it. And in the steam, pictures formed before his eyes. A huge castle, the size of Vichton and Kettlestan together, with rearing towers, battlements and spires. Outside, its standing army – bigger than Heartwood's Exercitus had ever been – guarded the castle and prepared for war, weapons shining, armour glinting. The picture moved as if he were a bird floating down on currents from high in the sky, and he descended through an arrow slit to the castle interior, into a sumptuous Great Hall.

The walls were hung with rich and colourful tapestries, the tables piled high with dishes full of cooked meats and fruit. Every seat was filled, and the mood was that of a celebration, music spiralling in the air along with the smoke from the hearth. Wine flowed, ale spilled, and women danced between the tables, dressed in thin gauze gowns that revealed their curvaceous bodies.

"Your castle," the firebird murmured. "All this and more."

Orsin watched the view before him, his mouth watering at the thought of owning a castle bigger than his father's and living a life of indulgence. So what if he didn't spend his days in battle, risking his life for stories to be related after his death? He would rather enjoy his life now, with the pleasures of the body.

A woman came towards him through the smoke, arms above her head, wrists crossed, baring the soft white skin under her arms. She danced in front of him, lips curving in a tempting smile, the fabric of her gown moving like silk ribbons around her curves. As she moved nearer, he closed his eyes, his lips parting as the gown whispered across his skin, arousing him and teasing his senses to dizzy heights of pleasure.

"All this and more," the King whispered again.

The sensations faded, and Orsin opened his eyes, disappointed and filled with a deep longing.

"I have to go now," the King said. "Others need my attention. But I will be back. I need a host, Orsin. I need to work on how to make my army flesh, and you are my first choice. Welcome me, join with me, and you will never want for anything ever again."

It lowered itself into the magma, its form dissolving into the liquid like a block of salt in a cooking pot. "Think on it," it murmured before its head disappeared, the words echoing around the chamber and joining with the whisper of coins.

Orsin's chest heaved. His body ached for the girl, yearned for the treasure. In his world, he was nobody and would never amount to anything – even his own mother had no respect for him. He thought of her, and anger grew inside him at the way she had dismissed him as if he had been something she had scraped off her boot.

The King had offered him a castle, riches, power and love, everything his heart craved.

How could he refuse an offer like that?

II

Tahir sat with his back to the wall, head drooping, too tired to sit up straight. He didn't think his heart could sink any more. He had never felt so alone, so frightened and so sure that the world as he knew it was coming to an end.

His guards had taken him back to his cell, chained him up and left. He was alone in the dark, cold stone room. His body ached from where Pyra had kicked him, and he pressed the heels of his hands into his eyes, fighting the urge to cry. Even though his parents had rarely shown him any affection, they had never beaten him, and nobody else had ever dared to touch a finger to him.

Except Catena. Once, many, many years ago when he was perhaps four or five, she had caught him climbing onto a well. He had dropped a penny into it to make a wish, and had wanted to look into the water to see if he could see the penny sparkling. She had pulled him back from the edge, put him across her knee and spanked him several times. He had never forgotten it, and he suspected she hadn't either. Part of him hated her for it, but strangely part of him also respected her for it, too. Nobody else had cared enough to berate him for endangering his life. He supposed that was why he had always had a soft spot for her, and she for him. Probably the only person who ever had.

Until he met Demitto. Just the thought of the emissary made him smile, even though it took an effort to curve his lips. He thought about the moment when Demitto had walked into the Hall, striding towards him with the full weight of Heartwood behind him. Later, he doubted his own senses, but at that moment the emissary had seemed filled with light that radiated from him to all four corners of the Hall, illuminating the room and everyone in it. Tahir thought he had never seen a man so handsome or charismatic, and even though he had tried to show his usual boredom and disdain, inside, his heart had pounded and his body had warmed.

"Tahir."

The sound of someone speaking his name jolted him out of his pleasurable semi-doze and made him open his eyes.

He looked around. How could anyone be talking to him? Achingly tired, he peered into the shadows in the corners, wondering if the girl Horada had returned to talk to him.

A figure moved in the shadows and came forward into the

light of the single lantern above his head. Tahir stared, and then joy burgeoned inside him like the flowering petals of a rose. "Demitto!"

The emissary dropped to his haunches before him and looked into his eyes. "Are you all right?"

"Yes... well no... well yes, I am tired, but I am not hurt really, I just..." Tahir's eyes filled with tears. "I do not understand. Why... how...?"

Demitto placed a finger against his lips and glanced up at the grating above the door. "I had to make sure the guards had gone. I am sorry to have made you wait for so long."

"It does not matter, now you are here..."

Demitto indicated with a twirled finger for him to turn around, and Tahir did so. The emissary fiddled at his manacles, and then the iron cuffs fell away.

Tahir rubbed his wrists and then pushed himself tiredly to his feet. "How are we going to escape? There are so many guards."

"Do not worry. I know my way out of here." Demitto held out a hand. "Come on."

The young lad's heart surged and he slid his hand a little shyly into the older man's grasp. His skin was warm and dry, and Demitto smiled as he led the Prince over to the door.

The emissary took a key from his pocket and slotted it into the lock. "Stole it from one of the guards," he whispered. He turned the key and, opening the door slowly so it didn't squeal, he inched it open.

The corridor was, surprisingly, empty.

"Where are the guards?" Tahir wondered, and then he realised. "Catena? Is she here?"

"Not far," Demitto said.

"And Atavus?" Tahir had tortured himself with the memory of his dog's high-pitched squeal, sure he had been killed. "Is he dead?"

Demitto's eyebrows rose. "No, no. He is here too, with Catena."

Tahir filled with joy. "Oh, thank the Arbor."

Demitto smiled. He waited a moment, listening, then slunk out into the corridor, holding tightly to Tahir's hand. "Come on."

With a flame dancing in the centre of the ambassador's hand, they crept along, Tahir's heart pounding so loudly, at first he thought drums were playing in another cavern. At the end of the corridor, Demitto turned right and they crept through another silent cave.

How deep did the cave system go? Tahir knew they must be well into the mountains, possibly miles in, and the thought of having to walk for a few hours made his heart sink, even though he was eager to escape.

"Are you tired?" Demitto asked, pausing to look around the corner of a corridor.

"I cannot remember the last time I slept," Tahir admitted.

Demitto turned back and motioned for silence, and the two of them waited in the darkness. Tahir could hear voices in the distance, and he panicked at the thought of being found, but the people must have chosen a different path because the voices grew no louder, and gradually faded away.

Demitto waited for a moment and then looked around the corner again. Still holding Tahir's hand, he led him out and away from the noise.

They walked for some time in semi-darkness, their feet scuffling on loose stones and fallen debris. Occasionally they passed the doorway to other caverns, lit with flame, from which voices echoed, but Demitto ignored them and stuck to the passageways, taking them even further from the centre.

"I long to see the sun again," Tahir confessed. "When it was there every day I did not give it a thought, but now I have no access to it, it is all I think about."

"That is always the way of things," Demitto said. "What else do you miss?"

Tahir thought about it. "The freedom, I suppose. I was very lucky – even though I was the King's son, I could do whatever

I wanted, within reason. I was not left by myself very often, but they did not stop me having the run of the castle and most of the city. I mean, I knew from an early age that my destiny lay in Heartwood, but for a long time it seemed very far away."

"And now it is so close." Demitto paused at a doorway. For the first time he didn't pass but instead walked inside.

Tahir followed him in. They were in a smallish, square chamber, the walls polished to a smooth sheen and painted with red and golden figures and patterns. In the centre was a round pool of water. It did not appear to be boiling, but the steam that arose from it suggested it must be hot.

A small torch had been placed in a bracket on each wall, and Demitto closed his hand and extinguished the light in his palm.

"Is Catena to meet us here?" Tahir asked.

"Yes." Demitto led him over to a bench on the opposite wall, and they sat, shoulders touching.

Tahir sagged against the emissary, wishing he could just lie down and go to sleep.

"Rest for a while," Demitto said. "You are young and not yet at your full strength. It is no wonder you are tired."

"I am tired," Tahir admitted.

Demitto touched his hair. "It is a shame to think you will not come of age. I am sorry for that."

Tears filled Tahir's eyes at both the words and the tender touch. Too tired to wipe them away, he let them trickle down his cheeks. "I knew I would never be a knight," he said. "I have neither the talent nor the ambition. And what was the point in training when I knew I would not live past my fourteenth birthday?"

"It must have been very difficult for you." Demitto's hand continued to stroke his hair.

"Yes." Tahir's throat tightened, so he chose not to elaborate.

"How much do you think the fact that your future had already been written affected your youth?"

He thought about it. "In some ways it made me careless, reckless. I did not care what I said to anyone or what they thought of me. But in other ways, it made me take fewer risks, because there seemed no point in training or trying new things because I knew I would not have the time to carry them through. Now I think maybe I should have been more adventurous, travelled more, but at the time I suppose I was angry. I did not want to see more of the world and know what I would be missing."

"I understand," Demitto said, "but it saddens me to think of all the things you will be missing. The thrill of battle. The delight of getting drunk."

Tahir's lips curved in spite of his sadness. "I suppose."

"Falling in love," Demitto said.

Tahir's smile faded. He concentrated on his hands, thinking how dirty his fingernails had got.

Demitto put a finger under his chin and lifted it so the lad had to look up at him. "You *have* fallen in love then?" he questioned.

Tahir's cheeks grew warm. He couldn't think what to say.

Demitto's expression softened. "Oh."

Tahir lifted his chin out of the man's hand, face now burning. "Please, I..." He cursed himself for not denying it. Would the man get angry or disgusted?

But Demitto just continued to stroke his hair. "Do not be embarrassed."

"You cannot ask that of someone," Tahir said, looking away and closing his eyes.

"Young prince, you have led a sheltered life with few heroes to idolise – it is only natural that you look up to me. I am not alarmed by it; only flattered."

Tahir didn't know what to say to that. He was conscious of the emissary's touch on his head. He had never been touched like that before.

Demitto picked up a stray hair and tucked it behind Tahir's ear. "It is not fair. You should have the whole of your life to explore love and sex."

The burning sensation slid down from Tahir's cheeks to his neck and chest.

The emissary continued to stroke him. "It is so sad to think you will never know another's touch."

Tahir's insides twisted, a mangled wreck of sadness and bliss. "Yes."

"You are a handsome young man. Your eyes are like twin suns – I have never seen anything like them."

Tahir raised his gaze. He knew people found his eyes unnerving. When he was younger, he had grown angry when other children stared at him, and pointed or giggled, but as he had grown older he had learned to use them to his advantage. Now he caught the emissary's gaze, and Demitto's own eyes locked on his.

"Sad to die so lonely," the ambassador murmured. "So unloved."

A fresh tear ran down Tahir's face. "Stop..."

Demitto cupped the lad's cheek and ran his thumb across it to wipe away the tear. "I cannot believe no one will ever love you."

Tahir's lip trembled. "Do not... I cannot bear it."

Demitto's eyes were clear. He leaned forward and, before Tahir could react, pressed his lips against the young prince's.

Tahir stilled, shocked, heart pounding at the feel of the man's warm lips against his own. Demitto waited a moment, thumb still stroking his cheek, before moving back. Tahir stared at him, face burning again, unsure what to do or say.

"Did you like that?" the emissary asked.

Half-afraid, half-excited, Tahir nodded slowly.

Demitto's mouth curved up. He looked across at the warm water, the heat rising slowly. "That looks so inviting. I think we should get in."

Tahir stared. "Now?"

The emissary shrugged. "Catena may be a while. I think we are safe here. Would you not like that?" He stood and began to undo his belt, the Heartwood buckle glinting in the light of the torches.

Tahir's jaw sagged. He got to his feet, eyes wide as Demitto undid the clasps on his leather tunic and then dragged it over his head. The sleeveless linen undertunic joined it, and Tahir stared at the man's glistening brown skin, his developed muscles.

The breeches joined the rest of his clothing, and then Demitto walked down the steps into the warm water. "Aaah!" Up to his waist, he smiled and held out a hand. "Join me!"

Tahir walked to the edge of the pool. He wanted nothing more than to plunge into the water, to watch it close over his skin. To feel the emissary's lips on his again. His hands rose to his belt, began to unbuckle it. Then he paused.

Demitto beckoned. "We do not have long. Come on. I know you wish to be with me." His wet arms gleamed and his long dark hair clung to his muscular neck. "Know some happiness before the end, young prince. Join me."

Tahir said nothing. His heart raced. "Your Heartwood belt buckle. You lost it at Realberg."

The emissary looked at his clothing and frowned. "It was found and returned to me."

Tahir shook his head, ice sliding down inside him. His head began to spin. "This is wrong."

"Tahir…"

The Prince closed his eyes. *Oh Arbor's roots, what have I done…*

Heat flared around him. His eyes shot open.

He stood on the edge of the pit of magma in front of the pyramid. His toes were burning, his skin scarlet from the heat. Gone was the room with the water pool – gone was Demitto.

Pyra stood beside him, face filled with fury. "Get in!" he yelled.

Tahir looked at the magma. He had been about to step into it of his own volition, talked into it by a vision of the man he loved. Shame and indignation shot through him that Pyra had used his idolism of Demitto against him, to try and talk him into killing himself.

He stumbled back, tripped and fell on the floor, cowering as the Incendi king towered over him.

"Get in!" Pyra screamed.

And suddenly Tahir understood. The King could not kill him. He may be able to physically hurt him, but he could not take away his life. The Arbor still protected him, even deep in the mountains, miles from Heartwood. He might be alone, he might never have known affection in his life, and he might die without ever knowing another person's touch.

But the Arbor loved him.

He pushed himself to his feet, rose up and stood before the King, and said one word.

"No."

III

Comminor and the other three members of the Umbra pushed onward, even though they were all tired and desperate for a rest.

Comminor had always considered himself a fit man. Although not as young as the rest of them, he swam daily in the palace pool, joined in the training most days, and still led small groups on hunting camps in the outer Embers where the salamanders and turtles grew big enough to wrestle. He had not gained his position as Chief Select through force, but nevertheless a ruler had to portray strength and competence, and he had worked hard to maintain that view of a leader.

Still, in spite of his fitness levels, he was tired, his body longing for rest. Sarra and the Veris couldn't be too far ahead of them, he thought. They had come upon the body of the young woman called Kytte, obviously injured in the fall from the Cataracta, so he knew he was on the right track. Sarra would have to rest at some point because of the baby. Therefore if he and the Umbra didn't rest, they would be able to close the gap that much sooner. So he pushed on, threading through the corridors without pause, laying his hands on the rock and feeling the passage of those before him like a murmur through his veins.

Not only a bard and a Select, Comminor was also a Saxum, sensitive to the voice of stone, able to hear the whisper in the rock of past millennia of inhabitants. Just like the faded pictures on the walls, the hum of voices spoke to him, telling him of the rise and fall of civilisations, a whole history laid out beneath his fingertips, with Sarra riding atop those voices like a reed on a river.

He could sense her, and her presence wrapped around him sensuously like smoke, creeping into his pores, his head, until he could think of nothing but her.

"Comminor."

The voice spoke loudly, a little impatiently, as if it had not been the first time it had called his name. He looked over his shoulder and slowed as he realised the Umbra had stopped outside a small room and were seating themselves on the floor inside.

He walked back to the doorway. "We must keep going."

"We have to rest for a while," Viel said. He had dark shadows under his eyes and his shoulders sagged.

Comminor stood with hands on hips. "We must press on. Get up."

Paronel said nothing, clearly too tired to even reply. Josse also looked exhausted. He raised his head, determination on his face, along with not a little wariness. "No."

Comminor said nothing. He demanded many things of his followers, and complete obedience was one of them. Usually he would have beaten Josse for that reply, and the man knew it. But this wasn't the Embers. And nothing would be served by using force at that particular moment.

Instead, he went into the room, gathered some of the dry moss from the back wall, brought it to the exhausted Umbra and lit it with a flame from his hand. The fire crackled merrily in front of them, and he sat down, taking comfort from the warmth.

Josse stared at him, obviously shocked he wasn't going to be reprimanded. But he said nothing, and the four of them sat silently for a while as their muscles gradually loosened.

"How are we going to get back?" Paronel said suddenly. "How will we make it up the waterfall?"

Comminor said nothing, just stared into the flames.

"You do not think we will return," Viel said softly. "Smoke and fire."

"Why?" Josse whispered. "Why is this so important that you would risk the Embers by never returning?"

"I am doing this to save the Embers," Comminor said. He did not know yet whether he would return, but he had left the city in the care of several other trusted Umbra. He had also left a letter declaring that they pick his successor if he did not return, and leaving instructions for their chosen person to read the *Quercetum* and learn the truth. One way or another, the Embers would continue.

"I do not understand." Josse's indignation burned as bright as the fire before them. "We have dedicated our lives to you. Are we so worthless that you would throw our lives away as if they are broken shell?"

Comminor smiled. "It is because you are so valuable to me that I asked you to come with me. This task is more important to the survival of our people than anything you could imagine."

"I do not believe you." Paronel looked near to tears, fists clenched with anger. "You wanted Sarra in your bed, and you were angry that she proved you a fool. You want to punish her for having a mind of her own."

"Part of me does," he admitted. The words did not come easy. He had never had a confidante and always kept his thoughts to himself. But the only way he was going to get them to come with him was by finally revealing the truth.

"But that is not all. The Veris must be stopped, or they will bring about the end of the Embers."

"How?" Josse looked curious in spite of his resentment, and both the others also gave him inquisitive looks.

"I have been charged with a task," Comminor said. "I am the last member of the Nox Aves, a group who have connected through the ages with one purpose – to keep our people alive."

And so he told them about the *Quercetum*, and the history of their ancestors. He told them about the balance of the elements, and the invasion of the Darkwater Lords, and the rise of the Incendi. He told them about the creation of the Embers and explained how it had remained safe for a thousand years, isolating itself from the rest of the world, protected by a line of Chief Select who knew the truth and vowed to protect the city, thus ensuring the survival of their race.

"So there is a Surface?" Paronel spoke in a hushed whisper.

"Yes," Comminor said.

The three of them stared at him, and he could only guess what they were thinking. Since they had heard of the Veris, there had been rumours about the other world, but everyone had assumed they were only that – rumours, and the Veris's tales were just stories told to make their dreary lives more exciting.

Viel leaned forward. "What is up there?"

"We do not know." Comminor warmed his hands and stared into the fire. That was one piece of information he was not prepared to share. "But we cannot risk the Incendi finding out about the existence of the Embers. If they know, they will come to destroy us, and I have vowed not to let that happen. I have dedicated my life to ensuring the Embers remains isolated, and I do not intend to stop now."

They all thought on that. Paronel drew her blanket around her shoulders and leaned her cheek on her arms. Comminor thought she slept, but when he looked closer, her eyes were open as she stared at the fire.

"You should have told us you did not think we would return when you asked us to come with you," Viel said.

"I did not know about the Cataracta," Comminor pointed out. "And nothing is certain. That much I have learned over the years."

"What do you intend to do when you catch them?" Josse's anger appeared to have faded.

"Persuade them to come back."

"And if they will not?"

Comminor met his gaze. He knew the answer, but did not want to put it into words, and the others fell silent.

For a short while, they rested. Comminor lay back and closed his eyes. *Just for a moment...* The cool stone seeped into his muscles, calming them, and even though the floor was hard, his body relaxed, and he slipped into an uneasy sleep.

He opened his eyes, and Sarra stood before him. She was large with child, and one hand rested on her sizeable bump. She wore a long blue tunic of a rare fine material she would not have had access to in the Embers, and a gold circlet set with gems. He recognised the circlet – it was in the palace vault. He had given it to her – she was his woman. His heart swelled.

Her other hand rested on the bark of a tree. Comminor tipped his head back and looked up at the branches. He had never seen anything like it before in the Embers, but he knew what it was. An oak tree. *The* oak tree. The Arbor.

Its leaves shook a little in the early morning breeze, almost as if it were beckoning him closer. He hesitated, then reached out a hand and rested it on the trunk. To his shock, the bark was warm, and beneath his fingers beat a slow, steady pulse.

"Can you feel it?" Sarra asked him.

He nodded, turning his gaze back to her. She smiled, her eyes filled with such love that it warmed his heart.

"I have something for you," he said, and unfurled his hand. A small flame danced there, and he offered it to her.

Sarra's smile slowly faded. "It burns," she said. "It burns because of you."

Against his will, the flame lengthened and above it, a leaf caught light. Alarmed, Comminor reached out to take it in his hand, but beside it another burst, then another. He went around the tree, trying to extinguish all the flames, but he could not move quickly enough. A chain of flames spread around the branches, leaves curling and crisping; soon twigs were catching light and then whole branches burst into flame.

The heat drove him back, and he held his arms up to his face as the fire spread down the trunk and soon the whole tree was burning. And now it was crying, its heart-wrenching sobs filling the air, tearing at his heart.

Then, to his shock, he saw that Sarra still stood beneath the branches, unmoving. Burning leaves fell onto her hair, setting it aflame, and her clothes caught light, enveloping her in a halo of orange. Comminor tried to get to her but the heat was too intense, and in the end all he could do was watch as her skin bubbled and blackened, and she collapsed to the floor, filling the air with the smell of roasted flesh.

The tree roared, burning fiercely, and he fell to his knees, tears running down his face. Sarra's voice continued to whisper in his ears, haunting him. *It burns because of you.*

"No!"

He opened his eyes, aware he had spoken out loud, and sat up. He was back in the small stone room, the fire nearly dead, and the others were sitting up and rubbing their eyes, awoken by his cry.

"Sorry." He ran his hands through his hair. "A dream."

"What did you dream about?" Josse took out his water bottle and had a mouthful. They all looked curiously at the Chief Select.

He shook his head, unable to voice the horror. Was it an omen? Was the Arbor trying to tell him he was going to be the downfall of his people? Or was it just a dream born out of his fear that he couldn't fulfil his role as protector of the Embers?

He pushed himself to his feet. "We should get going."

This time they didn't argue but rose with him and packed away their blankets. He shouldered his bag and walked to the doorway, raising his hand and producing a flame to light the way. He tried not to think of how the leaves had caught light when he had done that standing beneath the Arbor. It was just a dream, not a portent. It meant nothing.

They walked again for what felt like hours, threading through passages and caves, each as quiet and empty as the last, long since abandoned and left to the mosses, and spiders and insects that scurried away as their feet scuffed on loose stones and dirt.

Comminor continued to run his fingers along the walls, following Sarra's echo. Why he could feel her presence so clearly, he did not know. From the first moment he saw her, he had felt a special connection to her, but he could not have said why or put it into words.

The passageway opened up into a large room, the floor filled with cooled and folded sheets of rock. His fingers tingled and, heart pounding, he walked up the rising pathway and exited the doorway at the end.

The others came to stand beside him, mouths open as they looked down at the enormous cavern and the gigantic pyramid at the other end. The sheer scale of the place made him dizzy, and the faded pictures on the walls showed the history of the elementals he had read about in the *Quercetum* since he was a young man.

But in spite of the wondrous view, it was not this that drew his attention. That was captured by the sight of a figure standing in the huge doorway of the pyramid, looking up at him.

They stared at each other for a long moment, and then Sarra turned and disappeared into the pyramid.

CHAPTER FIFTEEN

I

Horada knelt on the rocky floor, head bowed, trying to control her shaking and failing miserably.

Sweat ran down her face and back, and her clothing stuck to her skin uncomfortably. In front of her, the magma pit swirled and spat occasional globs of burning rock at the path on which she knelt. So far none had landed on her, but she watched them bubble and hiss on the rock and knew it was only a matter of time.

In the pit, the giant firebird flapped its wings lazily, surveying her. She kept her eyes lowered, but could still see its scarlet form, could feel its glowing red eyes fixed on her.

The King of the Incendi. She could not believe she knelt before him. If only she could take a sword and thrust it into his heart and end this once and for all. But unfortunately she didn't have a sword. And even if she did, she wasn't sure he had a heart, or not one that could be hurt by a blade. He seemed made of fire, and although he appeared to have form, he had materialised from the liquid rock as if by magic.

Her wrists were chained to rock on either side, her arms stretched out, her knees hurt but she could not rise. She was totally at his mercy and wondered if at any moment she would feel the fire wash over her, burning flesh from bone and taking away her life in one brief burst of pain.

As if hearing her thoughts, the firebird moved towards her with a sweep of its wings, pausing just in front of her. He lowered his head, and a fiery tongue emerged to flick past her cheek. The heat made fresh sweat run down her neck, and she swayed with exhaustion.

"Water," said the King, and beside her one of the elementals brought in a bucket and tipped it straight over her head. The liquid evaporated almost immediately, but not before the wetness brought her to her senses like a sharp slap. She gasped and shook her head, droplets flying off and meeting the rock with a hiss.

The firebird lowered its head to look into her eyes. "Hello, Horada."

She moistened her lips. How did he know her name? His scarlet orbs, brilliant as rubies, hot as a forge, burned into her. "What do you want?"

His tongue curled out and then back. "You."

Her heart raced. She tried to look away from his stare, but found she couldn't, as if he was hypnotising her, keeping her entranced. "You cannot have me," she whispered, aware even as she said the words how feeble they sounded.

The tongue flicked in and out. "We will see." He sounded amused.

For the first time, indignation rose inside her. "You can do what you like to my body," she said firmly. "But you will never control my mind."

"That sounds like both an offer and a challenge," Pyra said.

Horada swallowed down the fear rising within her at the thought of what torture he could put her through, and lifted her chin to meet his gaze. "Take it whatever way you wish. You do not frighten me."

The firebird swept in a circle. "You have a very high opinion of yourself. Let me summarise my intentions by saying that by the end of our conversation, you will have submitted yourself to me willingly. Your body and your mind will be mine, to do with whatever I wish." His tongue flicked out. "I have a lot of ideas."

"Never," Horada whispered. "You cannot make me do anything I do not want to do." But she could not stop herself shaking. Could he control her mind – make her do things against her will? But he said she would submit willingly. That would never happen.

The King turned and breathed out a long, scarlet flame. Steam rose from it to form a white wall. On this screen, a picture began to form.

It took her a while to recognise the person. She could not understand how the picture was moving – she had seen painting and tapestries, but never a picture where the figures moved. It was as if Pyra had transported them to the scene, even though she could still feel the rock beneath her knees and the heat from his sour breath.

It was her brother, Orsin. He lay on his back on a sheet of rock, eyes half-lidded while in front of him danced a woman clothed in sheer layers of gauze. Around them, golden coins and ornaments glistened, and she could not mistake that look of lust in his eyes. She had seen it before late in the evening when, in his cups, he had grabbed one of the serving wenches before leading her off to one of the pallets where the household slept and sliding under the blankets with her. The dancer draped her gown across him and let the silky fabric trail across his face, and he arched his back in ecstasy.

"You are seducing him," she whispered, once again unable to tear her gaze away.

"Orsin was already halfway to being my follower," Pyra said scornfully. "He has been attracted to fire since he was a child, and none of you recognised it. His family have never tried to understand him, nor find his strengths. You also dismiss him as a fool, but he has power you could never dream of. Power that I now possess."

In spite of the heat, Horada went cold. Orsin was a follower of the Incendi?

"I do not believe it," she said, fighting against the tears that threatened to form. "He may not be religious, but he would not betray the Arbor or his people."

"You deny he is a slave to his senses?"

Orsin loved good food, fine ale and pretty women. There was no denying it. "That does not make him a traitor," she said.

"He is soundly connected to the physical world, which is what I desire. He is the perfect container for my spirit, and through him I shall conquer Anguis and all its people."

The firebird reared up, scattering flecks of magma across the room, and spread its wings, fire leaping from the ends. Horada cowered before it, squealing as boiling sparks landed on her skin. She shook them off but they left tiny blisters, and she sobbed, holding up her hands in defence.

"Stop, please stop."

"Then join with me." He lowered back into the magma. "The pain will be but momentary, and then we shall be one. I can show you bliss such as you have never experienced before, and you shall live forever!"

Horada leaned forward, head bowed, fingers digging into the hard rock. "No."

"You think you can refuse me?" The King laughed, his searing breath blasting her so she nearly fainted.

"I will not," she said, although her bottom lip trembled and she continued to shake.

"If you will not do it for Orsin, then do it for your other brother." Pyra beat his wings, and the scene on the sheet of steam cleared and was replaced by another.

This time she saw Julen. He was walking through the forest, the greenery painted with sunlight from the shafts that filtered down through the canopy of trees. It was difficult to see him as he wore clothes that blended with the colour of the trees, although she knew it was more than that because even his face and hands seemed to match the colours of the undergrowth. He was camouflaging himself, using his special talent to hide as he moved quickly, glancing occasionally over his shoulder.

"Clever," Pyra said. "What a wonderful gift that is. Amazing we can see him at all."

Horada said nothing. She watched as Julen reached the edge of a line of trees and dropped to his haunches. Ahead of him was a rockface darkened by the entrance to a cave. He had reached the mountainside, she realised. He was coming to find her.

Even as her heart leapt, she saw the two Incendi figures in the cave's shadows. They lay in wait, aware of his presence, ready to ambush him the moment he entered.

"Hmm," said Pyra. "They are waiting for my command. Do I tell them to move forward, or do I hold them back?"

Horada bit her lip and turned her gaze to the King. "Please. Do not harm him."

Flames ran down the elemental's form, glistening in gold and scarlet. "Then join with me."

Tears finally ran down her face. To save her brother, she would have to throw herself into the magma and join with the Incendi. But that would be the end of the Arbor, she knew it instinctively. In another age, another era, Tahir was nearby, and so presumably was the girl he spoke of, the girl from his future. They were coming together, about to join in location if not in time, and with the Apex formed, their destruction would be inevitable.

"I cannot." She lifted her chin, not ashamed to show her tears.

The King did not wait. Clearing the picture, he let another one form. This time of her mother, leaning close to the neck of the horse she rode, fleeing through the countryside at full pace. Her hair had escaped her usual tight knot and it trailed behind her like a pennant, snapping in the breeze. Trees and fields flashed by, cows and sheep a blur of colour. She glanced over her shoulder, and to Horada's alarm, fear lit her mother's face. She had never seen her mother scared before.

"Procella fears being caught by Hunfrith," Pyra said. "He wants her, in all the ways a man can want a woman. She knows he is stronger than her. She can remember that moment your father first bested her in mock combat – that moment of humiliation and fear that she could not hold her own. She will experience that tenfold with Hunfrith. Your father loved her, but Hunfrith will use her body with no sign of the tenderness that Chonrad felt towards her. Hunfrith will abuse her, rape her, then give her to his men to use in any way they wish. Do you want that for your mother?"

Tears streamed down Horada's cheeks. Her chains clanged as she moved her hands to dash them away. "No. Please..."

"Then join with me."

She closed her eyes. *Forgive me, Mother...* "I cannot."

Pyra roared, making her eyes snap open again. He cleared the scene. This time, the new picture puzzled her. It looked like a view of somewhere in the mountains, with more magma bubbling redder than blood. She blinked, trying to focus on the figure in the centre. He lay stretched out on a rock, arms and feet spread and tied, and he was naked. Fire elementals crawled over him, and his skin blistered, renewed and blistered again, accompanied by his cries of pain.

It was her father.

Horada's jaw dropped. Horror filled her. "Father?" She turned furious eyes to the King. "Now I know you lie. He is dead. I saw his body and buried it afterwards."

"But this is not his body," said the King. "This is his soul."

Horada stared. Since the beginning of time, scholars had debated the presence of a soul and whether it lived on when the body gave up its life. Current thought was that, like with trees, when the physical body died its energy returned to the ground and brought life to the new shoots in a circle that never ended. The existence of a person's mind, of their very being, outside of the body was not thought to exist.

And yet here was her father, his face clearly distinguishable, captured by the Incendi and kept to be tortured for all eternity.

Bile rose inside her and she vomited onto the ground.

The King lowered himself in the magma so he could look into her face. "Join with me," he whispered, "and I will end your father's suffering. I will return his spirit to the Arbor so he can rest in peace."

A fire elemental climbed onto Chonrad and stretched out along him, lying like a lover atop her partner's form. He screamed as the fire ate into him, arching his back in a spasm of pain.

"Stop," Horada whispered, curling up, her forehead almost resting on the ground. "Please, make it stop."

"Join with me…" His insidious voice crept over her like a warm blanket, promising an end to the suffering, an end to the pain.

She pushed herself up to her hands and knees. She would do it. She didn't care about the Arbor and Anguis, about the end of the world. She just wanted the pain to cease.

Ahead of her, the picture of her father evaporated, the steam dissipating as she crawled forward and Pyra sensed his victory.

And then she stopped. In the remnants of the mist, a final faint picture remained.

The hourglass filled, turned, filled again.

Timekeeper…

She caught her breath. The hourglass vanished. The King continued to stare at her – he hadn't seen the image. It hadn't been sent by him.

Cinereo?

He was still with her. And he was trying to tell her to keep her faith.

It didn't matter what Pyra had shown her. Whether the images were true or not – there was nothing she could do about it now. Her brothers, her mother, her father's poor soul, if there was such a thing, which she doubted – she was not responsible for their freedom or whether they lived or died. She had to trust that the Arbor would protect them too, that its love would keep them safe and bring them through this time of trial.

All that mattered was keeping the Arbor alive. She remembered her father telling her that. If the people loved the tree and worked with it to maintain Anguis, the tree would protect them and love them back, and the cycle would be complete.

She sat on her heels and tipped back her head. Too exhausted to stand, too tired to speak, she just looked up at the Incendi king and let him read the truth in her eyes.

II

Catena placed her palms on the stone wall and closed her eyes.

She didn't think she would ever get used to the sensation of communicating with the rock. Why had she never noticed it before? She had lived in a castle and usually rested one hand on the wall as she ascended or descended the spiral staircase to the battlements. Wouldn't she have noticed if she had this peculiar talent?

Demitto had suggested it was because the castle had been built from cut stones, whereas these caves were carved into the mountainside and thus still connected with the earth. That made some sort of sense. And anyway, she wondered if she had been ignoring her instincts all along. One reason she had worked so hard to become Chief of the Guard was because she loved the castle. As a child, she had spent hours walking around the battlements, talking to the guards. They had indulged her because it could be a lonely job, and she had listened to their grumbles as they patrolled in all weathers. But she had loved being way up high above everyone else, being able to look down upon the town, watching people go about their business as if she were a bird flying high in the clouds. And she had loved the feel of the stone beneath her fingertips, imagining all the people who must have touched it before her, and what stories it could have told, if it had been able to talk. Had she been communicating with it then, in some small way?

Her mind was wandering, and she brought it back to the present, trying to concentrate on Tahir's location. The rock warmed beneath her hand, but still her brain struggled to focus.

Part of the problem was having the emissary standing so close to her. Her skin prickled at his nearness, the memory of his brief kiss still fresh in her mind. Why had he kissed her? She hadn't picked up on any feelings of desire from him before. He usually radiated irritation and frustration rather than attraction.

His touch had completely taken her by surprise, and she didn't like being surprised in such a way. Not one bit. She could not understand him. One moment he was so irreverent and carefree, making light of the Arbor and their predicament, and the next he became all mysterious and gave the impression there was far more to him than met the eye. How was she to react to that? She didn't know where she stood with him, and she certainly had no interest in him as a mate.

She opened her eyes and glanced aside at him. He stood with one hand on his hip, head bowed as he waited for her to tell them which way to go. It had become so hot in the caves, he had finally removed the linen undertunic, and now his bronzed skin gleamed in the light of the flame dancing on his open palm, his sculpted muscles an exemplary display of masculinity. She knew if she touched them, they would be as hard as the rock beneath her fingers...

He looked up, meeting her gaze, and Catena's eyes widened. *Arbor's roots.* She looked back at the rock, her cheeks flaming. She was *not* going to let the man get to her like this! He had probably kissed her on purpose to make a point, although she could not think what the point was at that moment. Maybe to keep her interested so she didn't run off and leave him. His claustrophobia had been obvious, and she had comforted him more than once when his breathing became irregular. Well, no more! He could hyperventilate himself to oblivion as far as she cared from now on.

She formed an image of Tahir in her mind, forced herself to concentrate and immediately felt the ripple of connection brush across her nerve endings like a feather across her skin.

"This way," she said, and headed off to the right.

Demitto said nothing, but he was only a foot behind her, with Atavus a foot behind him, and when she stopped suddenly, he bumped hard into her. She swatted at him and scowled, although he wouldn't be able to see it in the semi-darkness.

"Sorry." He rested a hand on her hip so he could lean close to murmur in her ear. "Can you feel him?"

"Yes." She twitched her hips but his hand remained there, warm even through her breeches. "Demitto..."

"How far?"

She pushed her irritation aside. She had to focus on the Prince now – he was all that mattered. "Not far. Maybe one or two passages. And he is locked in."

Demitto nodded, took her hand, pulled her and the dog into an adjacent empty room and pushed the door almost closed. "We will wait here until the guards go past," he said. Reluctance flickering across his face, he closed his palm, extinguishing the flame.

They were plunged into darkness, and Catena felt his arm snake around her, his hand gripping hers as they both fought to retain their sense of balance. Atavus pressed against their legs, also clearly unsettled. It felt as if she had jumped into a vat of thick honey, and someone had placed a blanket over her head, extinguishing the light. The warm, humid air smothered her, and she wasn't surprised to hear Demitto's breathing speed up. In spite of her promise to herself to let him suffer, she tightened her hand and rubbed his arm, instinctively wanting to comfort.

Clearly they were in the area where the Incendi kept prisoners, perhaps before the elementals took over their bodies.

Cries and screams echoed occasionally along the corridors, and further along someone gave great, heart-rending sobs that brought tears to her eyes.

"We cannot leave these people here," she whispered, leaning her cheek against his shoulder, suddenly glad of his presence. "It is too awful to speak of."

"I know." His hand rested on her back. "But our first priority is rescuing Tahir. Maybe later we can come back for the others. But if we do not take him to Heartwood, then everything is lost."

She lifted her head to look up at him. A light sprang into being further along the corridor – from what she couldn't be sure – but she could just make out the glitter of his eyes. "I do not understand why it has to be him. I know the Arbor needs a sacrifice. But can you not just let us disappear and find someone else?"

His hand came up to cup her cheek, his thumb brushing her damp skin. "I wish I could, but I have sworn I will bring him there at all costs, and I must keep my promise. The very world depends on it."

"Why?"

He moved to look out of the grille in the door, then came back to stand close to her. Closer than was necessary, she thought with some irritation. But when he linked their fingers and she pressed her thumb against his wrist, she could feel his pulse racing, and so she didn't complain.

He leaned on the rock above her head, his cheek so close to hers that she could feel the roughness of his bristles. "I do not fully understand it all, Catena. But I will try to explain. Certain events in time are fixed, like towns in Anguis. You can take any road you like from one town to another, but all roads lead from town to town. Does that make any sense?"

She frowned. "Not really."

"From what I can understand, some moments in our history have already been written. The Arbor can see its past, its present and its future, and those moments of the Apex are unmoveable.

Everything we do and say is leading to those events."

"I do not like the feeling that I have no say in what happens in my life."

"I think it is up to us how we travel from town to town. We can walk, or take a slow horse and cart, or ride a fast horse to get there in a day. But the towns – the events – are fixed."

It was difficult to concentrate with his mouth only inches from hers, but she forced herself to think. "So what is the problem? If events are fixed, then obviously we will escape and Tahir will complete his destiny."

His lips brushed her cheek so lightly she couldn't be sure if he had done it on purpose or not. "The problem is that somehow the Incendi have found a way to travel along the timelines, and they are doing their best to sabotage the Apex. Is it possible? We are not sure, but we cannot jeopardise our future by being arrogant enough to assume everything will just work itself out. The Nox Aves have given me the task of escorting Tahir and you to Heartwood, and I have to do everything in my power to try to make that happen."

The hairs rose on Catena's neck at the feel of his warm breath on her skin. She raised a hand to rest on his chest, her breathing also growing faster at the feel of his damp skin.

Then his words registered and she frowned. "Wait... 'Tahir and you'?"

He went still. "What?"

"You said 'Tahir and you'. You mean just the Prince, surely? Why does it matter whether I get to Heartwood or not?"

He hesitated, and that brief moment of pause told her it had not been a mistake.

"Me?" she whispered. "Why me? What do I have to do with the Apex?"

His hand brushed her back. "I am sorry, but I cannot tell you."

She drew back sharply. "What do you mean? You are so arrogant! You think you are so important keeping all this knowledge to yourself."

"Catena, hush."

"Do not hush me!"

"I cannot tell you, because if I do, they could torture you to get the information."

She thumped his chest with her fist. "Do not be so infuriating! If I am to play a part in the Apex, I deserve to know."

He caught her wrists. "We will all play a part in the Arbor's future. You and I and Tahir."

Fury welled up inside her, born out of frustration and fear that the Incendi might be trying to hunt her down as well as the Prince. "Am I to be sacrificed too? Is that it? If my life is to come to an end, I should be told!"

"Seriously, you must keep your voice down."

Panic flooded her. "Am I to die with the Prince? Is that my destiny?"

"Catena…" Demitto pulled her to him and before she could vent any more frustration, he tightened his arms around her and kissed her.

Shocked, angry and scared, she struggled, trying to slap him, to push him away, but he was far too strong for her.

Tears poured down her cheeks, and as she ceased to fight him, so his arms relaxed, turning into a caress more than a restraint, his hand moving up to cup the back of her head as he deepened the kiss. Her hands splayed on his chest, moved up to his shoulders, crept around his neck.

When he finally lifted his head, she remained in the circle of his arms, all rebellion vanquished.

"Why?" she whispered.

He stroked her cheek. "I cannot tell you, Catena."

"No. I mean why did you kiss me?"

He gave a little chuckle. "To keep you quiet."

She looked up into the glitter of his eyes. "Is that the only reason?"

He kissed her nose. "No."

"I..." Her voice trailed off at the sound of voices in the corridor. She pulled back, heart beginning to pound again.

Silently, they drew their swords and took up a place on either side of the door, Demitto with one hand holding Atavus's collar. He touched a finger to his lips, and Catena nodded.

Demitto took a breath and yelled, "Guard!"

The feet outside stopped, and the two guards came into the cell. "What...?"

Before they could utter another word, Catena and Demitto swung as one, and Atavus leapt forward. The dog's jaws closed around the guard's arm, stopping him from swinging his blade. Demitto thrust his sword up under his armpit, almost to the hilt in his ribcage. Catena's blade neatly lopped off the head of the second, and it rolled onto the floor as he fell to his knees, then slowly forward onto his stomach.

They looked down at the fallen bodies.

"Nice," Demitto said.

She blew out a breath, blood racing around her body. Suddenly she felt a whole lot better.

He grinned at her. "Ready?"

She nodded. They were going to dress themselves in the guards' attire, and then try to get into Tahir's cell. It was a risky plan, but the only way they could think of to get close to him. And at that moment, watching Demitto's eyes glitter in the low light and remembering his lips on hers, she felt as if together they could conquer the world.

"All right, let's do it."

III

The inside of the pyramid was cool and quiet. Sarra and the other four Veris made their way through the maze of passages quickly, aware that Comminor was not far behind them. Still, as they passed, they couldn't stop themselves admiring the beauty of the rooms.

"Who did all this?" Nele paused briefly to admire an ornate pillar carved with the shape of flames, and Sarra stopped to run her fingers over the paintwork. She could see where once it had been brightly coloured, and flecks of gold leaf still glinted in the light from the acorn in the pouch around Betune's neck. This had been a magnificent place, she thought, looking up at the high painted ceiling. It would have been full of life and energy. Now it seemed sad, cold and distant, gradually fading into myth, disappearing like the rainbows Amabil had described from her dreams.

"It was the Incendi," said Geve.

Sarra looked across at him, startled. He had hardly said anything for the last few hours, although he hadn't ventured far from her side, and had been there several times to help her out with a steadying hand as she stumbled on loose rock. "Who?" she asked, puzzled.

The room had several large polished blocks of stone placed around a central square floor. A deep channel ran around the outside, filled with the same folded grey rock she had seen earlier. Geve sat on one of the blocks and put his head in his hands. Sarra hesitated, wanting to press on, the memory of Comminor standing at the top of the stairs in the distance haunting her. But her legs ached, and she sank onto the nearest block gratefully. A few seconds couldn't hurt.

The others sat beside them, all tired and weary. Amabil rested a hand on Geve's back. "What is it?"

He sank his hands into his hair. "I keep seeing images. Hearing voices in my ear. It is like the dreams, although I am awake. It is driving me mad."

"It is all right." Amabil stroked his back.

"It is not all right." He lifted his head, and his features were ravished with pain. "This place – it used to belong to our enemies. The Incendi were fire elementals, and they were the cause of our downfall. They were what drove us underground, all those thousands of years ago!"

They all stared at him. Sarra became aware that her jaw was sagging and snapped it shut. "What do you mean?" she whispered, shivering in the cool stale air.

He leaned forward, elbows on his knees, and sank his hands back into his hair. "I do not know. I see images... Burning buildings, people screaming... I just know that they caused our doom."

Betune looked around, her hand unconsciously straying to the pouch around her neck. "Where are they now? Are we to be attacked at any moment?"

"No. They have abandoned this place," Nele said. "It feels dead. Nothing lives here anymore."

"Maybe they died," Amabil suggested. "Perhaps there was a disease, or a civil war."

"I do not know. But this place is doing something to us. I know it feels dead, but it is still affecting us. We should go."

Sarra looked around the room. "I am not sure which way." Her previous certainty had deserted her. Suddenly every exit looked the same, and the instinctive tug she had felt to go in a particular direction had vanished.

Geve glanced across at her, his gaze challenging. "Is nobody going to comment on the fact that Sarra's baby is getting bigger?"

She held her breath as they all looked at her. Instinctively her hand strayed to her bump. At first she had thought she was imagining it, but it had soon become clear to her that the baby was growing much faster than it should. They had only left the Embers at the most two days ago, and the baby had grown enough for two months.

"I thought I had imagined it," Betune murmured.

"I did not want to say," Amabil added, "but I had noticed."

Nausea rose in Sarra's throat. No longer could she pretend it wasn't happening. "I am scared."

Nele stood and came over to sit beside her. He took her hand. "We know the baby is special. He is a bard, and he has been leading you out of the darkness and into the light. It is certain that the Arbor is behind this. The Arbor cares for your child, Sarra, and it knows he is in danger. Perhaps it is trying to bring him to term so his safety is ensured. Whatever is happening, we can be certain it is for the best."

Sarra nodded, although she felt anything but certain at that moment. Inside her, the baby kicked as if aware that everyone was talking about him.

And why was she so sure it was a "him"? She had no way of telling the sex of the child before birth. There were numerous old wives' tales about holding crystals above the mother's belly and seeing whether the crystal swung in a clockwise or anticlockwise direction, but nobody gave any credence to them, and Sarra had never tried it. And yet she was certain it was a boy.

Tears came into her eyes as she thought of Rauf. What would he have thought if he had known he had a son? She hoped he would have been pleased. In truth, she had not known him for very long before he was killed – just long enough, in fact, for him to have fathered the child. He had been fun-loving and impetuous, a risk taker, which was no doubt what had got him killed. They had not had enough time together to know whether they were compatible or not. She had found him attractive, had not protested when he asked her back to his rooms in the palace. But was that because she loved him, or because she had been excited at the thought of being courted by a Select, a privileged man who could give her the life she would otherwise never hope to have?

She looked across at Geve, who had loved her since childhood: a kind, loyal man she felt a deep affection for. He must have had other partners, but she had never seen him with a woman. He was hanging onto the hope that when they reached their destination, she would give herself to him as she had promised. But again, was that out of love, or because the thought of being alone with a child frightened her?

She closed her eyes, her chest heaving. They had to get going. Comminor was coming for them, and the thought of what he would do to her when he caught up with her sent icy fear trickling down her spine. He would kill her, she knew. He could be such a cruel man. And yet his tender touch had awakened in her something she had not known before, not even with Rauf. He had been so gentle, so considerate of her. He had told her how she had haunted his thoughts, and how he could bring himself to think of nothing else but her. Would he truly be able to kill her?

Did she love him?

Her thoughts whirled, her emotions spiralling. The baby moved inside her, and she felt a tug somewhere near her navel, uncomfortable enough to make her gasp and open her eyes.

For a moment she just stared, disorientated. The Veris had disappeared and she sat alone in the dimly lit and dusty room. Alone, except for the man who stood before her.

He was tall and slender, about her own age, with long brown hair braided and drawn back with golden clasps, and shining brown eyes. He wore a strangely colourful tunic over plain brown breeches, woven from a material finer than she had ever seen before, with gold rings on his fingers and an intricate circlet on his hair studded with sparkling jewels. His face was handsome and intelligent, and his lips curved in a faint smile.

He held a hand out to her. Without hesitation – which struck her as strange, even though it didn't stop her – she took it and let him pull her up.

"Walk with me," he said.

He pulled her hand into the crook of his arm, and they walked across the floor to a doorway on the other side.

"Where are you taking me?" she asked.

He just smiled at her, his look affectionate, teasing even. "Not far now."

She reached out her other hand to trail along the corridor walls, fingers tracing the faded paintings and gold leaf, admiring the strange figures and delicate brushwork. "Who made these? I have never seen anything like it before."

"The Incendi."

"Geve was telling us about them."

"Yes."

The patterns, lines and circles seemed to move before her eyes. "Do they tell a story?"

"Sometimes. The small pictures and shapes in a line are their language."

Of course, now she could see the occasional repeated symbol. "What do they say?"

"It tells of their history. Their myths and legends. It describes of their wish to be free."

"We all want to be free," she said.

"Yes, we do."

He turned into another corridor. The ground began to slope up, and her heart rate increased.

"What is that sound?" she asked, looking around to try and find the source of the strange twittering.

"Birds," he said.

Joy flooded her. "Real birds? Flying in the sky?"

He laughed. "Yes. Would you like to see them?"

"Yes, please."

She felt oddly light, as if she were floating. Her legs were hardly moving, and yet the corridor seemed to be growing lighter, the air fresher.

"Will there be stars?" she asked him.

"At night-time," he replied. "A million million, in a sky so large it will take your breath away."

"Show me," she said breathlessly, and he smiled.

"Nearly there."

The light brightened. She had lived in the semi-darkness for so long it hurt her eyes. They watered, tears streaming down her cheeks, and he stopped for a moment and brushed them free. "Do not cry."

She wanted to tell him she wasn't crying, but in truth the happiness welled in her so much that the tears became real. "I have waited so long for this," she told him.

"I know. We all have." He put an arm around her, guiding her forward. "Mind your step."

She stumbled and he steadied her. She put out her hands in case she fell, then stopped, shocked to see the ground not the usual grey colour but instead a vibrant green.

"Grass?"

"Yes."

She bent and felt it, brushing her fingers across its furry surface. More tears joined the first. "It tickles."

He laughed and brought her to her feet. "Come on. Someone wants to meet you." He turned her, and she blinked, rubbed her eyes, and then stopped, shocked.

The oak tree rustled in the early morning breeze. It reared above her head, much bigger than she had ever thought possible, all deep brown branches and rich green leaves. She reached up a hand to touch one of the leaves, mouth open as she traced its shape with its even lobes, and nestling in them a shiny brown acorn. The acorn reminded her of the man's eyes, and she turned to look at him to find him smiling at her.

"It is beautiful, is it not?" he asked her.

"It is." She rested a hand on the Arbor's trunk. The rough bark scraped the skin on her palm, but as she waited, she felt what she had somehow known existed – its slow, steady heartbeat.

"It is time to go," said the man.

She turned reluctantly to face him. He held out his hands, and she placed hers in them. She looked up into his eyes, not surprised to find in them the shining brown form of an acorn.

"It will not be easy," he said. "The future is not carved in stone. There are many trials to undergo yet. You must be strong. You must have hope."

A shiver went through her. "Will you stay with me?"

"Always." He squeezed her hands. "Close your eyes."

She did so. "I love you."

"I love you too, Mother."

"Stay safe, my son."

She felt his kiss on her cheek. And then the light faded.

Sarra opened her eyes with a jerk. The others were clustered around her, faces concerned. Geve looked almost tearful, and he knelt before her, his hand cupping her cheek.

"Are you all right?" His expression turned to relief as he saw her gaze focus. "I thought we had lost you. We could not wake you."

She took a deep breath. Her blood raced and her heart pounded. "He is here," she said.

"Who?"

She looked past him, and he glanced over his shoulder. Slowly, he pushed himself to his feet.

"Hello, Sarra," Comminor said.

CHAPTER SIXTEEN

I

Julen felt a peculiar sense of isolation in the mountain caves.

Part of it was due to the atmosphere: hot, humid and dark. The cloying warmth closed around him like a blanket, and he wanted to rip it apart with his hands to be able to breathe the fresh air once again. Part of it was being in a place where it had become clear to him that the Incendi had been existing all along, hidden deep within the mountains, in the bowels of the land. And part of it was not being able to contact Cinereo – in fact being completely isolated from all of his kind. He was alone, and the rescue of Horada rested entirely on his shoulders. Before he entered the caves, Cinereo had made it very clear that he *had* to rescue Horada if they were to save the Arbor in both this time and the future. He simply could not afford to fail.

His forehead beaded with sweat; he stopped to retrieve his leather water bag from his backpack. Why hadn't Gravis come with him? Julen had travelled a lot and was used to acting on his own, but he had never taken on a role with such importance before. Clearly the Peacemaker had been aware of the Incendi threat, and the Nox Aves were making preparations to save the Arbor. Why had they entrusted this essential task to him when he was as yet unproven?

He sank to his haunches and leaned back against the rock. Once he closed his fist to open his water bag, the flame that was lighting his way disappeared, plunging him into darkness. He was used to working in the shadows, however, and the darkness did not bother him, even though he disliked the humidity.

Of course, Gravis would not have thought twice about sending him on the journey. He and his twin, Gavius, had been Quest Leaders at the time of the Darkwater invasion, and they had undergone severe trials to activate the Nodes even though they were only a few years older than himself. Gavius had died shortly after completing his Quest. Gravis wouldn't have even considered that Julen might not be ready to handle such a role.

And yet the twins had been Militis, trained from the age of seven to handle a sword and to defend the Arbor. Julen may have been Chonrad and Procella's son, but he had been raised in a very different world to the twins. He had only ever known peace in Anguis, and although Wulfian lords stirred from time to time and young men hungered to prove themselves in battle, the odd skirmish was nothing compared to the way the four countries of Anguis had come together to defeat the Darkwater Lords.

He tied the top of his water bag and placed it in his backpack. Then he tipped his head back on the wall.

He must not give in to fear and doubt. He thought of his parents and what they would say to him now, were they standing before him. Chonrad would have knelt and looked him in the eye, told him to be strong of heart, told him he was his son and that together they could save the world. His father had had an innate goodness and belief in the triumph of good over bad, of righteousness over evil, as if a beacon of light had shone from him to illuminate the darkest parts of men's souls. Oh, he could be bad-tempered and grumpy as much as the next man, when he was tired or hungry or exasperated from the trials and tribulations of the day. But deep down he had a heart of gold, and even though he was gone, Julen felt his love enshroud him like a cloak every day of his life.

And his mother? Julen smiled wryly in the semi-darkness.

Procella would have given him a whack and told him to stop being such a baby. Emotions, she would have said, were for other people and had no place in battle. Sympathy for the enemy, guilt over one's actions, sorrow for a slain friend, anger over a soldier's death – none of these should be entertained in wartime. For although emotions could give a person a reason to fight, it also gave them a vulnerable point, made them weak.

With his father's staunch support and his mother's sometimes harsh but astute guidance, he had grown into an able member of the Peacemaker's team. He was kind but never gullible; fair but never weak; strong but never overbearing; ruthless but never cruel. He had killed those the Nox Aves considered a threat to the Arbor, and was relentless when given a task to complete. He had a wisdom way beyond his years and had thrown off the fears and daydreams of childhood a long time ago.

So why was he doubting himself now?

He pressed his palms against the rock floor, aware of the way his heart beat faster than usual, the race of blood around his veins. He was just nervous about being discovered. Worried about Horada, and fearful that the Incendi had already decided she was not worth keeping alive, that his journey into these caves was all for nothing.

It couldn't be due to the faint thrumming he could feel through his hands that vibrated all the way up to the base of his skull.

Wishing he could contact Cinereo, he pushed himself to his feet, shouldered his bag, conjured up the flame and started walking again.

He held the sunstone pendant in his left hand, and he rubbed his thumb across the wood. The thought that it came from the Arbor itself sent a warmth through him that had nothing to do with the humidity in the caves. *It will guide and protect you*, Gravis had said. Julen pondered on the words as he walked. Well it was definitely guiding him – his feet turned at corners without him having to think which way to go. He had yet to establish whether it would protect him. He had not yet had to fight any Incendi – although he had sensed their presence in the woods, he had managed to evade them and so far hadn't come across any in the caves.

In fact, where were they all? His feet slowed. He had expected to be challenged when he entered their kingdom, but apart from the rumbling beneath his feet, he had not heard or seen anything except dark, rough rock. It felt as if he had been walking for hours, although he had no way of telling. At first the tunnels had been long and meandering, but now they were shorter and straighter, almost like corridors in a castle. In fact it was a bit like a castle dungeon, he thought, noting that cells opened off the passage he walked down. They were all empty, though.

The pendant warmed in his hand as he approached the door to another cell. He edged to the wall and moved silently to the door, then peered through the grille, holding up his lantern.

His heart seemed to stutter to a halt. In the middle of the cell, Horada lay on a stone block. She lay on her back, legs straight, arms crossed over her chest. Her eyes were closed.

She looked dead.

Julen inhaled and leaned back against the corridor wall, looking up and down to make sure he was alone. But there were no guards, no sounds and no lights further along the passageway. He waited for a few moments, took a deep breath, and then looked through the grille again. His gaze searched the four corners of the cell, but there was nobody inside it but his sister.

He tried the handle of the door. It was not locked, so clearly they were not worried about her escaping.

She's not dead, he thought desperately. *She can't be dead. I would have sensed it.*

He went inside, pushed the door almost shut and moved quietly up to his sister.

Even before he reached her, he could see he had been fooling himself. Not an ounce of life remained in the young girl. Her face was bleached white, her lips dry, her blonde hair limp, and when he rested a hand on her arm, her skin was cold.

Finding it hard to breathe, he reached out to touch her face. She could not be dead. Cinereo would have seen it – the Arbor would have warned him.

But maybe they did not know? Maybe the Arbor's power did not extend into the mountains, where the Incendi had obviously staked their claim.

What did it mean for Anguis? Could the Apex still take place? Was Anguis and the Arbor lost?

He sank to his knees beside her. He didn't care about all that. His sister was dead.

His heart hollowed and filled with grief, and he buried his face in his hands.

They had been close ever since they were young. Julen loved all his family, but had a special fondness for his sister. He loved her innocence, her patience, her calm and her inner strength. Their mother was wrong to think Horada weak, just because she didn't enjoy swordplay. Horada harboured their father's warmth, wholesomeness and faith.

And now she was dead.

He had never before felt the hopelessness that washed over him now, wave after wave. Tears poured down his face, and he sank his hands into his hair. He had let her down – had let them all down: his family, Gravis, the Nox Aves, the Arbor, even Anguis itself. Cinereo had impressed upon him the necessity of rescuing Horada – that just like her father, she was the key to the Apex for reasons not yet clear, and that without her the future lay shattered. He should have been faster, worked harder... He should have tried more. He had failed.

He moved to lay on his front, prone by the side of Horada's bier, arms stretched out. What was the point in rising again? He rested his forehead on the floor, tempted to dash his brain out on the cool stone. He couldn't swallow, could hardly breathe, a whirlwind of emotions spinning inside him. Anger, frustration, grief, despair... How could he have let her die?

For a while, he didn't move. The stone, although initially cool, became warmed by his body, which grew stiff and unyielding as he continued to lie there. His head ached, and his breathing laboured through his tight chest.

It was the sensation of something touching his foot that brought him out of his melancholic stupor. He twitched automatically, lifted and turned onto his side to look down.

A green vine had wrapped around his foot.

He stared as the vine moved upward, and sat up, intending to move back, but the vine encircled his ankle, taut as an iron manacle, and he couldn't move.

Panicking now, he withdrew the dagger on his hip, but another vine snaked out and wrapped around his wrist and tightened, and the dagger fell from his fingers.

Vines crept over his torso, forcing him to lie on his back. He turned his head and saw they were emanating from the base of the stand on which Horada lay.

Wait a moment... Vines, underground?

For the first time, Julen stopped resisting. Although the tendrils felt insidious as they crept over him, he forced himself to lie still. Instinctively, he knew this wasn't the Incendi's doing.

This was the Arbor.

A thrill threaded through him. The Arbor hadn't deserted him. It still watched over him, even underground, even in this place when he was at his darkest, when his sister had left him alone...

A shadow loomed over him. A man, dressed in a grey cloak. Cinereo!

The cloaked figure extended a hand towards him and said one word.

"Wake."

Julen gasped and his eyes shot open. He wasn't in a dark cell. And the girl lying on the floor next to him stirred at his gasp and also opened her eyes. Horada was alive!

They lay in a ceremonial room filled with elemental forms, the whole place alight with light and fire. Gold, silver and gems decorated the painted walls and the stone pedestals, and the floor was laid with gold and red tiles. Magma boiled in a channel that ran around the room.

"Horada?" he asked urgently.

Her face lit up. "Julen?"

"Are you all right?"

She nodded, sitting up, and looked around her. "Where are we?"

He struggled to his feet, the manacles around his wrists making it difficult to rise where they were chained to the rock behind him. The elementals stirred, their voices – such as they were – filling the room with the roar of a billowing fire.

He moved forward to the edge of his chains and stood facing them, fury blazing through him.

"You thought you could fool me!" he yelled, straining at the chains, wanting to rip the Incendi apart with his bare hands. "You thought you could tell me my sister had died and make me give up hope? Well the Arbor watches over me, and it will not forsake me! You cannot touch me!"

The elementals stared at him. Then they started making a strange noise. Julen wasn't sure, but he thought it might have been laughter.

He clenched his fists and opened his mouth to shout again, but the words faded as he became aware of a burning sensation on his chest.

Afraid that one of the Incendi had touched him, or maybe that a fleck of the magma had landed on him, he looked down. But it wasn't magma. The thing that was burning him was the wooden pendant – and it burned so hot it had turned white.

It glowed, so dazzling he couldn't look straight at it. He remembered the way the vines had snaked around him, and he knew this was the Arbor reaching out for him, helping him during his hour of need.

The words his father had once told him about the Darkwater invasion rang in his head, almost as if his father were there, speaking in his ear. *You think the Arbor triumphed over the Darkwater Lords through strength of its weapons? No, it was strength of the heart that made us victorious. Power comes through love and trust. That is what we can give the Arbor. That is what won us the war.*

Julen closed his eyes and let his love for the tree and for Horada and his family sweep over him. It rushed through his veins, made his heart pump furiously, and he exclaimed in shock as it burst from him in a brilliant flash of white light that encompassed the whole room. The manacles around his hands fell away, and he raised his arms, revelling in the rush of joy at the thought that his sister was still alive, and he still had a chance to save the day.

Next to him, Horada exclaimed. The rush of light faded and he opened his eyes.

Around him, the elementals stood where they had been when the light hit them. They had been frozen, their forms locked in place by an icy casing.

Julen stared at them, then dropped to his knees to help Horada up. "Quick! We do not have long."

She got to her feet, but even as she did so, the ground trembled beneath them and she fell again. "Julen!"

He put a hand under her arm, but the trembling increased and the whole room shook.

"What is happening?" she whispered, looking down at her hands. They sparkled, and Julen went cold as around them the air turned thick and shone with glittering dust.

"I do not know…" The room darkened and to his shock, the elementals faded into shadow.

II

Tahir's bottom had gone numb. Standing up made his legs ache, and besides, he couldn't move far from where his manacles were linked to an iron ring in the wall, so he ended up sitting most of the time. But he couldn't lie down, and consequently he was beginning to feel sore. He didn't have a lot of meat on his bones anyway, he thought, pushing his back up against the wall and crossing his legs, and he had even less now as he had hardly eaten anything over the last few days.

Hunger gnawed at his stomach, but he was too tired and dispirited to worry about it. Standing up to the Incendi king had been uplifting and thrilling, but Pyra had promptly thrown him in a cell and forgotten about him. Nobody had come in for hours, maybe days – he had no way of telling. He had no light, no food, and no water. His mouth felt as if it were full of sand, and he was so tired he could barely lift his head up.

Pyra might not be able to kill him directly, he mused, but he was doing a pretty good job indirectly. At this rate, he would be dead before the end of the day. And for the first time, he thought he might welcome it.

He leaned his head against the stone and dozed.

A muffled yell from further down the corridor snapped him awake. How long had he slept? It could have been minutes or hours. And who had yelled? Since being in the cell, he had heard tortured screams and people crying, but this sounded different – nearby, an oath, cut off quickly. He sat up, tried to get to his feet and failed, too weak to rise.

Feet scuffed outside the door and a voice whispered, "Tahir?"

His heart swelled. He knew that voice! "Catena? It is I!"

A key turned in the lock and the door opened. The familiar form of Catena came through. She looked tired and dishevelled, streaked with sweat and dust, odd in the clothes of an Incendi guard, but her face lit up as she saw him.

She dropped to her knees before him and cupped his face. "Tahir? What have they done to you?"

He tried to shake his head. "I am all right."

"You are not all right." Her voice hitched. "My young prince. How could they?"

He felt too emotional to answer, and instead turned as Atavus pushed under her arm, tail wagging furiously, and shoved his nose into Tahir's face. The dog's warm tongue licked him, and Tahir threw his arms around Atavus's neck and buried his face in the dog's fur. "Oh I have missed you," he murmured, only then realising how much.

A dark shape filled the doorway, and Tahir pulled back as Demitto appeared. He looked down at the boy silently. Tahir looked up, seeing the emissary's handsome face and his dark eyes. The man also wore Incendi garb.

A twinge of doubt made Tahir stiffen in Catena's hands. "How do I know it is you?" he whispered.

She frowned and stroked his cheeks. "It is me, Tahir. Can you not tell?"

"I…" He swallowed. "He plays tricks on me."

Demitto lowered his bag from his back and retrieved his leather water bag. He passed it to Catena. "The boy's dehydrated and probably delirious. Do not let him drink it all. Just a bit at first."

Pushing the eager Atavus out of the way, she tipped up the bottle and the water slid between Tahir's lips. It was warm, but he drank it like it was cold and clear, fresh from a mountain stream, and he had never tasted anything so fine.

She lowered the bottle and handed it back to Demitto, who sank to his haunches before the Prince.

"We must go," he stated. "Can you stand?"

Tahir looked up at him. Embarrassment and shame filled him at the fantasy that Pyra had used to taunt and tempt him with. He could not shake the memory of the man's lips pressed against his. "How do I know it is you?" he whispered.

Demitto frowned. "If you ask me that again, I am going to slap you. Now get up. We have to go."

The man's obvious impatience filled him with relief and convinced him that this was the real Demitto more than anything else could have done.

He tried to push himself to his feet again, but his limbs shook and he fell to his knees. "I do not think I can walk..." His lip trembled. "I am sorry."

Demitto put an arm around his shoulders, bent and slid a hand under his knees, and hefted him into his arms. "You weigh almost nothing," he said, gesturing with his head for Catena to check the corridor. "We need to get you to eat."

Tahir leaned his head on Demitto's shoulder and let the tears trickle down his cheeks. They had risked their lives to find him and rescue him. He felt so humble he could not put it into words.

They rounded a corner and Demitto stopped at the sight of two guards in the corridor ahead of them. Catena passed him and drew her sword. Even before Atavus could leap at them, the guards were dead.

Tahir blinked at the speed with which she had despatched them. He had never seen her kill anyone before, had not been certain she was capable of it. He had always thought of her role as Captain of the Guard a sedentary one. Little happened down in Harlton – there had been no great invasions of the castle or local wars in Tahir's lifetime. She practised her sword skills on a daily basis and he had often watched her putting the guards through their paces, laughing as they tripped over their swords or dazed each other with mis-hits. The thought of them fighting in battle had amused him. And now here she was, fending off the enemy with ease.

She cleaned her sword on the guard's jerkin, stood and sheathed the blade, and looked down at the bodies for a moment. "I wonder where they were from," she murmured. "They were probably just farmers, brought here by the Incendi – their training could not match a Laxonian knight's."

"They hope to overwhelm with numbers," Demitto said. He nodded down the corridor. "Keep going."

She led the way, and the emissary followed. Tahir curled in the man's arms, drawing his feet in so they didn't knock against the walls of the passage. He let his hand drop, however, and felt Atavus's nose bump against it from time to time.

He had seen the elemental army preparing for battle, had counted their numbers. Anguis had not known a war like this for five hundred years. Heartwood had few defences. The people had grown soft and lazy after years of peace. What would happen when the Incendi rose?

Ahead of them, Catena paused, her palm resting on the wall. She bent her head in concentration, her dark hair falling across her face.

"What is she doing?" Tahir whispered.

"Listening to the rock," Demitto replied. "She is a Saxum."

Two revelations about Catena in the space of a few moments. Tahir watched her, seeing her hand glow with silver light. Her father was a miner, and his father before him. Had she somehow inherited a love of the rock in the blood?

She lifted her head and looked up at them. "Something is happening."

"Can you be more specific?" Demitto sounded exasperated. Tahir could feel the tenseness of the man's body, and an irritation that teetered on fear. He didn't like being underground.

She frowned. "Can you not feel it?"

Demitto opened his mouth to reply, then paused.

Tahir lifted his head. "What is it?"

The emissary slid his arm from under the boy's knees to let his feet drop to the floor. Tahir stood, albeit unsteadily, one hand resting on Atavus's neck as he came forward to support him. As he did so, he felt what the others had been able to feel – a deep vibration in the ground.

At the same time, the air about them turned crystalline, as if it were freezing cold, although the temperature and humidity remained so high that sweat poured down their faces. Tahir passed his hand in front of him, watching the sparkling dust move and swirl. "What is it?"

"I do not know." Demitto took his hand and moved forward. They walked to the end of the corridor and stood at the entrance to the next room.

They were in the heart of the enormous pyramid, Tahir thought, in some kind of large ceremonial room, with high ceilings and flat, polished walls painted in bright colours, highlighted with gold and silver, studded with sparkling gems. Magma ran in a channel around the edge, and steam curled from the boiling rock, lending the whole chamber a hazy air. It was empty of Incendi, as if the room were only used for important occasions. Tahir lived in a king's castle, but he had never seen anything as splendid as this place.

"We should go," Catena said, but Tahir pushed past her and, on shaky legs, walked into the room.

The air felt thick, like walking through honey. He could remember being taken to the sea once by a nurse, and she had led him out into the ocean until he could not touch the bottom. He had played often in the local river and could swim well enough, but the sensation of being out of his depth had made him panic, and it was a similar feeling now. He moved his arms, watching the silver dust swirl around them, conscious of breathing it in, although it did not appear to be affecting his lungs. He splayed his fingers, and spirals of silver wove between them, entrancing and terrifying at the same time.

"Tahir." Demitto spoke firmly. "We are leaving."

But Tahir ignored him. He felt a strange attraction to the centre of the room, as if he were being drawn there by invisible hands. He walked down the wide steps to the tiled floor, hands brushing the elaborately carved statues and stone furniture.

"Tahir," Catena snapped in her best do-as-I-say-or-there-will-be-trouble voice, but he ignored her too.

Something was shifting inside him. He stopped in the middle of the floor, heart pounding, slightly dizzy. Was that just the lack of food and water or something more? He raised his hands in front of him. They sparkled too; in fact as he looked down he could see the whole of him sparkling.

"Tahir…" Catena's voice sounded as if from a long way away. He closed his eyes.

The world turned. He felt as if he were sinking into the ground, into the earth, separating into a billion tiny pieces that were travelling along the energy channels from the Arbor to all corners of Anguis.

Above him, the stars wheeled, the sun rose and set, clouds scudded across the sky and birds dipped and soared on the currents. Trees grew, and died; animals lived, and died. Their energy seeped into the channels, circled the world, joined with him in this journey from coast to coast. Men loved women, made babies; they grew in the womb, were born. It was all a circle – a cycle – and Tahir felt a part of it for the first time in his life. No longer was he a small, thin, rather insignificant young man – he was the food for the world, the breath of life.

This can all be yours…

The Arbor loomed large in his mind, towering over him. The rich, thick leaves rustled in the breeze. Tahir put his arms around the trunk and rested his cheek on the bark. The heartbeat sounded in his ears, slow and steady. Faces flashed through his mind, including one similar to his own, with dark hair, golden eyes. Was it someone else or was he looking into a mirror?

Overhead, the sky rumbled. Thunder – a storm coming. He watched the clouds gather, curling, darkening, brooding. The tree rustled. Something was coming. His breathing quickened, and he stepped away from the trunk. He felt empty inside, like a mother whose newborn has been snatched from her arms. The tree faded, and his consciousness withdrew like a sailor pulling in the mooring ropes before setting sail.

Once again, he became aware of the ground trembling beneath his feet. The air swirled around him, thick and humid. Voices whispered in the darkness, tugging at his mind. The world spun.

Tahir opened his eyes.

III

Comminor walked down the steps into the large ceremonial room. He glanced around it briefly, seeing the faded paint, the beautifully carved statues, the stone furniture. Ice settled in his stomach. He hated it, hated all of it. He wished he could tear it down with his bare hands.

The five members of the Veris stood in a line on the other side of the room. They had all drawn small blades and held them like dining knives. They would be no match for his trained Umbra. The journey was over.

He moved closer and noticed with shock that Sarra's pregnancy had advanced far more than it should have done in the days since they had left the Embers. Why was that? What strange phenomenon could be causing the baby to grow?

She saw him looking at her bump and crossed her arms over it protectively. "Please do not harm the baby," she whispered.

He frowned. "I will not harm it if you do as you are told." His gaze rested on her face and he could not stop the sweep of longing that overcame him. He loved her – he could not deny it. "I do not want to harm any of you. You are my citizens. I just want you to return with me." He thought briefly of the waterfall and the hanging rope, then brushed it away. He would worry about how they were to return later.

"We are not going back," the apothecary known as Nele said.

Comminor turned his hard gaze to him. "I will not let you leave."

Frustration filled the other man's face. "What are we to you? Nothing. Why can you not just let us go?"

"You belong to me. And it is my duty to keep you all safe." Sarra moved forward. "You do not understand. There is a way out, Comminor. A way to the Surface. The baby knows – it is a bard. I have spoken to him. He is connected to the Arbor – he is showing me the way out! Do you not want to see the Surface? To know what is out there? To see the Arbor?"

Comminor kept his face impassive. "You must come back with me."

She walked up to him and stood before him, then took his hands in hers. "Please."

He looked into her eyes. Love swept over him, and he wished he could just pick her up and carry her back, and live with her in his palace for the rest of his days. He cupped her cheek, brushing it with his thumb, aching to hold her, wishing he didn't have to say the words. "I cannot."

Geve came down the steps and took Sarra's hand. "Come on."

"You are not taking her anywhere," Comminor said, moving to confront the other man.

They faced each other, Geve's face showing determination. "I will fight you. I will not let you take her."

Behind Comminor, Viel, Josse and Paronel fanned out to meet the other members of the Veris as they came down the steps, swords drawn.

"I would like to see you try," Comminor said, amused.

Geve opened his mouth to reply. And then the ground trembled.

Comminor's eyes met Sarra's again, and she must have read the uncertainty in his because it mirrored in her own. "What was that?"

"I do not know." They looked around as the trembling continued, seeing clouds of dust arising from the statues and pillars, the vibration travelling up through their feet into their bones.

The air became thick and filled with glistening dust, and as Comminor moved his hand in front of him, the glitter stirred in whorls of silver and gold.

He held his breath, shocked. Surely not...

He had read about this in the *Quercetum*. This happened when time was being manipulated. And it had happened when the Apex had occurred.

The *Quercetum* had stated that the third phase of the Apex would occur in the future. Of course the book had been written in the First and Second Age, and those who played a part in the second phase had not been able to tell how far in the future the third phase would be. Comminor had assumed it was hundreds if not thousands of years ahead – had never thought to play a role in it.

Was it really happening now?

The room – already in a half-light that Comminor noticed now came from a bag around Betune's neck – darkened. His stomach knotted the way it did when he jumped into the palace pool from the diving board, as if he were falling. Around them, the air stirred, grew thick as stew, shone silver.

And then figures appeared out of the darkness, standing beside them, their shimmering forms hardening, solidifying, until the room was full of people, staring at each other in shocked disbelief.

Comminor looked at the men and women who had appeared and knew immediately that they were those mentioned in the *Quercetum* as having taken part in the Apex. The blonde, small young woman was Horada, the angry dark-haired man her brother Julen, both children of Chonrad, the great knight who had helped to save the Arbor from the Darkwater Lords. And the boy with the black hair and golden eyes the same as his own was the young prince, Tahir, while the couple standing by him must be the emissary and the boy's guard, Demitto and Catena. Next to the Prince stood the dog that the *Quercetum* had stated was the father of all the dogs who had lived in the Embers ever since.

Comminor stared at them all, shocked into silence, confused beyond belief. The Apex had occurred outside, hadn't it? In front of the Arbor, at Heartwood. How could it be happening now, underground?

Horada grabbed hold of her brother. "The Apex," she said urgently. "He is trying to move the Apex. To force it to happen now!"

"Who is?" Comminor demanded.

Julen studied him cautiously, then stepped forward. "Pyra, the King of the Incendi."

"We cannot let it happen," Demitto said.

"I think it is too late." Prince Tahir dropped to his knees as the ground shook again. "We have failed."

"No!" Comminor let out a bellow. He had not worked all these years to protect his people only to have them destroyed. "We must call for help."

"I have tried," said Demitto, "but the Arbor cannot help us in here. It cannot hear us."

"Yes, it can." Julen's eyes lit up. "I thought the same, but it has just helped me turn the Incendi elementals to ice and it freed me from the manacles." He looked down and clasped the wooden pendant around his neck. "It was this. It is a part of the Arbor."

The trembling increased, and to their left a statue tumbled to the ground, breaking into half a dozen pieces. Amabil, standing nearby, squealed and rubbed her arm where the rock had struck her. Everyone moved, clustering in the centre.

Demitto fumbled in his linen shirt and withdrew his own pendant. "Here is mine."

Comminor pulled out his. "And mine."

"What do we do with them?"

"I do not know." Comminor lifted the cord over his head, as did the others. They tightened their fists and placed their hands together. "Think of the Arbor," he commanded.

They all concentrated, but nothing happened. To his surprise, he felt Sarra's hand creep into his. "What is happening?" she whispered.

He realised she knew nothing of the Apex, nor of the time before the Embers. But it would take too long to explain now. "You must believe me," he said. "We have to stop this convergence. It is not time."

She met his gaze. He saw it dawn in her eyes that he knew more than he had revealed to her. Slowly, she nodded. "Betune," she murmured.

Comminor's head snapped around to the woman who held the tiny bag in her hand. "What is in there?"

Betune's gaze flicked to Nele, who nodded. "It is an acorn from the Arbor," she said reluctantly, as if worried he would take it away from her.

But Comminor just beckoned her forward. "Hold it here."

It was becoming hard to stand upright, and everyone reached out to hold onto one of the stone blocks as the tremors increased and more statues fell, the dust making everyone cough.

Betune stumbled to them, opening the tiny bag, and let the acorn drop onto her palm. She closed her fingers around it and placed her hand on top of the others.

Comminor waited, but nothing happened. Huge chunks of stone fell all around them, as if the whole world were breaking apart. Sarra's hand tightened in his, and beside her he heard Geve curse under his breath as fragments of falling stone chipped and flew to sting their skin.

They couldn't die here, not after everything he had done. He had worked so hard, studied the histories, made decisions that had kept him awake at night just to keep the Embers at peace. *Please*, he thought. *Do not let us all die here. I have kept us safe for so long.* He thought of the Arbor. *Please, help us.*

His pendant grew warm. He opened his eyes and stared at their hands. Demitto and Julen were doing the same. A glow emitted from the acorn, passing through the sunstones in the pendants. All three brightened, first to an orange glow, then to a brilliant white light.

Suddenly, beside them all, a figure appeared, making them jump. A tall man in a long grey cloak, the hood pulled over his head, arms covered with leather bracers, body criss-crossed with leather straps. A holy man who nevertheless was ready for action.

Comminor's heart leapt. *Cinereo?*

The figure brought his hand down in a sharp slash and, at the same time, the world exploded. Bright light from the sunstones shot out across the room, which crumbled around them, and all of them instinctively ducked and covered their heads as stone rained down. Comminor pulled Sarra into his arms and they crouched by the side of a huge stone block that didn't look as if an earthquake could move it. Well, they would soon find out, Comminor thought, because it felt as if they were having an earthquake. The ground shook, pillars fell and dust rose to choke them all. The noise was deafening, and for a while he was sure it was only a matter of time before a huge lump of stone would squash them flat.

He covered Sarra's body with his own, and did his best to protect the baby.

It felt as if the earthquake went on forever. But gradually, the noise and commotion died down. The trembling stopped. The clouds of dust settled.

Comminor waited to make sure it was really over. Then he lifted his head.

The other people who had slipped through the barrier of time had disappeared.

He pushed himself to his feet and lifted Sarra with him, relieved to see she was unharmed. Around them, the others stirred too, coughing and groaning as they checked damaged limbs and found blood. Viel's left hand had been damaged in the falling debris and he cradled it to his chest, wincing with pain. Amabil's left arm was covered in blood where a sharp piece of chipped rock had wounded her shoulder. But amazingly, nobody had been killed.

Comminor looked around the room. Debris littered the floor, and statues and pillars had fallen everywhere, but the most shocking sight was the far wall. It had completely crumbled, and behind it, a staircase of stone steps curved upwards, out of sight to the right.

Comminor's gaze met Sarra's. Defiance leapt in her eyes.

"No!" He drew his sword and made a grab for her, but she was already moving away to the stairs. "Sarra, wait!"

"This way!" she yelled to the others.

Viel, Josse and Paronel moved to stop the Veris as they scrambled to follow her. Geve vaulted over a fallen statue, but Comminor moved to meet him, blocking his exit.

"Get out of my way," Geve snarled, drawing his own sword.

"Do not go up there," Comminor said, unable to stop the desperation entering his voice. "Please."

Geve's brow flickered with confusion, but Comminor saw him look past to where Sarra was already mounting the staircase, pushing bits of stone aside as she climbed.

"This is the way out!" Her voice rang with excitement. "Hurry!"

Comminor met Geve's blade with a parry of his own and pushed him back, and the two men circled. To his right, the others scuffled, but the Veris were no match for the trained Umbra and were quickly restrained.

Angry now, Comminor swung his sword and knocked Geve's aside, but the young man leapt out of his way before he could attack again, regaining his balance and crouching as Comminor approached for another blow.

"We have to protect Sarra," Geve said. "This is madness. Why do we not all go with her?"

Comminor hesitated. It was true that it did not matter whether one or all of them made it to the Surface. However many, it was the beginning of the end. He opened his mouth to speak, and at that moment, a scream cut through the silence.

As one, the two men turned and raced up the staircase, the others close behind. Comminor ran beside Geve, taking two steps at a time, holding onto the wall as the staircase curved up and to the right.

"We are coming, Sarra!" yelled Geve, but there was no reply.

They climbed higher and higher, Comminor privately musing at Sarra's sprightliness at climbing so quickly considering she was so heavily pregnant.

More steps and yet more, and then they turned the corner and saw above them the end of the steps. They climbed the last few and found themselves in a large room.

They came to a halt. In front of them, Sarra had collapsed onto the floor, faced with the scene on the far side. Comminor stared, vaguely aware of the Veris and the Umbra coming up behind him and fanning out to his left and right. Everyone fell silent and stared too.

The wall on the opposite side of the room had crumbled and fallen down a slope, leaving the view wide open. They stood about a third of the way up a mountain, the panorama before them stretching away as far as the eye could see. Comminor's head spun and he almost fell over as his brain tried to make sense of the perspective. He had never seen such a vast distance.

He had known what to expect – the *Quercetum* had made it quite clear what had happened after the second phase of the Apex. He had known that the bards of the Embers saw not the present, but the glorious past: a time when there were birds and the grass and trees, when the land was whole and the Arbor still existed, when Anguis was a place for the living.

He had known it had all come to an end, but even so, seeing it was almost the hardest thing he had ever done. Except for watching the others around him see it too. Especially the Veris – those who had also dreamed of the land of green and blue.

Because the vista before them held only one colour.

The brilliant red of fire.

PART FOUR

CHAPTER SEVENTEEN

I

Procella warmed her hands around the soup bowl, making sure to keep her eyes lowered as she sipped the hot broth.

The inn was practically empty, but a woman on her own could never feel completely safe in Wulfengar, and Procella wasn't exactly unknown in the borderlands. She had pulled her nondescript cloak closely around her shoulders and wore the hood up, hoping she could remain unnoticed. She hadn't eaten all day, and she didn't want to fall off her horse through lack of nourishment.

The west border of Wulfengar loomed temptingly close, only half a day's ride away, but as she'd walked through the small hamlet Yenston, she'd overheard talk of the presence of an army outside the westernmost fort on Isenbard's Wall. Rumours were that the Wulfengar lord of the Lowlands was planning a raid on Setbourg. No doubt they were taking advantage of the unease caused by the Incendi, she thought, as she'd listened to the town traders gossiping about the increasing fires and strange sightings of flaming figures in the night. Most of them scoffed at such notions, but Procella knew the truth that lay behind them.

She finished her broth, her eyelids drooping, and wished she could just rent a room for the night and rest. But Hunfrith still hunted her, and the Incendi were also literally hot on her trail. She had to keep going west until she could find a place to cross the Wall. She had to get to Heartwood. Only then would she be safe.

And maybe not even then. As she sipped her ale, she wondered how Dolosus – Imperator at Heartwood – had reacted to the apparent Incendi threat. After the Darkwater Lords had been vanquished and the Arbor destroyed its own defences, they had not been rebuilt. The fortified Temple had been demolished, and the tree now stood in an open area, ringed only by a simple wooden fence. Around this complex a trading settlement had grown and developed into a small town. Dolosus and the Custodes who used to man the defences now merely controlled the traffic of those wishing to visit and pay their respects to the tree rather than protect it. True, Dolosus ensured that the Custodes were still trained for battle, as it was difficult for everyone for whom the invasion existed in living memory to completely throw off the fear of another threat. But it would be difficult – if not impossible – for them to ward off a direct assault on the tree.

She stared into the fire, musing on the events of the invasion over twenty years ago. Chonrad had descended into the labyrinth, found the fifth node and communicated with the Arbor, which had told him it did not need defending and could look after itself. It had then proceeded to destroy the stone walls surrounding it. So what did that mean for the Wulfengar and Incendi threat? Would the Arbor be able to protect itself again?

Procella loved the Arbor – had spent most of her life defending it – and the thought of it now being defenceless sent a chill through her. The memory of what had happened all those years ago had faded, and she could no longer feel as strongly the thrill of when it had burst forth from its confinement and doubled in size, defeating the Darkwater Lords in the process. Every day, people went to Heartwood to touch the holy tree and feel its Pectoris beating. It remained tall and strong, and there was no doubt from its size and the energy that radiated from it that it was special, more than just one of the many oak trees that grew in the land. But she couldn't imagine that it would respond in the same way to another attack. It felt like a dream, a myth to keep the younger generation in line if they threatened to forget the old ways.

Her eyelids drooped. She couldn't exist forever without sleep. And anyway, it was early evening and it would be better if she rode in the darkness. It was going to be difficult enough to get across the Wall without having to do it in broad daylight.

Her breathing slowed, and she dozed.

She wasn't sure what jerked her awake. The lanterns in the inn had been lit and through the open doorway she could see the daylight had faded, although it wasn't completely dark. The innkeeper had even lit the fire without waking her. She'd been curled in the chair, and she straightened, a little stiff from the position she had taken, blinking as she looked around.

Everything looked the same – a couple of customers at the bar, a young girl sweeping the floor, noises and mouth-watering smells emanating from the kitchen, the twitter of birds outside. And yet her senses prickled. The fire leapt in the hearth. The shadows seemed darker than normal, stretching towards her like giant claws. In spite of the fire, a cold breeze ran through the inn.

What had awoken her? She rose slowly to her feet, years of battle training snapping her out of her slumber, honing her senses. Her gaze focussed on a corner of the room, and for a brief moment she thought she saw a man standing there, dressed in a grey cloak, the hood over his face. Cinereo? She caught her breath. A warning?

"There she is!"

Her head snapped around. A figure appeared silhouetted at the door, backlit by the setting sun, almost filling the doorway with his huge frame. Hunfrith! Two more came through behind him, henchmen who fanned out at his command, approaching her with sneering grins. Their bare blades glinted in the firelight.

The innkeeper squealed and pulled the young girl into the corner with him. The other guests in the room downed their ale and made a hasty exit.

Hunfrith approached, the two men on either side of him. He adopted a forlorn face. "You ran away. And I was so looking forward to spending some time together."

Procella drew her sword. "Go fuck your mother, you ugly bastard son of a rancid dog."

Hunfrith laughed at the guttural Wulfian words, although his eyes narrowed at the insult. "Such spirit." His gaze bore into her, lust sparking the green orbs. "It will be interesting to see if that fire still burns after every man in Wulfengar has taken his pleasure out on you."

"I will kill myself before I let any Wulfian scum touch me." She tossed the sword from right hand to left and back again, reminding herself of the weight, forcing herself to relax. Refusing to let his taunts rile her, she ran through the mental list she made before every fight – weight on the balls of her feet, stance wide, deep breaths, chin up, shoulders loose. Exhilaration flooded her. She had been made for battle. Even the mighty Valens had struggled to best her on a good day, and Chonrad had pronounced her the best knight he had ever met. She would not be intimidated by a trio of jackasses.

Still, the Wulfian lord was exceptionally tall and well-built, bigger than both Valens and Chonrad had been, and he had already almost bested her in a fight. She tried not to look at the bulging muscles in his arms and the width of his thighs, focussing instead on his self-assured grin, and letting her indignation rise to fuel her.

"We will see," Hunfrith said. He grabbed his crotch and massaged it. "It has been a while since I have seen action. I think I will keep you to myself for a while. I will chain you to my bed and rape you until you beg me to stop. And then rape you a few times more." The men with him laughed.

Her heart raced, blood thundering through her veins, and she began to feel the battle rage taking her over. It had been a while, and she welcomed the scarlet veil as it descended upon her. Her senses sharpened, and she became aware of every little noise – the scrape of a chair as the innkeeper barricaded himself into a corner; the murmur of the two cooks in the kitchen; the clatter of a mouse's paws as it ran across the floor to a hole in the opposite wall. Her gaze flicked from man to man, judging their size and strength, noting the way the fellow on her left shifted his weight, signifying a troublesome knee, and how the right eye of the other man was discoloured, suggesting partial blindness.

That man now sniggered and said, "Do not wear her out, Hunfrith, I want her to have some life left in her when I–"

He didn't have time to finish the sentence. Procella lunged forward onto his blind side, caught him by surprise and jammed her sword in his stomach up to the hilt. Drawing the blade out swiftly, she moved back out of range of the others, swinging the sword around her, to the left, to the right, behind her, to the front, enjoying the weight of the blade, the buzz of adrenalin bringing her body to life. She met Hunfrith's furious gaze and held it, challenging him.

"He will die slowly," she announced as the man's screams rang through the inn. "The bowel will suppurate and the wound will fester. It will be very painful. At least, I hope it will."

Hunfrith's eyes narrowed, and the man beside him snarled. Do your worst, she thought, hoping that Chonrad's spirit would stay with her and Valens would lend his strength to her arms. But she said nothing more, waiting for the attack she knew would come.

The man next to the Wulfian lord moved forward. His smile had faded, and he approached her more cautiously, obviously aware her skill was not to be treated lightly. She moved across the room, pushing aside tables and chairs, not taking her eyes off him. He swung at her and she dodged the blow neatly, then did the same the other side. He was testing her, trying to get the measure of her skill and find a weakness. She almost laughed. He wouldn't find one. He was about half her age, and although he probably had the edge on her when it came to speed, she had fought in more battles than he had teeth in his head.

She let him play for a bit, and then, when she had got bored and he had tired from his constant movement, she darted forward, caught the hilt of his blade with hers as he brought it up instinctively to protect himself, and twisted it, causing the sword to fall from his hand and skitter across the floor. His eyes lit with alarm, but they barely had time to register the fear before she grabbed a fistful of his tunic, knocked aside his raised arm and shoved the blade up under his arm and into his ribcage. Blood bubbled from his mouth, and his eyes widened, then went gradually glassy before he fell silently to the floor.

Procella moved backwards, wiping her sword on a cloth she had picked up from the bar. She threw the bloodied material onto the nearest table and swung the blade around her again, her wrist loose, the pommel keeping the weight even. How wonderful it felt to fight. She had forgotten how good at it she was.

Hunfrith came forward slowly, his blade across his body. She wiped the back of her hand across her forehead, removing the sweat, and wondered why he didn't seem angrier. Then she realised – he had sent in the other two so he could watch her, ascertain her style, tire her a little. They had been expendable, although hopefully he hadn't expected her to dispatch them quite so effortlessly.

They circled, and she watched him carefully. He was taller, younger, heavier and stronger than her, so she wouldn't win the fight with physical power. She had to be quicker, and she had to be smarter.

He feinted, ducked to her right; they parried and she leapt back. They circled, clashed weapons, and the steel rang as the blades skidded across each other. Again and again they met, moving around the room, lunging, side-stepping, swinging, and thrusting.

He was good – fast and agile for a big man. But Procella had trained with the best, and her reactions were still second to none.

Even so, she was having trouble finding a way through his defences. Because of his height and weight, she knew she couldn't afford to indulge in a physical lock. She had to keep moving to have any chance of winning this, and so she kept light on her feet and circled him continuously, keeping him off-balance, not letting him widen his stance.

Briefly she wondered why he didn't just have one of his followers come up behind her and knock her out, but she knew that he wanted to do this himself. Wulfians prided themselves on their masculinity, and Hunfrith would not be able to return to his followers with the news that he had been bested by a woman.

The blow, when it came, took her by surprise, his hand moving so fast she barely saw it before the hilt connected with her nose. The bone cracked and blood spurted, spraying like a fountain over them both, making her cough and splutter.

She stumbled back and tried to wipe her hands on her leather tunic, aware the blood would make the hilt of the sword slip in her fingers.

"Aw, poor little lady," Hunfrith taunted. "Does she have a bit of blood under her fingernails? Does she want to go wash her pretty little face?"

The patronising taunt got to her more than the blow. She had been lucky throughout her career in the Exercitus and had never broken a limb nor suffered a long-lasting wound, but she had known her fair share of cuts and bruises, and had long since ceased to worry about the sight of blood.

Rage spiralled through her, and with it came carelessness.

She swung, missed as he side-stepped, and then he was on her, his weight pushing her so she backpedalled, crashing into tables and chairs until she met an unmoveable one. He bent her backwards, his sword across her throat and his face inches from hers, lips pulled back in a snarl like a dog's.

"*Pawes!*" he growled, breathing the Wulfian swear word over her like a spell he thought would charm her into submission. "I am Lord of the Plains. You think you can best me?"

She struggled, but the blade bit into her skin, forcing her back. He was too heavy and she could not throw him off.

Panic shot through her. She could not let him win. She could not! She had never been bested in battle, had never been touched by a man other than her husband, other than by Hunfrith with his forced kiss, and she was not going to start now, with this heaving oafish hulk who smelled of fish and whose confidence oozed over her like sap.

He laughed and fumbled at the tie at the top of her breeches. His hips pressed hers into the table, his body crushing hers into the wood, and she could feel him hard against her.

"No!" She tugged futilely at his jerkin, braced her hands against his shoulder, but to no avail. She would not scream; she would not give him the satisfaction. Blood continued to flow from her nose, and she coughed and spat as she struggled. She was losing. Arbor's roots, she was losing.

And then Hunfrith stopped. No; correction, he was still moving, but he looked as if he had been thrown into deep water, his movements slow and ponderous. Procella blinked, caught her breath as around them the twilight air sparkled with fine dust. She turned her head on the table and only then saw the figure standing to one side, dressed in a grey cloak.

"Cinereo?"

"Playing games, Procella?" He sounded amused.

"I cannot..." She pushed at Hunfrith, tried to heave him off, but couldn't.

"Where is your fight? Your passion?"

She punched the big man furiously in the shoulder, angry at the cloaked man's words. And yet… Was he right? Was she fighting as hard as she could? Or had she half given up, too tired and demoralised to fight on?

"Your children need you," Cinereo said.

Her children? In her mind, scenes flashed by. Horada, chained and kept in the dark. Julen, surrounded by flaming elementals. Orsin, tempted and tormented, about to give up everything he believed in because he felt so unloved.

Her chest tightened. "Help me," she whispered.

"Help yourself." His voice hardened.

She stared at him, then back at Hunfrith. He was in the process of undoing the ties on his breeches, his fingers moving a tenth of their normal speed.

Help yourself…

She gritted her teeth. Had she ever done anything but? She had never needed a man to rescue her, and she wasn't going to start now.

She spat blood, shifted beneath the hulk and brought up a knee. At the same time, the glittering dust faded, and Hunfrith's movements returned to normal.

With every ounce of strength in her body, she connected her knee to the precious part of his body he was just trying to release.

His eyes popped, he let out a low groan and stumbled back. Procella leapt up, launched herself at him and pushed him onto the floor. Straddling him, letting her full fury flood her, she hit him several times across the face, giving a satisfied yell as teeth loosened and something snapped. Then, grabbing the hilt of the dagger on her hip, she ripped it out and pressed the point into the flesh of his neck.

Hunfrith's eyes met hers. To her delight, fear sparked in them.

Keeping her eyes locked on his, she pushed the blade up into his throat, and deep into his brain, leaning all her weight on it until the hilt met his neck.

When he was dead, she got to her feet and looked around, wiping her nose on her sleeve. Half a dozen of his followers had come through the doorway, but they stopped as they saw Hunfrith on the floor, unmoving.

Victory flooded her veins, made her swell. "Do you want to join him?" she demanded of the men, gesturing to the body. "Anyone?"

The men looked at each other, unsure. One turned and fled. The others gradually lowered their swords.

She raised her blade high. "I am Procella, Dux of the Exercitus!" She glared at them and let her triumph radiate through her. Nobody was going to stop her when her children needed saving. "Never forget it!"

II

The journey out of the mountains was fast and furious, and it passed by mostly in a blur for Tahir. Still in need of food and drink, hazy with confusion about what had just happened, he let Demitto half-carry him through the passageways. Catena walked in front, her hands brushing the walls on either side, guiding their way out. Atavus trotted by their side, inseparable now from the master he had missed so much.

They met Incendi-possessed guards more than once, but each time Demitto and Catena despatched them with speedy ruthlessness, Atavus snarling and biting; then they picked Tahir up and moved on. They wove through the maze of corridors, and at some point exited the pyramid and plunged deep into the heart of the mountain. Tahir lost track of time, of distance, of everything but the sound of feet scuffling on loose stone, the smell of rock dust, the heat and the stifling, oppressive air. At some point, Demitto picked him up completely and carried him, and he lay limp in the emissary's arms, barely lucid.

And he began to dream. He was back at Harlton, nine years old, and, as usual, he was alone. The other children in the castle had gone down to the river to fish, and they had not asked him to go with them. Perhaps they thought he was busy with princely duties, or maybe they just didn't know how to speak to the boy whose life was doomed to end on his fourteenth birthday. But at the time he had watched them walk into town with a heavy heart, lonely resentful tears he refused to shed pricking his eyes.

He walked to an oak tree in the castle grounds and lay beneath it, the grass soft like velvet under his back. The sun was high in the sky, and filtered through the tree's lobed leaves to cast warm patches like drops of melted butter across him, while at the same time a refreshing zephyr brushed his skin. The air smelled clean, of loam and growth, and he could hear birdsong from the branches, the hum of people talking in the distance.

He knew he should be happy. He was privileged – he didn't want for food, shelter or clothing. He had seen some of the children dressed in rags as he rode through the town, so thin their bones seemed to protrude through their flesh. Catena had once snapped at him when he complained that he didn't like the venison they had served for dinner, saying at least he had venison, and that as a child, meat for her had been a rarity, with the same bit of bacon boiled umpteen times in a stew to give the vegetables flavour. He hadn't talked to her for a week after she told him off, but as usual her words had struck home and for some reason played on his mind. The children in the town may have looked thin and scruffy, but they had also looked happy, running away from the royal party to play hopscotch together. He had craned his neck to watch them as his horse plodded towards the castle, and at that moment he would have given anything to have been one of those poor children.

He closed his eyes, trying to let the dappled sunlight soothe him. He was destined to be alone – he just had to come to terms with it.

Someone called his name, and he cursed at this interruption of his peace and sat upright, his irritation fading as he realised it was Catena. She carried a large wooden box, and she was smiling.

"Hey, young prince." She knelt beside him. "I have something for you."

He looked at the box with interest. Although he rarely wanted for anything, he rarely received personal presents. "What is it?"

"I am not going to spoil it for you. Open it and see."

His fingers fumbled on the lid and he looked up at her, startled as he felt movement in the box. He lifted the lid, and stared with delight.

It was a puppy. One of the castle guard dogs had recently given birth to a litter, and he recognised the light grey fur.

"Go on," Catena said. "Pick it up."

Tahir stared at her. "Is it... mine?"

She smiled. "All yours."

He looked down at the puppy, which sat and scratched its ear then jumped up and put its front paws on the edge of the box. It scrabbled to get its hind leg up, but couldn't quite make it, and gave a short, annoyed yap.

"Father would not like it," he said, careful to keep the emotion from his voice.

For a moment, Catena said nothing. Then she rested a hand on his shoulder. The rare contact brought tears to his eyes. "I have discussed it with your father," she said. "I suggested to him that now you have been named the Selected, it is imperative we keep you safe. And he agreed it would be a good idea for you to have a guard dog." Her words were matter-of-fact, but her eyes showed a softness the statement didn't convey. That was not why she had given him the puppy – even he in his immaturity recognised that. She had recognised his loneliness and was hoping to remedy it.

He reached out a hand to the puppy, and it licked and nibbled his fingers with tiny teeth. "He is really mine?"

"All yours, my prince."

He lifted the puppy out. It was a boy, with ears too big for his head and paws too big for his legs. It scrambled over him, turned around and around in his lap, plonked its bottom down at an uneven angle and fell off Tahir's leg onto the ground.

Tahir laughed and picked him up again. "He is like a court jester."

"It is good to see you smile," Catena observed.

Tahir clasped the puppy close and buried his nose behind a velvet ear. "Thank you."

"You are welcome." She pushed herself to her feet and gave the puppy's head a parting ruffle. "Now you must give him a name."

"Atavus," he whispered, realising as she walked away that he would never be alone again. "I shall call him Atavus."

He opened his eyes. He lay on his side. It was dark, but he could feel a body pressed alongside his stomach, warming him in the cool night. He didn't realise until that moment how much he had missed the dog.

He buried a hand in Atavus's fur, and the dog raised his head and nuzzled his hand before lying back down again. Where were they? The light breeze playing across his face suggested they had left the mountains. A light glow from behind him told him he was lying with his back to a fire. He was about to lift himself and turn over, but then he heard murmured words, and he lay still, trying to hear what they were saying.

Demitto and Catena were talking.

"...Cinereo that brought it to a close," Catena was saying. "I do not know how that happened."

"Somehow we contacted the Arbor by placing those pendants together," Demitto murmured. "I had not thought it would work in the mountains as I was told the pendant had to be pushed into the earth to access the Arbor's channels, but maybe we all just made such a strong connection it did not matter."

"I cannot believe we actually saw Horada and Julen,"

Catena said. "And those people from the future. Who was the man with the silver hair?"

"I do not know. The *Quercetum* carries some information from the third phase of the Apex – that which was recorded in Horada's time – but as far as I am aware, it is very limited."

"What happens when the Apex occurs?"

"Catena…"

"It is just the two of us here, Dem. Does Tahir truly have to die? Is there no way we can save him?"

Demitto was silent for a while. Then he said simply, "No."

Tahir lay as still as he could, but his hand fisted in Atavus's fur.

"I wish there was something I could do," Catena said softly. "He has had such a difficult time, living under the shadow of his fate. He is only a boy – he does not deserve it."

"He is more than a boy," Demitto said, and his deep voice seemed to ring in the young prince's ears. "He holds the fate of the whole world in his hands. Why do you think we went to such trouble to rescue him?"

"I know," she said. "But Tahir will think you did it because you like him, and you must not take that away from him, not now, with Heartwood only days away."

"I do like him."

"Not in the way that Tahir would wish it."

The Prince closed his eyes, shame and embarrassment washing over him.

"He is very… fond of you," Catena continued.

Tahir waited for the emissary to exclaim in disgust. But instead Demitto said, "I know. You think I am not aware?"

"It does not bother you?"

"Why would it? Love is love, Catena, a precious jewel, and it should be treasured, whatever the source." The emissary's words wove around Tahir's heart and tempered his shame.

Catena gave a soft laugh. "I never thought to hear you speak thus."

"You thought I did not understand love?" Demitto sounded amused.

"I thought it was very low priority for you."

"I have been in love," he protested.

It was Catena's turn to sound amused. "With your reflection?"

"You mock me. A Hanairean princess broke my heart several years ago and I have never recovered."

"Was she very beautiful?" Catena sounded wistful.

"Like a princess should be. Blonde hair in long braids, fair skin."

"What happened?"

"I escorted her to her new husband's home. And left her there."

"There has got to be more to the story than that," Catena scoffed.

He chuckled. "That would be telling."

"I envy you."

"You have never been in love?"

"No." The fire hissed as Catena obviously threw a twig or clump of grass on it. "Never."

"Catena, now you are breaking my heart."

"I do not need your pity."

"It is not pity. Well, all right, maybe a little. Everyone deserves to have some love in their life."

"I am not saying I am a virgin." She sounded indignant.

And now he was amused again. "I see."

Tahir stroked Atavus's flank, hardly breathing, caught up in what he realised was a courtship ritual, something he had never witnessed before. He had seen the castle guards creep under the kitchen maids' blanket at night where they slept in the hall, and he thought he knew how babies were made. But he had never seen his father touch his mother other than to hold her hand as they descended from the dais. He had never even seen him kiss her. He had never been party to the rite of seduction, and it made his heart pound and his eyes sting at the same time, as he realised he would never undertake the ritual himself.

"If I wanted a man, I could have him," Catena said.

Demitto was laughing. "I am certain of that. You are a very determined woman."

"You are mocking me."

"No." Someone shifted on the grass, presumably Demitto. "I would not do that. You fascinate me. You are so strong and self-assured, and yet vulnerable at the same time."

"I am not weak–"

"Not weak, vulnerable. It is a compliment, Catena. You have the heart of a warrior and the gentleness of a lady. It is a very alluring combination."

She went quiet for a moment. "Nobody has ever called me alluring before."

"I am shocked. It was the first word that came to my mind when I saw you."

She gave a girlish giggle Tahir had never heard her give before. "Stop flattering me."

"I like flattering you."

"Demitto… the boy!"

"He is asleep. Do as you are told for once and come here."

The two of them went quiet, and soon the sounds of lovemaking filled the evening: rustling clothing, hushed whispers, sighs and appreciative murmurs.

Tahir buried his nose in Atavus's fur, inhaling his deep, doggy scent, taking comfort in his warmth. He wanted to hate Catena for accepting Demitto's affection, but found he could not. The end of the world was coming, and he was glad they had each other.

Love is love… a precious jewel, and it should be treasured.

He closed eyes, and went back to sleep.

III

They camped that night in what they came to call the Broken Room, all nine of them, Veris and Umbra alike, bound together by misfortune and a rising sense of despair as to what they were going to do now their dreams had been destroyed.

They had built a fire from dry brush and a few larger logs left lying around. From looking at the landscape, it seemed that wood was in short supply, most trees and plants having long since been burned away. Raging fires tore across the countryside, ravaging everything in their paths, and the lakes of lava poured down from the numerous volcanoes, flooding the land with scarlet. But up here, scattered around the Broken Room, odds and ends of wood still remained.

"I do not think the Incendi know of this room," Geve remarked. "Surely they would have razed it by now."

Most of them sat in a circle around the fire. Sarra was the only one who had removed herself from the others, and she now lay to one side, lying down, curled up. The fire was for light more than comfort, as the whole place was hot and humid and the flames only made the heat worse. It was almost dark, although the fires lit the sky with a yellowish-grey haze, little different to the day.

"What is to raze?" said Josse. "A few lumps of wood and dried mosses?"

Geve said nothing, turning instead to Sarra. "Would you like something to eat?"

She tried to give him a smile, but could only manage a twitch of her lips. "No, thank you."

"You should eat," Comminor said. "You need your strength."

Several of them glanced at her stomach, and she had to fight not to cover herself with her hands. Not that she could have. In two days it looked as if the baby had grown enough for two months, and if she looked closely she could almost see the bump burgeoning. She swallowed down the fear and looked away.

The rest of them passed around a small amount of dried salamander meat, and they broke off pieces of one of Amabil's cakes, washing it down with a swig of water. None of them mentioned that their supplies would not last more than a few days.

Geve finished his mouthful, swigged the water and wiped his mouth on the back of his hand. "So. I think it is probably time you told us what you know." Sarra saw him look directly at Comminor.

The Chief Select glanced at her, and she pushed herself upright.

"Yes," she said. "We are all in this together now. We deserve to know."

He looked into the flames. Then he nodded.

"It is a burden I have carried for a long time. Maybe too long. I am the latest in a long line of Chief Selects, and all those who came before me passed on their knowledge to the next in line. What we call Chief Selects were once called the Nox Aves – the Night Birds. The Nox Aves have been scholars for thousands of years. They were holders of sacred knowledge before the Embers was formed, and they wrote this knowledge down in two volumes of a book they called the *Quercetum*. I have these books in my rooms in the palace. They contain a history of many things that have happened to this land, which was once called Anguis."

He proceeded to tell them some of its history, and Sarra listened to the fantastical tale with growing shock. Comminor told of a war between the elements, of the superiority of earth, of the rise of water leading to the invasion of the Darkwater Lords, and then the rise of fire, which had brought about the Incendi superiority. He told them of the God Animus who had cried tears that fell to the earth, and how the Pectoris had grown around the tears and become the heart of the Arbor, and how the Arbor had spread Animus's love to all corners of the land through its roots.

He told them that they now lived in the Third Age of Anguis, and that the Arbor connected not only space but time, and that it could remember its past and see into its future. It had foreseen the rise of the Incendi, and although it could not stop it, it had the power to bring together a triumvirate of events that had occurred in three different Ages to form the Apex – a peak of energy that could ultimately bring about the fall of the element of fire and the rise once again of the element of earth.

The trouble was, Comminor explained, that the writers of the *Quercetum* knew only of the events of the first two parts of the Apex. They could neither see when the third part would occur, nor what the final outcome would be.

"So do *you* know when this third part is supposed to happen?" Nele asked.

"No," said Comminor. "I have no idea."

"Could it be now?" Betune asked.

Comminor hesitated. He looked across at Sarra. She did not miss the softening of his expression. "Maybe. The growth of Sarra's child and the strange events that have occurred leading up to this point suggest that could be the case. But I do not know how this will play out. Or whether it will be successful."

"So the dreams we have all had," said Amabil softly, "of the grass and the sky and birds... We were not seeing the future? We were seeing the past?"

Again he hesitated. "I do not have all the answers. Perhaps we *were* seeing the future, and the land will be returned as it once was. I do not know."

"But the Arbor," Betune said in a small voice. "The Arbor is gone."

Comminor looked out across the barren land. "Yes."

Sarra caught her breath. She had known, of course, that there was no way the tree could have survived in that desolate landscape. But hearing the words made an ache grow inside her that wouldn't go away.

"So these Incendi," said Josse, "they once existed inside the mountains, in the Embers?"

"Certainly in the caves surrounding the Embers," Comminor replied. "I do not know if they ever lived in the Embers itself. There is no evidence for that, none of their paintings or carvings. And many of our caves we dug out for ourselves. The Embers was made to be isolated and self-sufficient, that is why our forebears created it. We were a pocket of resistance against the Incendi invasion, and were meant to survive to fight back one day."

"If the Nox Aves knew about the Apex and what was going to happen to the Arbor, why did they not try to stop it?" Amabil looked near to tears.

Comminor ran his hands through his hair – a gesture that Sarra knew meant he was struggling to hide his impatience. "Because the Apex cannot be stopped. It is set in time and space, a fixed event. If the Nox Aves attempted to stop it, it would forever alter the path of time and the way events transpired, and they could not know whether this would mean the Incendi would forever remain in the ascendant. All they could do was let the Arbor guide us in all three ages to come together to try to defeat them when the moment arose."

They all fell silent, lost in their thoughts as they stared into the flames. Sarra moved to sit with her back against the wall, rubbing her bump tiredly. She closed her eyes, wishing she had never started out on this journey. How foolish she had been, to follow her dreams, to believe her son was going to lead her to the Surface. Well, of course, it could be argued that he had, but none of it had turned out as she had thought it would.

And she had only had dreams of the green and blue land for the last few months. How awful must it be for the other Veris, who had dreamed of the Arbor since childhood? The hope of finding it had sustained them all their lives, and now they had discovered their dreams were like burnt paper, flying away in the wind.

She wished she understood the things Comminor talked about – convergences of time, connections, and the Arbor's plans for the Incendi, but her brain hurt and she was so tired that everything seemed to merge together, like when she had tried to paint and the wood was wet, and the colours had blended into one. All she could think about was her son, that she had failed him, because what kind of life could she give him in this world?

They would have to go back. The realisation dawned on her slowly. There was no other option – here they had no food, and she had seen no sign of a river in the landscape before it got dark. But if they went back, what would happen to her baby? If it were any other woman, Comminor would demand the pregnancy be terminated, although she was much further along now than when it usually happened. Would he be able to bring himself to kill a newborn baby? Would he be able to bring himself to kill *her* baby? She had seen the way he looked at her, his expression softening. He loved her. Before he knew about her being part of the Veris, he had promised to treat the child as his own. Had that changed?

What option did she have? If she stayed here, they would both die, her and the baby.

She opened her eyes and looked out across the bleak landscape. Through the darkness, volcanoes spat lava and fires leapt in a brief blaze of light before succumbing to the night again. Small, glowing forms moved across the parched earth, Incendi elementals, scorching everything in their path. The world looked dead, defeated.

She had never felt so low. She had really believed she would find the Arbor and the land she had dreamed about over the past few months. *Why?* She whispered the word as she stroked her belly. Why had she had those visions of her child? Had it all been an amazing creation conjured up by her mind? A tear ran down her cheek. She had been so foolish. Convinced she was special, she had risked the lives of herself and her baby, as well as the other people who had followed her there. Amabil and Betune, trusting Nele, poor Kytte who had died as well as the member of the Umbra who had also hit the rock, and Geve… She bit her lip. Poor Geve. He had once told her he would follow her to the end of the world. Well, now he had, hadn't he?

A hand touched her face and brushed away the tear and she opened her eyes, expecting to see Geve, surprised to find it was Comminor.

"Do not cry," he murmured.

Another tear joined the first. "I cannot help it."

"I tried to stop you," he said.

"Perhaps you should just have told me the truth," she snapped.

"And what do you think the truth will do to the people of the Embers?" He bent his head to look at her, and a fire leapt in the distance, highlighting his silver hair with orange. "Do you think it will lift their spirits to know they were driven underground by a creature that roams the land they once stood on? That there is no hope of them ever seeing the sun and the grass again?"

"What about the Apex?" she whispered. "You said it will happen one day."

"It could be thousands of years in our future. Which is why I and the other Nox Aves who came before me have done our best to keep our people safe until it happens, and that means hiding the truth, and keeping them in the dark, metaphorically as well as literally, until the time comes."

Sarra closed her eyes. "I am tired."

"I will leave you to sleep." He leaned forward and kissed her forehead, then moved away.

She squeezed her eyes shut and bit her lip. *That means hiding the truth.*

They couldn't go back. Comminor would not let them return. Because if they did, he ran the risk that one of them would tell the others what they knew, and the truth would be out.

She opened her eyes and watched a fire briefly flare in the distance. And as the flames flickered out, so did the last remnant of hope.

CHAPTER EIGHTEEN

I

Horada crouched low in the semi-darkness and felt Julen slip down the wall to the ground beside her. She knew they should keep running and put as much distance between them and the Incendi as they could, but something was bothering her, and she couldn't keep it to herself any longer.

"I have something to tell you," she said to her brother.

"What is it?" He moved the hand that held the flame closer to her so he could see her face. She had been startled by the fact that he could create fire, but after seeing what else the pendants could do, it no longer seemed so shocking.

She took comfort from his deep voice, his reassuring presence, the familiar, strong features of his face. He had ventured alone deep into the mountains to rescue her, had been guided by the Arbor, had frozen the elementals and been part of the connection with the people from the future. She had always felt a kind of awe toward him, but that had now increased a hundredfold with the events of the past few hours.

"It is Orsin," she said. "When Pyra tried to tempt me to give in, he showed me a vision of my family in trouble – you surrounded by elementals, Mother being chased by a Wulfian lord, and Orsin... I saw Pyra tempting him with visions of earthly pleasures, things Orsin is going to find very difficult to refuse. Julen, I think Pyra has somehow possessed him."

Julen fell silent for a while. Then he said, "Why? What would the Incendi king possibly want with our brother?"

Horada heard the scorn in his words. "You should not think so little of him," she scolded.

"He is weak and foolish," Julen snapped. "I should have foreseen this."

"He is neither weak nor foolish. It is just that he has not yet found his purpose. He misses our father. Although he is his heir, and although our mother has little respect for him too, I think he has her love of adventure and the open road. But he has not been allowed to embrace that. He lives – or has lived up until now anyway – in a time of peace, and so he has not been able to fully hone his talents which, I am sure, lie in the art of war. He was born into the wrong time, and Pyra has taken advantage of his restlessness and lack of direction by appealing to his love of wine and women."

"Like I said, he is weak."

"Julen!" She sighed. "Not every man has your inner strength. Orsin needs focus, and he does not have that at the moment."

"That, my dear, is the understatement of the year."

She pushed herself to her feet crossly. "Do not be so patronising. Orsin does not have your special talent – he has rarely been made to feel special. Do you think he finds it easy to watch you go off with the Peacemaker to do dangerous missions Arbor-knows-where? He craves that excitement but has nothing apparent to offer."

He stood next to her. "And neither have the majority of people who lived in Anguis, but they do not defect to the enemy. Orsin is spoilt and he is throwing his rattle out of the bassinet. He is flattered by Pyra's attention and, as you say, is enjoying feeling special. He does not realise the King is just using him, and that when Pyra is finished, he will chew him up and spit him out and that will be the end of him, if not the end of all of us."

Horada studied her brother silently, noting his furious features, his lowered voice that held a hint of menace. His use of the word defect told her that he was angry that Orsin had gone over to the other side, and concerned as to what this meant for their cause. She had only been thinking about her brother, but Julen had greater things on his mind. He was old beyond his years, and carried a weight that a young man should not have to convey on his shoulders.

"What do you want to do?" she asked quietly.

He looked at his feet and took a couple of deep breaths, calming himself. Then he bent and picked up the lantern. "We shall have to go and rescue him."

She stared at him. Then she walked forward and slid her arms around him.

Still holding the lantern, he put his arms around her and hugged her. "We will find him, do not worry."

She said nothing, briefly overwhelmed with emotion, mainly with relief that he wanted to rescue their brother, although she could not suppress a shiver of fear at the thought of going back into the heart of the place.

"You can stay here if you wish," he said, reading her mind.

She shook her head. Her heart pounded, but she said, "No. It is better if we stay together."

Their minds made up, they moved into the heart of the Incendi caves. Repeatedly they saw the corridors ahead blaze with the presence of fiery elemental forms, but each time Julen pulled them aside into empty cells, warned by the warmth of the pendant he held in his hand.

To Horada – already lost in the vast network of caves – Julen's turns left and right could have been guesses as far as she knew, and she followed him blindly, holding on to his arm, hoping he wasn't imagining the way the Arbor led him through the tunnels.

It felt like hours passed, but ultimately they found Orsin quicker than she had expected. Julen pressed her back against the wall of a corridor, gestured to the right and whispered, "He is just down there."

They waited, and she could see in the light of the flame the way the pulse beat rapidly in his throat. He remained calm, however, showing no signs of the panic she herself felt. He had done this often, she thought, acted in tense situations, and he was used to thinking on his feet. He had led such a different life to her, and she envied him for his freedom and the excitement that he must have experienced in his adventures.

"Where are we?" she whispered.

"Some kind of antechamber. He is surrounded by elementals."

Her heart pounded. "How will we get close to him?"

He clasped the pendant around his neck, closed his eyes and murmured something beneath his breath. She remembered the way he had done the same in the chamber where she had been imprisoned, how light had radiated from him, turning the room to ice. Somehow, he had connected to the Arbor, had forged a link and the holy tree had helped him. Would he do it again?

"Now," he whispered, and together they stepped into the chamber.

The stone under Horada's feet vibrated – not like in the grand ceremonial chamber where Julen had rescued her and the barrier between the times had been opened – it was much more subtle than that. It was like a cart rumbling along the ground towards them, and she felt it pass under her, then fan out into the room. She opened her mouth to ask what it was, then saw the sunstone in Julen's pendant glowing and remembered what he had told her about energy travelling through the Arbor's roots. Was that what was happening here?

The room was similar to the ceremonial one, slightly smaller but still ringed with a channel of slowly moving magma that swirled into a large central pit. To one side a large chair stood filled with plump cushions and beside it a table stacked with a plate of luxurious food and flasks of ale and wine. In the chair sat Orsin, slightly slumped, and in front of him two young semi-naked women were dancing in a rather lewd manner, Horada still managed to think through the fear.

Around the room, half a dozen elementals stood watching the scene before them. Horada could not make out their faces, but she sensed somehow that the emotion they exuded was disdain.

As she and Julen moved into the room, the elementals saw them and emitted a loud crackling sound. The magma pit stirred, and to Horada's horror the magma rose, took shape and formed the firebird king, who had obviously been relaxing in the pit as he watched Orsin be tantalised and teased.

Orsin glanced over and sat up hurriedly, food falling from his lap onto the floor. Pyra turned towards them and hissed, breathing a long column of flame that shot in their direction. Julen passed his hand from left to right across his chest in front of the pendant, and the air filled with a glittering dust.

Horada had backed up against the wall and could feel the onset of panic at the realisation that the Incendi king was in the room, but even as a terrified scream rose in her throat, she saw that the elementals and the girls stood like statues, and the stream of flame that emitted from Pyra was moving at a fingernail's distance at a time. So slowed, then, not stopped.

"What..?" she began, but Julen interrupted her.

"We do not have long." He strode towards his brother. "What in Arbor's name do you think you are doing?"

Orsin pushed aside the plate on his lap and stood. "Do not use that tone of voice with me."

Julen stepped up onto the small dais and faced his brother. Orsin was taller and broader than Julen, but somehow Julen managed to hold his own as he stared up at Orsin with barely held back contempt. "Oh, you think you deserve respect, sitting here indulging your earthly pleasures with our enemies?"

"Your enemies," Orsin corrected. "Not mine."

"By the Arbor, you are the biggest coward I have ever met."
Julen stepped closer to him. His eyes filled with menace, and
Horada caught her breath. Those eyes had clearly observed death
and pain, had been made to watch things other young men of his
age were lucky they never got to see. Her hand crept up to cover
her mouth. Maybe she should not envy Julen so much after all.

Julen had always had a way of sliding beneath Orsin's
defences to annoy him, and Horada expected her eldest
brother to react as he usually did, by exploding with anger,
and for the confrontation to quickly turn physical.

Instead, however, Orsin just smiled, which unnerved her
far more than anything else could have done.

"Say what you will, little brother." He pointed at the
pendant. "That will not last forever, and then when its magic
runs out, Pyra will turn you to flame and reduce your skinny
little frame to ash and bone."

Julen hesitated, and Horada could see their brother's answer
had thrown him. Orsin did not look as if he were under some
kind of spell, or as if the Incendi king were controlling him,
as she had thought. His eyes were clear, and she had the
sudden, horrible notion that all Pyra had done was appeal
to the decadent side of Orsin's nature that craved gluttonous
pleasures. That was all it had taken.

Seeing Julen apparently lost for words, she moved forward
to stand before them. "Orsin," she whispered, "please, come
with us. I cannot believe Pyra has promised you so much that
you will betray us all."

For the first time, he looked at her, his eyes travelling slowly
as if he were reluctant to look at her. His gaze rested on her
for a moment, and then dropped. "You should go," he said,
"before the magic wears off and Pyra awakes."

"You cannot mean to stay." Her throat tightened and tears
pricked her eyes. "Please, Orsin. What would Father say if he
knew what you have done? What is Mother going to say?"

His head lifted, and his expression turned to rage. "Father would not give a pig's spit for what happens to me, and Mother does not care whether I live or die!"

"That is not true," Horada protested, but he slashed his hand in the air as if he could cut off her words.

"It is true. She despises me. Father despised me – he thought me of little use as an heir and parcelled me off to someone as soon as I was old enough to sit on a horse."

"Orsin!" She was openly sobbing now.

"Oh, Horada, grow up," he said impatiently. "I am under no illusion that they didn't both favour Julen – he is the golden boy, the acorn of Father's eye. I came to terms with that years ago."

"This very conversation proves you did not," she snapped, dashing away her tears.

He glared at them both. "I am of no consequence to them or to anyone else in Anguis. I am worthless and have nothing to offer, according to the rest of the world."

"That is not true," said Julen at last, but Orsin ignored him.

"Our father may have been the key to helping the Arbor, but I do not have his strength or his goodness. I am like a copper ring tossed in the sea – tarnished with verdigris, unused, unwanted. But Pyra sees something within me that is useful to him. For once, I am needed, I am wanted. So tell me why I should turn my back on him."

Horada stared at him, appalled. "Because it is *wrong*."

"Horada!" Julen snapped, shocking her. "Do not be so damned naïve." He turned back to Orsin. "Life is what we make it, brother, and we do not need others to tell us our usefulness. It might be true that our parents did not see much of worth in you. It might be true that you have not proved yourself indispensable to others. But it is *your* task to show us what your strengths are and to prove your worth – that task does not belong to others."

Orsin studied him, his jaw working. For a brief moment, Horada thought they had reached him. But then his gaze slid to the beautiful dancing girls, to the flagons of ale and the rich pastries, and all emotion disappeared from his eyes.

"Go," he said. "Before it is too late for you to leave."

And he turned back to the chair, slumped down in it, picked up a goblet and drained its contents.

Julen stared at him for a moment. Then he turned and marched past Horada back to the doorway, catching her wrist and dragging her with him.

"Wait!" she screamed, resisting and stopping him. "We cannot leave him here!"

"He has made his choice," Julen snapped. "What do you suggest we do, carry him out?"

"I do not know… the pendant…"

"Has done its work." In the chamber, the scene flickered, the glittering dust fading. "We have to go," he said to his sister, his grey eyes like steel. "Are you coming or do I have to put you over my shoulder? Because I will."

She glanced back once more at Orsin, sitting on the chair, staring mutely at the dancing statues. The scene flickered again, the statues moving briefly. Orsin did not look over at her.

"No. Let us go." Tears pouring down her face, she followed Julen out. As they ran down the corridor, behind them she heard Pyra bellow.

And she knew her hollowed heart would never be whole again.

II

They walked to Hicton, and there, at night, Demitto stole some horses, promising Tahir he would send money back for them once they arrived at Heartwood.

Tahir didn't believe him. The emissary didn't appear to have a conscience. Plus, as the days went by, he seemed to be adopting a reckless profligacy that Tahir, in his youth, found both exciting and disturbing. It could have been due to the thrill of escaping from the Incendi, Tahir thought, or maybe from the knowledge that they were approaching Heartwood and knowing what was to come, but Demitto rode and drank hard, got into fights just because he felt like it, made love to Catena every night and carried within him a wild excitement that began to be infectious.

Tahir felt he'd crossed a bridge and put his fears behind him. He had undergone a terrifying trial, had been captured, starved, beaten and restrained, but he had escaped and gone on to live another day. Even though his death was now imminent, it was the right death, not an accident over which he would have no control. The event that he had been groomed for was looming, and for maybe the first time in his life he saw it as a good thing.

Early in the morning, while they rode and Catena and Demitto talked, and Atavus trotted alongside sniffing at trees and chasing rabbits, Tahir spent his time looking around at the changing countryside. They had left the jungle behind a while after Lornberg, and the land stretched out to his right in a patchwork of fields, hills and forests. He knew from his tutor's history lessons that, once upon a time, the dominant colour would have been green, with maybe yellow from the growing corn and a deep red-brown from ploughed fields. But now everything was a dull grey-brown, parched and scorched from the growing heat. In spite of the fact that they had only just entered The Stirring, the land was clearly confused by the changing seasons. Although some trees had shed their leaves, many were budding and some even had glossy leaves, although they were not evergreens. Crops sprouted in all stages of growth, growing half the size they would have done several hundred years before, and drooped miserably in the hot and humid weather. As they passed close by to a field of wheat, Tahir could see the blight growing on the new sheaves, cultivated by the hot, damp conditions. The country was suffering, and Demitto had told him that it would not be long before food would start to become scarce and the poor would begin to starve.

They had passed little traffic really from Harlton all the way up to Cherton, the number of carts and horses increasing as they approached towns and then dwindling as they left for the open countryside. Now, the gradual growth of people riding or walking told Tahir that they couldn't be far from Heartwood. The roadside became peppered with stalls, with merchants selling fruit and vegetables, baked goods and small wares, and offering various entertainments.

The other sign that they must be nearing the great city was the sight of the mountain rising to the left in the distance. Once it had been snow-topped, according to Tahir's tutor. Now, all snow had vanished and a plume of smoke spiralled from the top. Every now and again, a deep rumble shook the earth, although nobody around them seem to take any notice of it.

Tahir's heart rate began to increase and his mouth went dry. "How long before we get to the palace?" he asked the emissary, who sat straight in the saddle, eyes alight with an emotion Tahir could not decipher.

Demitto looked at him then. His expression softened. "We will not go straight to the palace," he said.

"Why?"

"My young prince, as a Selected, your entry to the city demands great pomp and ceremony. Nobody would believe any of us is anything special at the moment! We are going to visit the Nest, that is the Nox Aves's buildings, have a bath, change into more suitable clothing, rest, and then give you the entrance you deserve."

Tahir's pounding heart slowed a little, and he took a few deep breaths. Almost as if his execution had been delayed, he thought wryly. Which was pretty much the case, when he thought about it.

The traffic intensified, and their horses had to weave between the carts filled with loaves of bread, barrels of salted pork and beef, fish from the coast, finely woven cloths, and all manner of merchants carrying their wares into the big city.

At one point, everyone had to move off the road to let pass a huge cavalcade of riders in the midst of which rode what could only be a king, Tahir thought, dressed in a fashionable long overtunic in fine green wool embroidered with gold threads, the circlet on his brow studded with gems that winked in the sunlight. The crowd cheered as he passed. The King barely gave them a second look, his face showing his boredom.

"Who was that?" Tahir asked as the last of his retinue passed and the guards allowed them back onto the road.

"The King of Dorle," Demitto said. "An ignorant oaf. I do not think his oak tree has many acorns growing on it."

Tahir giggled at his irreverence, while Catena's lips curved wryly.

"Demitto," she scolded. "Honestly."

He stuck his tongue out at her and they all laughed. A bubble of excitement rose inside Tahir and burst from him in a childhood song. Catena joined in with it and eventually so did Demitto, and when Atavus barked it seemed as if he too, wanted to sing along.

As they neared the city walls, however, the tune faded from Tahir's lips. The walls rose high and intimidating, built from grey stone from the north. They looked formidable, but to Tahir's surprise there was no moat or drawbridge and the gates remained wide open.

"It is mainly for show," Demitto said in response to the look on Tahir's face. "The King does not truly believe anyone would ever attack Heartwood."

"But have the Nox Aves not told him about the Incendi threat?" Catena asked incredulously.

"Yes. The King did not believe them."

They both stared at him in silence.

"Does he know about the Apex?" Tahir asked. "That the Arbor is under threat?"

Demitto shrugged. "The King sees the religious significance of the tree as completely separate to his governance of the city. The Arbor is almost an irritation, although he likes the way it draws visitors to Heartwood."

"You do not think very highly of him," Catena remarked.

"I will let you make your own minds up when you meet him," Demitto said.

Tahir said nothing, his attention drawn by the looming gate and the throng of people. Atavus stayed close to his horse's legs, skilled at weaving without being kicked. Tahir's heart raced as they passed beneath the gate into the city proper, and he had a sudden sense of foreboding, his previous burst of happiness dimming like a cloud passing over the sun.

Demitto took the main road into the heart of the city, and Tahir trailed along behind him, silently looking around at the buildings and people. Stalls lined the road filled with every kind of goods he could have imagined, and the noise was deafening, merchants yelling their wares, children screaming, dogs barking, people talking.

Tahir had been often into Harlton, including on market day, but he had never seen anything like this. Harlton had wide, open streets and a huge market place, and the smell of the sea wafted across with the cry of seagulls. Here, the only smell that arose from the rubbish-infested gutters was foul, and it felt as if all his senses were under attack: his ears ringing and his nose stinging from the awful stench.

The buildings towered high on either side, mostly lodgings above shops, the balconies strung with limp washing that dried crisp within minutes from the overbearing heat. Red-faced women poured liquid from buckets over the side of the balconies occasionally, and it seemed pot luck as to whether a person would get hit below.

Ahead, the road widened out into the main market place, and further on from that Tahir could see the spires and battlements of the palace rearing above the houses on higher ground, but Demitto turned off on a road to the left, leaving the raucous bustle behind and heading down the narrower street.

Tahir let out the breath he didn't realise he had been holding. "It is so busy!" he exclaimed, glancing back over his shoulder. "Is it always like this?"

"Yes, although at the moment it does seem worse than usual."

"Why?"

Demitto smiled. "Because of you, young prince. Everyone has come to watch the Veriditas."

Tahir stared, mouth open. "For me?"

"The Veriditas is the King's excuse to hold a huge party. Nobles are invited from all over the land to come and watch the event. Of course the ceremony is just a pretext for the King to get everyone here to make negotiations and discuss trade and other matters." He winced as Catena kicked out at him from the saddle, glanced at her, then looked back at Tahir. "Although the King is very much in the minority. Most people take the ceremony very seriously."

Tahir's lips curved. "You are a terrible liar."

Demitto smiled wryly and slowed his horse to ride beside Tahir's. "Actually, I speak the truth. At the moment of the sacrifice, there will not be a dry eye in the house. The Veriditas speaks to our own Pectoris – the part inside us that belongs to Animus alone. It may be that ten minutes later everyone will try to forget what they have seen because they do not want to feel they are bound by their religion in the way it was in the old days. But in that moment when you become one with the Arbor, nobody will be able to look away."

Tahir swallowed and nodded. His heart rate began to speed up again. It was nearly time, he thought. Only a few days and he would no longer be living and breathing fresh Anguis air.

Not that it was very fresh at that moment. He couldn't believe how much the place stank. Human and animal excrement littered the streets, along with rubbish thrown out by shops and houses, fish heads, meat bones, and the rotting tops of vegetables. Dogs snarled and snapped at one another as they picked out the best pieces. Atavus carefully avoided them as if they were beneath him, but he stopped frequently to investigate the smells that must have been overwhelming to his sensitive nose.

As they neared the end of the road and turned left again into a narrower cobbled street, it grew quieter, and the houses looked neater and more cared for, the roads less littered. Demitto led them through a maze of roads, announcing that this was called the Scholars' District. This was where those people who had travelled specifically to see the Arbor and to find out more about their religion came to stay.

They rounded the corner and Tahir's eyebrows rose at the sight of the tall, elegant stone wall with its wide arched doorway, the top engraved with a beautiful carving of an oak tree.

"This is the Nest, the headquarters of the Nox Aves." Demitto dismounted and reached up a hand to help the Prince. Catena jumped down beside them too, and they led their horses beneath the archway.

"This is the nearest thing in Anguis you will find to Heartwood as it used to be," Demitto said. He gestured around, taking in the square open yard flanked by well-kept cells, and the building at the end with its domed roof, which reminded Tahir of the pictures in his history books of the ancient Temple that had been destroyed after the invasion of the Darkwater Lords.

A young stable lad came out to take their horses. The boy looked curiously at Tahir with his black hair and golden eyes, but didn't say anything and led the horses away.

Demitto crossed the yard to an open doorway on the far side and stuck his head in. Tahir heard a male voice call with delight, "Demitto!" and the emissary smiled and went inside.

Tahir hovered outside with Catena, his hand buried in Atavus's fur. He felt shy, nervous, excited and panicky all at once. These were the men and women who understood the Veriditas, who knew about the Apex and were trying to ensure everything happened when it should. What if they took one look at him and realised he wasn't up to the job?

He glanced at Catena, who gave a small smile. She had been very quiet since they had left the mountains, and although she had obviously found pleasure in Demitto's attentions at night, during the day she kept herself to herself. Tahir often found her watching him. He knew she had doubted him back in Harlton – that although she had a certain fondness for him because she had known him for so long and felt sorry for him, she hadn't been sure he would make a good Selected. Did she feel the same way now?

"I am scared," he said, surprising himself. He had not meant to voice his thoughts. But now he couldn't stop. "What if they do not think I am good enough?"

Catena's gaze slipped over his shoulder for a moment, and then came back to him. Her smile widened.

He turned and stared. The man to whom Demitto had been talking had come out of the building, along with half a dozen others, who now fanned out to either side, staring at him.

"He is here!" called one of the men, and more men and women came out of other cells, stopping as soon as they saw him.

Tahir's mouth went dry. What was he supposed to do? Were they all sizing him up? Would they burst into laughter? Yell at Demitto scornfully for bringing him there?

The man next to Demitto came forward to stand before him. He stared solemnly into Tahir's golden eyes. And then he dropped to one knee before him.

As one, every other member of the Nox Aves did the same, bowing to the new Selected.

Tahir's eyes filled with tears.

III

Geve's stomach was rumbling. He did his best to ignore it, although he was so hungry he was pretty sure they'd be able to hear it all the way down in the Embers. But it was useless to think about it. Their food supply was alarmingly low, and they had to save what they had until they figured out what they were going to do.

"Cannot sleep?"

He turned, surprised to see Comminor awake. The others, including Sarra, all slept, exhausted by their long journey, worn out with emotion.

"No." He pushed himself up to a sitting position and ran his hands through his hair. "I am tired and my body aches. But sleep will not come."

Comminor, too, pushed himself up, and the two men stared at the dying remains of their small fire.

Geve's gaze crept over to the older man. He had hated him for so long it was difficult to feel any other emotion. In the Embers, fear of the Select kept everyone in their rightful place, and he suspected Comminor encouraged that fear, maybe even spreading rumours about himself and his followers to keep rebellions to a minimum.

In truth, although Geve had succumbed to that fear and hatred, deep down he had understood the reasons behind some of the Chief Select's decisions. The strict control of births had been unpleasant, but he knew it was necessary to keep control of the birth rate because of their limited resources. That wasn't necessarily what had bothered Geve – it was more the manner in which the elite few who lived in the palace had privileges that men and women in his own situation could never hope to achieve. But then what was the answer to that? He did not think he himself could have governed a whole city. Hard decisions would have to be made, and he did not have the toughness required for that.

He glanced out at the landscape. As long as he could remember, he had dreamed of rolling green hills and blue skies, birds floating endlessly on the currents, and the oak trees swaying gently in a morning breeze. He could not match the visions with the view before him. What was it he had dreamed of? The past? The future? Or had it all been a figment of his imagination?

But if that was the case, how come Nele and Kytte and Amabil and Betune, and of course Comminor, and probably countless others who had kept it to themselves, had dreamed about it too? They had no histories, no stories to tell of days of old. Life as they knew it had begun in the caves, and everything else had gradually faded into myth and then into oblivion. So why had they all dreamed of the green world? Was it some sort of collective memory? Or had the Arbor been trying to send them a message?

"If you were in my position, would you have done things differently?" Comminor asked softly.

Geve raised his eyebrows, surprised by the Chief Select's willingness to accept there could have been a different way to do things. "What sort of things?"

"Telling the people of the Embers the truth about their past and their future."

Geve hesitated. "I do not know. I understand your reasoning for keeping it to yourself. If everyone had known there had been a world outside the one we existed in, a better world, there would definitely have been more dissatisfaction, a desire to find a way out. But then if you suspected what we would find is this," and he gestured to the barren countryside, "what would be the point? I do not like being kept in the dark, metaphorically or literally, but I do not know any other way it could have been done." He said the words regretfully, not wanting to agree with the man who had tried to capture Sarra's heart, but he could not lie.

Comminor nodded. "It has weighed heavy on my mind since the moment I first read the *Quercetum* and discovered the truth. I ruled under the instruction of all the Nox Aves who had gone before me. My predecessor made me swear to abide by the Nox Aves's rules. As you say, I still do not see how I could have done things differently. But still, doubts plague me."

He looked up at Geve then, and said, "Does she love you?"

Geve met his gaze. The Chief Select's golden eyes unnerved him. He wanted to say yes, to make the man think he had no chance with her, to prove that the history he himself had with Sarra was worth more than the moments Comminor had snatched from her. But once again, he could not bring himself to lie.

"No."

Comminor stared at him for a moment. And then he blew out his breath in a low, slow exhalation. "It is of no consequence. We cannot return to the Embers, and if we stay here it will mean certain death. Love and a future is not a possibility anymore."

Geve's heart seemed to shudder to a stop. "What do you mean, we cannot return to the Embers?"

"Can you think of a way back up the waterfall?"

Geve honestly hadn't thought about it. "No... I... well, there must be another way."

"I know of no other."

"We have to look!"

Comminor's expression reflected his impatience. "Do you think we will have the strength to search the labyrinth of caves beneath us to find ways back in? We have a few scraps of meat and half a dozen cakes left!"

"We have to try," Geve said earnestly. An idea came to him. "How did the people who originally formed the Embers get into the caves?"

Comminor frowned. "Why?"

"Can we not find that entrance?"

"It was completely blocked. They tried for years to remove the debris but it appears half the mountain collapsed and blocked the way out. That is not an option."

Geve's mouth had gone dry. "You cannot just sit here and admit defeat. You are supposed to be our leader."

"And as leader, it is sometimes my job to state the truth, even when it is not what everyone wants to hear." Comminor turned his back. "Go to sleep."

Do not tell me what to do! Geve wanted to yell the words, but he knew he was being childish. Instead, he lay back and tried to get comfortable. The blanket he had carried in his bag was a little damp still, but actually it felt nice under his back, cooling his warm skin. He rested his head on his bag and closed his eyes.

He fell asleep almost immediately. And then he began to dream.

He stood beneath the Arbor, the huge tree's branches rearing above his head, the glossy green leaves shivering in the morning breeze. Reaching out, he rested a hand upon the trunk, his fingers running over the rough bark. Slowly, he moved forward and wrapped his arms around it, resting his cheek against the wood. As if a drum played softly inside, the tree's heart beat rhythmically, regular and reassuring.

He moved back, uplifted by the experience, to find there were others standing on the grass around the tree. He recognised some of them. Sarra was there, and Comminor, and Betune, in fact all of them who at that moment lay in the warmth of the Broken Room. And also the faces of those with whom they had connected down in the ceremonial room – the young boy who bore Comminor's golden eyes. The tall, lean man with the scruffy dark hair who had stood by the boy protectively. The dark-haired woman whose hand had rested on the pommel of her sword, clearly a soldier. The blonde-haired young woman, who looked so like the man standing by her side that Geve knew they must have been related.

And there were others – a tall man with brown hair and a beard, and gentle, friendly eyes. Another golden-eyed man, holding the hand of a beautiful woman who rested her head on his shoulder. A young man with curly hair, a lock falling across his forehead even though he pushed it away impatiently. A thickset, muscular older man with grey hair whose face reflected his obvious position of authority.

They and many more stood in a ring around the Arbor and, as Geve watched, they all stretched out their arms and everyone held hands.

He had always been a loner, which was unusual in the Embers. The mayors in each sub-district organised many events and people found comfort in being together and sharing their lives. But he had never been that way. Maybe because he was a bard and he had always been conscious of there being a hidden world that only he seemed to know about. Maybe because he spent most of his time watching Sarra instead of talking to others. Or maybe he was just destined to be alone.

But for perhaps the first time in his life, Geve felt he belonged. He was linked to all these people through his love for the Arbor, and he could feel its love for him radiating out with each slow heartbeat, washing over him like a wave. He closed his eyes, enjoying the warmth of the hands of those next to him, feeling this new connection running from person to person, energising them all.

When he opened his eyes, he was surprised to see a man standing in front of the Arbor, in the middle of the ring of people. He wore a long grey cloak with the hood raised and his head was bowed. Leather straps crossed his body and bracers covered his arms. He held out his hands, and Geve felt himself lift into the air.

He rose above the land and looked down with awe to see the radiant green grass and the Arbor growing smaller beneath him. The higher he went, the more of Anguis he could see. Hills and valleys sprinkled with grazing sheep and cows. Thick, lush forests crowding the edge of the mountains, which reared up with their shining grey slopes and snow-topped peaks. Villages and towns and cities, filled with people living their lives, every one precious to the Arbor.

Higher he went, and higher still. He saw the sea, a deep, glittering blue, maybe the most beautiful thing he had ever seen. Waves crashed on the golden shores, and in the deep, white horses rode atop the swells. Fish leapt out, dolphins played near boats, and the flukes of whales rose gracefully before sliding back into the ocean.

And he rose higher still. The sky was an even more brilliant blue than the sea. Birds flew past him, and the warm sun shone down on his hands and face, filling him with a joy he had never experienced in his life. He passed through the clouds, the nebulous white threads wrapping around him like spiders' webs, and then he was through and climbing higher still.

The blue faded, darkened to black, and then he was amongst the stars. A million, million sparkles of white, like the glitter of minerals in a rockface, all trying to outdo each other with their brilliantness.

He encompassed all of this and more, he was Anguis and the sea and the sky and everything in it that walked or crawled or flew. He was the universe, and he was loved.

He opened his eyes and sat up with a gasp. Around him, everyone was doing the same. They all stared at each other with startled eyes.

"I had a dream," he said, not really surprised to see everyone else nod.

"The Arbor," Nele said.

"We were all there," Amabil said.

Josse nodded. "I rose above the ground."

"And flew," Betune said, eyes shining.

"We all had the same dream," Comminor said as everyone nodded their agreement. His expression filled with hope. "That has to mean something."

Geve turned to Sarra. But the spot where she had lain the night before was empty.

He looked around the room. "Where is Sarra?"

Everyone glanced around. "Perhaps she went downstairs to relieve herself," Amabil suggested. "I will check." She rose and ran down the steps back into the caves, disappearing around the corner.

Geve got to his feet, the joy he had felt fading. Outside, the sky had lightened, although he could not see the sun, the air still choked with a red, smoke-filled haze. Pillars of flame lit occasionally across the burnt, barren landscape, and more smoke billowed. The air smelled of sulphur and tasted of ash.

In the distance, something moved, and he blinked and tried to focus. The shape almost filled the horizon, and he had thought it a river of lava, but as he watched it rose up high above the ground. Molten rock dripped from it, leaving behind a long, low body and huge wings that beat slowly, lifting its body above the horizon.

"She is not there." Amabil's voice echoed from behind him, filled with panic. "Where has she gone?"

Geve already knew the answer. He could see her in the distance, scrambling down the side of the mountain, falling occasionally but picking herself up and continuing to climb down to the blackened land.

He turned and looked over his shoulder at Comminor. "She has gone."

CHAPTER NINETEEN

I

Procella reached the last fort on Isenbard's Wall at sunset.

She approached from the north, deciding that if anyone were waiting for her, they would not expect her to come from that direction. The road wound south through the Wall to Laxony, a wide open trackway easily visible from the fort, so she turned off a few miles north, cut across a field, past some startled cows, then dismounted and shadowed a hedgerow until she had the fort in sight.

The road that ran from Cherton in Laxony past Heartwood and the Wall and there on to Redgar in Wulfengar was a popular trade route, as well as being the main road for pilgrims and other visitors to the Arbor. Ever since the defeat of the Darkwater Lords and the start of the Second Era, the fort had remained open, manned by little more than a handful of members of the new Heartwood Council, who provided mainly an economic presence, charging a small toll to pass, which was used primarily to maintain the busy road.

However, sure enough, just as she had suspected, on this side of the Wall on both sides of the Flumen river, the place seethed with Wulfian soldiers, and from the armour they wore, the way they had stationed scouts at the perimeter, and the air of excitement about the place, she knew they were waiting for her.

She swore violently, and the horse gave a whinny as if in disapproval. She leaned her forehead on the saddle. So near and yet so far!

She raised her head and peered through the hedgerow to the far side of the Wall. Although Heartwood's Temple had been destroyed after the invasion, the large defensive walls remained standing, and she could just see the battlements of the amber stone walls, glowing almost red in the last remnants of the setting sun. She had spent a good proportion of her early years patrolling those walls, and a nostalgic longing filled her, so strong it almost made her weep.

Her fist tightened in the horse's mane as she remembered the visions Cinereo had shown her of her children in trouble. She had not come so far to fall at the last hurdle. She was not some feeble court lady who needed rescuing, or a simpering maid ready to shed tears when the going got rough. She had been the Dux of Heartwood's Exercitus. Men and women alike had looked to her to lead them into battle, to show a good example.

She would not fail now.

The sun set slowly, darkness laying its cloak over the land. Procella waited until the soldiers had lit their torches and the night watch had begun in the Wulfian tradition – two-thirds sleeping with one-third to stay on duty.

While she waited, she pondered on whether to remove her chainmail. No doubt she would have to fight at some point as she tried to pass through the fort, and the chainmail would give her necessary protection. Equally, it slowed her movements, made noise, and could reflect light when she needed to remain in shadow. In the end, she chose to remove it, placing the bits and pieces of buckled plate in the horse's saddlebags, and laying the mail shirt across the saddle. When she'd done, she wore dark brown breeches and a brown leather jerkin over a short-sleeved green tunic. She scooped some mud from a nearby puddle and rubbed it on her face to hide her pale skin, and did the same to her forearms before drawing her brown cloak close around her and raising the hood.

Finally, she led the horse to a small tributary from the Flumen and reluctantly let it loose, hoping someone would find him the next day and be glad for a free new mount and the money they would raise from selling the armour.

Then she crept back to the hedge.

The fort had grown quiet, the majority of soldiers sleeping either in hastily erected tents or snoring out in the open. Leaving her sword sheathed, she drew her dagger, feeling less nervous with a blade in her hand, and crept as close to the fort as she could until the hedge ran out by the bridge over the Flumen.

They only had one guard stationed on the bridge. He looked half-asleep, and she waited for him to stretch and yawn, then move to one side to relieve himself against a tree before she slipped across the bridge, careful to walk by the edge so the boards didn't squeak. So easy! But somehow she didn't think the rest of her journey would be so simple.

From there, she began to make her way to the fort using trees, tents, carts and whatever else she could find as cover. When she had been in the Exercitus, before she became Dux, Valens had placed her with a spy for a week, and he had taken her on several missions to show her ways of hiding herself in plain sight, including making their way into both castles and military camps without being noticed. She employed those techniques now, moving silently from point to point, resisting the urge to attack anyone she came across as that could lead to them making a noise and alerting others around them, and being patient when her progress was halted by a patrol, waiting and growing stiff and cold until the guards moved on rather than being hasty and risk being seen.

In this manner she made it all the way to twenty feet from the fort before two guards appeared around a tent out of the darkness, surprising her.

Speed will keep you alive. She could hear the spy's words almost as if he stood beside her, whispering in her ear. As the two guards stared at her, confused by her appearance and presumably not even sure if she were a man or woman from her clothing, she moved forward. Before he even saw the dagger in her hand, she cut the first guard's throat and he fell to the ground, fingers clutching uselessly at his neck before collapsing face down.

The other guard stepped back as she approached and exclaimed out loud in shock, although he didn't shout a warning as he should have done. Backing away, he knocked her arm as she brought the dagger up to grant him the same fate as his friend, and he drew his own blade. Desperate to ensure he didn't make any more noise, she advanced quickly, swapping her dagger to her left hand and drawing her sword, then stabbed the dagger swiftly towards his chest. As she'd hoped, he reacted to it and knocked her hand away again, and at the same time she brought up her right hand and bashed the hilt of the sword into his face. His arms came up, and she thrust the dagger in the gap to the right of his breastplate and into his heart.

He fell back, gasping, and she pushed him onto the ground and used her weight to lean on the blade, covering his mouth so he couldn't call out, making sure he was dead before she got back to her feet. She was sweating, her heart pounding, but she didn't have time to recover. His exclamation had been heard, and voices sounded from inside the tent.

She backed away into the shadows and circled the tent, heading for the Wall as the two soldiers inside came out, shouting. Men moved from the fort towards the source of the noise, and she flattened herself to the Wall and moved quickly towards the building, keeping in the shadows.

A bell rang. More soldiers poured from the fort. She waited in the corner where the Wall met the square building, heart pounding, as men fanned out, meeting others who had spoken to those who'd heard the exclamation of the man she'd killed. She couldn't afford to wait any longer. At the moment all was confusion and they weren't even sure there was an intruder; as soon as they thought she might be on the site they would close the fort and she'd never get through.

Heart in her mouth, she moved out of the shadows and walked around the corner.

Clearly, they never expected her to just walk right up to them. Men bumped into her, ran past her, but she kept her head down and moved through them into the fort.

The Wall itself was eight feet thick and fifteen feet high, but the fort jutted out either side and was big enough to house a dozen soldiers on two floors, with a command room beneath and a gate that could be lowered to block the passage of travellers should the need arise. The gate had not been lowered for years, but still she was glad to pass under the rusty portcullis, knowing at that point she was on Laxonian ground. Although a Wulfian herself, she had lived the vast majority of her life in Laxony. She was glad to have an insight into Wulfian life as it had helped on many occasions, but she had no desire to remain there until she died.

She glanced up at the portcullis as she passed under it. And in doing so, she bumped straight into the back of a Wulfian lord, solid as a tree trunk, about as wide as he was tall.

He swore in Wulfian, turned to see who it was, and for a moment Procella stared right into his face, shocked into silence. It was Grimbeald, the Lord of the Highlands, who had been instrumental in the defeat of the Darkwater Lords over twenty years before. He had returned to his home in Calemar and married the Heartwood knight Tenara who he had fallen in love with on his journey to open the portal at the Tumulus, and since then Procella had only seen him twice, both times up in the Highlands when she'd done a tour of Wulfengar with the Peacemaker to encourage peaceful relations between the two nations.

Grimbeald stared at her. His black hair and wild beard were threaded with grey, but his eyes were sharp as ever. She gave a small shake of her head, worried that he would speak to her and announce her presence. His expression flickered with exasperation then, as if he were angry that she'd thought he would do that to her. Turning, he walked south through the fort, and Procella walked close behind him in his wake, the other soldiers there barely giving her a glance as she was obviously with him.

They weren't challenged until they went to pass under the portcullis on the Laxonian side. A hand shot out and tightened around her arm, and someone shouted. Her heart raced in alarm. A Wulfian soldier tugged at her hood, which fell back and exposed her braided hair, and more shouts ensued.

Grimbeald caught her hand and tugged her beneath the portcullis, but the other soldier's hand was still tight on her arm and she couldn't move. Soldiers poured into the fort, surrounding them.

Equally, behind Grimbeald she saw both men and women approaching the kerfuffle from tents pitched on the Laxonian side. Some of these Wulfians bore Grimbeald's badge on their tabards; others were clearly Laxonians. One raised his hand to call others over to them, and she saw the distinctive oak-leaf tattoo on his wrist, which meant he had once been a Militis, a Heartwood holy knight. Relief flooded her.

But the Wulfians were not going to let her go easily. One pushed forward – a captain judging by the gold buttons on the sleeve of his jerkin – a tall, broad-shouldered man with the distinctive Wulfian bushy beard and wild hair. He placed a large, heavy hand on her shoulder. "This woman is wanted in connection with the death of Hunfrith, Lord of the Plains," he announced. Procella tried to shake off his hand, but he'd clamped it to her like a vice.

"She is coming with me," Grimbeald said, his voice brooking no argument.

The captain just glared at him. "She killed Hunfrith in front of witnesses in a tavern."

Grimbeald glanced at her. She gave a little shrug. Exasperation crossed his features again briefly before he turned back to the captain. "Then you may petition Heartwood to have her extradited. But for now she is in Laxonian territory."

They all glanced down. Procella hadn't realised, but in the commotion they had passed beneath the portcullis, and her feet now stood on Laxonian ground.

Grimbeald moved towards the captain. For the first time, the captain saw the gold embroidery on his tabard that marked him as a lord, and uncertainty stirred in his eyes.

"Do you really want to cause a national incident?" Grimbeald spoke softly. "The vast presence you have on the other side of the Wall is already inflammatory to relations between our two countries. Do you really want to be the one responsible for tipping the scales into outright war? Because I will not let this woman go without a fight."

The captain hesitated. Procella could understand his predicament. He had been instructed to capture her at all costs, and if they had been standing on the Wulfian side of the Wall things would have been very different. But for him to fight Laxonian soldiers – especially those from Heartwood, a supposedly neutral territory – on Laxonian soil, that would be an outright declaration of war.

In a battle, Procella had always been able to sense that moment when the scales were tipping towards either success or failure. And so she recognised the moment when the captain made up his mind. She twitched her shoulder and he dropped his hand, and she walked past Grimbeald to the group of waiting Laxonians.

Grimbeald waited there a moment longer, face to face with the captain, and then without another word he too turned and walked to join her.

"Do not look back," he murmured as they moved away from the fort towards the Laxonian camp of tents and horses.

"Thank you," she said, looking across to her right and feeling a swell of relief at the familiar sight of Heartwood's walls about a half a mile to the west.

"Did you have to kill Hunfrith?" he said, his voice filled with irritation.

"He was trying to rape me."

He stopped walking. She glanced over her shoulder, stopped and turned to face him, seeing his expression. Anger, pure and bright, radiated from him, and his hand rested on the pommel of his sword.

"You are the Dux," he said through gritted teeth. "How could he have made such a blatant mistake?"

She wasn't sure whether he meant because Hunfrith had underestimated her skill with a sword or because attacking such a prominent figure was political suicide. Ultimately, she didn't care. Weariness swept over her and suddenly she longed for a good meal and a night's sleep.

"I *was* the Dux," she said softly. "And anyway, 'tis done. Hunfrith paid for his transgression – I made sure of that."

Grimbeald met her gaze. Then he nodded. "I am glad to see you safe, my lady. And I would like to pass on my condolences in person for the death of your husband. He will be sorely missed." He had sent gifts via his ambassador at the time of Chonrad's passing, but it was the first time she had seen him since.

"Thank you." Her throat tightened. It had been a long journey, she thought.

Grimbeald touched her arm lightly. "Then come. It is but a brief ride to Heartwood, and I know there are many who will be glad to see you. You are amongst friends now. You can relax."

The knot inside her loosened. She had made it. For the first time, hope glimmered inside her like the stars beginning to appear in the dusky sky.

II

Catena soaked in the hot bath and watched Demitto lazily as he finally got out and began to dry himself. The water for the baths was directed in from large, hot pools situated just behind the Nox Aves buildings they called the Nest. Catena had never seen natural geysers, and had been both fascinated and slightly alarmed by the way the steam rose sporadically in jets around Heartwood as the pressure built beneath the surface.

For the first time in a week, though, her muscles felt free of tension, and the scholars had allowed her access to their herb garden, which meant the water smelled of jasmine and lavender, familiar smells to help her relax.

Demitto – naked as the day he was born – finished drying and lifted his arms above his head, stretching the muscles in his back. Catena admired his physique: his toned arms, his taut stomach, his strong legs. Bathing was a ritual both sexes shared and was thus not a place she usually associated with sexual urges, but the relationship they had begun over the past few days meant she could not completely stop herself thinking of him in that way when he stood all brown and muscular before her.

He didn't look over at her now, however, and she kept her thoughts to herself as he began to dress, a slight frown marring his brow. She had no illusions about their relationship. She had proved a moment of distraction for him, a few nights of fun to ease the stress of the moment, and she had no objections to that. When he had first pulled her into his arms that night after rescuing the Prince, she had neither fought him off nor demanded a declaration of intent when he kissed her. She had known what he wanted, and had desired the same. And so now she could hardly complain if he ignored her as if it had never happened.

To her surprise, though, once he had finished pulling on his breeches and linen tunic, he came over to her tub and smiled, his hands on his hips. "Come, fair lady," he said, holding out a hand.

"You have been in there so long you will turn into a prune."

"I intend never to get out," she stated, sinking in even further. "I did not think I would ever get clean again."

He laughed and flicked his fingers, beckoning her. "Come on. We have to deliver the Prince in the proper fashion today. We must not keep the King waiting."

"Of course not," she grumbled, but she rose and accepted the towel he held out for her.

"As to your attire," he said, calling over a young squire to help him start buckling on his armour, "Manifred has provided you with a few items you might wish to don for the procession."

She opened her mouth to say she didn't need any handouts thank you very much and she certainly didn't want to garb herself in some frivolous lady's gown, but the words refused to come as a female squire brought across a selection of the items Demitto had been referring to. Catena fingered the linen tunic embroidered with silver thread, and the finely woven thin woollen breeches. It was the expensive ceremonial clothing a respected female knight would wear, not the kind of thing a lady would wear to court. She caught her breath as Demitto's eyes twinkled, and she realised how well he had grown to know her in such a small space of time.

"Maybe I could borrow one or two things," she said, and he nodded, pleased.

In the end she dressed entirely in the new items, thinking if she was going to wear one piece, she might as well wear the whole lot. So she finished with the fine breeches, a dark green long-sleeved tunic with embroidered cuffs, and topped it with the white linen short-sleeved tunic bearing the beautiful silver embroidery.

"I will not need armour?" she queried, feeling light and a little uneasy without her chain mail.

Demitto shook his head. "This is but ceremonial," he explained as the squire buckled on the highly decorative breastplate he had arranged to be sent back from Lornberg. "And besides, I think you will be glad to be free of mail today."

It was true; it was already exceptionally warm. She walked to the doorway and looked up at the mountain, observing the spiral of smoke that curled up into the sky. A scatter of rocks rolled down the side at the same time that a nearby geyser erupted in a high spray, startling her. Although Harlton had a sub-tropical climate, it did not experience this kind of seismic activity, and for a moment unease boiled in her stomach in the same way that the thick mud boiled around the hot pools behind the buildings.

But she had too much on her mind to dwell on it for long. As she turned back to the room, Tahir came in, and she smiled to see him rested and dressed ready for his ceremonial procession into the city.

The Nox Aves had managed to find some beautiful clothes fit for a prince. He wore a knee-length sky-blue tunic embroidered with silver and gold thread and tiny silver discs, which glittered in the sunlight. His dark blue undertunic and breeches provided an attractive contrast. The simple silver circlet on his brow announced his status as a prince representing one of the Laxonian lands. The shining oak-leaf pendant set with gems pronounced him the Selected for that year's Veriditas.

Even Atavus had been dressed up, with a silvery-blue kerchief tied around his neck.

Catena came forward and took Tahir's hands in hers. "How are you feeling?"

"Well enough." His eyes looked bright and his smile unforced. The Nox Aves's reaction to him on his arrival had completely thrown him, but she sensed he felt reassured by their veneration, as if his presence there truly was of some importance.

Demitto slotted his sword into his scabbard. He looked magnificent, she thought, in his polished armour with the oak tree engraved on the breastplate, and once again he seemed to radiate the power and eminence of the place he represented. He came to give the young prince a hug, and Catena stepped back, allowing them this special moment.

As yet, she remained uncertain of her role in the days to come. She had left Harlton thinking that after delivering Tahir to Heartwood, she would return there to continue her duties living the same life she had always done. Now, she wasn't so sure. Demitto had implied she was an important figure in the Apex, and although he had refused to give her more information about what it involved, he had implied she would play more than a passing role. This had been confirmed when they arrived at Heartwood because, after Manifred had acknowledged Demitto and bowed to Tahir, he had come to Catena and kissed her hand, saying her name, and his eyes had told her that he knew who she was and was also aware of her future in a way she was not.

But there had been no time to question him the night before as they had all been exhausted, and now it was too late. The squires wrapped them all in plain woollen cloaks, and then other members of the Nox Aves came to take them outside.

"You will be taken via the postern gate back to the main road into Heartwood," Manifred informed them, his curly brown hair blowing across his youthful face in the warm breeze.

The lines around his eyes suggested he wasn't quite as young as he seemed at first, she thought, and the others certainly seemed to defer to him as if he was their leader, which surprised her. As if reading her thoughts, Tahir said, "When do we get to meet Cinereo? I assumed he would be here."

Manifred's eyes met Demitto's in a glance so brief Catena wondered whether she'd imagined it. "Later. We have told everyone that you are arriving this morning. We will smuggle you out of the city, and then we will arrange for your arrival to be announced to the King, who will come to meet you and invite you to the palace." He smiled at Tahir. "You will get the proper welcome you deserve. And I will see you later, young prince."

Tahir nodded, and they all mounted their horses. Catena turned her mare and followed the member of the Nox Aves as he led them out, but she puzzled on the brief glance she'd caught as they rode. The mysterious way in which Cinereo had appeared to Demitto suggested there was something... unusual about the man. But what exactly that was remained to be seen.

They exited Heartwood via the postern gate without any ado, took a back road through the village that lay outside the main walls, headed south for a few miles and then circled back to approach once again via the main road. The Nox Aves member took their cloaks, and this time, as they approached Heartwood, horns rang out across the city and the waiting crowd began to turn and stare as they approached.

"It is the Selected!" someone yelled, and a huge cheer went up. Young girls waiting with baskets full of rose petals threw them in the air so they scattered the floor in white and pink. Horns blared. People screamed and cheered, and Catena was genuinely touched by the hope and respect on their faces. Demitto may have painted the aristocracy as indifferent to the religious purpose of the Veriditas, but the people still obviously understood the importance of the ceremony.

As they approached the main gates, more fanfares sounded and a man appeared beneath the raised portcullis. He sat astride a shining white mare, and there could be no mistaking his role. His clothes dripped with gold and jewels, and more precious gems glittered on his fingers and around his neck. On his hair he wore an elaborate crown, and his horse bore the livery of Heartwood – a green oak leaf sewn with gold thread and emeralds.

Catena and Demitto flanked Tahir as they approached. For the first time she became aware of the years of training Tahir had undergone in his princely role at Harlton, because the pomp and ceremony did not faze him, and he lifted his chin and sat straight in the saddle as they neared the King.

The Queen sat sidesaddle on her horse just beside the King, and behind them rode several other obviously important dignitaries, dressed in their best finery and wearing imperious expressions. Pride surged through Catena as Tahir nudged his horse forward and announced his name in a loud, clear voice as if determined he would appear as important as any of the kings he faced.

A herald called a welcome to the new Selected, and the King gave a brief dip of his head. He did not speak, though, and without further ado he turned his horse and led the cavalcade back into the city.

Catena stared, feeling the King had snubbed her prince, but Tahir just waved to the crowd and followed. She glanced across at Demitto, who just raised an eyebrow. He had warned them many times about the King's boorish ways, and she was beginning to understand what he meant.

They rode through the town, the air filled with more flower petals and streamers thrown from the high balconies. Performers danced and juggled and breathed fire in the streets to entertain the crowds, and stalls sold cinnamon apples and meat pies that filled the air with mouth-watering aromas.

Tahir smiled and waved, and Catena wondered how much of his apparent enjoyment of the parade was real. Perhaps he really was enjoying it.

Personally, she had enjoyed the previous day's entry to the city more. Today, her head ached from the humid weather and the too-bright sun. She hadn't eaten and felt a little queasy, and the noise and crush of people made her uneasy. She looked across at Demitto, a smile creeping to her lips as she thought that he in no way seemed daunted by the attention. In fact she thought he probably thrived on it. As if someone had switched on a light within him, the distracted apprehension he had exhibited over the past few days had disappeared, and now he radiated power, and those in the crowd had to shade their eyes from the blinding light reflected from his armour as he rode by.

Just then, he glanced at her and caught her watching him. She blinked, a little embarrassed, but pleasure rushed through her as his lips curved and he winked. She looked down demurely, but her heart raced.

And that in itself was enough of a sign to confirm to her what she had been thinking since the moment she first set eyes on him outside Harlton. He had captivated her heart as easily as catching a butterfly in a net, and that was a huge mistake.

Because something was approaching. She could see it in the air, which seemed to shimmer with anticipation and the promise of an event that would make Anguis tremble. She could feel it in her body, which tingled with expectation, like when a lover blows across the skin and hairs rise in response. And she could read it in Demitto's eyes. As if he stood on a high hill looking into the distance, and could see the approach of something so momentous it was going to change their world forever.

No, today was not a good day to have discovered she was in love.

III

Sarra had never been more scared in her entire life. Maybe the moment she had climbed down the ladder from her room in the Embers and had seen Comminor waiting at the bottom had come close to it, up until the moment she realised he wasn't there to take away her baby, anyway. But life in the Embers had been relatively safe. People rarely died from accidents or physical confrontation. Death came through disease, or sometimes hunger, which had been one of the major problems: in the safe atmosphere everyone lived longer, causing the environment to become increasingly more crowded. But she had never felt her life to be in danger. And thus she was completely unprepared for the panic that enveloped her as she descended down the mountain.

Part of the problem was the fact that the baby had grown to such an extent that her swollen belly made movement very difficult. She had not had the usual months to get used to her change in weight as most pregnant women did, and several times she fell, unaccustomed to having to adjust her centre of gravity. And the going was not easy anyway. When she first slipped from the Broken Room it was dark, and although the sky remained a dull grey-red from the sporadic fires that had erupted across the land, the ground was shrouded in shadow, and she had no lantern or other method of lighting her way.

The mountainside was steep, filled with loose rock and ash that soon blackened her hands and stuck to her sweat-soaked skin. She was sure she must look a fright, but that was the last of her worries at that moment. Someone would eventually notice she had gone, and then they would try to come after her. And she had to get as far away as she could before that happened.

She had no idea where she was going or why she had to flee. She did so from some deeply embedded instinct that told her she had to distance herself from the others before they made her return to the Embers. She had no doubt that Geve and Comminor were going to try to find a way back to the underground city, because what possible life could there be for them all in this lifeless place? It made perfect sense, and yet in her heart she knew she could not return.

The ground trembled beneath her feet, throwing her off centre again, and she fell onto her hands and knees. Pain shot through her, radiating out from her stomach, and she clutched her bump with one arm, crying out as it felt as if someone had slid a knife above her pubic bone and twisted it.

She waited, panting, and gradually the pain faded, but that only made her worry more. She had listened to the mothers talk in the common rooms, relating their tales of pregnancy and childbirth, and so she knew what was supposed to happen before the child was born. Her hand clenched into a fist in the soft ash and she cursed under her breath. *No, no, no!* She could not be in labour. Although she didn't know where she was going, she knew she had to keep walking. And besides, she couldn't have the baby here! She lifted her head and looked around at the boiling lava that bubbled and spat in the valleys, at the spurting geysers, the jets of flame erupting from the hundreds of volcanoes that littered the landscape. "No!" she wailed. What possible good could come of the baby arriving in this terrible place?

Pushing herself to her feet, she struggled further down the mountainside. Ahead of her, the slope began to shallow, leading to an uneven landscape scattered with boulders and cooled lava flows, the occasional stump of old, burnt trees poking through the surface. Small creatures like the crabs in the Great Lake skittered across the grey rock, but she could see no other sign of life.

Where was she going? Her feet slowed, and eventually she stopped walking and stared around hopelessly. The urge to continue filled her; she stubbornly ignored what she was beginning to think was an irrational hope – that she would somehow find something to make her believe the journey had not all been for nothing. Hope wasn't a good enough reason to risk the life of her baby.

The ground trembled and shook again and she fell once more, this time drawing blood on her right knee as it hit the rock. She cried out and sat back, unable to stop tears forming. She had never felt so lonely, so hopeless and helpless. "I wish you were here," she whispered, although she wasn't sure to whom she was referring. Geve? Comminor? The Arbor? Or something else?

A blast of heat warmed the already-humid air, and she gasped as she looked up at the sky to see a huge shadow approaching from the north. *A firebird...*

The creature loomed large in the sky and swooped towards her, only a few feet from the ground. She could not even conceive how big it must be as she had known nothing in her experience to compare it to. It was longer than the Great Lake, maybe even bigger than the whole of the Embers, and just as wide as it reached out its gigantic wings. Lava dripped from the flaming red and gold feathers, and she cowered close to the ground while it skimmed past her. Heat rose to engulf her, and for a moment it was difficult to breathe, the air so hot it burned her lungs as she breathed in, the ash so thick it stung her eyes and choked her.

Had it seen her? She must be so small and insignificant crouched on the ground, her skin and hair probably now as black as the rock around her. She tucked her chin against her chest and curled into a ball, remaining there even as the heat intensified and sweat poured from her, drying on her skin in seconds. *Please do not let it see me...* She wasn't sure to whom she prayed, but she begged whoever was watching her – if there were indeed anyone – to help her.

If the firebird had flown over her, it would have turned her to ash in seconds. But when it was only a few miles away, for no apparent reason it suddenly changed direction and banked, turning to the south-west. The intense heat lessened, and she lifted her head cautiously to see the creature growing gradually smaller as it flew, before it finally disappeared, leaving only a glow of orange light on the dark horizon.

She exhaled – not realising until then that she'd been holding her breath – only to catch it again as her stomach cramped, the pain radiating out across her abdomen. She forced herself to breathe through it, but the ache was like nothing she'd experienced before, and by the end of it she was drenched in sweat and tears.

How could she go through with this on her own? She glanced over her shoulder, shocked at how far she had travelled. She couldn't possibly make it back up the slope to the Broken Room. She should have discussed it with the others – they wouldn't have made her go back if she were in labour. They were in it together, weren't they? Surely one of them would have understood her urge to stay?

She wiped her face, forgetting until she saw her hand how it was covered in ash, and sobbed even more at the thought of how she must look. Yes, she'd coped on her own pretty much all her life, but this was different. She was truly alone, she was scared, she was tired, and she was in pain. How was she ever going to make it through?

"You are not alone."

She looked up sharply at the voice and stared with shock at the sight of the man standing before her. He had not been there a few moments before – she was sure of it. He wore the same clothing he had worn the previous time he appeared to her: plain brown breeches and a colourful tunic, an intricate circlet on his braided brown hair.

"My son," she whispered.

He smiled. "Hello, Mother."

Wonder filled her. "Am I dreaming?"

"Do I feel like a dream?" He held out his hand.

She grasped it, and his skin was warm and firm. It grounded her in reality, and at that moment she knew he must be real.

He pulled her to her feet and placed an arm around her waist, supporting her as they walked forward and continued down the slope.

"I do not know where I am going," she said, glancing around the landscape. One feature looked the same as another – everything was rock grey or lava red. The sun must be rising, she thought, noticing that the sky had lightened, although she could not see the yellow orb she had dreamed of since being pregnant.

"You will know when you get there," he said.

She glanced over her shoulder again at the Broken Room, not sure if she could see a figure standing in the darkness looking at her. "He will be angry with me," she said.

"He will understand."

"I should have told them where I was going."

"They will follow." He spoke with such certainty that she ceased to worry and turned her attention to the landscape ahead of her.

The parched brown ground spread out from the mountain in a large circle. It seemed to be ringed by a collection of low boulders. As she approached them, she saw they were vaguely rectangular in shape, although they were now broken and pitted.

"It looks like they were once a wall," she observed.

"You may be right."

"Was it...?" Her voice faded out as another contraction seized her, and she doubled over in pain.

He helped her lower herself to the ground, and she rode the pain out on hands and knees, blowing out each breath in a long exhalation that seemed to help. When she was done, she sat back, exhausted, relieved as the discomfort abated.

He knelt by her side and stroked her hair back off her face, murmuring calming words. She looked up at him, touched by his gentleness and obvious love for her.

"What is your name?" she whispered.

He gave her a cheeky smile. "You have not given me one yet."

She smiled back tiredly. "Are you really here?"

"Can you not touch me?"

"How can you be here?"

He stroked her forehead. "I do not know."

Tears formed in her eyes and trickled down her cheeks. She was so tired... "I am scared."

"You have to be strong."

"I am trying."

"I know." He leaned forward and kissed her cheek.

"I miss him," she said, and again wasn't sure herself if she was referring to Rauf, Geve or Comminor.

"He will come."

"I am so tired…"

"Then sleep." He stroked her hair. "Sleep…"

Comforted and secure in his arms, she closed her eyes, and slept.

CHAPTER TWENTY

I

Procella hadn't been to Heartwood in over two years. When Chonrad had felt called to the Arbor just over a year before, she had stayed in Vichton as there had been a spate of coastal raids by what had been rumoured to be Wulfian pirates, and with the first rumblings of trouble after such a long peace, Chonrad had been worried the raids presaged a full-blown attack on the towns just south of the Wall.

She had been to Heartwood several times since she gave up the role of Dux, though, and had seen the place change gradually. After the Darkwater Lords had been defeated and the Arbor itself destroyed the Temple that had been built around it, the Militis had been disbanded and the gates on the massive Porta gatehouse taken down on Chonrad's instructions: the tree did not need to be defended in the way they had thought. Some of the Militis had remained at Heartwood, however, and had formed the Council with the intention of looking after the holy site, controlling the flow of pilgrims and providing shelter and amenities for those who wished to travel to see the tree.

Of course it hadn't turned out to be as simple as it had sounded at the time they conceived the idea. The members of the Council required a place to live, offices in which to work and a place to grow food and keep livestock to feed themselves and the pilgrims. As stories of the great victory over the Darkwater Lords and the amazing growth of the Arbor spread, so visitors to the site grew exponentially, and it didn't take long for people to realise this growth in traffic to the region granted them increased opportunities.

Merchants began to travel from near and far to sell wares to the visitors. It began with food and clothing, and grew to include the kind of goods people required when travelling, such as cooking utensils, simple medicines in case people took ill on the journey, and tools to mend broken carts. That led to small workshops opening up for blacksmiths and carpenters to offer their services to mend the broken carts, while others set up stalls selling simple souvenirs for visitors to take back to give to their loved ones as proof that they had visited the famous Arbor, such as carved wooden pendants, clothing embroidered with oak leaves and wooden ornaments imbued with oils to make the home smell sweeter. The travelling merchants discovered they made more money when selling outside Heartwood than when they travelled to other cities, and decided to settle there permanently. They had to live somewhere, so clusters of small dwellings began to sprout around the walls.

And gradually, Heartwood grew into a small town.

In the last rays of the sun, Procella followed Grimbeald and the others through the streets towards the main dwellings of the Council. She fell silent as she observed how much the place had grown over the last few years. It had a good feel: everyone seemed happy, there was no sign of violence or arguments in the streets, and the place looked well-kept and thriving. But as she rode past the First Acorn – the first tavern to be raised on the site – and heard raucous singing spill out from the open doors like the lantern light that lit up the street, her brow darkened. The Arbor had informed them that it didn't want to be defended and it didn't want to be worshipped. Nevertheless, it continued to be a holy site.

It housed the Pectoris, granted to them by Animus itself, and it remained the source of Anguis's growth and prosperity. To treat it so... lightly seemed wrong somehow.

And yet she had been brought up a Militis, trained since the age of seven to venerate the tree. Twenty-two years had passed, and men and women much more dedicated and wise than herself had formed the Council that maintained the new town. Perhaps she was being overcautious and old-fashioned.

They approached the old walls that circled the site of the Temple, and to Procella's surprise and shock, she saw they were in the process of being dismantled. Most of the eastern part of the wall had already vanished, and the western section had large pieces missing.

"What in Anguis's name...?"

Grimbeald heard her and followed her startled gaze. "Dolosus has instructed the removal as they are starting to build new houses and they need the stone. The wall is irrelevant anyway as it is not supposed to be needed for defence. They are going to build a wooden fence, I believe, mainly to control access to the tree."

She noted his used of the word 'supposed'. Chonrad had written down in the *Quercetum* what the Arbor had passed onto him, and instructed that the defences not be rebuilt, but even though he was her husband and they had discussed it many times over the years, still she felt a tremor of fear at the thought of the Incendi threat and the knowledge that they could no longer defend the holy tree with a physical presence.

Not that it did much good last time, she thought. The Darkwater Lords had merely risen above the walls, although it was true that the Temple had held them at bay long enough for Chonrad to activate the final node, deep in the labyrinth beneath the tree.

Her head ached and she was too tired to think on it further, so she kept quiet as they followed the main road around to the west where the Council buildings now nestled against the base of the mountain.

She dismounted and left her horse in the hands of one of the young stablehands, and then followed Grimbeald and the others into the small complex of buildings that housed the Council members and those scholars she now knew to be members of the Nox Aves.

Even as she walked into the courtyard, a man emerged from one of the buildings with outstretched arms, smiling broadly. "Procella!"

"Dolosus." She came forward and received his hug, smiling as he stepped back. He didn't seem to have aged much since the last time they met, although his once-dark brown hair had lightened with grey, as had his trimmed beard. "You look well."

He tipped his head. "I am not sure I can return the compliment," he teased.

She looked at her arms and remembered she had covered them and her face with mud to camouflage herself in the darkness. "Ah, yes. I think maybe a bath is in order."

"I barely recognised her," Grimbeald stated. "I thought she was a Komis at first."

Dolosus snorted at the mention of their brown-skinned neighbours. The Komis had sent an army to invade Heartwood at the same time as the Darkwater invasion, but the majority of their soldiers had been washed away in the floods. Politically the two countries had been at peace for over twenty years, but for those who had seen friends wounded in the original Komis attack – like Dolosus – forgiveness still did not come easy.

"Is there any news of my children?" she asked hopefully.

He shook his head. "We have scouts trying to find their location. As soon as we hear anything, we will let you know. Please, come in and we will let you have a very brief bath. But then you must join us – there are many others here who wish to greet you."

She pondered on his words as she soaked in the bath in one of the guest rooms. Her curiosity made her get out quicker than she might otherwise have done, as the hot water soaked into her aching bones, and it was tempting to stay there all night. But eventually she forced herself out, dried and dressed, and then left her room and walked along the corridor to find the source of the voices that echoed further along.

It turned out they came from a long room with tables laid end-to-end: a dining hall. Most of the tables were empty, but one was filled with half a dozen people who all seemed to be talking at once.

She stopped in the doorway, unnerved by the noise. She had never been comfortable with social gatherings, being much more at home on the battlefield than at court, and although she had forced herself to play the role of the wife of a Laxonian lord and entertain with Chonrad when the need arose, since his death she hadn't socialised at all.

But as she looked along the line of seats, she realised she knew all the people present. Joy radiated through her, and she walked into the room to a chorus of cheers.

"I did not know you were all coming," she exclaimed, walking across to the blonde-haired couple of Hanaireans who rose as she approached and kissed her on the cheek.

"The Peacemaker asked us to come but suggested we did not announce it," said Fionnghuala, still beautiful and elegant even though ten years or so had passed since Procella had travelled with Chonrad to Hanaire to visit them.

"It does not pay to declare one's actions at the moment," her husband, Bearrach, said as he kissed Procella also.

"Indeed." Procella turned to greet Gravis, the Peacemaker, then moved past him to kiss her old friend from Heartwood – Nitesco, now a great scholar. She nodded to Grimbeald and then took a place at the table next to Gravis.

"So why are we all here?" She helped herself to some of the cooked meat and bread on the platters before her, realising she was ravenous. When was the last time she had eaten a full meal?

The others gradually settled, and Gravis pushed his plate away and sat back in his chair. He didn't seem to have aged at all, Procella thought, hiding a smile at the way his hair continued to curl on his forehead the way it had when he was in his twenties all those years ago. Then, he and his twin brother Gavius had been mischievous and permanently cracking jokes, and Gravis had been so unsure of himself and his abilities. Now when he spoke he did so confidently, wearing his authority with obvious ease.

"I think by now we have all heard of the rising problems," he began. "And I think I have personally spoken to most of you about the fact that Nitesco has created the Nox Aves, a group of scholars whose focus has been on trying to understand and make sense of everything that happened in the days of Darkwater, and to try to fathom what is happening now."

Nitesco nodded. "You will all have heard of the rise of the element of fire. The Nox Aves do not believe that at this time the Incendi pose the same threat as Darkwater did twenty-two years ago. I do not believe we are under the threat of an imminent invasion. But equally, I believe the time *is* fast approaching when an event will occur that will be crucial for the survival of Heartwood, the Arbor, and indeed the whole of Anguis in the future. We have named this event the Apex."

Murmurs arose around the table, but Procella remained quiet, thinking of what Julen had told her about the strange fires that had been springing up around the country. "When will this event occur?" she asked.

"We are not sure," Nitesco replied. "Soon. Unfortunately we have no way of knowing exactly when."

"Julen told me that you think the Arbor's roots conduct not only energy but also time," she said.

"That is true. In this way, it seems the Arbor has seen something in its future – possibly even its own death."

Everyone fell quiet, digesting that.

"Well, we must stop it," Procella said, appalled. "We have done so before. We can do so again!"

Nitesco poured himself a cup of wine before continuing. "Actually, we believe that the event in the future that the Arbor has foreseen – whatever it is – is fixed in time. It cannot be changed. In effect, it *has* to happen the way it is supposed to happen. It is our role to ensure that it *does* occur, and that the Incendi do not change it."

"They wish to stop it happening?" Procella said, confused.

"Maybe they want to change the way these events occur and thus change the future. We cannot know. But we do know that they have been eliminating people who they think could have played a role in the Apex. They have come after many of us, and some of us have barely escaped with our lives."

Procella thought of how close she had come to death and nodded. "Who has fallen?"

Nitesco named two Laxonian lords and one Wulfian one; some dignitaries who had risen to prominence over the past few years; and then sadly he told her of the death of Niveus and Terreo, two Militis who had helped on the quests all those years ago, and of the passing of Silva, the Komis woman who had been in charge of the Arbor for many years.

"That is terrible," Procella said, her fists clenching as sorrow swept over her.

Nitesco exchanged a glance with Gravis. Then he said, "There is one more…"

She held her breath as coldness filtered through her. *Not my children…* "Who?"

Nitesco ran a hand through his hair. "I am sorry, Dux, but we think it was the Incendi who killed Chonrad."

Procella stared at him as her heart seemed to shudder to a halt. "What makes you say that?"

"We think that when the Arbor called for him, it might have tried to inform him what was going to happen during the Apex and ask him for help. The Incendi would no doubt have been aware of Chonrad's part in defeating the Darkwater Lords and that he had a special connection with the tree. And I think they managed to use the Arbor's roots to stop the tree communicating with him. We are not sure if they brought about his demise, or if he sacrificed himself to the Arbor."

She opened her mouth, horrified to think of what he might have gone through before he died, but at that moment someone burst through the door and announced, "Imperator!"

Dolosus stood. "What is it?"

Procella recognised the messenger – he had once been a Militis and like many others, he must have stayed behind after the Militis were disbanded in order to work for Dolosus. He looked across at Procella and his face now broke into a smile, his words confirming their previous relationship. "The Dux's children – Julen and Horada – they are here!"

II

Demitto poured himself another cup of ale and sat back in his chair, longing once again for the end of the day so he could remove his ceremonial armour and relax.

The large hall was incredibly hot and stuffy, even though they had opened the doors, and about two dozen children stood behind the tables attempting to cool the guests with large fans of peacock feathers.

He looked up at the dais where King Varin of Heartwood and his queen sat with a number of visiting dignitaries, kings and queens from other lands and important officials. Tahir sat at the end as if he had been added as an afterthought. Clearly Varin knew he had to accommodate the Selected – supposedly the most important figure in the coming Veriditas – at the high table, but equally as clearly the fact that he had placed the boy at the far end and ignored him for the entire evening emphasised what little importance the King placed on the ceremony.

Tahir had accepted his fate with grace, however. To Demitto's relief and admiration, even though he'd been separated from the only people he knew in the city, the young prince hadn't made a fuss when shown his place, had eaten quietly with one hand buried in Atavus's fur and answered any questions asked of him, and generally acted more like royalty than any of the other pompous fools sitting along the table from him.

Demitto stifled a sigh, aware of his cynicism and knowing it was unfair. He had met many of the other kings on his travels and none of them were really that bad. Most of them would be respectful during the ceremony, and he thought that privately they all admired Tahir for his sacrifice.

No, the only person he really disliked was Heartwood's own king. Granted, the man did not mean to be cruel or heartless. But he was stupid, bombastic, pleasure-loving and self-indulgent. He cared only for appearances, was not religious in the least and seemed completely ignorant of the fact that he was responsible for the huge tree that resided in his city. Did Varin ever visit the Arbor except at the Veriditas? Demitto thought probably not. He couldn't imagine the King stirring himself to do something that didn't in some way grant him either fame or fortune.

To all appearances, though, it seemed as if he considered the Veriditas of utmost importance, and the party he had thrown that evening in the Selected's honour was magnificent, complete with an elaborate show by one of the country's most revered playwrights, entertainment by the court's musicians – each of whom were known to be exceptionally skilled in their instruments – enough food to feed an army for a fortnight, and enough gold and silver scattered around the room to ransom a dozen kings. But Demitto knew it was all for show, to impress his visitors and prove his influence. None of it was related to the fact that, the following day, Tahir was to gift the most important thing a person possessed to the Arbor – his life.

Demitto glanced at Catena. Her expression – as it had been all evening – was stony, and those who sat either side of her had long since turned away after finding she had no desire for conversation. His lips curved a little. Ninety percent of the time her face was marred by a scowl, but he adored her in spite of that, knowing that beneath her harsh countenance lay a tender heart and a caring personality.

When he had first met her, he had been completely puzzled by the thought that this was the woman with whom he was supposed to spend the rest of his days. He had known many women in his life: princesses, whores, knights and merchants, dancers and singers, young and old. The dark-haired, seemingly permanently angry young woman had not particularly attracted his interest at all, and for the first few days he had tried to tell himself that Cinereo was mistaken, and she could not be the vitally important person he had made her out to be. But as the days had passed, she had gradually proven herself to be even more solid, capable, loving and strong. She had accepted his advances wholeheartedly, and had made no demands of him, nor any declarations of undying love. But still, he knew she had feelings for him. And that, at least, was a good thing.

He glanced around the room. The party was far from over: wine flowed, the dancing had begun, and he knew that before long men and women alike would be making fools of themselves from being drunk and over-excited.

He caught Catena's eye, gestured with his head towards Tahir, and her features lit with relief. She nodded, and together they rose and walked across to the King's table, carefully avoiding the wild dancers who spun in the centre of the room.

"Your Highness," Demitto said, raising his voice about the musicians, who were also getting carried away.

Varin looked up, annoyed at being interrupted. "What?"

"The Selected grows tired after his long journey, my king.

We request your permission to take him back to the Nest for the night so he can be ready and refreshed ready for his big day tomorrow."

The King waved his hand, bored, impatient. "Whatever you want. I care not."

Standing beside Demitto, Catena bristled, but Demitto held her hand and just bowed. "Thank you, my king. We will see you tomorrow."

The King said nothing – he had already turned away.

Catena opened her mouth to say something, but Demitto directed her to the other end of the table towards Tahir.

"He is so rude!" she exclaimed.

"He is. But it would do no good to mention it now."

He stopped in front of the Prince, whose face lit with relief at the sight of him. "Ready for bed?" Demitto asked. He had wondered if Tahir would be fearful to think his evening was already over, but the Prince nodded eagerly and rose to join him.

Nobody took any notice of the three of them and the dog as they made their way along the edge of the hall and exited the room. And that, Demitto thought, was probably the saddest thing of all.

Outside, however, Tahir seemed to take the first deep breath he'd had all night. "At last," the Prince murmured, stretching up his arms.

"I am sorry for that," Demitto muttered, leading them through the palace grounds. Trimmed hedges and borders filled with limp flowers could not distract him from the smoking mountain that reared behind the spires of the palace. He tore his eyes away and instead smiled at Tahir. "You deserve so much more."

"It is of no concern," Tahir said, looking down and stopping to pick a flower. "I am just glad it is over."

Demitto couldn't think of anything to say to that.

They approached the palace gates leading to the town, and Tahir glanced to the right at the high wooden fence that Demitto had told him earlier encircled the Arbor. "I do not suppose we could stop and see it?" he asked quietly.

Demitto shook his head. "I am sorry. The Selected are forbidden to visit the Arbor before the Veriditas."

Tahir nodded, and they walked on.

Demitto knew they should have called for a royal carriage to take them to the Nest, but the city was in celebration mode and he thought it would be nice for the boy to spend his last evening outside. Besides which, the heat was unbearable, and he thought he might pass out if he had to sit in a carriage in his armour. He glanced over at Catena, seeing how the strands of hair that had escaped the knot at the nape of her neck curled from the heat, and how her skin was flushed pink. A tenderness he had not expected swept over him. None of them had asked for this. If given the choice, they would all have chosen a different future.

They walked through the streets, and although Tahir wasn't hungry, Demitto bought him a candied apple to nibble, and Catena bought him a stuffed toy dog that looked like Atavus.

Tahir looked up at Demitto. "I would like him to be there tomorrow."

Demitto hesitated, knowing the King didn't like animals at the ceremony, but he did not have the heart to tell the Prince that. "Of course," he said, promising himself that he would find a way to smuggle the dog in.

He had wondered if the people in the streets would recognise them from the procession into the city, but oddly it was as if the three of them were invisible as they walked back to the Nest. Even though he still wore his ceremonial armour, and all of them wore clothes clearly too fancy for them to be ordinary citizens, they passed through the throng untouched, and it wasn't long before the crowds thinned out and the walls of the Nest rose before them.

Demitto glanced to the right of the complex, noting the flurry of activity outside the mouth of the Cavus as the Nox Aves carried out last-minute preparations. Catena looked over too; she caught his eye and raised an eyebrow, but he gave a little shake of his head and was relieved when she said nothing.

The guard on the gate recognised them and let them in, surprise flitting across his features at the realisation that they had walked back alone.

It was nearly dark, the courtyard lit by lanterns, and as they approached the buildings and Manifred came out to welcome them, it obviously hit Tahir for the first time that this would be his last night on Anguis, because he went completely white and began to shake.

Manifred smiled, though, and several other members of the Nox Aves came out, and together they took Tahir to his room, gave him some mulled wine to calm him, helped him out of his clothes, dressed him in a cool linen gown, and put him to bed.

At this point, the Nox Aves standing around the bed bowed their heads, and Manifred spoke a prayer. Demitto dipped his head, but he could not take his eyes from the boy's face. Tahir blinked rapidly, his golden eyes wide, the pulse racing his throat, and that made up Demitto's mind. He had hoped to spend the last night alone with Catena, but at that moment he knew he could not leave the boy.

Manifred and the Nox Aves withdrew, but Demitto continued to talk about the day as he unbuckled his armour, about how fat the King was, about how hot it had become, and how Atavus's breath smelled from the meaty bones he'd eaten. Catena took the hint and chatted too, and after they'd tidied away Tahir's clothes and there was nothing more to do, they removed their own clothing leaving on just their linen undershirts and climbed onto the bed with the Prince, one on either side. Atavus leapt up onto the bed and lay across Tahir's feet.

Catena talked about Harlton, about the river threading through the city, about the smell of metal in the air and the way the seagulls dipped over the castle, and she stroked Tahir's dark hair as she talked, bending occasionally to plant a soft kiss on his forehead. Tahir continued to shake, however, and as Catena noticed his distress her voice petered out as emotion overwhelmed her too, so Demitto took over.

As he talked, he made up a future for Tahir. He spoke of what adventures the boy would have, of the battles he'd fight, the warriors he'd best, the dragons he'd defeat, and how one day he'd find his one true love. He talked about the places he'd visit – the hills of Wulfengar's highlands, the patchwork quilt of Laxonian fields, the glittering blue of the sea off Hanaire's coast, the forests of Komis with their avenues of carved trees. He spoke of a life of beauty, of excitement, of love and of triumph. He made him seem a hero, and Tahir listened with glistening eyes.

Demitto knew he had a talent for storytelling, and as the lanterns were extinguished outside and their room faded into darkness with the only light coming from a lone candle on the table, he let his voice soothe the troubled prince until finally, late into the night, the boy's eyelids drooped.

He just thought Tahir had dozed off when the boy whispered, "Demitto? Do not leave me."

His throat tightened. "Never, young prince. I will be there until the end, I swear."

Tahir's eyes closed.

Demitto began to hum a song he remembered from his childhood: an old hymn about the Arbor that his mother used to sing to him. He sang all five verses softly, emotions stirring within him at the memory of the days when he had thought the whole world consisted of his parents and the house by the lake.

By the time he'd finished, Catena's cheeks were wet, and Tahir finally slept.

"You have magic in your voice," she whispered, wiping away the tears with a hand.

He reached across the sleeping prince and brushed a few she'd missed with his fingers. "Do not cry."

"I cannot help it. It is a terrible crime." She looked down at Tahir. "He does not deserve to die."

"It is his destiny," he said simply.

"But…"

"Catena. You do not rail against the setting of the sun or the leaves that fall from the tree in The Falling."

She frowned at the analogy. "It is not the same."

"It is the same."

Her green eyes shone in the candlelight. "What are you trying to tell me?"

"I do not know." And he didn't – he was not a scholar. All he knew was that the events of the following day were as inevitable as the sunrise. But something within him – something as magical as the night had turned out to be – urged him to say, "It is all a cycle, Cat. Life and death. The fools in the palace understand nothing, but the Nox Aves know. At this moment in time, Tahir is the most important person in the world. He stands at the centre of the wheel of fate, and he holds the future of the whole of Anguis in his hands."

"And what of us?" she whispered. "Tell me my fate, Demitto."

He hesitated. Manifred had sworn him to secrecy, had instructed him never to share his knowledge of what was to come.

But it was the night of nights, and Catena was scared, and he wanted to comfort her.

He reached out a hand and – to her obvious surprise – rested it on her belly.

"This is your future," he said. "As one life ends, another begins, sweet Cat."

And while the Prince slept, Demitto linked their fingers, and told her everything.

III

Geve clenched his fists, anger rising within him and making it difficult for him to hold back from knocking Josse flat on his back.

"We are not leaving her!" he yelled.

Josse glared at him. "Sarra's overactive imagination has led us away from our home to this terrible place. It is her fault we are here. We do not even know if we can get back to the Embers yet. We could be lost here forever!"

"Then what is wrong with spending another day to persuade her to come with us?" Geve snapped.

"Why should we? She clearly does not want to come with us. She wants to be alone. So let us leave her alone!"

Geve opened his mouth to retaliate, but Comminor cut him off.

"We stay together," the Chief Select said flatly, picking up his bag and slinging it over his shoulder. "There is nothing else to say."

For once, however, the usually obedient Josse stood his ground. "This is foolishness." He gestured out at the scorched landscape. They had all watched the firebird swoop across the barren land, and Geve's heart had risen in his throat as he'd seen it pass so close to Sarra that he was sure he saw her hair glow scarlet. Josse's face now reflected his fear. "Why should I risk my life for her?"

Geve looked down at the scene. They could just see Sarra in the distance. She had stopped walking and appeared to be lying on the ground. Geve wasn't sure if she was injured or just tired, but his heart went out to her to think of her in pain and alone.

He wanted to beg the others to help her, but deep down he could understand why they felt like that. She hadn't lied –

she had led them to the Surface. But what was the point of it all when the world was dead? Why had they been led to this place? What was the point?

Still, a tiny part of him believed in her. There was something about her, something special that he couldn't define. Yes, he loved her, but it wasn't just that. Comminor could see it, and he thought the other members of the Veris could too. They had followed her unquestioningly, as if an inner instinct had convinced them she was telling the truth. And he couldn't just stop now, even though despair kept threatening to overwhelm him whenever he looked out and saw burnt rock instead of grass.

"Well I am going down there," he said, picking up his bag. "I understand if you do not wish to follow. But on the small chance that it is not all over yet, I am willing to give her one last try."

He turned and walked over to the lip of the room, climbed over, and began to descend the mountain.

A moment later, Comminor slid down beside him, and the two of them began walking together.

When he looked over his shoulder, his throat tightened at the sight of everyone else following not far behind.

They slipped and skidded down the steep slope on the loose stones, and before long his skin became streaked with ash and dirt. He glanced across at Comminor, silent and solid beside him, and smiled wryly at the sight of the older man's face streaked with black. He wanted to hate Comminor, but in truth he was just thankful he'd backed him up. Although Geve was jealous of the other man's relationship with Sarra, at that moment he just wanted her safe, and the more people who could help with that, the better.

It took them a long time to reach her, and by then the sun had obviously risen, even though all it did was lighten the red fog that hung in the air. Geve eyes – used to a lifetime of semi-darkness in the Embers – watered continuously, and when he looked around at the others, he saw their soot-marked faces also streaked with tears. Everyone looked exhausted, but they all pressed on, presumably filled with the same sense of determination he himself felt.

The slope began to level out, and he and Comminor picked up speed and almost ran the final mile or so, eager to get to the prone form of Sarra ahead of them. They ran up to her, chests heaving, and dropped to her side, and Geve lifted her limp body into his arms. Her hair stuck to her damp skin, and he tried to smooth it away from her forehead, although all he succeeded in doing was smearing the black on her face even more.

"Sarra?" He patted her cheek lightly, panic filling him as she didn't stir. "Sarra?"

She jerked then, and her eyes opened and she looked up at him. She blinked a few times, and then her mouth curved. "Geve?"

"It is me."

She looked around, saw Comminor on the other side of her, then tried to look past him. "Where is he?"

"Who, my darling?"

Her eyes came back to him. "Help me up."

He lifted her to a sitting position, watching as she looked around for someone. But all she said was, "It does not matter."

The others arrived, dropping to the ground around her.

"Are you all right?" Amabil asked, resting a hand on Sarra's swollen stomach.

"I think it has begun," Sarra said. "The pains are regular and close together now."

Geve exchanged a glance with Comminor. If she were in labour, that changed everything. Now they had to get her to safety.

"Listen, we are going to try to think of a way to get you back to the Broken Room," he said. He looked around. "Maybe if we scavenge for wood or anything else that could be used as a stretcher, we could—"

"I am not going," Sarra said.

Comminor took her hand in his. "You cannot have your baby here, Sarra. It is too dangerous. The firebird might come back, and other Incendi could appear at any moment." As if illustrating his words, a spurt of flame erupted from the ground not far away from them, making them all jump and filling the air with an even more intense heat.

"I am not going," she said again. She would have added more words, but at that moment another contraction began, and she gripped Geve's hand hard as she rode out the pain.

Panic filled him. He knew nothing about childbirth at the best of times, but even he knew this was not the place to bring a baby into the world. "Sarra, please. I will carry you..."

The contraction released its grip on her, and she lay back, exhausted. But still she shook her head. "I have to stay. I do not expect you to stay with me, though."

"I cannot leave you," he said, near to tears. It had been such a long journey, both literally and metaphorically, from meeting Nele, to forming the Veris, to finding out Sarra was also having the dreams, to leaving the Embers. He could not bring himself to abandon her, but equally the thought of staying out in the burnt wilderness terrified him.

Next to him, however, the women were already getting organised.

"Take out all your blankets," Amabil instructed, "and we'll make a bed for her."

Betune lifted the strap of her bag over her head and extracted her blanket, gathered the blankets from the others as they unpacked, and with Paronel began to lay them out in a rectangle to soften the ground. Comminor and Nele formed clothing wrapped in a blanket into a makeshift pillow, and then they moved her onto the 'bed'. Josse and Viel took all the food and began to discuss how much they should ration and how long it could last.

Choked at the fact that in spite of their misgivings and their own fear, everyone had decided they were going to support

Sarra, Geve sat cross-legged beside her and took her hand. "We are all here for you," he said. "I will not leave you. I promise."

She bit her lip and her eyes glistened as she glanced around at them all. "I am so sorry. But I cannot explain. I have to..." Her words faded out as another contraction overtook her.

Geve saw the women exchange glances and knew it meant things were speeding up. It wasn't really surprising considering the speed with which her pregnancy had developed. Her hand crushed his, but he bore the discomfort and spoke soothing words as he encouraged her to ride it out. Betune moistened a cloth with a tiny amount of their precious water, and he used it to wipe her face and cool her brow.

She sank back, breathing more regularly as the pain eased. A tear rolled down her face. "I do not think I can do this."

"Of course you can. We will all help you."

"You are right – he should not be born here." She looked around at the blackened landscape. "This is a place of death."

"Not anymore," he said firmly.

"This was meant to be," Comminor said. He stood a few feet away, looking out across the broken rocks and scorched earth. "We have been led here, and all we can do is take our places on the stage and watch the events unfold."

He turned back to face them, and Geve saw that the man's eyes were lit with a strange excitement. "Can you not feel it?" he said. "Can you not see it?"

Geve frowned, puzzled, but as he opened his mouth to ask what Comminor meant, a sudden glimmer of the air around them made him stop. "What was that?" he whispered.

"It is beginning," Comminor said.

Sarra's hand tightened on Geve's again and she cried out. Amabil moved quickly to her side, and they held her as the next contraction began. Amabil raised Sarra's dress, and the men politely averted their eyes as she inspected the mother-to-be.

An exclamation from Amabil caused Geve to look back, however, and he saw the blanket between Sarra's pale thighs soaked with liquid.

"Her waters have broken," Amabil clarified. "It will not be too long now."

They waited for her contraction to stop and then removed the sodden blanket. Nele took a fresh one and went to replace it.

And then he stopped and stared at the ground.

Comminor frowned. "What is it?" He looked, and his eyes widened too. Everyone crowded round, following their gaze.

Geve's jaw dropped.

A tiny green shoot protruded from out of the blackened earth.

For a long time, none of them said anything.

Then Nele bent closer and touched the shoot with the tips of his fingers. "It is alive," he said, his voice filled with wonder.

Betune cried out, her hand moving to her breastbone as Geve had seen it do regularly on their journey. She searched for the bag that hung around her neck, but couldn't find it. She moved another blanket and found the bag there, its strap broken. "It must have snapped when I removed my backpack." She picked up the tiny bag – its neck had loosened. She tipped it up.

It was empty.

"The acorn," Viel said breathlessly.

Geve's heart pounded. "But why..."

"The birthing fluid," Amabil cried out. "It soaked into the earth, right over the acorn."

Comminor instructed them to move Sarra a little to the side so she did not have to worry about damaging the new shoot. Geve continued to hold her hand, watching as the Chief Select and Nele bent to examine the shoot again.

"Is it growing?" Josse asked.

"I am not sure."

Geve's head spun. Sarra's hand tightened on his, and he turned to her, thinking she was having another contraction, but he found her gaze fixed on him, her eyes alight.

"The Arbor," she whispered. "It is a new Arbor!"

His heart thundered. "I do not know... It could be..."

Her eyes drifted past him, and then fear lit her face. "We must protect it," she said fiercely. Her hand clenched as a new pain started. "Geve..."

"Do not think about it," he told her. "You must concentrate on the baby now – that is all that matters."

"No, you do not understand!" She clenched her teeth and tried to gesture past him. "Look!"

He turned his head. And his heart seemed to shudder to a stop.

Because in the distance, the horizon blazed with flame as the firebird swooped down towards them.

CHAPTER TWENTY-ONE

I

Orsin knelt before Pyra, the Incendi king.

The firebird hovered in the air before him, dripping golden lava, the heat scorching his face.

"Can you do it?" Pyra asked.

Orsin swallowed. "Can you not send your elementals in to kill them all?"

"We cannot yet leave the mountain. Small fires are all we have been able to conjure. But it is imperative that we do our best to create chaos during the Apex. You *must* do this for me."

Orsin shook. "Of course, my king."

"You must go back into the world of the earth elementals, and destroy what must be destroyed. You will not fail me again?" The firebird's hot breath scorched Orsin's skin.

"No! No, of course not."

"Your reward will be great. Everything you desire!"

Orsin thought of the joy of the past few days. He had existed in a haze of wine, rich food and women, everything he had ever desired brought to him with no effort on his part at all. He would never have to worry about anything ever again. "Yes, please. I would like that."

"You think you can do this? You can fight against your family? Your countrymen?"

The firebird's words engendered a surge of indignation and anger in Orsin. Along with providing pleasurable ways for Orsin to pass the time, the firebird had spent the past few days encouraging Orsin to remember how his family had made him suffer over the years. Memories had floated past his eyes like puppets in a show – times when Julen had mocked him, when his mother had sneered at him and called him a coward, when his sister had been exasperated at his refusal to talk seriously with her. None of them had thought he would amount to anything, and he owed them nothing. He wanted to see them suffer as he had suffered, to know the loneliness that dwelt deep inside him.

"I can do it," he said, meaning it.

"Then open yourself to me." The firebird breathed out.

Like flaming snakes, fire licked up Orsin's body, crawled across his torso, slid into his mouth and burned down inside him. It ran through his veins and blazed in his eyes, shot from his fingertips and wrapped scarlet fingers around his heart. The pain was excruciating, but equally he had never felt such pleasure, and his body twisted and shuddered, his mouth emitting screams and moans of desire in turn.

How long it lasted, he could not tell. He wanted it to stop – but he also wanted it to go on forever.

Eventually, however, the pleasure/pain died away and left only darkness.

Orsin opened his eyes. His head ached, and he felt as if he stared at the world through a piece of fogged up stained glass. Days of overindulging himself with wine and women had numbed his senses, and it took a while for everything to come into focus.

Gradually, his confusion subsided. He sat up, more than a little shocked to find himself in the middle of a forest. Slowly, still slightly dizzy, he pushed himself to his feet and looked around. Behind him, he could just see the sheer side of the mountain through the trees.

He scrubbed his eyes then dropped his hands, wondering how he had got to the forest. Had it all been a dream? Had he invented everything, from the dancing women to the wine and food to the presence of the mighty King of the Incendi?

As he thought of the firebird, a sudden burst of heat rushed through him. He raised a hand and stared at it in shock. For a brief moment, fire danced from the tips of his fingers.

He squealed and immediately the fire vanished.

His heart pounding, he held his hands up before his face. Again, he thought of Pyra. And again heat rushed through him, and his hands leapt with flames.

His lips curved in a slow smile. And now he knew what he had to do.

Turning away from the mountain, he began to walk north.

He walked all day, most of the night, and then most of the following day as well. But by the time the light started to fade, the buildings of the new town of Heartwood lay in the distance.

The road into the town was lined with stalls and newly built houses that had not been there the last time he visited Heartwood several years before. Most of the traders had closed for the night, but a couple were still touting their wares. He bought a hot meat pie and a tankard of weak ale, and ate and drank as he covered the final distance to the centre of the town.

The lights from the tavern beckoned him closer, but he reluctantly ignored them and headed for the stone buildings to one side of the wall, which he noted with surprise and not a little pleasure was being dismantled. Did they really think they did not need defences anymore? He could not believe they were being so foolish. It was his father's fault – he had stuffed their heads full of nonsense about the Arbor being able to take care of itself. That hadn't helped against the Darkwater Lords, had it? And even with all its Nodes operational, he couldn't see how the Arbor could defend itself against an army of fire elementals when they were eventually able to leave the mountain.

His anger growing at the arrogance of those who thought themselves strong enough to stand up to the Incendi king, he stormed up to the complex Julen had told him they were calling the Nest. To his amazement, there were no guards, no defensive doors, and no sentries looking out for possible intruders. He walked straight into the courtyard and looked around him, bewildered and laughing at their idiocy. What was to stop him using the power Pyra had given him and razing the whole place to the ground? The whole city? Exultancy flooded him, and as he thought of the King, heat roared through his veins. He would do this in the blink of an eye, without a moment of opposition – he would turn the place to ash and they would never be able to sneer at him again.

He raised his hands, and lava poured from his fingertips and flames leapt from his fingers.

And then something smashed into the back of his head with a crack louder than thunder. Pain shot through him, and he fell to the ground.

When he came to, he was sitting in a chair, his hands bound tightly behind him, head bowed.

"He is awake," someone said, and he saw the feet of someone walk towards him. The man dropped to his haunches so he could look up into Orsin's face.

It was Julen.

Orsin let saliva pool in his mouth and spat at his brother. Julen recoiled, then gave a humourless laugh as he wiped the spittle from his cheek.

"I should have let Pyra kill you in the caves," Orsin snarled.

"And I should have drowned you at birth." His mother's voice sounded from beside him, bitter and hard.

He turned his head to look at her, pain exploding at the base of his skull. "Was it you who whacked me?"

"Unfortunately not." Her eyes were icy. "I would have enjoyed that."

He looked around the room, realising as his vision cleared that it was filled with people. He recognised some of the faces – the Peacemaker, the Imperator and Nitesco the scholar. His sister stood to one side, her expression guarded.

Dolosus came forward. "Why are you here?"

Orsin just laughed.

Dolosus struck him across the face, and Orsin shook his head, tasting blood.

He tested his lip with his tongue gingerly as he eyed the Imperator. "I thought you had put violence behind you."

Dolosus's eyes gleamed. "Oh, I never said that. I ask you again. What are you doing here? Does your coming herald an Incendi invasion?"

"No," Orsin said.

The people in the room exchanged glances. "We cannot believe anything he says," Dolosus announced in disgust. "This is pointless."

"I am not lying," Orsin said. "I have no need to lie. The Incendi have no plans to invade Anguis now."

"But they will in the future," Nitesco stated.

Orsin shrugged.

"You are here to try and stop the Apex," Julen stated. "How did you plan to do that?"

Orsin tested his lip again, but remained silent.

"This is pointless," Dolosus said again. "It is a needless distraction. We should move on."

Julen stayed where he was, though, his eyes blazing. "He is here for a reason – we need to find out what that reason is."

Horada came forward at that point and bent to look in his eyes. "Help us, Orsin," she said softly. "Now you are here, join with us to defeat Pyra."

Indignation shot through him. "Why should I? What do you have to offer me that I should do as you say?"

"What do we have to offer?" Procella looked aghast. "You are my son! You are Chonrad's son!"

"So?"

Procella looked lost for words, and the room fell silent. Eventually, Horada whispered, "It is your duty."

"My duty?" He spat a mouthful of blood-stained spittle onto the floor. "You all treat me like an idiot, as if I had nothing to offer, as if I were something you scraped off your shoe." He couldn't help it – hurt rose within him at the scornful look on his mother's face. "You have never thought me worthy of anything – even Father sent me away because he did not wish to be around me."

"He sent you away to keep you safe," Horada said, but Orsin shook his head.

"It was just an excuse." He looked at his mother. "And you did not try to stop him. You despise me – you look at me as if I am lower than an insect crawling on the ground."

Procella's expression hardened. "You cannot demand respect in this world. You have to earn it. And what have you done to earn my respect? Drunk and whored your way through life."

"You never loved me!" he yelled.

"Because you took me away from what I loved most!" she yelled back. "Do you think I wanted to give up being Dux of Heartwood's Exercitus for a life wiping arses and playing at being a wife? I am a soldier. But you took me away from all that!"

"It was not my fault you finally opened your legs and let yourself be mounted like a mare!"

A sharp crack sounded in the room as her fist met his jaw. She stood over him, grabbed his face in one hand and bent until her nose was only inches from his. "I have killed men for saying less than that to me," she whispered, her fingers pinching his cheeks.

Ice slid down inside him – at that moment he had no trouble believing she had led a whole army into battle.

"It is not my fault," he whispered back, and to his shame, a tear slid down his cheek.

She looked deep into his eyes. Then, abruptly, she turned and walked out of the room.

Orsin dropped his head. His chest heaved as he struggled to rein in his emotion. Around him, voices murmured and people gradually left the room. He heard Dolosus order a couple of men to stand guard before leaving.

Eventually, only his brother remained.

Julen sat on the table at the other side of the room and folded his arms. "I am sorry," he said.

Orsin glared at him. "Do not feel pity for me."

"She is a soldier, Orsin. She did not find it easy to adjust to a civilian's life. She loved our father, but I think she always blamed him, too, for taking her away from Heartwood."

"The Militis was disbanded," Orsin said hoarsely. "It was not Father's fault either."

"I know. But she never saw it that way. She is not a scholar – she does not have the ability to reason and weigh the arguments around a subject. She works on instinct."

Frustration surged through Orsin. "You should not make excuses for her. She is my mother, and yet do you know that I can never remember her giving me a hug or a kiss? I can never remember her showing me affection." Heat ran through his veins, but he kept a tight hold on it. "I swear she will regret it, Julen. I will make her pay for what she did to me."

Julen pushed himself off the table. "Be a man, Orsin. Take responsibility for your own life and stop blaming your failures on someone else."

Orsin's gaze dropped to the pendant lying on Julen's chest. In the middle, the sunstone glowed briefly in response to the fire in his veins, but his brother didn't notice.

"Go fuck yourself," Orsin said.

Julen said nothing. Then he turned and walked out of the room.

II

Tahir stood at the window of his room in the Nest and thought that really there should be a tremendous storm – there should be thunder and lightning and tremendous gales and sheets of rain to mark the fact that, today, he was going to die. People should be weeping and wailing, and everyone should be dressed in white to mark his passing. But instead, the sun shone brightly, and even through the small window, he could hear that outside the party had already begun.

He turned as footsteps sounded outside and saw Catena in the doorway. She looked solemn, dressed surprisingly conservatively considering today was the Veriditas, a day when most people brought out their finest clothes. Although the previous day for the procession she had borrowed an outfit from the Nox Aves, today she wore her usual plain brown breeches and a leather jerkin over a plain green tunic.

"No shiny clothes today?" He made his voice light.

"Why?" she said. "I am not celebrating."

He smiled. "I will miss you."

She met his gaze, then looked away and changed the subject. "Here, boy." She shooed Atavus into the room, who sat at the end of the bed, looking sheepish. "I found him having his wicked way with one of the bitches that happened to be in heat. Honestly."

Tahir giggled. "I think he has been with Demitto too long."

Catena's lips curved, but as she went to reply, the emissary appeared behind her in the door.

"What is the joke?" Demitto asked as they both started laughing.

"Nothing." Catena kissed him on the cheek.

Tahir smiled at them both as the emissary whispered something in her ear. He had thought that when he feigned sleep the night before, they would both remove themselves and head off together to their own room. To his surprise, instead they had stayed by his side all night, talking into the early hours of the morning before they had finally dozed off. Tahir had listened with a racing heart as Demitto told the Chief of Guard what he knew about the events that were to unfold that day. He found it difficult to believe that everything was going to change so much, and that he would play such a big role. But ultimately there was nothing he could do about it either way now. He had to let events unfold and do the best he could.

The two of them stopped talking, and turned to face him, their smiles fading and hesitancy replacing the humour.

"It is time?" he asked.

Demitto nodded.

Tahir took a deep breath, let it out slowly, and turned to Atavus. One of the Nox Aves was bringing the dog along, but he would not be allowed to stay at the Prince's side. He had spent a good portion of the night holding the dog, which had crept up from his place at the bottom of the bed to huddle by his side. Now, he bent and buried his face in the dog's fur, kissed his ears and snout, and whispered goodbye. He did it quickly, knowing that if he stayed, he would never be able to let him go.

Finally, holding back tears, he straightened his white tunic embroidered in silver with an oak tree and fingered the silver pendant of the Selected around his neck. He was as ready as he would ever be. "Then let us go."

He left a whimpering Atavus behind in the room, and did not look back.

Accompanied by a dozen members of the Nox Aves, including Manifred, all dressed in white, they rode through the streets accompanied by the cheers of the people. Some of the women cried as he passed, and he felt that they at least understood his sacrifice.

They entered the busy market square, and from there rode past the palace and onto the street fronting the large wooden fence surrounding the Arbor. There they reined in their horses, and the Nox Aves formed two lines leading to the large doors in the centre of the wooden fence.

Today, the doors stood open. Inside, Tahir could see that what looked like temporary wooden stands had been set up in a mock-amphitheatre style to house hundreds of privileged spectators at the Veriditas ceremony. Music blared, and the sound of everyone talking at once was deafening.

He dismounted and stood in a daze as people moved around him, preparing for his grand entrance to the arena. Closing his eyes, he tried to ground himself. He had to focus, or he wasn't going to make it through this.

He concentrated on his breathing, and as he did, so the noise around him seemed to fade away until all he could hear was the beating of his heart in his ears.

He stilled, aware that something was happening. Beneath his feet, the ground seemed to vibrate with his heartbeat, but that couldn't possibly be happening, could it? He could feel it though, a rhythmic pulse that sent a shiver up his legs and spine to the roots of his hair. It couldn't be his own heart. Was it the pounding of feet from the crowd? No, it was too regular. But it was coming from inside the arena...

He opened his eyes and raised his gaze to the skies. Crows wheeled above his head like black threads weaving the clouds together. Far above Heartwood, the mountain coughed up a plume of steam and a shower of ash rained down like snow. Nobody seemed to notice, however. He frowned, feeling his heart thud under his ribs, matching the beat beneath his feet. Something was happening...

"Tahir."

He snapped to attention to see Demitto standing on his right, looking down at him, concerned.

"Are you ready?" Demitto asked, raising his voice above the noise of the crowd.

Tahir felt a pressure on his left and realised Catena stood the other side of him. In front, the Nox Aves waited expectantly, Manifred at the end, his gaze steady.

Tahir nodded. "I am ready."

"I will be at your side the entire time," Demitto said as they walked forward.

"As will I," said Catena. "My prince. I am so proud of you."

"Thank you," Tahir whispered, his throat tight.

They passed between the two lines formed by the Nox Aves. As he felt their respectful gazes on him, Tahir's final fears fell away. He straightened and lifted his chin.

They approached Manifred who stood in the doorway. Manifred nodded across the arena, and somebody must have signalled something inside because the crowd suddenly hushed. A deep bell sounded from the Nest's tower, and at the same time, trumpets rang out across the town.

Demitto on his right, Catena on his left, Manifred in front carrying a white flag embroidered with a silver oak tree, Tahir walked forward.

The trumpets continued as he walked along the white carpet. To his left and right, he was aware of the stands rising in tiers, filled with hundreds of people who watched him, silent as the solemnity of the occasion finally reached them. To his right, King Varin and his queen sat on a raised dais at the front of the stands. Somewhere in the stands was Atavus, although he could not see him.

All eyes were on him, and for the first time in his life, he became the focus of everyone's attention. But he hardly noticed as his gaze fell on the reason for his visit to the city.

Towards the back, the Arbor watched him approach.

Tahir had not known what to expect of the tree. There were oaks all over Anguis, of course, including a large one in Harlton, and he had lain under it many times, staring up into its branches as he pondered on whether the Arbor looked anything like it.

Now, he realised that had been like wondering whether a cupful of water looked like the ocean.

The tree reared above him – above them all – its trunk so wide that five men linking their arms around it would not be able to make their hands meet. Its branches arched across the span of the arena, filled with glossy green leaves in spite of the fact that they were just coming out of The Sleep.

But its size was not the only thing that made him hold his breath in awe. As he slowed and came to a halt where the carpet came to an end in the centre of the arena, the tree shivered, and once again he became aware of the slow, steady beat in the ground through his feet.

It is the Pectoris, he realised with shock. The beat he could feel was from the Arbor's own heart.

The trumpets fell silent, and Manifred walked forward to a podium in front of the tree and turned to address the audience.

"My friends," he called, his voice ringing out across the lawn to the tiers, reaching the ears of those listening, enthralled. "We come here today to pay homage to the Arbor, and to offer it this year's Selected as a token of our gratitude for its care and protection of Anguis and its people. We give thanks to Tahir, Prince of Harlton, for graciously giving up his life for us, and we recognise the solemn sacrifice he is making for the good of the land."

He continued on talking about King Varin's graciousness in allowing them all to witness the ceremony, and then he opened the large book that lay on the podium, which Tahir realised was the *Quercetum* – the book that held the history of the last few thousand years of Anguis. He started to read out the names of all those Selected recorded in the pages.

As Tahir listened to the names, once again the hushed whispers around the arena disappeared and even Manifred's voice faded. At the same time, Tahir's senses seemed to turn crystal sharp. He could feel Demitto on his right, Catena on his left, their combined presence giving him strength and courage. He could feel the light brush of flakes of ash on his skin as they floated down from the mountain. The ground rumbled, disturbing the steady heartbeat for a moment, but then it returned, stronger than ever, drowning out every other sound in the arena. Could nobody else hear it? He glanced around, but everyone seemed to be listening to Manifred, and Tahir knew he was the only one aware of it.

His attention came back into focus again as he became aware that Manifred was concluding his speech. "...And Tahir, Prince of Harlton," he read from the *Quercetum*, finishing off the list of Selecteds. He closed the book and rested a hand on it for a moment.

This time, when the ground rumbled, everyone seemed to hear it. Demitto stiffened beside Tahir, and Catena muttered something beneath her breath. Tahir looked up at the emissary and saw his pulse beating rapidly in his throat. He remembered what Demitto had told Catena the previous night, about the arrival of the Apex, and his own heartbeat quickened.

Manifred looked across at Demitto, and Tahir felt the emissary's hand come to rest in the small of his back. The Nox Aves moved forward once again to form a walkway to the Arbor's trunk. Demitto, Catena and Tahir walked between them towards the tree.

Music spiralled around the arena, a haunting melody of *a cappella* voices, male and female. Tahir's breath caught in his throat at their beauty, and he glanced around but could not see the source.

"Who is singing?" he whispered to Demitto, his feet carrying him ever forward to the tree.

Demitto bent closer and whispered in his ear. "It is the Arbor. It is calling you home, young prince."

His breathing quickened, and as he came to the end of the line of Nox Aves, he looked up and realised he stood beneath the Arbor's branches.

The Nox Aves withdrew. Demitto and Catena remained, as they had promised, a pace or two away.

What was he supposed to do? He stood there, uncertain, waiting to be told. The voices rose around him, heart-rendingly beautiful.

Something touched his shoulder. He looked, thinking it was Demitto's hand, but to his shock saw it was a tree branch. It had dipped, and the leaves now brushed his upper arm affectionately.

Breathless, he watched as the branch dipped lower and the leaves stroked his arm, gentle and persuasive at the same time.

Something touched his foot, and he looked down to see that one of the tree roots had snaked across the ground and now curled around his ankle. The singing intensified, and as he looked up at Catena, he saw tears pouring down her face at the beauty of it.

The tree tugged gently, and he walked forward, up to the trunk, and placed his hands on the bark. It felt rough beneath his fingers, but to his amazement it was warm. Beneath his fingertips beat the steady pulse of the Pectoris, in time with his own heart.

Whispers echoed around the arena – or was it the rustle of the leaves above his head? He closed his eyes, feeling the roots wrap around him, pulling him close. He put his arms around the trunk and rested his cheek against the bark. The tree tightened its grip, and its sharp edges bit into his soft skin.

Beside him, Demitto swore loudly, the curse ringing out across the quiet arena.

Tahir opened his eyes, a small part of him wanting to laugh at the emissary's irreverence. But the laughter faded at the sight of the sunstone in the pendant around Demitto's neck glowing scarlet.

Behind him, the King's expression grew incensed at his ambassador's disrespect. But at the same time, the crowd began to mutter and voices rose. Tahir followed their gazes and pointing fingers, craning his neck. He could just see, way up above them, a column of flame erupting from the peak of the mountain.

The Arbor wrapped its roots tighter around him, and Tahir closed his eyes again.

It begins, the Arbor whispered.

III

Comminor followed Geve and Sarra's horrified gazes and saw the horizon spread with scarlet as the firebird rose in the sky.

It was too far away for him to see in which direction it was flying. It was coming vaguely towards them, but he couldn't be sure if it had seen them yet. Despair filled him. How could he protect her and the new shoot against something so powerful? If the firebird flew directly over them, he had no hope of stopping it from turning them all to ash with one blast of fiery breath.

"We have to get her back to the Broken Room," yelled Josse.

Comminor hesitated, wishing he had made that decision earlier. He had thought he was doing the right thing, but now he realised he had just put all their lives in danger. He looked up the slope of the mountain, wondering if they could make it back there if they ran. But even as the thought entered his head, he knew the answer. "We would never make it in time," he said. "It is too far."

The hope faded from everyone's eyes, and frustration filled him. He had led them all for so long in the Embers, for years and years. Even though many had hated him, they had trusted him to keep them safe.

In the distance, the firebird blasted the landscape with scorching heat. Dry dust rose in a sandstorm and swept over them, choking him, searing his lungs and stinging his eyes.

He closed them against both the dust and the fear, his hand moving automatically to cover the pendant on his chest.

What was he to do? Had he travelled this far, worked so hard, only to fall right at the end?

Sarra's cries filled his ears as she became gripped with another contraction. He wanted to move, to be at her side to comfort her and help her through this, but something made him remain where he was. His head was spinning. At first he'd thought it was panic confusing his senses, but as pressure built on his ears and the noises around him faded, he realised something was happening.

He held his breath, holding one hand out in front of him as his balance failed and he swayed. He was vaguely aware of the dust blowing across his skin, of the faint cries of Sarra as if from far off in the distance, of the voices of the others rising as they argued about what to do. The world went quiet. His pulse echoed in his ears.

Or was it his pulse? It was not just in his ears, he could *feel* it, like when he'd stood near the Magna Cataracta and felt the thunder of the water as it cascaded down the rockface. The regular, rhythmic beat pounded against his feet, shooting up through his legs and knees, into his hips and spine, until his bones seemed to vibrate with it, and his heart slowed to match the beat.

He felt himself expand, his consciousness scatter like a handful of blown dust. For a brief moment, he became aware of the passage of time, of history, of the whole timeline of the world stretching back into the past. Suddenly he knew what the Arbor had seen when it was alive – how it had stretched through time and space, how it had *known* everything there was to see and hear and taste and smell.

It is time, a voice whispered in his ear.

He opened his eyes.

The dust in the air before him shimmered silver the way it had in the ceremonial room. Those around him didn't seem to notice. Betune and Amabil knelt by Sarra, holding her hands as she grimaced in pain. Geve stood arguing with Josse, looking like he was about to punch him at any moment. Nele, Paronel and Viel looked nervously through the dusty wind at the approaching firebird, seemingly unaware of anything else.

Comminor blinked. Someone was singing. Above the rising bellow of the whirling wind, he could hear voices raised in song. He caught his breath at the beauty of it, not understanding the words, but the melody brought tears to his eyes. The mouths of those around him weren't moving – at least certainly not in song. Who was it?

The air glittered, glimmered. As in the ceremonial room, figures flickered, the barrier between times thinning, parting. He saw the faces he had seen before loom out of the darkness, then disappear again, the moment not quite ready, the time not quite right. He wanted to yell, to tear apart the fabric of time and let them through, but he couldn't move, couldn't do anything but stand there like a useless statue, his head spinning.

He looked at his feet, his mouth opening as he stared at the green shoot. It had risen by a foot and now reached almost to his knee. The ground around it crumpled as its roots spread. The shoot waved in the breeze, growing even as he watched, trying so hard to establish itself.

And then he glanced up at the horizon, and the hope faded, and his heart sank. It did not matter – the firebird loomed above the ground, approaching them at a fast pace. It had seen them. It would turn them all to cinders before the shoot could grow its first leaves.

They were too late. The Apex wasn't going to happen. Through time, everyone was coming together, trying to save the world, to save Anguis, and he was going to be the one who'd let them all down. A sob tore from his lips, but still he could not move.

It was only gradually that he became aware that the pendant in his hand was growing hot. He glanced down at it, confused. The wood remained untouched, the faded deep brown it had always been. But inside it, the oval sunstone glowed as if it had been placed in a fire. He frowned, lifting it up before him, startled as the glow intensified. It burned red, then orange, then a bright yellow-gold, the light hurting his eyes so much that he had to avert his gaze as it brightened.

He looked back up and saw Viel, Josse and Paronel staring at their own pendants, which also glowed a bright red-gold.

Something rushed through him, not quite heat, not quite light, making his spine stiffen, his head tip back, his heart pound along with the beat that vibrated through his feet. A shaft of light shot out of the sunstone at the same time that the other three also ejected a beam, and the four rays joined and brightened, spreading above their heads in an arc of golden light.

Everyone exclaimed, even Sarra, and they all stared in wonder at the dome above their heads. Comminor's chest heaved, and he tried to keep calm, knowing this was meant to be – this *was* the Apex, happening exactly when it was supposed to happen.

Above them, the firebird loomed, and it exhaled a wall of fire that swept over them. Heat scorched his skin, hot dust flurried around his face, but when it had passed, they all remained standing, protected by the dome of light.

The firebird bellowed, its frustrated screech ringing out above the sound of the singing, and the dome above them flickered, although it didn't break.

"It is not enough," Josse yelled. "It will not hold."

Comminor looked down at Sarra in despair. Her baby had led her here, and she had followed, full of hope that it was leading her to a better life. This couldn't be the end of them all.

He glanced at the seedling still growing by his side. It was a miracle – a new Arbor, born in this land of fire and darkness with the belief that it could grow and conquer the Incendi elementals. He couldn't bear to think he had failed it. He had dreamed for so long of its shining leaves, of the sun and the sky.

But what could he do about it?

The singing grew louder, insistent, haunting, distracting him from the view, in spite of the imminent danger.

He closed his eyes, and in his mind, a picture formed of his room in the Embers. In the middle, on the table, rested the *Quercetum*, open to reveal the stories of the past, of Teague and Tahir and all the others, of those who had died to give the Arbor life.

He remembered the paragraph written all those years ago by Oculus, the man who had begun the *Quercetum*, who had been responsible for originally building the Temple around the Arbor in the ancient town of Heartwood.

"'The Arbor brings life, but it also brings death. Because essentially life is about balance. What is given in one way has to be taken in another. It is all a cycle – everything lives, and dies, and lives again. For there to be light, there has to be darkness. For there to be day, so equally there has to be night. And to create, we have to destroy. This and this alone lies at the heart of the Arbor's place in the world.'"

Yes… whispered the tree, the singing dying away.

Comminor opened his eyes. "A sacrifice," he whispered.

It barely sounded above the noise of the flapping firebird, the howling wind and the cries of Sarra, who strained again with another contraction. He clenched his hands in frustration, knowing what had to be done, urging himself to move. But he seemed frozen in place, his feet nailed to the ground, unable to do anything but let the sunstone draw energy from him to cast the dome above their heads.

And then he looked up and met Geve's eyes. He saw immediately that Geve had heard him, and that he understood.

Josse continued to argue, but Geve fell silent, and he nodded.

"I am sorry," Comminor said, meaning it, but Geve shook his head.

"We all have a part to play," he said.

Josse stared at him in confusion. "What?"

Geve ignored him and came forward to stand by the seedling, in the middle of the rays of light beaming from the four sunstones.

Sarra stared at him. "What are you doing?" she demanded.

He looked down at her and smiled. "Good luck with the baby."

Sarra's eyes widened. She looked up and met Comminor's gaze and tried to struggle to her feet, but at the same time a contraction gripped her and she doubled over, crying out in physical and emotional pain. "Do not go," she sobbed, reaching out towards him, but he turned away.

Instead, he met Comminor's gaze. "Look after her," Geve said, and Comminor nodded.

Geve raised his arm, took a deep breath and plunged his hand into the dome of fire above their heads.

PART FIVE

CHAPTER TWENTY-TWO

I

The Heartwood Council were deep in consultation, seated around the large round wooden table in the meeting room in the main building.

Horada hovered in the doorway, uneasy and distracted. She had been offered a place at the table along with her mother, brother and the other visitors, but she had declined, feeling awkward placing herself amongst those who clearly knew much more about the matter than herself.

Strangely, the one person who seemed to be missing was the mysterious Cinereo. Julen had asked Gravis where he was, but Gravis and Nitesco had just exchanged a glance and said he would appear later, and they had to be content with that.

Now, they were all discussing the Wulfian presence on the Wall and listening to Procella talk about her experiences at Kettlestan. Horada listened for a while, but kept finding her gaze drawn to the room down the corridor where two men stood outside guarding her oldest brother. The accusation that her mother had thrown at him – that it was his fault she had been forced to leave the Militis – had shocked Horada. Although she had always found Orsin irreverent, she had never quite understood her mother's imperious attitude towards him. Now it made sense – except it didn't. It wasn't

Orsin's fault that her mother became a wife and mother. In that sense, Orsin's lewd comment had been right – she only had herself to blame.

The Council were now discussing the Incendi threat and when they thought the Apex might occur. Horada turned from the room and began to walk towards the doorway outside. It was uncomfortably warm in the buildings and she longed for some fresh air. Plus, there was somewhere she wanted to visit alone.

Outside, she crossed the courtyard, left the complex and made her way through the buildings along the busy main road. She could see where they were taking down the wall now, removing it stone by stone. People crowded the streets but, to her surprise, the gates to the new wooden fence inside the old wall were shut. She stopped outside where two guards stood on duty.

"Why are the doors closed?" she asked.

"Access to the Arbor is restricted for the foreseeable future," stated one of the guards sounding bored, seemingly reciting a well-rehearsed warning.

The second guard – an older man with grey hair – looked at Horada quizzically. After a few moments, his eyes widened. "Are you... You are not Chonrad of Barle's daughter by any chance?"

She smiled. "Yes. Did you know my father?"

"I did. You look very like him! I travelled with him to Vichton on the Quest to Darkwater. My name is Solum."

Her smile broadened. "My father told me all about that adventure. And my mother speaks very highly of your fighting abilities as well as your calmness and patience."

Solum nodded his head. "Procella was a great Dux, and Chonrad was a great man. I was very sorry to hear of his loss."

"Thank you." She swallowed and looked away. Being here, in Heartwood, the place that she had heard so much of during her life and that had played such a big part in her father's world, had brought her emotions bubbling to the surface.

"Have you come to see the Arbor?" Solum spoke softly.

She nodded. "I have never seen it."

"You can go in," he said. The other guard started to object, but Solum held up a hand. "This is Chonrad's daughter. Of all the people in Anguis, she is one whom I would trust."

The other guard nodded reluctantly and opened the door. Solum smiled and gestured for her to enter.

Suddenly uncertain, Horada hesitated, but she couldn't back out now. Giving them both a brief smile, she slipped through the door and they closed it behind her.

She stood in a wide open space, the site of the old Heartwood complex, just inside the walls. Although she could still hear the city outside – including the complaints of those visitors who had seen her slip in but were being stopped from following – inside it seemed peaceful, as if more than a mere wooden fence separated her from the outside world.

The fence ringed the grassy area, meeting the mountain on both sides, the rocky face rearing above her, solid and impenetrable. Sparrows and finches hopped across the grass, and to one side in the sun, a lone cat stretched out, oblivious to anything else. The inside of the fence panels had been carved with intricate engravings of oak leaves, acorns and trees, and at any other time she would have exclaimed and stopped to admire the workmanship.

But she could not tear her eyes away from the Arbor.

It stood in the centre and slightly towards the back, its branches casting a shadow across a good third of the grass. Her father had told her many stories about it, and she had heard Julen and Orsin, her mother and many travellers also talk about it, but nothing could have prepared her for the sight of it. Three times as big as she had imagined, it appeared imposing for more than just its size. Thick with green leaves, full of ripe acorns, it arched towards her as if reaching out for her. Even above the noise of the city, the whisper of its leaves reached her ears.

She stood motionless, though, fear freezing her feet to the floor. Chonrad had told her about the moment when the Arbor had reached out for him that first time during the Last Stand. He had explained his fear, the pain that had coursed through him when he opened the Node, the sheer terror that he had felt that he would not live to see the next day. And then, of course, he had visited the Arbor again the year before, only for it to end with his death.

Horada's mouth had gone dry. But it was pointless to avoid walking forward. She had come all this way – was she really going to pretend this wasn't the reason she had come, the reason for what was right and wrong in the world, the reason for everything?

She walked slowly forward to the middle of the grassed area. The morning sun beat down on her face and arms, and she hovered on the edge of the shade. The leaves on the old oak stirred and fluttered, although she could feel no breeze on her skin.

Heart pounding, she closed her eyes.

The sounds of the city faded completely. The birdsong faded. And then, as if from a long way away, came the sound of voices raised in song.

She listened for a while, lips slightly parted, entranced by the beautiful, haunting melody. And then she opened her eyes.

The source of the voices was a line of people walking from somewhere behind the tree trunk. She stared at them, mouth still open in wonder as she looked at their faces and watched them walk and sing.

She recognised some of them. The man with the long dark hair and golden eyes was Teague, the Komis Virimage who had given up his life for the tree all those years ago. Walking with him, holding his hand, was the young, beautiful knight Horada was sure was Beata, who had also given her life at the Last Stand. Behind them walked a tall man with huge shoulders, a shock of thick grey hair and piercing eyes that could only be the mighty Valens from Procella's long descriptions of him. The young man whose hair curled in exactly the same way as his twin brother's had to be Gavius who had died after completing his quest.

Behind them walked more people Horada was sure she recognised from descriptions given by her parents over the years. More and more people followed behind them. Gradually the people began to look different, their clothes old-fashioned, and Horada realised she was seeing all those who had given their lives in service to the tree, stretching back in time hundreds if not thousands of years.

They walked around her in a circle, then made their way back to a figure standing beneath the tree. Dressed in a long grey cloak, his hood pulled over his head, he held out his hands as if in welcome. To her shock and bewilderment, one by one the people walked right up to him and *vanished* into his billowing cloak.

Stunned, scanning the figures and trying to make sense of it all, only as the last person in the line passed around her and walked towards the tree did she see his face.

It was her father.

Emotion welled inside her and made her catch her breath. She wanted to run up to him, to throw her arms around him, but her feet wouldn't move, frozen to the floor as if held by invisible hands. He smiled at her, but continued walking until he reached the grey-cloaked figure, at which point he, too, vanished into the grey cloak.

She stared, tears coursing down her cheeks, realisation making her feel as if shutters had been removed from her eyes.

Cinereo was not one person – he was *all* the people who had given their lives for the Arbor. So maybe in that sense he even *was* the Arbor, which in itself was formed from the energy and life given to it by all its sacrifices and all those who had helped it over the years of its existence.

Cinereo stretched his hands out to her, and she walked forward. Her heart pounded – was she to be welcomed into his arms too? Was she that year's sacrifice?

As she approached him, however, he dropped his hands, and she came to a halt before him. They stood six feet from the base of the tree, and as she glanced at the trunk, she saw that one side of it had been carved to represent two figures – Teague and Beata, the wood worn smooth and shiny over the years as countless people touched the loving couple.

Voices sounded from behind her, and she saw the side doors leading to the Nest open and people come running in, spilling onto the green grass to stand before her in shock.

Everyone was there, including her mother – who looked alarmed to see her daughter standing with Cinereo right by the Arbor – and Julen, who walked forward until he stood near her, his eyes alight with excitement and caution.

"Horada?" he said, glancing over his shoulder as Nitesco and Dolosus also approached. "What are you doing?"

"It called me," she said, breathless, something rising inside her and sending the blood shooting around her veins. "I think it is beginning."

They all looked shocked – clearly they had thought to have more warning, or that they would all be aware and ready when something finally happened.

More people came forward – all the council members, including Grimbeald, Fionnghuala, Bearrach and Gravis the Peacemaker – to stand in front of the Arbor with wide eyes.

Horada stared at Julen. He was watching her, so he wasn't aware of what had started happening to his pendant. The sunstone in the middle glowed orange-red, and as it brightened, so he looked down and exclaimed, holding it out before him.

"She is right – it is beginning," said Dolosus, gesturing for everyone to fan out in an arc around Horada and Cinereo, who still stood silently, his face covered by the grey cloak. "It is too late to do anything now. We must assume the Arbor is ready to start, and we will have to follow its lead."

Horada's chest rose and fell with her rapid breaths. Julen walked forward a few steps to stand before her, and they both watched as the sunstone brightened even more, seemingly carrying within it a piece of the sun, which continued to bathe them in warmth.

Before them, the air shimmered the same way it had in the room deep inside the mountain, and Horada caught her breath. Tiny specks of dust glittered like when sunlight falls through a curtain in a forgotten room, and as she passed her hand before her, the air stirred as if it were smoke.

Her head lightened and spun. Next to her, Cinereo's hand drew a sign in the air, and she saw the image of an hourglass appear, the sand trickling through from the top glass to the bottom.

"You are the Timekeeper," he said.

I am the connection, she thought. I am the one to connect all three sides of the Apex.

A shaft of light shot from the sunstone in Julen's hand towards her, hitting her solidly in the heart.

Immediately, the scene flickered. Once again, she saw images of the people she had seen in the mountain – the young man Tahir with long dark hair and golden eyes standing with his arms around the Arbor, and through a misty red fog, the woman they had called Sarra lying on the ground, her stomach swollen, obviously about to give birth.

In both times, just like Julen, others stood with glowing pendants, the sunstones sending beams of light that formed a shining web, centring within Horada. It burned white-hot, making her gasp, but she stood transfixed, unable to do anything but let the energy surge through her.

It was only then that she looked up and glanced past the arc of men and women who were watching her with bated breath.

To her shock, behind them stood another figure, the remnants of his iron manacles hanging around his wrists – Orsin.

She opened her mouth but nothing came out, and she could only watch in stunned silence as he lifted his hands and they balled with leaping flame.

Some of the others had finally seen Orsin too, and shouts rang out around the grassy area in warning. But even as a couple of the nearest members of the council approached Orsin, he let out a bellow and the flame in his hands shot across the grass towards his sister.

Horada inhaled sharply, but fixed as she was to the ground, there was nothing she could do, and the firebolt enveloped her in a sheet of flame.

II

Tahir felt more than saw Demitto's sunstone burn brighter than the sun. Fire shot up in the air, and with alarm he felt the ground tremble as the mountain above them shook and finally blew its top completely. Large pieces of rock showered on the crowd, and hot ash began to rain down, burning everything it touched.

Tahir cried out from where he stood with his arms around the Arbor's trunk and went to step back. Shocked, he found that he couldn't let go.

As screams arose around him and people began running across the grass, Tahir's heart pounded, and he howled as he tried to pull back from the trunk. But the roots that wrapped around his legs had crept up his body, and all they seemed to do was pull him tighter.

"Let me go," he sobbed.

He didn't hear the tree answer. Instead, the Arbor's words crept into his mind, the whisper louder even than the noise arising from the chaos around him.

I need you…

He didn't want to be needed. He wanted to escape. But beside him, Demitto appeared unable to move, his sunstone still emitting light and fire, and next to him Catena was yelling and trying to get the pendant from around his neck. The King and Queen had vanished along with most of the dignitaries, and the Nox Aves in their grey robes were running around trying to shepherd people out of the arena. Nobody was paying attention to him. He was all alone.

Alone, except for the small warm body that pressed against his legs.

His heart pounding and panic rising within him, Tahir managed to look down, and he caught his breath at the sight of Atavus curled up by his feet. In spite of the noise, the fire, and the white-hot ash that was starting to settle on the grass, Atavus refused to leave his side.

The dog's brown eyes looked up, but he didn't rise or fuss. He just lay there, as if he knew exactly what was happening, and had already come to terms with his fate.

Tahir went still and ceased to struggle. This was what he had waited for his whole life. The day was finally here. He had known this was going to happen – all right, maybe not *exactly* this way, but he had known the Apex would bring with it a momentous time of struggle, a battle that needed to be fought. And he was part of that battle. There was no point in denying it now.

Catena had finally managed to get the pendant over Demitto's head, and they let it drop to the ground and backed away, trying to cover their heads as the sunstone grew even brighter and more ash rained down.

"You cannot help him," Demitto yelled as Catena tried to pull away from his tight grip. His eyes met Tahir's, full of sorrow.

Tahir couldn't speak but tried to convey his thoughts in his gaze. It is all right. I understand. Go!

As they turned and ran, Tahir pushed away the worry of what would happen to them. They had delivered him to the Arbor – their role was done. Now he just had to finish it.

Through the misty haze of time, he could see Horada channelling the Arbor's power, connecting them with Sarra in the future, who lay on the ground, crying out as pain racked her. Beside her stood the man with the silvery hair, his sunstone also blinding, and before him another man stood with hands plunged into a fiery dome above their heads. Everyone was in their rightful place, playing their part.

Tahir closed his eyes against the dazzling brightness. He had to focus now on how he could help.

He concentrated on his body and the tree in his arms. On what he could feel and what he could touch. As he calmed himself, he realised that he had already begun to join with the Arbor without noticing it. The rough edges of the bark bit into the soft skin of his cheek, his arms and his tummy where he pressed against it. As the roots tightened around him, his skin broke in several places and blood flowed, but he felt no pain, only a flood of exultancy that at last it was beginning.

The sound of singing rose again and, as the voices soothed him, so the roots touched his feet, wriggled through the gaps in his leather shoes, wrapped around his ankles, penetrated between his toes. They forced their way into his skin, crept into his body, spread up through his calves, his knees, his thighs, into his stomach. He felt them slide into his skull, close around his heart, joining it with the thousands of others it had absorbed over the years, making them into one – the Pectoris, the heart of the Arbor.

Ash poured down, coating the dog at his feet, the bodies of those who had fallen. Demitto and Catena ran across the arena. Now a part of the tree, Tahir was aware that they had reached Manifred where he stood by the entrance to a hole in the ground. Steps led downwards, into the darkness, and Manifred and other Nox Aves were trying to get as many people as possible down the steps.

A refuge, he thought. They were trying to hide them from the Incendi.

Even as he thought their name, through the mists of time he saw the man standing near Horada, hands raised in flame as he called the Incendi king into the world. And in his own time, as the volcano began to spit rocks and lava across the countryside, so the Incendi soldiers began to pour from their city beneath the mountain.

Through the Arbor's roots, Tahir saw it all happen. The volcano had tipped the balance of the elements in the Incendi's favour. With fire surging through the land, they were finally able to break through the tree's control. Hidden within the thousands of men, the elementals streamed forth, and as the temperature rose and a pyroclastic flow of liquid rock poured down sweeping everything in its wake, the men were engulfed and the elementals released to burst forth into this new fiery land.

Hot ash curled the Arbor's leaves, turning them to dust. At his feet, Atavus lay buried beneath the growing carpet of white. Tahir saw people screaming, dying, and he wept for them, for the Arbor and for himself. The elementals were closing on Heartwood, spreading through its streets. Liquid rock sped down from the volcano, and people ran, crying and yelling, only to be incinerated as they met the elementals coming the other way.

The city was going to fall, Tahir thought. The tree would burn. And all those who were trying to hide underground would be taken by the elementals. Earth would be destroyed, and fire would remain supreme forever and ever. And he was powerless to do anything to stop it.

Wasn't he?

III

Sarra screamed as Geve plunged his hands into the fiery dome above their heads. She had seen the look in his eyes as he stared at her – he had been saying goodbye. He had known this would lead to his death. But still he had done it, aware that this was what the seedling needed – a sacrifice, a burst of life in this land of dust and death.

Still, she did not want to accept it. She had known him since childhood and loved him like a brother, and the thought of him giving up his life wrenched her heart in two. But she couldn't do anything about it. Racked with labour pains, she could only lie there and scream and clench her fists and sweat as the dome glowed even brighter, somehow managing to keep the firebird at bay.

Her head was full of noise and light, her ears ringing. Betune and Amabil were yelling instructions to each other; Viel, Josse and Paronel were standing before Comminor, shocked at the power emitting from their sunstones, and Nele had crossed to the seedling, trying to support it as it struggled to keep growing.

Her present contraction faded, and Sarra let her head fall back, now completely exhausted. This baby was never going to be born. Had she known it would be this painful, she would never have lain with Rauf. "It hurts," she sobbed, only vaguely aware of Betune wiping her brow with a welcome damp cloth, her skin drying the moment the cloth was lifted.

"It will not be long now," Amabil said from the other side of her.

Sarra couldn't believe her words. She felt stuck in time, caught in a loop of events that went around and around with no beginning or end. Things would always be like this – hot, intense, her body taut with pain like a fishing line, filled with a hope that things would come to a conclusion, but they never did, they just went on and on and on...

The air shimmered in the heat, and she became aware of ash falling softly around her. When it touched her skin or the ground, however, it vanished. To either side, figures appeared as if out of a mist, only to fade away again. Images flickered, and she couldn't be sure whether she was delirious or whether they were actually there.

Another contraction began, and she squeezed her eyes shut as it swept over her. All her concentration focussed on her body, and the world faded away. It didn't matter that beyond the dome, the firebird swooped in a circle, screeching and threatening to incinerate them all in a blink of an eye, or that her favourite person in the whole world was going to die, or that everything else was falling apart. All she could think about at that moment was the pain.

And this time, the pain had changed. She felt an unavoidable urge to push, and when the contraction finally lessened, she told the women what had happened.

"It is time," Amabil said, gesturing for Paronel to ready the last few blankets. "Your baby will be born soon, Sarra." She smiled, although Sarra could see the fear and worry deep in her eyes. "Do not think of anything else – let us just get the baby out of you."

"I cannot do it," Sarra sobbed. The thought of trying to get a whole person out of her seemed impossible. "Do not make me do it."

"It is all right." They soothed her, stroked her brow. "This is normal, Sarra," Amabil told her. "You are in transition. It means you are nearly there. Think of your baby in your arms!"

Sarra lay back, conscious once again of the figures fading in and out around her. She had been led to this place – why? She had thought her baby was supposed to save the world. But how could that happen now? The dreams she'd had of the Surface – she'd assumed they had meant she would be bringing the child up in a land full of grass and sun, not fire and death. If she'd stayed in the Embers, Comminor would have taken her as his mate and the baby would have been safe. What had she done?

Figures appeared once again through the mist. Through the falling ash, she could see the young woman she remembered from the ceremonial room. Sarra could see the light beams from all the sunstones passing through her, as she realised that this woman was the key to them all connecting. And beside her, the one they called Cinereo stood, fading in and out of each scene, bringing them all together.

Sarra was not a scholar, and she did not fully understand everything Comminor had tried to explain to them about time and the events that had led to this day. But she did realise that this was the Apex he had spoken of. Right now, somehow, all three times had become one, the events simultaneous. What was happening all those hundreds and thousands of years ago was somehow having a direct effect on what was happening here. Time had disappeared.

And suddenly she realised she was not alone. The Arbor had seen its death all those years ago and somehow it had managed to engineer this culmination of events. It wanted them to work together to save it, to save the world. She could see the people in each time period working together, and she was at the end of the line, the last of those on whom the Arbor was relying.

But what would the outcome be? Was that future fixed, or still uncertain?

Behind the young woman standing by the Arbor, Sarra could see a man. Fire erupted from his hands, building, burning, travelling along the timelines into the future. He was the reason the ash was falling; because of him the Arbor's control on the world had slipped. She could see the lava pouring down the mountainside. It was going to flood Heartwood – it was going to burn the tree.

Next to her, Geve cried out, the dome above their heads flickering. Pain etched his face, but still he stood there as if holding the dome up, and she knew he would not move until his strength gave out.

Their world teetered on a knife edge, and she could not see the way clear. It helped to know she was not alone, but the firebird's breath repeatedly blasted the dome that was keeping them safe, and she could not envisage a future that did not involve fire and flame. How could they all make it out of this alive?

Another contraction claimed her, this one more powerful than the last, and again she felt the unavoidable urge to push.

Gritting her teeth and holding on to Amabil's hand, she let the world fade away and bore down as hard as she could.

CHAPTER TWENTY-THREE

I

Orsin had never felt so exultant, so wonderfully alive. Fire poured through his veins and lit up the world in a blaze of gold, and he could hear the roar of the Incendi echoing through the Arbor's roots, across land, across time. For the first time in his life, he felt powerful and strong. No one could say he was insignificant, that he did not have a part to play in the world. Nobody could ignore him now.

Around him, he was vaguely aware of figures trying to get him to stop – he could see his brother, Dolosus and Gravis all trying to approach him, but the flames pushed them back, and even though they threw water on him, it evaporated before it even touched his skin. Hate billowed through him like the flame – hate and resentment over everything they had said or done to him in the past to make him feel insignificant and small. Now they would pay for what they had done. No longer could they pretend as though he didn't exist.

Through the mists of time, he saw the people running across the wide, grassy space heading for the darkness of a cave entrance, but he could see they were not going to make it. The liquid rock ran down the mountainside like water, and the ash that fell on hair and shoulders made the men and women scream in pain.

Hidden in the depths of his heart like a jewel amidst the darkness of his pain and hate, something glittered.

Orsin jerked and opened his eyes. Julen, Dolosus and all the others had moved away to leave a single person standing before him. Dressed in a cloak of grey, the hood covering his head, the man they called Cinereo stood silently, and waited.

Orsin let the fire rage through him. "Nobody can stop me!" he yelled. He watched as his sister trembled in the distance from the effort of keeping the Apex together. She looked very young and small. How could she possibly think she could be strong enough to keep it up?

In front of him, Cinereo raised his head, and for the first time pushed the hood from his face.

Orsin stared, shocked. It was his father.

Chonrad studied his son, and his strong, handsome features portrayed his hurt and disappointment. "My son," he said, his voice ringing clear about the noise of the fire and the screams of the people echoing through time. "What are you doing?"

"Get away from me," Orsin snarled, bringing his hands before his face to channel flame in the man's direction. Fire billowed from him, but although it swept right over his father, when the flames finally died down, he remained untouched.

"You cannot hurt me," Chonrad said calmly.

"Because you are not really here," Orsin said through gritted teeth.

"I am here. I just do not have physical form."

Orsin closed his eyes. They were trying to force him to stop by appealing to his past, to his grief and love for the man who had died, but he would not let them.

"They have not brought me here," Chonrad said as if reading his mind. "I am here of my own free will."

"You cannot be," Orsin snapped. "You are a figment of my imagination. How can you possibly be here?"

"When we die, we do not just disappear. Our bodies are returned to the earth, but our souls live on, Orsin."

Orsin stared at him. "What do you mean?"

"The Arbor absorbs our energy. It is all a cycle, Orsin, life and death. Like the trees in the forests that lose their leaves in The Falling; they do not die. They just rest in the darkness and wait for The Stirring to come. And when it arrives, they begin their growth again. And when eventually they fall, they lend their energy to the next tree that takes its place."

He moved closer to his son, and although Orsin went to take a step back, he found he could not move his feet. Fire still raged through him and his form leapt with flame, but his father seemed oblivious to it. His eyes fixed on his son's face, he walked forward until he stood only a couple of feet away.

"I live within you," he said, his voice so soft that Orsin could not understand how the words rang in his ears like a bell. "I will always be with you, my son."

"You left me," Orsin yelled. "First you sent me away, and then when I finally came back, you left me!"

Chonrad's forehead creased. "The Arbor needed me, and I could not refuse. I tried to help it, but the Incendi were waiting and they destroyed my link with the tree before I could stop them. I did not mean to leave you, Orsin. I love you."

"Say no more!" Orsin's chest hurt, so full of grief and sorrow it felt as if his heart would burst.

"You must stop this," Chonrad said gently.

"I cannot. I will not! Pyra is the only one who has treated me with respect – who believes I am worthwhile."

Chonrad's expression hardened. "You think he has welcomed you into his arms because he loves you? He sees you as a doorway through which he can bring his army into the world – nothing more."

"That is not true!"

"Orsin. It is time you stopped demanding respect from everyone else, and expecting them to bring your world to rights." Concern lit Chonrad's eyes. "You are so full of hurt and hatred that you cannot see the way clearly. You need to take your fate in both hands and do what is *right*."

"Who is to say what is right? I do not care anymore. You all abandoned me, but Pyra accepted me – he is the only one who has ever made me feel I *matter*."

In spite of his words, however, once again Orsin felt the glitter of something deep within him. The fire flickering around his hands faltered, and he cursed and urged it through him.

"You matter to me," Chonrad said softly.

"You sent me away."

"To keep you safe." Chonrad hesitated. "I have always known that my children would play an instrumental role in the Arbor's future. It told me, the day of the Last Stand when I opened the fifth and final Node. And I could not bear to think that you might suffer."

"You did not send Julen or Horada away," Orsin said, aware as he spoke that he sounded like a petulant child.

"That is because you are my eldest son and heir," Chonrad said. And he smiled. "You will always be special to me because of that. And nobody can take that relationship away from us."

To Orsin's shock, Chonrad walked forward into the flames leaping around him. "Keep away!" he said in alarm, but his father put his arms around him and drew him close.

"My son," said Chonrad. "I am so sorry."

Deep inside, Orsin felt something give, like a tree branch that has been bearing the weight of too many leaves for too long. "Do not," he said hoarsely as the guilt and remorse that had nestled within him finally broke free and flooded through him. "I cannot bear it."

But his father refused to let him go. The flames licked over them both, but all Orsin could feel were his father's strong arms holding him tightly, his presence unlocking the chains that had held everything in.

Orsin looked around at the distraught faces of his family and friends, at the pain and suffering of those in other times

as the ash came down and covered their world, at those who
had emerged from the darkness hoping to find freedom.

"What have I done?" he whispered.

"All life is a cycle," Chonrad said. "Life leads to death, and
from death springs life."

Behind him, Orsin saw the woman lying on the ground,
struggling to bring forth a child, and next to her the slim green
shoots of a new tree.

"Let us end this," Chonrad murmured in his ear.

"I do not know how," Orsin whispered.

"I will help you." Chonrad tightened his arms.

Behind him, the Arbor shook in the wind, and Orsin finally
understood. Tears coursed down his cheeks, and he closed his
eyes and finally let go.

The small part of Tahir's consciousness that still remained saw
Orsin finally give in to his father and submit himself to the
light. At the precise moment that he joined with Cinereo, there
was a rush of fire like a backdraft and the volcano behind the
Arbor completely exploded, scattering the remnants of its top
across the city. Ash came down like snow, a hot, thick carpet
that covered the world in grey and white.

But for the first time, Tahir could see what he needed to do.

Cinereo turned and spread out his arms. Every man and
woman who had lived and who had loved the Arbor came
together as one in a glorious explosion of blinding light. Orsin,
Tahir and Geve joined hands, and as they touched, their
physical forms crumbled and became the ash blowing across
the arena. They gave up their lives to the tree, and the energy
flooded through the sunstones to Horada, and through Horada
to the tree's roots and thence to all corners of the world.

Tahir's mind joined with the others, with Chonrad, Valens,
Gavius and everyone else who had gone before him, and

with the soul of the tree itself, to become Cinereo, the guide who had worked so hard to bring the three sides of the Apex together, and to try to ensure the fire elementals did not destroy the world forever.

Cinereo saw Demitto, Catena and Manifred backing away into the depths of the cave, driven there by the fire and ash that threatened to choke the entrance. At the same time, he could see that all across Anguis, Incendi soldiers were emerging from caves and tunnels into the sun. Battles broke out across the land – battles that could only be resolved in one way, as the heat built and the elementals turned the bodies of those they inhabited to ash and covered the world in flame.

Drawing the power from the lives that had been sacrificed, Cinereo reached out and curled the Arbor's roots around the foot of the mountain. The roots tore at the mountainside, bringing rocks crashing down, covering the mouth of the cave and burying the people inside the mountain for the next few thousand years. But he did not worry. He had watched the Nox Aves prepare the old Cavum beneath the Arbor for years, hoarding supplies and preparing the Night Birds for a lifetime below ground, so that one day they would be ready – like the Arbor – to rise again.

The screech of the firebird cut across the Apex and made them all cower for a moment. For even as the mighty Pyra emerged from the mountainside to swoop exultantly across the land, so it saw its doom thousands of years in the future, a fixed point in time that it could not change, no matter how hard it tried.

Cinereo could feel himself beginning to suffer from the weight of the ash falling across Heartwood. His leaves had crumbled, the branches and twigs burning and disintegrating, and now all that remained was the great trunk, holding the Pectoris containing the loving hearts of every man and woman who had died in its name.

Drawing on that love, Cinereo gathered his strength and sent the remainder of his power through Horada to the sunstones. Energy poured into the golden gems and radiated out, blinding everyone who stood nearby. Horada screamed, her voice ringing out across the arena, and as the final moments of the Apex approached and the timelines converged, her scream turned into the cry of a newborn baby, the sound travelling through the sunstones to echo through space, through time.

That high-pitched cry bounced between the sunstones, gathering speed and strength, and then burst through from the pendant in Comminor's hand until it brightened a hundredfold, making him hold up an arm to shield his eyes. The light engulfed the shoot at his feet, and with a tearing crack, the shoot exploded into life.

Roots sunk down into the ground, deeper and deeper, spreading at an incredible speed through the land, breaking up the burnt ground and crumbling the scorched earth. And still they spread, racing beneath the surface across miles and miles of ash and blackened ground.

Above the surface, the shoot began to grow. It surged upwards, and as it grew taller, so it began to sprout tiny, thin branches and small, waving leaves. The shoot broadened, thickened, grew strong and supple, developed a thick skin to protect its vulnerable heart. The shoot turned into a narrow stalk, the narrow stalk into a slender stem, the slender stem to a slim trunk. The trunk expanded, branches lengthening. Twigs grew from the branches, stiffened and sprouted thick, glossy leaves, which unfurled as if stretching their arms after a long sleep.

Nele backed away, pulling the others with him, and Amabil and Betune covered Sarra and the newborn baby as the tree reared above their heads.

The new branches penetrated the dome that had protected them, and beyond it Pyra surged forward eagerly as if certain this indicated his chance to attack, but the new tree had other ideas. Its growth quickened, and those watching gasped as it doubled in size, almost exultantly, as if overjoyed at finally being able to grow after so long in the darkness.

Pyra swooped and breathed fire over it and the flames scoured the earth. Without the dome, he had clearly hoped to incinerate those who remained, but the tree arched its branches over them as they huddled beneath it, keeping them safe. And although its leaves curled and died and fell as ash to the floor, new ones immediately grew to replace them, growing quicker than before, and Pyra circled and hesitated in the air.

The tree's roots reached the coast on all four sides of Anguis, and Cinereo waited as its power built within its new, huge heart. Then it erupted forth in a burst through its roots.

Across the land, the crumbling, broken earth cracked, and new shoots appeared. At first they were barely noticeable, only tiny green specks on the black and brown, but the shoots lengthened into blades of grass that rapidly spread in a carpet of green.

Pyra bellowed and turned a broad swathe to ash, but they merely grew again, grass and flowers and trees, burgeoning and blooming in a riot of colour that dazzled those who watched the explosion of growth.

Cinereo concentrated on the sunstone in Comminor's hand and drew his consciousness along the rays of light that still connected them, away from the old disintegrating tree and into the flourishing new one.

The old one crumbled and died, buried beneath a blanket of ash and molten rock, and lava coated the city and killed everyone it touched: the King and Queen, the shopkeepers and guards, rich and poor alike. Across the land, fire flourished. Forests burned, houses collapsed, animals and people died amidst the fire and flame. The world turned black, and the Incendi spread joyously into their new domain, ready to begin their reign.

Pyra saw it happen through the mists of time, even as his own death loomed. He rose higher in the air with a mighty flap of his wings, hoping to escape the new tree's rising power, but he was too late.

The tree's loving life-force expanded from it in a widening ring, clearing the air of the fog and ash and smoke, and letting the full, clean heat of the sun break through. As one, every blade of grass, every petal on every flower, turned towards it, and Pyra cried out as the green energy engulfed him. The firebird expired in a billow of flame, falling to the ground in a shower of ash that sank quickly into the earth.

The new Arbor arched above the land. Its new heart beat deep within its trunk, safe and secure, the love of its followers contained in its beating form. It reached out its roots, spread its branches, turned its leaves up to the sun, and let out a shivering sigh. And as Cinereo broke into song, his voice splintered and became a thousand, thousand voices, echoing through time to the ears of those who would carry its memory through the dark years until it could rise again.

The lava buried Demitto's sunstone where he had dropped it on the ground as he fled the falling ash, and with its disappearance, Horada's connection with the other timelines dissolved, and the Apex collapsed.

She crumpled to the ground in a heap. Figures rushed to lift her, but grief and loss combined with physical exhaustion overwhelmed her, and she passed out.

When she came to, she lay on a bed in a darkened room. It was empty, apart from one person sitting in a chair by the bed, his head in his hands.

She turned onto her side, her whole body aching, and looked at him fondly. "Hello, Julen."

His head snapped up and relief flooded his face. "You are awake!"

"So it seems." She smiled tiredly. "How long have I been out?"

"Two days." He picked up her hand and pressed it against his cheek. "I thought I had lost you."

"It was not I who fell." Grief rolled over her and tears trickled down her face.

"Horada…" He moved close and pulled her into his arms.

She cried for a while as she thought of her oldest brother, remembering the way his form had suddenly seemed to take all the fire into itself and had disintegrated into ash that blew away in the wind.

"All those people," Horada whispered, burying her face in Julen's tunic. She could not shake the memory of the ash falling and smothering the bodies.

"I know." He stroked her back.

"I cannot believe Orsin was responsible for it, Julen. How can we live with the fact that we let him down so badly?"

He hesitated, and then he pulled back to look at her. She pushed herself up to a sitting position, and he took her hands. "The thing is," he said, "the Nox Aves are certain that the Apex *needed* to happen. Nitesco described it to me as how sometimes a field of wheat stubble has to be burned and the field rested before the crop is grown again. In the future, for whatever reason, the Arbor knew that fire would rise and it had to die. Because of this, the Nox Aves believe that it engineered for the events to happen the way they did."

"You mean it *made* Orsin betray us?" Her voice filled with horror.

He tipped his head from side to side. "Not made him betray, exactly, but I suppose it knew he had the strange connection with fire and it contrived for him to be tempted, because it suspected what would happen. Orsin fulfilled his purpose the same as we all did."

She clenched her fists. "The Arbor made him kill all those people. How could it have done that?"

"I cannot pretend to understand its reasoning. I am not a scholar."

"We are just pawns in its game of life," she snapped, dashing away more tears. "If the future is so set in stone then why do we think we have any say over what happens to ourselves at all?"

"It is the price we pay for its love," said a new voice from behind them. They turned to see their mother standing in the doorway. Horada stared – Procella wore a simple green gown, and her long blonde hair, peppered with grey, hung loose around her shoulders. She looked beautiful, but exhausted.

She came forward and sat on the side of the bed, taking her daughter in her arms. She kissed her forehead. "How are you feeling?"

"I ache, but my head is clear." Horada fingered her mother's gown. "Why are you dressed like this?"

"I have been holding a vigil," Procella said.

"For Orsin?"

"Yes." Procella's eyes brimmed with sorrow, but she looked calm. "I know I failed him, and I cannot make any excuses for that. When I saw him fall, I was filled with such guilt that I did not think I could survive the pain. I spent two days and nights by the Arbor, battling with my feelings, trying to understand. I hated the tree for taking your father from me, for what it has done to us all, and now for taking Orsin from us. For a while I did not want to live. It hurt too much."

Procella's gaze had drifted away, her eyes shining. Horada bit her lip and squeezed her mother's hand, and Procella's eyes focussed. She smiled. "But last night, your father appeared to me."

Horada's eyes widened. "Truly?"

"Yes. He told me I must not blame the Arbor for the events that have unfolded. Our connection with the tree is a special, holy one, and it called on us because it knew we were able to help. I thought it treated our lives lightly, but Chonrad helped me understand how much value it places on our sacrifices, and how much it loves us."

She took a deep breath and let it out slowly. "I regret not being able to see Orsin again, and to tell him that I do love him and I am sorry for not treating him better. But Chonrad assured me he is at rest now, and he will always be a part of us, here." She touched above her heart.

"And what now?" murmured Horada. "The second phase of the Apex – Tahir told me he lived five hundred years in the future. Can we not warn them? Tell them to prepare an army, ready themselves for the Incendi invasion?"

Julen shook his head. "They will record much of what happened in the *Quercetum* for future generations. But what we must take away from this is that we cannot – *must* not – try to change the future. Heartwood *will* fall, and the Arbor *will* die. Nitesco has said that we must not talk about what we have seen to anyone. The Nox Aves will record what they think future generations need to know. And we have to trust in them."

"It is strange to think of the people we saw in the future," Horada murmured. "Those who were banished underground – how will they fare? And the woman with the baby. What will happen to her?"

Procella smiled. "We may never know. But we must rest assured that we have fulfilled our role in the course of history, and that is all we can do."

She and Julen continued to talk about future events, but Horada lay back and closed her eyes, tired again. She thought of Cinereo – of the fact that he had been formed from all those who had gone before. Orsin would now have joined them, and one day she herself would become part of him too.

All life is a cycle...

She yawned and stretched, turned over and settled down to sleep. She would grieve for her brother in the proper manner, but deep down, she had seen enough of death. She rested a hand on her belly as she thought of the baby that had been born beneath the new Arbor's leaves. Perhaps one day she would get married and have children. And maybe those children would be the ancestors of those who played a part in the Apex.

Life leads to death, and from death springs life…

It was time to start living.

II

Deep in the mountainside, Demitto sat with his back against the wall of the cavern and drew Catena into his arms. She sat with her back to his chest, and where he rested his hand on her ribcage under her breast, he could feel the steady, reassuring beat of her heart.

It had been a chaotic day. As the cave entrance had collapsed and filled with rubble, the refugees had moved deeper into the cave system and waited for the clouds of dust to clear. Sunstone pendants crafted by the Nox Aves and hung around the caves provided them with a source of light.

As the dust settled and they went back to investigate, it had soon become clear that they would not be able to clear the cave entrance. Hundreds of massive boulders that they would not be able to move filled the way out. Manifred, Demitto and the other Nox Aves members had gone through the supplies that had been stored away for the past few hundred years, but although they had tools and weapons and plenty of building supplies, they knew they would not be able to make anything strong enough to lift the heavy stone.

They had come to that conclusion with a positive outlook, however. They had suspected this would happen, and presumed that the Arbor had blocked them in on purpose to keep them safe from the volcanic lava as well as to make sure the Incendi elementals did not discover their presence as they took over Anguis. Now all that remained was to speak to the people who had followed them down into the caves, and to allay their panic and explain that they had prepared for this eventuality.

"My friends," Manifred began, and waited for the talk to die down. He stood atop a flat shelf that protruded from the cavern's edge, and widened his arms to encompass the hundreds of people sitting huddled in small groups. They were from all walks of life – some were rich dignitaries who had been visiting Heartwood for the Veriditas, others were town guards or council members, some were merchants and ordinary townspeople, even some of the poorer folk from the outer districts of the town. Old and young alike, they comforted each other during this hour of need.

"My friends," Manifred said again as everyone fell quiet. "I think by now most of you will be aware of the events of the day. The volcano above Heartwood has erupted, and we believe the lava has completely destroyed the city."

Shock registered on everyone's faces. Demitto tightened his arms around Catena and touched his lips to her shoulder, thanking the Arbor that she was safe.

But of course, the Arbor was dead. He screwed his eyes shut, unable to believe it had actually happened.

Manifred continued, "The cave entrance has been blocked by boulders too heavy for us to clear. We have no way of knowing what is happening outside, so for now we have to come to terms with the fact that we will be here for some time."

He waited a moment for everyone to digest that news. Demitto opened his eyes and glanced around, wondering what they were all thinking. The Nox Aves had come to the decision that they would not discuss the Apex with everyone. They would keep to themselves the news that they were probably the only remaining people alive in the whole of Anguis. Hope would be the single most important thing that would keep everyone alive now. Hope that one day they would make it to the surface again.

"However, it is not all bad news," Manifred continued. "At it happens, the Nox Aves have been using these caves for storage for some time. We have supplies, tools, materials and food. We have been investigating the plants and animals that live within these caves, and we managed to bring many things down with us as we fled." Secretly, the Nox Aves had been working to discover what kinds of animals – from dogs to goats to chickens – would survive in the caves, and whether plants that usually flourished on the surface could grow in the dark, moist depths.

"We are well prepared for our new life," Manifred said. "We *will* survive."

"What of the Arbor?" someone called out. "Is it... Is it dead?"

Manifred's face remained impassive. "We cannot know. We need to have hope that the Pectoris is safe – that the tree will regrow. My friends, I know many of you have lost people close to you. Tonight, we will sing songs and shed tears to mourn them."

Catena wiped a tear from her cheek, and Demitto knew she must be thinking about Tahir. He swallowed down the lump in his throat that appeared as he thought of the young lad and how bravely he had offered himself to the Arbor. How different would things have been if he, Demitto, had joined Catena and spirited Tahir away instead of delivering him to his fate? Surely he would still have died? Manifred had assured him that the world above their heads was now destroyed – that they were indeed all that remained. Tahir's sacrifice to the Arbor had enabled the tree to keep them safe in the mountains, and the Apex had ensured that, in the future, a new Arbor would grow. He had to hope that was the case, and the boy hadn't died in vain.

"So tonight we will mourn," Manifred said. "But tomorrow, we will rise from the ashes and our life will begin anew." He glanced across at the two volumes of the *Quercetum* that Demitto knew lay in a wooden box. Manifred had rescued them, determined that their history would not be forgotten, that the Nox Aves could continue to exist to guide their people.

Someone started singing, and voices gradually rose around them, even as tears flowed down everyone's cheeks as they remembered loved ones they had lost in the great fire.

Catena sang with them, but Demitto stayed silent, too overwhelmed with emotion. He leaned his head back on the cave wall and let the tears come. Sorrow for Tahir, for Atavus who had lain at Tahir's feet and refused to move, for the Arbor, for all those who had fallen around him and who he hadn't been able to get to the Cavus in time.

The wave of grief swept over him, and then it passed by, leaving in its wake a lightness of heart he had not expected. He thought of the visions he had been shown of the future – of the baby being born, the new tree taking roots and the green grass growing through the blackened earth.

Catena took Demitto's hands and rested them on her stomach, and he understood what she was trying to say. One day, their children's children would rise again and banish fire back to the mountain. The Arbor lay dormant for now, silent as The Sleep, but one day The Stirring would come and their people would climb out of the caves and find their true place in the world. This was a temporary state of affairs, and no matter how long it took, they would reclaim what was rightfully theirs. The part they had all played in the Apex had ensured their future, even as it doomed them to darkness. But it would come to an end.

One day.

III

Sarra walked down the grassy bank and sat on a flattened boulder by the water's edge.

It was nighttime. The sun had set, flooding the horizon with red, which had sent them all into a panic for a while, thinking that the firebird was returning, but the red had faded to purple, then to dark blue, and at the same time the Light Moon had risen in the sky to shine its pale light down across the new world.

She looked up at the white sphere, remembering the way everyone in the Embers had been awestruck to see it appear in the Caelum. What would they think if they could see it now? And the stars – she tried to count the twinkling forms but there were too many of them, scattered across the blackness and glittering the way minerals had glittered in the rockface deep in the caverns.

Would they ever cease to compare everything on the Surface to what they had known below ground? It must be natural to find comfort in what was familiar. And this was their first experience of night-time, after all. Oddly, she felt more at ease now than she had felt in the daytime. The bright sun had hurt her eyes and the whole dramatic events of the day had been overwhelming.

But now she felt at peace, tired and ready for sleep, but wanting to spend just a few more moments enjoying the view before she returned the small distance to the makeshift camp they had created beneath the new tree.

Thinking of the Arbor brought tears to her eyes as she thought about the fact that Geve would never get a chance to stand beneath its branches. She felt a huge sense of loss at his death and the knowledge that she would never again see his bright smile. She couldn't help feel a swathe of guilt too because he had loved her, and she had never been able to return his love in the way he had wanted. And he had known that – she had seen that resignation on his face when he had surrendered to the Arbor and given up his life. He had accepted his fate because he had known that even though she had promised herself to him, she had not felt in her heart the same way he had felt about her.

The grief washed over her, and she closed her eyes. The night air brushed across her lids, cooling her skin. By her feet, the new stream tinkled away merrily, sounding strangely like singing. No, in fact it *was* someone singing, she could hear them.

Sarra held her breath as she listened. She had heard the same melody at the moment that the Apex had broken and the connection with the past had severed – they had all heard it, and had been certain it was the Arbor itself breaking into song. Now, she could hear lots of voices joined in harmony. Gradually, one grew louder than the rest. She recognised the voice, had listened to him sing to her many times in the common rooms. It was Geve.

A tear ran down her cheek, but it was a tear of joy, not sorrow. He was letting her know that he was all right. Though his physical form had perished, his soul had gone on to live within the Arbor, and at that moment she knew she would carry a little piece of him forever in her heart.

A hand touched her shoulder, and the singing voices grew quieter until the only sound was the bubbling stream.

She turned to look up at the person and saw it was Comminor, and he held her baby in his arms, wrapped tightly in a blanket.

"He is hungry," Comminor said with a smile.

She smiled back, took the baby and put him to the breast. He suckled hungrily, and she stroked his thatch of dark hair, thinking of the way it would grow into brown curls like Rauf's. The man who had led her out of the darkness and into the light had looked healthy, affluent and happy, and it gave her hope that the future was going to be bright.

Comminor lowered himself down next to her, sitting close, his arm brushing hers. They sat contentedly and listened to the bubbling brook, bathed in the silver moonlight.

"I never knew the Light Moon would be so beautiful," he said, looking up at it.

"It is all beautiful," she said, glancing up from the baby's face to see the small plants and flowers growing at the water's edge, at the trees that were now waist-high in the fields. Their growth was slowing, but they could still see leaves unfurling, almost joyful in the cool light.

She lifted her head to look at him. "What will we do about all the people still in the Embers? We cannot leave them there."

"Of course not. I do not know how, yet. But we will find a way to get a message to them. Every single one of them deserves to see the sun."

Sarra opened her mouth to reply, but beneath her the boulder shifted and she stood, startled, the babe in her arms still sucking at her breast. "What was that?"

Comminor stood too and turned to look at the rock. A crack had appeared in the top, and as he pushed down on the front half, it gave way and broke into pieces, falling into the river. His eyes widened with surprise. "Look!"

Sarra walked forward and bent down. The middle of the rock was hollow, and it formed the distinct shape of a dog, lying curled up.

They stared at it in wonder. "Do you think this was once a real dog?" Sarra whispered. "From the past?"

"Who knows?" Comminor dropped to his haunches and brushed his fingers on the inside of the rock, following the shape. "Perhaps he guarded the old Arbor. He might have been here at the end."

They studied it for a few moments, and then Comminor pushed himself to his feet. They turned to look at the new tree.

It arched up into the night sky, way above their heads, its branches stretching across the grassy slope, its thousands of glossy leaves shimmering.

Beneath it, Nele, Josse, Viel, Paronel, Amabil and Betune sat curled up around the sunstones, which still held a remnant of their fiery glow.

"I am sorry about Geve," Comminor said, surprising her.

She dropped her gaze back to the baby and stroked his cheek.

"I will miss him. But his sacrifice will enable us all to live again."

She took a deep breath and looked back at the man beside her, whose grey hair seemed to reflect the silvery moonlight above them. "I did not love him, you know."

Comminor went still, and then he looked down at her.

"I mean, I did love him, but not in the way..." She swallowed. "Not in the way I love you."

His eyes searched her face. Hope blossomed within them like the flowers that bloomed by the water's edge. And he lowered his head and touched his lips to hers.

The Arbor rustled, and Comminor lifted his head and laughed. Sarra smiled, hoping that Geve could be happy for them. One day she would join him in the tree's embrace. Until then, she would give Comminor her heart.

Life leads to death, and from death springs life...

Cinereo watched Comminor bring Sarra beneath the branches and settle around the sunstones, the baby safe and secure in her arms. A thousand different emotions moved through him, but the greatest of all was joy.

The world was at peace, and the element of earth was in the ascendant.

For now.

ACKNOWLEDGMENTS

I'd like to acknowledge those people who matter most to me.

My parents – my lovely mum, Jan, who first interested me in historical fiction and who can still remember that story I wrote about King Arthur; and my dad, Barry, who reads all my books, and who got me hooked on sci-fi and fantasy. Thank you for following me to the other side of the world – I love you both.

My parents-in-law – Ann, who made me feel so welcome from the first time we spoke on the phone and who is still so encouraging; and John, a real old-fashioned gentleman whose love for science and inventions gives me so many ideas. I love you and your chickens.

Mark and Jo, Lucy and Ben – our best friends. We've known you for so long and we've had such fun together. Long may it continue.

This book is for all of you.

ABOUT THE AUTHOR

Freya Robertson is a lifelong fan of science fiction and fantasy, as well as a dedicated gamer. She has a deep and abiding fascination for the history and archaeology of the middle ages and spent many hours as a teenager writing out notecards detailing the battles of the Wars of the Roses, or moping around museums looking at ancient skeletons, bits of rusted iron and broken pots. She also has an impressive track record, having published over twenty romance novels under her pseudonym, Serenity Woods.

She lives in the glorious country of New Zealand Aotearoa, where the countryside was made to inspire fantasy writers and filmmakers, and where they brew the best coffee in the world.

freyarobertson.com
twitter.com/EpicFreya